Kent Knowles
Quahaug

by

Joseph Crosby Lincoln

Double 9
BOOKS

Kent Knowles
Quahaug
by Joseph Crosby Lincoln

Copyright © 2024

All Rights reserved.

ISBN: 978-93-62769-81-7

Published by

DOUBLE 9 BOOKS

2/13-B, Ansari Road
Daryaganj, New Delhi – 110002
info@double9books.com
www.double9books.com
Tel. 011-40042856

ABOUT THE AUTHOR

Joseph Crosby Lincoln was an American novelist, poet, and short story writer, with many of his works situated on a fictional Cape Cod. Lincoln was born in 1870 in Brewster, Massachusetts, on Cape Cod, and after his father died, his mother relocated the family to Chelsea, Massachusetts, an industrial community outside of Boston. Lincoln's writing career extolling "old Cape Cod" can be viewed as an attempt to return to an Eden that he had fled due to familial sorrow. Lincoln's work was frequently featured in renowned journals like The Saturday Evening Post and The Delineator. Lincoln was aware of contemporary naturalist writers like Frank Norris and Theodore Dreiser, who utilized American literature to delve into the depths of human nature, but he rejected the creative exercise. Lincoln stated that he was content "spinning yarns" that made readers feel good about themselves and their neighbors. His work served as the basis for six films and a short.

CONTENTS

CHAPTER I
Which is Not a Chapter at All

It was Asaph Tidditt who told me how to begin this history. Perhaps I should be very much obliged to Asaph; perhaps I shouldn't. He has gotten me out of a difficulty—or into one; I am far from certain which.

Ordinarily—I am speaking now of the writing of swashbuckling romances, which is, or was, my trade—I swear I never have called it a profession—the beginning of a story is the least of the troubles connected with its manufacture. Given a character or two and a situation, the beginning of one of those romances is, or was, pretty likely to be something like this:

"It was a black night. Heavy clouds had obscured the setting sun and now, as the clock in the great stone tower boomed twelve, the darkness was pitchy."

That is a good safe beginning. Midnight, a stone tower, a booming clock, and darkness make an appeal the imagination. On a night like that almost anything may happen. A reader of one of my romances—and readers there must be, for the things did, and still do, sell to some extent—might be fairly certain that something WOULD happen before the end of the second page. After that the somethings continued to happen as fast as I could invent them.

But this story was different. The weather or the time had nothing to do with its beginning. There were no solitary horsemen or strange wayfarers on lonely roads, no unexpected knocks at the doors of taverns, no cloaked personages landing from boats rowed by black-browed seamen with red handkerchiefs knotted about their heads and knives in their belts. The hero was not addressed as "My Lord"; he was not "Sir Somebody-or-other" in disguise. He was not young and handsome; there was not even "a certain something in his manner and bearing which hinted of an eventful past." Indeed there was not. For, if this particular yarn or history or chronicle which I had made up my mind to write, and which I am writing now, had or has a hero, I am he. And I am Hosea Kent Knowles, of Bayport, Massachusetts, the latter the village in which I was born and in which I have lived most of the time since I was twenty-seven years old. Nobody calls me "My Lord."

Hephzy has always called me "Hosy"—a name which I despise—and the others, most of them, "Kent" to my face and "The Quahaug" behind my back, a quahaug being a very common form of clam which is supposed to lead a solitary existence and to keep its shell tightly shut. If anything in my manner had hinted at a mysterious past no one in Bayport would have taken the hint. Bayporters know my past and that of my ancestors only too well.

As for being young and handsome—well, I was thirty-eight years old last March. Which is quite enough on THAT subject.

But I had determined to write the story, so I sat down to begin it. And immediately I got into difficulties. How should I begin? I might begin at any one of a dozen places—with Hephzy's receiving the Raymond and Whitcomb circular; with our arrival in London; with Jim Campbell's visit to me here in Bayport; with the curious way in which the letter reached us, after crossing the ocean twice. Any one of these might serve as a beginning—but which? I made I don't know how many attempts, but not one was satisfactory. I, who had begun I am ashamed to tell you how many stories—yes, and had finished them and seen them in print as well—was stumped at the very beginning of this one. Like Sim Phinney I had worked at my job "a long spell" and "cal'lated" I knew it, but here was something I didn't know. As Sim said, when he faced his problem, "I couldn't seem to get steerage way on her."

Simeon, you see—He is Angeline Phinney's second cousin and lives in the third house beyond the Holiness Bethel on the right-hand side of the road—Simeon has "done carpentering" here in Bayport all his life. He built practically every henhouse now gracing or disgracing the backyards of our village. He is our "henhouse specialist," so to speak. He has even been known to boast of his skill. "Henhouses!" snorted Sim; "land of love! I can build a henhouse with my eyes shut. Nowadays when another one of them foolheads that's been readin' 'How to Make a Million Poultry Raisin'' in the Farm Gazette comes to me and says 'Henhouse,' I say, 'Yes sir. Fifteen dollars if you pay me cash now and a hundred and fifteen if you want to wait and pay me out of your egg profits. That's all there is to it.'"

And yet, when Captain Darius Nickerson, who made the most of his money selling fifty-foot lots of sand, beachgrass and ticks to summer people for bungalow sites—when Captain Darius, grown purse-proud and vainglorious, expressed a desire for a henhouse with a mansard roof and a cupola, the latter embellishments to match those surmounting his own dwelling, Simeon was set aback with his canvas flapping. At the end of a week he had not driven a nail. "Godfrey's mighty!" he is reported to have exclaimed. "I don't know whether to build the average cupola and trust to a hen's fittin' it, or take an average hen and build a cupola round her. Maybe I'll be all right after I get started, but it's where to start that beats me."

Where to start beat me, also, and it might be beating me yet, if I hadn't dropped in at the post-office and heard Asaph Tidditt telling a story to the group around the stove. After he had finished, and, the mail being sorted, we were walking homeward together, I asked a question.

"Asaph," said I, "when you start to spin a yarn how do you begin?"

"Hey?" he exclaimed. "How do I begin? Why, I just heave to and go to work and begin, that's all."

"Yes, I know, but where do you begin?"

"At the beginnin', naturally. If you was cal'latin' to sail a boat race you wouldn't commence at t'other end of the course, would you?"

"*I* might; practical people wouldn't, I suppose. But—what IS the beginning? Suppose there were a lot of beginnings and you didn't know which to choose."

"Oh, we-ll, in that case I'd just sort of—of edge around till I found one that—that was a beginnin' of SOMETHIN' and I'd start there. You understand, don't you? Take that yarn I was spinnin' just now—that one about Josiah Dimick's great uncle's pig on his mother's side. I mean his uncle on his mother's side, not the pig, of course. Now I hadn't no intention of tellin' about that hog; hadn't thought of it for a thousand year, as you might say. I just commenced to tell about Angie Phinney, about how fast she could talk, and that reminded me of a parrot that belonged to Sylvanus Cahoon's sister—Violet, the sister's name was—loony name, too, if you ask ME, 'cause she was a plaguey sight nigher bein' a sunflower than she was a violet—weighed two hundred and ten and had a face on her as red as—"

"Just a minute, Ase. About that pig?"

"Oh, yes! Well, the pig reminded me of Violet's parrot and the parrot reminded me of a Plymouth Rock rooster I had that used to roost in the pigpen nights—wouldn't use the henhouse no more'n you nor I would—and that, naturally, made me think of pigs, and pigs fetched Josiah's uncle's pig to mind and there I was all ready to start on the yarn. It pretty often works out that way. When you want to start a yarn and you can't start—you've forgot it, or somethin'—just begin somewhere, get goin' somehow. Edge around and keep edgin' around and pretty soon you'll fetch up at the right place TO start. See, don't you, Kent?"

I saw—that is, I saw enough. I came home and this morning I began the "edging around" process. I don't seem to have "fetched up" anywhere in particular, but I shall keep on with the edging until I do. As Asaph says, I must begin somewhere, so I shall begin with the Saturday morning of last April when Jim Campbell, my publisher and my friend—which is by no means such an unusual combination as many people think—sat on the veranda of my boathouse overlooking Cape Cod Bay and discussed my past, present and, more particularly, my future.

CHAPTER II
Which Repeats, for the Most Part, What Jim Campbell Said to Me and What I Said to Him

"Jim," said I, "what is the matter with me?"

Jim, who was seated in the ancient and dilapidated arm-chair which was the finest piece of furniture in the boathouse and which I always offered to visitors, looked at me over the collar of my sweater. I used the sweater as I did the arm-chair when I did not have visitors. He was using it then because, like an idiot, he had come to Cape Cod in April with nothing warmer than a very natty suit and a light overcoat. Of course one may go clamming and fishing in a light overcoat, but—one doesn't.

Jim looked at me over the collar of my sweater. Then he crossed his oilskinned and rubber-booted legs—they were my oilskins and my boots—and answered promptly.

"Indigestion," he said. "You ate nine of those biscuits this morning; I saw you."

"I did not," I retorted, "because you saw them first. MY interior is in its normal condition. As for yours—"

"Mine," he interrupted, filling his pipe from my tobacco pouch, "being accustomed to a breakfast, not a gorge, is abnormal but satisfactory, thank you—quite satisfactory."

"That," said I, "we will discuss later, when I have you out back of the bar in my catboat. Judging from present indications there will be some sea-running. The 'Hephzy' is a good, capable craft, but a bit cranky, like the lady she is named for. I imagine she will roll."

He didn't like that. You see, I had sailed with him before and I remembered.

"Ho-se-a," he drawled, "you have a vivid imagination. It is a pity you don't use more of it in those stories of yours."

"Humph! I am obliged to use the most of it on the royalty statements you send me. If you call me 'Hosea' again I will take the 'Hephzy' across the

Point Rip. The waves there are fifteen feet high at low tide. See here, I asked you a serious question and I should like a serious answer. Jim, what IS the matter with me? Have I written out or what is the trouble?"

He looked at me again.

"Are you in earnest?" he asked.

"I am, very much in earnest."

"And you really want to talk shop after a breakfast like that and on a morning like this?"

"I do."

"Was that why you asked me to come to Bayport and spend the week-end?"

"No-o. No, of course not."

"You're another; it was. When you met me at the railroad station yesterday I could see there was something wrong with you. All this morning you've had something on your chest. I thought it was the biscuits, of course; but it wasn't, eh?"

"It was not."

"Then what was it? Aren't we paying you a large enough royalty?"

"You are paying me a good deal larger one than I deserve. I don't see why you do it."

"Oh," with a wave of the hand, "that's all right. The publishing of books is a pure philanthropy. We are in business for our health, and—"

"Shut up. You know as well as I do that the last two yarns of mine which your house published have not done as well as the others."

I had caught him now. Anything remotely approaching a reflection upon the business house of which he was the head was sufficient to stir up Jim Campbell. That business, its methods and its success, were his idols.

"I don't know any such thing," he protested, hotly. "We sold—"

"Hang the sale! You sold quite enough. It is an everlasting miracle to me that you are able to sell a single copy. Why a self-respecting person, possessed of any intelligence whatever, should wish to read the stuff I write, to say nothing of paying money for the privilege, I can't understand."

"You don't have to understand. No one expects an author to understand anything. All you are expected to do is to write; we'll attend to the rest of it. And as for sales—why, 'The Black Brig'—that was the last one, wasn't it?—beat the 'Omelet' by eight thousand or more."

"The Omelet" was our pet name for "The Queen's Amulet," my first offence in the literary line. It was a highly seasoned concoction of revolution and adventure in a mythical kingdom where life was not dull, to say the least. The humblest character in it was a viscount. Living in Bayport had, naturally, made me familiar with the doings of viscounts.

"Eight thousand more than the last isn't so bad, is it?" demanded Jim Campbell combatively.

"It isn't. It is astonishingly good. It is the books themselves that are bad. The 'Omelet' was bad enough, but I wrote it more as a joke than anything else. I didn't take it seriously at all. Every time I called a duke by his Christian name I grinned. But nowadays I don't grin—I swear. I hate the things, Jim. They're no good. And the reviewers are beginning to tumble to the fact that they're no good, too. You saw the press notices yourself. 'Another Thriller by the Indefatigable Knowles' 'Barnacles, Buccaneers and Blood, not to Mention Beauty and the Bourbons.' That's the way two writers headed their articles about 'The Black Brig.' And a third said that I must be getting tired; I wrote as if I was. THAT fellow was right. I am tired, Jim. I'm tired and sick of writing slush. I can't write any more of it. And yet I can't write anything else."

Jim's pipe had gone out. Now he relit it and tossed the match over the veranda rail.

"How do you know you can't?" he demanded.

"Can't what?"

"Can't write anything but slush?"

"Ah ha! Then it is slush. You admit it."

"I don't admit anything of the kind. You may not be a William Shakespeare or even a George Meredith, but you have written some mighty interesting stories. Why, I know a chap who sits up till morning to finish a book of yours. Can't sleep until he has finished it."

"What's the matter with him; insomnia?"

"No; he's a night watchman. Does that satisfy you, you crossgrained old shellfish? Come on, let's dig clams—some of your own blood relations—and forget it."

"I don't want to forget it and there is plenty of time for clamming. The tide won't cover the flats for two hours yet. I tell you I'm serious, Jim. I can't write any more. I know it. The stuff I've been writing makes me sick. I hate it, I tell you. What the devil I'm going to do for a living I can't see—but I can't write another story."

Jim put his pipe in his pocket. I think at last he was convinced that I meant what I said, which I certainly did. The last year had been a year of torment to me. I had finished the 'Brig,' as a matter of duty, but if that piratical craft had sunk with all hands, including its creator, I should not have cared. I drove myself to my desk each day, as a horse might be driven to a treadmill, but the animal could have taken no less interest in his work than I had taken in mine. It was bad—bad—bad; worthless and hateful. There wasn't a new idea in it and I hadn't one in my head. I, who had taken up writing as a last resort, a gamble which might, on a hundred-to-one chance, win where everything else had failed, had now reached the point where that had failed, too. Campbell's surmise was correct; with the pretence of asking him to the Cape for a week-end of fishing and sailing I had lured him there to tell him of my discouragement and my determination to quit.

He took his feet from the rail and hitched his chair about until he faced me.

"So you're not going to write any more," he said.

"I'm not. I can't."

"What are you going to do; live on back royalties and clams?"

"I may have to live on the clams; my back royalties won't keep me very long."

"Humph! I should think they might keep you a good while down here. You must have something in the stocking. You can't have wasted very much in riotous living on this sand-heap. What have you done with your money, for the last ten years; been leading a double life?"

"I've found leading a single one hard enough. I have saved something, of course. It isn't the money that worries me, Jim; I told you that. It's myself; I'm no good. Every author, sometime or other, reaches the point where he knows perfectly well he has done all the real work he can ever do, that he has written himself out. That's what's the matter with me—I'm written out."

Jim snorted. "For Heaven's sake, Kent Knowles," he demanded, "how old are you?"

"I'm thirty-eight, according to the almanac, but—"

"Thirty-eight! Why, Thackeray wrote—"

"Drop it! I know when Thackeray wrote 'Vanity Fair' as well as you do. I'm no Thackeray to begin with, and, besides, I am older at thirty-eight than he was when he died—yes, older than he would have been if he had lived twice as long. So far as feeling and all the rest of it go, I'm a second Methusaleh."

"My soul! hear the man! And I'm forty-two myself. Well, Grandpa, what do you expect me to do; get you admitted to the Old Man's Home?"

"I expect—" I began, "I expect—" and I concluded with the lame admission that I didn't expect him to do anything. It was up to me to do whatever must be done, I imagined.

He smiled grimly.

"Glad your senility has not affected that remnant of your common-sense," he declared. "You're dead right, my boy; it IS up to you. You ought to be ashamed of yourself."

"I am, but that doesn't help me a whole lot."

"Nothing will help you as long as you think and speak as you have this morning. See here, Kent! answer me a question or two, will you? They may be personal questions, but will you answer them?"

"I guess so. There has been what a disinterested listener might call a slightly personal flavor to your remarks so far. Do your worst. Fire away."

"All right. You've lived in Bayport ten years or so, I know that. What have you done in all that time—besides write?"

"Well, I've continued to live."

"Doubted. You've continued to exist; but how? I've been here before. This isn't my first visit, by a good deal. Each time I have been here your daily routine—leaving out the exciting clam hunts and the excursions in quest of the ferocious flounder, like the one we're supposed—mind, I say supposed—to be on at the present moment—you have put in the day about like this: Get up, bathe, eat, walk to the post-office, walk home, sit about, talk a little, read some, walk some more, eat again, smoke, talk, read, eat for the third time, smoke, talk, read and go to bed. That's the program, isn't it?"

"Not exactly. I play tennis in summer when there is anyone to play with me—and golf, after a fashion. I used to play both a good deal, when I was younger. I swim, and I shoot a little, and—and—"

"How about society? Have any, do you?"

"In the summer, when the city people are here, there is a good deal going on, if you care for it—picnics and clam bakes and teas and lawn parties and such."

"Heavens! what reckless dissipation! Do you indulge?"

"Why, no—not very much. Hang it all, Jim! you know I'm no society man. I used to do the usual round of fool stunts when I was younger, but—"

"But now you're too antique, I suppose. Wonder that someone hasn't collected you as a genuine Chippendale or something. So you don't 'tea' much?"

"Not much. I'm not often invited, to tell you the truth. The summer crowd doesn't take kindly to me, I'm afraid."

"Astonishing! You're such a chatty, entertaining, communicative cuss on first acquaintance, too. So captivatingly loquacious to strangers. I can imagine how you'd shine at a 'tea.' Every summer girl that tried to talk to you would be frost-bitten. Do you accept invitations when they do come?"

"Not often nowadays. You see, I know they don't really want me."

"How do you know it?"

"Why—well, why should they? Everybody else calls me—"

"They call you a clam and so you try to live up to your reputation. I know you, Kent. You think yourself a tough old bivalve, but the most serious complaint you suffer from is ingrowing sensitiveness. They do want you. They'd invite you if you gave them half a chance. Oh, I know you won't, of course; but if I had my way I'd have you dragged by main strength to every picnic and tea and feminine talk-fest within twenty miles. You might meet some persevering female who would propose marriage. YOU never would, but SHE might."

I rose to my feet in disgust.

"We'll go clamming," said I.

He did not move.

"We will—later on," he answered. "We haven't got to the last page of the catechism yet. I mentioned matrimony because a good, capable, managing wife would be my first prescription in your case. I have one or two more up my sleeve. Tell me this: How often do you get away from Bayport? How often do you get to—well, to Boston, we'll say? How many times have you been there in the last year?"

"I don't know. A dozen, perhaps."

"What did you do when you went?"

"Various things. Shopped some, went to the theater occasionally, if there happened to be anything on that I cared to see. Bought a good many books. Saw the new Sargent pictures at the library. And—and—"

"And shook hands with your brother fossils at the museum, I suppose. Wild life you lead, Kent. Did you visit anybody? Meet any friends or acquaintances—any live ones?"

"Not many. I haven't many friends, Jim; you know that. As for the wild life—well, I made two visits to New York this year."

"Yes," drily; "and we saw Sothern and Marlowe and had dinner at the Holland. The rest of the time we talked shop. That was the first visit. The second was more exciting still; we talked shop ALL the time and you took the six o'clock train home again."

"You're wrong there. I saw the new loan collections at the Metropolitan and heard Ysaye play at Carnegie Hall. I didn't start for home until the next day."

"Is that so. That's news to me. You said you were going that afternoon. That was to put the kibosh on my intention of taking you home to my wife and her bridge party, I suppose. Was it?"

"Well—well, you see, Jim, I—I don't play bridge and I AM such a stick in a crowd like that. I wanted to stay and you were mighty kind, but—but—"

"All right. All right, my boy. Next time it will be Bustanoby's, the Winter Garden and a three A. M. cabaret for yours. My time is coming. Now—Well, now we'll go clamming."

He swung out of the arm-chair and walked to the top of the steps leading down to the beach. I was surprised, of course; I have known Jim Campbell a long time, but he can surprise me even yet.

"Here! hold on!" I protested. "How about the rest of that catechism?"

"You've had it."

"Were those all the questions you wanted to ask?"

"Yes."

"Humph! And that is all the advice and encouragement I'm to get from you! How about those prescriptions you had up your sleeve?"

"You'll get those by and by. Before I leave this gay and festive scene to-morrow I'm going to talk to you, Ho-se-a. And you're going to listen. You'll listen to old Doctor Campbell; HE'LL prescribe for you, don't you worry. And now," beginning to descend the steps, "now for clams and flounders."

"And the Point Rip," I added, maliciously, for his frivolous treatment of what was to me a very serious matter, was disappointing and provoking. "Don't forget the Point Rip."

We dug the clams—they were for bait—we boarded the "Hephzy," sailed out to the fishing grounds, and caught flounders. I caught the most of them; Jim was not interested in fishing during the greater part of the time.

Then we sailed home again and walked up to the house. Hephzibah, for whom my boat is named, met us at the back door. As usual her greeting was not to the point and practical.

"Leave your rubber boots right outside on the porch," she said. "Here, give me those flatfish; I'll take care of 'em. Hosy, you'll find dry things ready in your room. Here's your shoes; I've been warmin' 'em. Mr. Campbell I've put a suit of Hosy's and some flannels on your bed. They may not fit you, but they'll be lots better than the damp ones you've got on. You needn't hurry; dinner won't be ready till you are."

I did not say anything; I knew Hephzy—had known her all my life. Jim, who, naturally enough, didn't know her as well, protested.

"We're not wet, Miss Cahoon," he declared. "At least, I'm not, and I don't see how Kent can be. We both wore oilskins."

"That doesn't make any difference. You ought to change your clothes anyhow. Been out in that boat, haven't you?"

"Yes, but—"

"Well, then! Don't say another word. I'll have a fire in the sittin'-room and somethin' hot ready when you come down. Hosy, be sure and put on BOTH the socks I darned for you. Don't get thinkin' of somethin' else and come down with one whole and one holey, same as you did last time. You must excuse me, Mr. Campbell. I've got saleratus biscuits in the oven."

She hastened into the kitchen. When Jim and I, having obeyed orders to the extent of leaving our boots on the porch, passed through that kitchen she was busy with the tea-kettle. I led the way through the dining-room and up the front stairs. My visitor did not speak until we reached the second story. Then he expressed his feelings.

"Say, Kent" he demanded, "are you going to change your clothes?"

"Yes."

"Why? You're no wetter than I am, are you?"

"Not a bit, but I'm going to change, just the same. It's the easier way."

"It is, is it! What's the other way?"

"The other way is to keep on those you're wearing and take the consequences."

"What consequences?"

"Jamaica ginger, hot water bottles and an afternoon's roast in front of the sitting-room fire. Hephzibah went out sailing with me last October and caught cold. That was enough; no one else shall have the experience if she can help it."

"But—but good heavens! Kent, do you mean to say you always have to change when you come in from sailing?"

"Except in summer, yes."

"But why?"

"Because Hephzy tells me to."

"Do you always do what she tells you?"

"Generally. It's the easiest way, as I said before."

"Good—heavens! And she darns your socks and tells you what—er lingerie to wear and—does she wash your face and wipe your nose and scrub behind your ears?"

"Not exactly, but she probably would if I didn't do it."

"Well, I'll be hanged! And she extends the same treatment to all your guests?"

"I don't have any guests but you. No doubt she would if I did. She mothers every stray cat and sick chicken in the neighborhood. There, Jim, you trot along and do as you're told like a nice little boy. I'll join you in the sitting-room."

"Humph! perhaps I'd better. I may be spanked and put to bed if I don't. Well, well! and you are the author of 'The Black Brig!' 'Buccaneers and Blood!' 'Bibs and Butterscotch' it should be! Don't stand out here in the cold hall, Hosy darling; you may get the croup if you do."

I was waiting in the sitting-room when he came down. There was a roaring fire in the big, old-fashioned fireplace. That fireplace had been bricked up in the days when people used those abominations, stoves. As a boy I was well acquainted with the old "gas burner" with the iron urn on top and the nickeled ornaments and handles which Mother polished so assiduously. But the gas burner had long since gone to the junk dealer. Among the improvements which my first royalty checks made possible were steam heat and the restoration of the fireplace.

Jim found me sitting before the fire in one of the two big "wing" chairs which I had purchased when Darius Barlay's household effects were sold at auction. I should not have acquired them as cheaply if Captain Cyrus Whittaker had been at home when the auction took place. Captain Cy loves old-fashioned things as much as I do and, as he has often told me since, he meant to land those chairs some day if he had to run his bank account high and dry in consequence. But the Captain and his wife—who used to be Phoebe Dawes, our school-teacher here in Bayport—were away visiting their adopted daughter, Emily, who is married and living in Boston, and I got the chairs.

At the Barclay auction I bought also the oil painting of the bark "Freedom"—a command of Captain Elkanah Barclay, uncle of the late Darius—and the set—two volumes missing—of The Spectator, bound in sheepskin. The "Freedom" is depicted "Entering the Port of Genoa, July 10th, 1848," and if the port is somewhat wavy and uncertain, the bark's canvas and rigging are definite and rigid enough to make up. The Spectator set is chiefly remarkable for its marginal notes; Captain Elkanah bought the books in London and read and annotated at spare intervals during subsequent voyages. His opinions were decided and his notes nautical and emphatic. Hephzibah read a few pages of the notes when the books first came into the house and then went to prayer-meeting. As she had announced her intention of remaining at home that evening I was surprised—until I read them myself.

Jim came downstairs, arrayed in the suit which Hephzy had laid out for him. I made no comment upon his appearance. To do so would have been superfluous; he looked all the comments necessary.

I waved my hand towards the unoccupied wing chair and he sat down. Two glasses, one empty and the other half full of a steaming mixture, were on the little table beside us.

"Help yourself, Jim," I said, indicating the glasses. He took up the one containing the mixture and regarded it hopefully.

"What?" he asked.

"A Cahoon toddy," said I. "Warranted to keep off chills, rheumatism, lumbago and kindred miseries. Good for what ails you. Don't wait; I've had mine."

He took a sniff and then a very small sip. His face expressed genuine emotion.

"Whew!" he gasped, choking. "What in blazes—?"

"Jamaica ginger, sugar and hot water," I explained blandly. "It won't hurt you—longer than five minutes. It is Hephzy's invariable prescription."

"Good Lord! Did you drink yours?"

"No—I never do, unless she watches me."

"But your glass is empty. What did you do with it?"

"Emptied it behind the back log. Of course, if you prefer to drink it—"

"Drink it!" His "toddy" splashed the back log, causing a tremendous sizzle.

Before he could relieve his mind further, Hephzy appeared to announce that dinner was ready if we were. We were, most emphatically, so we went into the dining-room.

Hephzy and Jim did most of the talking during the meal. I had talked more that forenoon than I had for a week—I am not a chatty person, ordinarily, which, in part, explains my nickname—and I was very willing to eat and listen. Hephzy, who was garbed in her best gown—best weekday gown, that is; she kept her black silk for Sundays—talked a good deal, mostly about dreams and presentiments. Susanna Wixon, Tobias Wixon's oldest daughter, waited on table, when she happened to think of it, and listened when she did not. Susanna had been hired to do the waiting and the dish-washing during Campbell's brief visit. It was I who hired her. If I had had my way she would have been a permanent fixture in the household, but Hephzy scoffed at the idea. "Pity if I can't do housework for two folks," she declared. "I don't care if you can afford it. Keepin' hired help in a family no bigger than this, is a sinful extravagance." As Susanna's services had been already engaged for the weekend she could not discharge her, but she insisted on doing all the cooking herself.

Her conversation, as I said, dealt mainly with dreams and presentiments. Hephzibah is not what I should call a superstitious person. She doesn't believe in "signs," although she might feel uncomfortable if she broke a looking-glass or saw the new moon over her left shoulder. She has a most amazing fund of common-sense and is "down" on Spiritualism to a degree. It is one of Bayport's pet yarns, that at the Harniss Spiritualist camp-meeting when the "test medium" announced from the platform that he had a message for a lady named Hephzibah C—he "seemed to get the name Hephzibah C"—Hephzy got up and walked out. "Any dead relations I've got," she declared, "who send messages through a longhaired idiot like that one up there"—meaning the medium,—"can't have much to say that's worth listenin' to. They can talk to themselves if they want to, but they shan't waste MY time."

In but one particular was Hephzy superstitious. Whenever she dreamed of "Little Frank" she was certain something was going to happen. She had dreamed of "Little Frank" the night before and, if she had not been headed off, she would have talked of nothing else.

"I saw him just as plain as I see you this minute, Hosy," she said to me. "I was somewhere, in a strange place—a foreign place, I should say 'twas—and there I saw him. He didn't know me; at least I don't think he did."

"Considering that he never saw you that isn't so surprising," I interrupted. "I think Mr. Campbell would have another cup of coffee if you urged him. Susanna, take Mr. Campbell's cup."

Jim declined the coffee; said he hadn't finished his first cup yet. I knew that, of course, but I was trying to head off Hephzy. She refused to be headed, just then.

"But I knew HIM," she went on. "He looked just the same as he has when I've seen him before—in the other dreams, you know. The very image of his mother. Isn't it wonderful, Hosy!"

"Yes; but don't resurrect the family skeletons, Hephzy. Mr. Campbell isn't interested in anatomy."

"Skeletons! I don't know what you're talkin' about. He wasn't a skeleton. I saw him just as plain! And I said to myself, 'It's little Frank!' Now what do you suppose he came to me for? What do you suppose it means? It means somethin', I know that."

"Means that you weren't sleeping well, probably," I answered. "Jim, here, will dream of cross-seas and the Point Rip to-night, I have no doubt."

Jim promptly declared that if he thought that likely he shouldn't mind so much. What he feared most was a nightmare session with an author.

Hephzibah was interested at once. "Oh, do you dream about authors, Mr. Campbell?" she demanded. "I presume likely you do, they're so mixed up with your business. Do your dreams ever come true?"

"Not often," was the solemn reply. "Most of my dream-authors are rational and almost human."

Hephzy, of course, did not understand this, but it did have the effect for which I had been striving, that of driving "Little Frank" from her mind for the time.

"I don't care," she declared, "I s'pose it's awful foolish and silly of me, but it does seem sometimes as if there was somethin' in dreams, some kind of dreams. Hosy laughs at me and maybe I ought to laugh at myself, but some dreams come true, or awfully near to true; now don't they. Angeline Phinney was in here the other day and she was tellin' about her second cousin that was—he's dead now—Abednego Small. He was constable here in Bayport for years; everybody called him 'Uncle Bedny.' Uncle Bedny had been keepin' company with a woman named Dimick—Josiah Dimick's niece—lots younger than he, she was. He'd been thinkin' of marryin' her, so Angie said, but his folks had been talkin' to him, tellin' him he was too old to take such a young woman for his third wife, so he had made up his mind to throw her over, to write a letter sayin' it was all off between 'em. Well, he'd begun the letter but he never finished it, for three nights runnin' he dreamed that awful trouble was hangin' over him. That dream made such an impression on him that he tore the letter up and married the Dimick woman after all. And then—I didn't know this until Angie told me—it turned out that she had heard he was goin' to give her the go-by and had made all her arrangements to sue him for breach of promise if he did. That was the awful trouble, you see, and the dream saved him from it."

I smiled. "The fault there was in the interpretation of the dream," I said. "The 'awful trouble' of the breach of promise suit wouldn't have been a circumstance to the trouble poor Uncle Bedny got into by marrying Ann Dimick. THAT trouble lasted till he died."

Hephzibah laughed and said she guessed that was so, she hadn't thought of it in that way.

"Probably dreams are all nonsense," she admitted. "Usually, I don't pay much attention to 'em. But when I dream of poor 'Little Frank,' away off there, I—"

"Come into the sitting-room, Jim," I put in hastily. "I have a cigar or two there. I don't buy them in Bayport, either."

"And who," asked Jim, as we sat smoking by the fire, "is Little Frank?"

"He is a mythical relative of ours," I explained, shortly. "He was born twenty years ago or so—at least we heard that he was; and we haven't heard anything of him since, except by the dream route, which is not entirely convincing. He is Hephzy's pet obsession. Kindly forget him, to oblige me."

He looked puzzled, but he did not mention "Little Frank" again, for which I was thankful.

That afternoon we walked up to the village, stopping in at Simmons's store, which is also the post-office, for the mail. Captain Cyrus Whittaker happened to be there, also Asaph Tidditt and Bailey Bangs and Sylvanus Cahoon and several others. I introduced Campbell to the crowd and he seemed to be enjoying himself. When we came out and were walking home again, he observed:

"That Whittaker is an interesting chap, isn't he?"

"Yes," I said. "He is all right. Been everywhere and seen everything."

"And that," with an odd significance in his tone, "may possibly help to make him interesting, don't you think?"

"I suppose so. He lives here in Bayport now, though."

"So I gathered. Popular, is he?"

"Very."

"Satisfied with life?"

"Seems to be."

"Hum! No one calls HIM a—what is it—quahaug?"

"No, I'm the only human clam in this neighborhood."

He did not say any more, nor did I. My fit of the blues was on again and his silence on the subject in which I was interested, my work and my future, troubled me and made me more despondent. I began to lose faith in the "prescription" which he had promised so emphatically. How could he, or anyone else, help me? No one could write my stories but myself, and I knew, only too well, that I could not write them.

The only mail matter in our box was a letter addressed to Hephzibah. I forgot it until after supper and then I gave it to her. Jim retired early; the salt air made him sleepy, so he said, and he went upstairs shortly after nine. He had not mentioned our talk of the morning, nor did he until I left him at the door of his room. Then he said:

"Kent, I've got one of the answers to your conundrum. I've diagnosed one of your troubles. You're blind."

"Blind?"

"Yes, blind. Or, if not blind altogether you're suffering from the worse case of far-sightedness I ever saw. All your literary—we'll call it that for compliment's sake—all your literary life you've spent writing about people and things so far off you don't know anything about them. You and your dukes and your earls and your titled ladies! What do you know of that crowd? You never saw a lord in your life. Why don't you write of something near by, something or somebody you are acquainted with?"

"Acquainted with! You're crazy, man. What am I acquainted with, except this house, and myself and my books and—and Bayport?"

"That's enough. Why, there is material in that gang at the post-office to make a dozen books. Write about them."

"Tut! tut! tut! You ARE crazy. What shall I write; the life of Ase Tidditt in four volumes, beginning with 'I swan to man' and ending with 'By godfrey'?"

"You might do worse. If the book were as funny as its hero I'd undertake to sell a few copies."

"Funny! *I* couldn't write a funny book."

"Not an intentionally funny one, you mean. But there! There's no use to talk to you."

"There is not, if you talk like an imbecile. Is this your brilliant 'prescription'?"

"No. It might be; it would be, if you would take it, but you won't—not now. You need something else first and I'll give it to you. But I'll tell you this, and I mean it: Downstairs, in that dining-room of yours, there's one mighty good story, at least."

"The dining-room? A story in the dining-room?"

"Yes. Or it was there when we passed the door just now."

I looked at him. He seemed to be serious, but I knew he was not. I hate riddles.

"Oh, go to blazes!" I retorted, and turned away.

I looked into the dining-room as I went by. There was no story in sight there, so far as I could see. Hephzy was seated by the table, mending something, something of mine, of course. She looked up.

"Oh, Hosy," she said, "that letter you brought was a travel book from the Raymond and Whitcomb folks. I sent a stamp for it. It's awfully interesting! All about tours through England and France and Switzerland and everywhere. So cheap they are! I'm pickin' out the ones I'm goin' on some day. The pictures are lovely. Don't you want to see 'em?"

"Not now," I replied. Another obsession of Hephzy's was travel. She, who had never been further from Bayport than Hartford, Connecticut, was forever dreaming of globe-trotting. It was not a new disease with her, by any means; she had been dreaming the same things ever since I had known her, and that is since I knew anything. Some day, SOME day she was going to this, that and the other place. She knew all about these places, because she had read about them over and over again. Her knowledge, derived as it was from so many sources, was curiously mixed, but it was comprehensive, of its kind. She was continually sending for Cook's circulars and booklets advertising personally conducted excursions. And, with the arrival of each new circular or booklet, she picked out, as she had just done, the particular tours she would go on when her "some day" came. It was funny, this queer habit of hers, but not half as funny as the thought of her really going would have been. I would have as soon thought of our front door leaving home and starting on its travels as of Hephzy's doing it. The door was no more a part and fixture of that home than she was.

I went into my study, which adjoins the sitting-room, and sat down at my desk. Not with the intention of writing anything, or even of considering something to write about. That I made up my mind to forget for this night, at least. My desk chair was my usual seat in that room and I took that seat as a matter of habit.

As a matter of habit also I looked about for a book. I did not have to look far. Books were my extravagance—almost my only one. They filled the shelves to the ceiling on three sides of the study and overflowed in untidy heaps on the floor. They were Hephzy's bugbear, for I refused to permit their being "straightened out" or arranged.

I looked about for a book and selected several, but, although they were old favorites, I could not interest myself in any of them. I tried and tried, but even Mr. Pepys, that dependable solace of a lonely hour, failed to interest me with his chatter. Perhaps Campbell's pointed remarks concerning lords and ladies had its effect here. Old Samuel loved to write of such people, having a wide acquaintance with them, and perhaps that very acquaintance made me jealous. At any rate I threw the volume back upon its pile and began to think of myself, and of my work, the very thing I had expressly determined not to do when I came into the room.

Jim's foolish and impossible advice to write of places and people I knew haunted and irritated me. I did know Bayport—yes, and it might be true that the group at the post-office contained possible material for many books; but, if so, it was material for the other man, not for me. "Write of what you know," said Jim. And I knew so little. There was at least one good yarn in the dining-room at that moment, he had declared. He must have meant Hephzibah, but, if he did, what was there in Hephzibah's dull, gray life-story to interest an outside reader? Her story and mine were interwoven and neither contained anything worth writing about. His fancy had been caught, probably, by her odd combination of the romantic and the practical, and in her dream of "Little Frank" he had scented a mystery. There was no mystery there, nothing but the most commonplace record of misplaced trust and ingratitude. Similar things happen in so many families.

However, I began to think of Hephzy and, as I said, of myself, and to review my life since Ardelia Cahoon and Strickland Morley changed its course so completely. And now it seems to me that, in the course of my "edging around" for the beginning of this present chronicle—so different from anything I have ever written before or ever expected to write—the time has come when the reader—provided, of course, the said chronicle is ever finished or ever reaches a reader—should know something of that life; should know a little of the family history of the Knowles and the Cahoons and the Morleys.

CHAPTER III
Which, Although It Is Largely Family History, Should Not Be Skipped by the Reader

Let us take the Knowleses first. My name is Hosea Kent Knowles—I said that before—and my father was Captain Philander Kent Knowles. He was lost in the wreck of the steamer "Monarch of the Sea," off Hatteras. The steamer caught fire in the middle of the night, a howling gale blowing and the thermometer a few degrees above zero. The passengers and crew took to the boats and were saved. My father stuck by his ship and went down with her, as did also her first mate, another Cape-Codder. I was a baby at the time, and was at Bayport with my mother, Emily Knowles, formerly Emily Cahoon, Captain Barnabas Cahoon's niece. Mother had a little money of her own and Father's life was insured for a moderate sum. Her small fortune was invested for her by her uncle, Captain Barnabas, who was the Bayport magnate and man of affairs in those days. Mother and I continued to live in the old house in Bayport and I went to school in the village until I was fourteen, when I went away to a preparatory school near Boston. Mother died a year later. I was an only child, but Hephzibah, who had always seemed like an older sister to me, now began to "mother" me, the process which she has kept up ever since.

Hephzibah was the daughter of Captain Barnabas by his first wife. Hephzy was born in 1859, so she is well over fifty now, although no one would guess it. Her mother died when she was a little girl and ten years later Captain Barnabas married again. His second wife was Susan Hammond, of Ostable, and by her he had one daughter, Ardelia. Hephzy has always declared "Ardelia" to be a pretty name. I have my own opinion on that subject, but I keep it to myself.

At any rate, Ardelia herself was pretty enough. She was pretty when a baby and prettier still as a schoolgirl. Her mother—while she lived, which was not long—spoiled her, and her half-sister, Hephzy, assisted in the petting and spoiling. Ardelia grew up with the idea that most things in this world were hers for the asking. Whatever took her fancy she asked for and, if Captain Barnabas did not give it to her, she considered herself ill-used. She was the young lady of the family and Hephzibah was the housekeeper and drudge, an uncomplaining one, be it understood. For her, as for the Captain, the business of life was keeping Ardelia contented and happy, and they gloried in the task. Hephzy might have married well at least twice, but she wouldn't think of such a thing. "Pa and Ardelia need me," she said; that was reason sufficient.

In 1888 Captain Barnabas went to Philadelphia on business. He had retired from active sea-going years before, but he retained an interest in a certain line of coasting schooners. The Captain, as I said, went to Philadelphia on business connected with these schooners and Ardelia went with him. Hephzibah stayed at home, of course; she always stayed at home, never expected to do anything else, although even then her favorite reading were books of travel, and pictures of the Alps, and of St. Peter's at Rome, and the Tower of London were tacked up about her room. She, too, might have gone to Philadelphia, doubtless, if she had asked, but she did not ask. Her father did not think of inviting her. He loved his oldest daughter, although he did not worship her as he did Ardelia, but it never occurred to him that she, too, might enjoy the trip. Hephzy was always at home, she WAS home; so at home she remained.

In Philadelphia Ardelia met Strickland Morley.

I give that statement a line all by itself, for it is by far the most important I have set down so far. The whole story of the Cahoons and the Knowleses— that is, all of their story which is the foundation of this history of mine— hinges on just that. If those two had not met I should not be writing this to-day, I might not be writing at all; instead of having become a Bayport "quahaug" I might have been the Lord knows what.

However, they did meet, at the home of a wealthy shipping merchant named Osgood who was a lifelong friend of Captain Barnabas. This shipping merchant had a daughter and that daughter was giving a party at her father's home. Barnabas and Ardelia were invited. Strickland Morley was invited also.

Morley, at that time—I saw a good deal of him afterward, when he was at Bayport and when I was at the Cahoon house on holidays and vacations— was a handsome, aristocratic young Englishman. He was twenty-eight, but he looked younger. He was the second son in a Leicestershire family which had once been wealthy and influential but which had, in its later generations, gone to seed. He was educated, in a general sort of way, was a good dancer, played the violin fairly well, sang fairly well, had an attractive presence, and was one of the most plausible and fascinating talkers I ever listened to. He had studied medicine—studied it after a fashion, that is; he never applied himself to anything—and was then, in '88, "ship's doctor" aboard a British steamer, which ran between Philadelphia and Glasgow. Miss Osgood had met him at the home of a friend of hers who had traveled on that steamer.

Hephzy and I do not agree as to whether or not he actually fell in love with Ardelia Cahoon. Hephzy, of course, to whom Ardelia was the most wonderfully beautiful creature on earth, is certain that he did—he could not help it, she says. I am not so sure. It is very hard for me to believe that Strickland Morley was ever in love with anyone but himself. Captain Barnabas was well-to-do and had the reputation of being much richer than he really was. And Ardelia WAS beautiful, there is no doubt of that. At all events, Ardelia fell in love, with him, violently, desperately, head over heels in love, the very moment the two were introduced. They danced practically every dance together that evening, met surreptitiously the next day and for five days thereafter, and on the sixth day Captain Barnabas received a letter from his daughter announcing that she and Morley were married and had gone to New York together. "We will meet you there, Pa," wrote Ardelia. "I know you will forgive me for marrying Strickland. He is the most wonderful man in the wide world. You will love him, Pa, as I do."

There was very little love expressed by the Captain when he read the note. According to Mr. Osgood's account, Barnabas's language was a throwback from the days when he was first mate on a Liverpool packet. That his idolized daughter had married without asking his consent was bad enough; that she had married an Englishman was worse. Captain Barnabas hated all Englishmen. A ship of his had been captured and burned, in the war time, by the "Alabama," a British built privateer, and the very mildest of the terms he applied to a "John Bull" will not bear repetition in respectable society. He would not forgive Ardelia. She and her "Cockney husband" might sail together to the most tropical of tropics, or words to that effect.

But he did forgive her, of course. Likewise he forgave his son-in-law. When the Captain returned to Bayport he brought the newly wedded pair with him. I was not present at that homecoming. I was away at prep school, digging at my examinations, trying hard to forget that I was an orphan, but with the dull ache caused by my mother's death always grinding at my heart. Many years ago she died, but the ache comes back now, as I think of her. There is more self-reproach in it than there used to be, more vain regrets for impatient words and wasted opportunities. Ah, if some of us— boys grown older—might have our mothers back again, would we be as impatient and selfish now? Would we neglect the opportunities? I think not; I hope not.

Hephzibah, after she got over the shock of the surprise and the pain of sharing her beloved sister with another, welcomed that other for Ardelia's sake. She determined to like him very much indeed. This wasn't so hard, at first. Everyone liked and trusted Strickland Morley at first sight. Afterward, when they came to know him better, they were not—if they were as wise and discerning as Hephzy—so sure of the trust. The wise and discerning were not, I say; Captain Barnabas, though wise and shrewd enough in other things, trusted him to the end.

Morley made it a point to win the affection and goodwill of his father-in-law. For the first month or two after the return to Bayport the new member of the family was always speaking of his plans for the future, of his profession and how he intended soon, very soon, to look up a good location and settle down to practice. Whenever he spoke thus, Captain Barnabas and Ardelia begged him not to do it yet, to wait awhile. "I am so happy with you and Pa and Hephzy," declared Ardelia. "I can't bear to go away yet, Strickland. And Pa doesn't want us to; do you, Pa?"

Of course Captain Barnabas agreed with her, he always did, and so the Morleys remained at Bayport in the old house. Then came the first of the paralytic shocks—a very slight one—which rendered Captain Barnabas, the hitherto hale, active old seaman, unfit for exertion or the cares of business. He was not bedridden by any means; he could still take short walks, attend town meetings and those of the parish committee, but he must not, so Dr. Parker said, be allowed to worry about anything.

And Morley took it upon himself to prevent that worry. He spoke no more of leaving Bayport and settling down to practice his profession. Instead he settled down in Bayport and took the Captain's business cares upon his own shoulders. Little by little he increased his influence over the old man. He attended to the latter's investments, took charge of his bank account, collected his dividends, became, so to speak, his financial guardian. Captain Barnabas, at first rebellious—"I've always bossed my own ship," he declared, "and I ain't so darned feeble-headed that I can't do it yet"— gradually grew reconciled and then contented. He, too, began to worship his daughter's husband as the daughter herself did.

"He's a wonder," said the Captain. "I never saw such a fellow for money matters. He's handled my stocks and things a whole lot better'n I ever did. I used to cal'late if I got six per cent. interest I was doin' well. He ain't satisfied with anything short of eight, and he gets it, too. Whatever that boy wants and I own he can have. Sometimes I think this consarned palsy of mine is a judgment on me for bein' so sot against him in the beginnin'. Why, just look at how he runs this house, to say nothing of the rest of it! He's a skipper here; the rest of us ain't anything but fo'most hands."

Which was not the exact truth. Morley was skipper of the Cahoon house, Ardelia first mate, her father a passenger, and the foremast hand was Hephzy. And yet, so far as "running" that house was concerned the foremast hand ran it, as she always had done. The Captain and Ardelia were Morley's willing slaves; Hephzy was, and continued to be, a free woman. She worked from morning until night, but she obeyed only such orders as she saw fit.

She alone did not take the new skipper at his face value.

"I don't know what there was about him that made me uneasy," she has told me since. "Maybe there wasn't anything; perhaps that was just the reason. When a person is SO good and SO smart and SO polite—maybe the average sinful common mortal like me gets jealous; I don't know. But I do know that, to save my life, I couldn't swallow him whole the way Ardelia and Father did. I wanted to look him over first; and the more I looked him over, and the smoother and smoother he looked, the more sure I felt he'd give us all dyspepsy before he got through. Unreasonable, wasn't it?"

For Ardelia's sake she concealed her distrust and did her best to get on with the new head of the family. Only one thing she did, and that against Motley's and her father's protest. She withdrew her own little fortune, left her by her mother, from Captain Barnabas's care and deposited it in the Ostable savings bank and in equally secure places. Of course she told the Captain of her determination to do this before she did it and the telling was the cause of the only disagreement, almost a quarrel, which she and her father ever had. The Captain was very angry and demanded reasons. Hephzibah declared she didn't know that she had any reasons, but she was going to do it, nevertheless. And she did do it. For months thereafter relations between the two were strained; Barnabas scarcely spoke to his older daughter and Hephzy shed tears in the solitude of her bedroom. They were hard months for her.

At the end of them came the crash. Morley had developed a habit of running up to Boston on business trips connected with his father-in-law's investments. Of late these little trips had become more frequent. Also, so it seemed to Hephzy, he was losing something of his genial sweetness and suavity, and becoming more moody and less entertaining. Telegrams and letters came frequently and these he read and destroyed at once. He seldom played the violin now unless Captain Barnabas—who was fond of music of the simpler sort—requested him to do so and he seemed uneasy and, for him, surprisingly disinclined to talk.

Hephzy was not the only one who noticed the change in him. Ardelia noticed it also and, as she always did when troubled or perplexed, sought her sister's advice.

"I sha'n't ever forget that night when she came to me for the last time," Hephzy has told me over and over again. "She came up to my room, poor thing, and set down on the side of my bed and told me how worried she was about her husband. Father had turned in and HE was out, gone to the post-office or somewheres. I had Ardelia all to myself, for a wonder, and we sat and talked just the same as we used to before she was married. I'm glad it happened so. I shall always have that to remember, anyhow.

"Of course, all her worry was about Strickland. She was afraid he was makin' himself sick. He worked so hard; didn't I think so? Well, so far as that was concerned, I had come to believe that almost any kind of work was liable to make HIM sick, but of course I didn't say that to her. That somethin' was troublin' him was plain, though I was far enough from guessin' what that somethin' was.

"We set and talked, about Strickland and about Father and about ourselves. Mainly Ardelia's talk was a praise service with her husband for the subject of worship; she was so happy with him and idolized him so that she couldn't spare time for much else. But she did speak a little about herself and, before she went away, she whispered somethin' in my ear which was a dead secret. Even Father didn't know it yet, she said. Of course I was as pleased as she was, almost—and a little frightened too, although I didn't say so to her. She was always a frail little thing, delicate as she was pretty; not a strapping, rugged, homely body like me. We wasn't a bit alike.

"So we talked and when she went away to bed she gave me an extra hug and kiss; came back to give 'em to me, just as she used to when she was a little girl. I wondered since if she had any inklin' of what was goin' to happen. I'm sure she didn't; I'm sure of it as I am that it did happen. She couldn't have kept it from me if she had known—not that night. She went away to bed and I went to bed, too. I was a long while gettin' to sleep and after I did I dreamed my first dream about 'Little Frank.' I didn't call him 'Little Frank' then, though. I don't seem to remember what I did call him or just how he looked except that he looked like Ardelia. And the next afternoon she and Strickland went away—to Boston, he told us."

From that trip they never returned. Morley's influence over his wife must have been greater even than any of us thought to induce her to desert her father and Hephzy without even a written word of explanation or farewell. It is possible that she did write and that her husband destroyed the letter. I am as sure as Hephzy is that Ardelia did not know what Morley had done. But, at all events, they never came back to Bayport and within the week the truth became known. Morley had speculated, had lost and lost again and again. All of Captain Barnabas's own money and all intrusted to his care, including my little nest-egg, had gone as margins to the brokers who had bought for Morley his worthless eight per cent. wildcats. Hephzy's few thousands in the savings bank and elsewhere were all that was left.

I shall condense the rest of the miserable business as much as I can. Captain Barnabas traced his daughter and her husband as far as the steamer which sailed for England. Farther he would not trace them, although he might easily have cabled and caused his son-in-law's arrest. For a month he went about in a sort of daze, speaking to almost no one and sitting for hours alone in his room. The doctor feared for his sanity, but when the breakdown came it was in the form of a second paralytic stroke which left him a helpless, crippled dependent, weak and shattered in body and mind.

He lived nine years longer. Meanwhile various things happened. I managed to finish my preparatory school term and, then, instead of entering college as Mother and I had planned, I went into business—save the mark—taking the exalted position of entry clerk in a wholesale drygoods house in Boston. As entry clerk I did not shine, but I continued to keep the place until the firm failed—whether or not because of my connection with it I am not sure, though I doubt if my services were sufficiently important to contribute toward even this result. A month later I obtained another position and, after that, another. I was never discharged; I declare that with a sort of negative pride; but when I announced to my second employer my intention of resigning he bore the shock with—to say the least—philosophic fortitude.

"We shall miss you, Knowles," he observed.

"Thank you, sir," said I.

"I doubt if we ever have another bookkeeper just like you."

I thanked him again, fighting down my blushes with heroic modesty.

"Oh, I guess you can find one if you try," I said, lightly, wishing to comfort him.

He shook his head. "I sha'n't try," he declared. "I am not as young and as strong as I was and—well, there is always the chance that we might succeed."

It was a mean thing to say—to a boy, for I was scarcely more than that. And yet, looking back at it now, I am much more disposed to smile and forgive than I was then. My bookkeeping must have been a trial to his orderly, pigeon-holed soul. Why in the world he and his partner put up with it so long is a miracle. When, after my first novel appeared, he wrote me to say that the consciousness of having had a part, small though it might be, in training my young mind upward toward the success it had achieved would always be a great gratification to him, I did not send the letter I wrote in answer. Instead I tore up my letter and his and grinned. I WAS a bad bookkeeper; I was, and still am, a bad business man. Now I don't care so much; that is the difference.

Then I cared a great deal, but I kept on at my hated task. What else was there for me to do? My salary was so small that, as Charlie Burns, one of my fellow-clerks, said of his, I was afraid to count it over a bare floor for fear that it might drop in a crack and be lost. It was my only revenue, however, and I continued to live upon it somehow. I had a small room in a boarding-house on Shawmut Avenue and I spent most of my evenings there or in the reading-room at the public library. I was not popular at the boarding-house. Most of the young fellows there went out a good deal, to call upon young ladies or to dance or to go to the theater. I had learned to dance when I was at school and I was fond of the theater, but I did not dance well and on the rare occasions when I did accompany the other fellows to the play and they laughed and applauded and tried to flirt with the chorus girls, I fidgeted in my seat and was uncomfortable. Not that I disapproved of their conduct; I rather envied them, in fact. But if I laughed too heartily I was sure that everyone was looking at me, and though I should have liked to flirt, I didn't know how.

The few attempts I made were not encouraging. One evening—I was nineteen then, or thereabouts—Charlie Burns, the clerk whom I have mentioned, suggested that we get dinner downtown at a restaurant and "go somewhere" afterward. I agreed—it happened to be Saturday night and I had my pay in my pocket—so we feasted on oyster stew and ice cream and then started for what my companion called a "variety show." Burns, who cherished the fond hope that he was a true sport, ordered beer with his oyster stew and insisted that I should do the same. My acquaintance with beer was limited and I never did like the stuff, but I drank it with reckless abandon, following each sip with a mouthful of something else to get rid of the taste. On the way to the "show" we met two young women of Burns' acquaintance and stopped to converse with them. Charlie offered his arm to one, the best looking; I offered mine to the discard, and we proceeded to stroll two by two along the Tremont Street mall of the Common. We had strolled for perhaps ten minutes, most of which time I had spent trying to think of something to say, when Burns' charmer—she was a waitress in one of Mr. Wyman's celebrated "sandwich depots," I believe—turned and, looking back at my fair one and myself, observed with some sarcasm:

"What's the matter with your silent partner, Mame? Got the lock-jaw, has he?"

I left them soon after that. There was no "variety show" for me that night. Humiliated and disgusted with myself I returned to my room at the boarding-house, realizing in bitterness of spirit that the gentlemanly dissipations of a true sport were never to be mine.

As I grew older I kept more and more to myself. My work at the office must have been a little better done, I fancy, for my salary was raised twice in four years, but I detested the work and the office and all connected with it. I read more and more at the public library and began to spend the few dollars I could spare for luxuries on books. Among my acquaintances at the boarding-house and elsewhere I had the reputation of being "queer."

My only periods of real pleasure were my annual vacations in summer. These glorious fortnights were spent at Bayport. There, at our old home, for Hephzibah had sold the big Cahoon house and she and her father were living in mine, for which they paid a very small rent, I was happy. I spent the two weeks in sailing and fishing, and tramping along the waved-washed beaches and over the pine-sprinkled hills. Even in Bayport I had few associates of my own age. Even then they began to call me "The Quahaug." Hephzy hugged me when I came and wept over me when I went away and mended my clothes and cooked my favorite dishes in the interval. Captain Barnabas sat in the big arm-chair by the sitting-room window, looking out or sleeping. He took little interest in me or anyone else and spoke but seldom. Occasionally I spent the Fourth of July or Christmas at Bayport; not often, but as often as I could.

One morning—I was twenty-five at the time, and the day was Sunday—I read a story in one of the low-priced magazines. It was not much of a story, and, as I read it, I kept thinking that I could write as good a one. I had had such ideas before, but nothing had come of them. This time, however, I determined to try. In half an hour I had evolved a plot, such as it was, and at a quarter to twelve that night the story was finished. A highwayman was its hero and its scene the great North Road in England. My conceptions of highwaymen and the North Road—of England, too, for that matter—were derived from something I had read at some time or other, I suppose; they must have been. At any rate, I finished that story, addressed the envelope to the editor of the magazine and dropped the envelope and its inclosure in the corner mail-box before I went to bed. Next morning I went to the office as usual. I had not the faintest hope that the story would be accepted. The writing of it had been fun and the sending it to the magazine a joke.

But the story was accepted and the check which I received—forty dollars—was far from a joke to a man whose weekly wage was half that amount. The encouraging letter which accompanied the check was best of all. Before the week ended I had written another thriller and this, too, was accepted.

Thereafter, for a year or more, my Sundays and the most of my evenings were riots of ink and blood. The ink was real enough and the blood purely imaginary. My heroes spilled the latter and I the former. Sometimes my yarns were refused, but the most of them were accepted and paid for. Editors of other periodicals began to write to me requesting contributions. My price rose. For one particularly harrowing and romantic tale I was paid seventy-five dollars. I dressed in my best that evening, dined at the Adams House, gave the waiter a quarter, and saw Joseph Jefferson from an orchestra seat.

Then came the letter from Jim Campbell requesting me to come to New York and see him concerning a possible book, a romance, to be written by me and published by the firm of which he was the head. I saw my employer, obtained a Saturday off, and spent that Saturday and Sunday in New York, my first visit.

As a result of that visit began my friendship with Campbell and my first long story, "The Queen's Amulet." The "Amulet," or the "Omelet," just as you like, was a financial success. It sold a good many thousand copies. Six months later I broke to my employers the distressing news that their business must henceforth worry on as best it could without my aid; I was going to devote my valuable time and effort to literature.

My fellow-clerks were surprised. Charlie Burns, head bookkeeper now, and a married man and a father, was much concerned.

"But, great Scott, Kent!" he protested, "you're going to do something besides write books, ain't you? You ain't going to make your whole living that way?"

"I am going to try," I said.

"Great Scott! Why, you'll starve! All those fellows live in garrets and starve to death, don't they?"

"Not all," I told him. "Only real geniuses do that."

He shook his head and his good-by was anything but cheerful.

My plans were made and I put them into execution at once. I shipped my goods and chattels, the latter for the most part books, to Bayport and went there to live and write in the old house where I was born. Hephzy was engaged as my housekeeper. She was alone now; Captain Barnabas had died nearly two years before.

Among the Captain's papers and discovered by his daughter after his death was a letter from Strickland Morley. It was written from a town in France and was dated six years after Morley's flight and the disclosure of his crookedness. Captain Barnabas had never, apparently, answered the letter; certainly he had never told anyone of its receipt by him. The old man never mentioned Morley's name and only spoke of Ardelia during his last hours, when his mind was wandering. Then he spoke of and asked for her continually, driving poor Hephzibah to distraction, for her love for her lost sister was as great as his.

The letter was the complaining whine of a thoroughly selfish man. I can scarcely refer to it without losing patience, even now when I understand more completely the circumstances under which it was written. It was not too plainly written or coherent and seemed to imply that other letters had preceded it. Morley begged for money. He was in "pitiful straits," he declared, compelled to live as no gentleman of birth and breeding should live. As a matter of fact, the remnant of his resources, the little cash left from the Captain's fortune which he had taken with him had gone and he was earning a precarious living by playing the violin in a second-rate orchestra. "For poor dead Ardelia's sake," he wrote, "and for the sake of little Francis, your grandchild, I ask you to extend the financial help which I, as your heir-in-law, might demand. You may consider that I have wronged you, but, as you should know and must know, the wrong was unintentional and due solely to the sudden collapse of the worthless American investments which the scoundrelly Yankee brokers inveigled me into making."

If the money was sent at once, he added, it might reach him in time to prevent his yielding to despondency and committing suicide.

"Suicide! HE commit suicide!" sniffed Hephzy when she read me the letter. "He thinks too much of his miserable self ever to hurt it. But, oh dear! I wish Pa had told me of this letter instead of hidin' it away. I might have sent somethin', not to him, but to poor, motherless Little Frank."

She had tried; that is, she had written to the French address, but her letter had been returned. Morley and the child of whom this letter furnished the only information were no longer in that locality. Hephzy had talked of "Little Frank" and dreamed about him at intervals ever since. He had come to be a reality to her, and she even cut a child's picture from a magazine and fastened it to the wall of her room beneath the engraving of Westminster Abbey, because there was something about the child in the picture which reminded her of "Little Frank" as he looked in her dreams.

She and I had lived together ever since, I continuing to turn out, each with less enthusiasm and more labor, my stories of persons and places of which, as Campbell said but too truly, I knew nothing whatever. Finally I had reached my determination to write no more "slush," profitable though it might be. I invited Jim to visit me; he had come and the conversation at the boathouse and his remarks at the bedroom door were all the satisfaction that visit had brought me so far.

I sat there in my study, going over all this, not so fully as I have set it down here, but fully nevertheless, and the possibility of finding even a glimmer of interest or a hint of fictional foundation in Hephzibah or her life or mine was as remote at the end of my thinking as it had been at the beginning. There might be a story there, or a part of a story, but I could not write it. The real trouble was that I could not write anything. With which, conclusion, exactly what I started with, I blew out the lamp and went upstairs to bed.

Next morning Jim and I went for another sail from which we did not return until nearly dinner-time. During that whole forenoon he did not mention the promised "prescription," although I offered him plenty of opportunities and threw out various hints by way of bait.

He ignored the bait altogether and, though he talked a great deal and asked a good many questions, both talk and questions had no bearing on the all-important problem which had been my real reason for inviting him to Bayport. He questioned me again concerning my way of spending my time, about my savings, how much money I had put by, and the like, but I was not particularly interested in these matters and they were not his business, to put it plainly. At least, I could not see that they were.

I answered him as briefly as possible and, I am afraid, behaved rather boorishly to one, who next to Hephzy, was perhaps the best friend I had in the world. His apparent lack of interest hurt and disappointed me and I did not care if he knew it. My impatience must have been apparent enough, but if so it did not trouble him; he chatted and laughed and told stories all the way from the landing to the house and announced to Hephzy, who had stayed at home from church in order to prepare and cook clam chowder and chicken pie and a "Queen pudding," that he had an appetite like a starved shark.

When, at last, that appetite was satisfied, he and I adjourned to the sitting-room for a farewell smoke. His train left at three-thirty and it lacked but an hour of that time. He had worn my suit, the one which Hephzibah had laid out for him the day before, but had changed to his own again and packed his bag before dinner.

We camped in the wing chairs and he lighted his cigar. Then, to my astonishment, he rose and shut the door.

"What did you do that for?" I asked.

He came back to his chair.

"Because I'm going to talk to you like a Dutch uncle," he replied, "and I don't want anyone, not even a Cape Cod cousin, butting in. Kent, I told you that before I went I was going to prescribe for you, didn't I? Well, I'm going to do it now. Are you ready for the prescription?"

"I have been ready for it for some time," I retorted. "I began to think you had forgotten it altogether."

"I hadn't. But I wanted it to be the last word you should hear from me and I didn't want to give you time to think up a lot of fool objections to spring on me before I left. Look here, I'm your doctor now; do you understand? You called me in as a specialist and what I say goes. Is that understood?"

"I hear you."

"You've got to do more than hear me. You've got to do what I tell you. I know what ails you. You've buried yourself in the mud down here. Wake up, you clam! Come out of your shell. Stir around. Stop thinking about yourself and think of something worth while."

"Dear! dear! hark to the voice of the oracle. And what is the something worth while I am to think about; you?"

"Yes, by George! me! Me and the dear public! Here are thirty-five thousand seekers after the—the higher literature, panting open-mouthed for another Knowles classic. And you sit back here and cover yourself with sand and seaweed and say you won't give it to them."

"You're wrong. I say I can't."

"You will, though."

"I won't. You can bet high on that."

"You will, and I'll bet higher. YOU write no more stories! You! Why, confound you, you couldn't help it if you tried. You needn't write another 'Black Brig' unless you want to. You needn't—you mustn't write anything UNTIL you want to. But, by George! you'll get up and open your eyes and stir around, and keep stirring until the time comes when you've found something or someone you DO want to write about. THEN you'll write; you will, for I know you. It may turn out to be what you call 'slush,' or it may not, but you'll write it, mark my words."

He was serious now, serious enough even to suit me. But what he had said did not suit me.

"Don't talk nonsense, Jim," I said. "Don't you suppose I have thought—"

"Thought! that's just it; you do nothing but think. Stop thinking. Stop being a quahaug—a dead one, anyway. Drop the whole business, drop Bayport, drop America, if you like. Get up, clear out, go to China, go to Europe, go to—Well, never mind, but go somewhere. Go somewhere and forget it. Travel, take a long trip, start for one place and, if you change your mind before you get there, go somewhere else. It doesn't make much difference where, so that you go, and see different things. I'm talking now, Kent Knowles, and it isn't altogether because it pays us to publish your books, either. You drop Bayport and drop writing. Go out and pick up and go. Stay six months, stay a year, stay two years, but keep alive and meet people and give what you flatter yourself is a brain house-cleaning. Confound you, you've kept it shut like one of these best front parlors down here. Open the windows and air out. Let the outside light in. An idea may come with it; it is barely possible, even to you!"

He was out of breath by this time. I was in a somewhat similar condition for his tirade had taken mine away. However, I managed to express my feelings.

"Humph!" I grunted. "And so this is your wonderful prescription. I am to travel, am I?"

"You are. You can afford it, and I'll see that you do."

"And just what port would you recommend?"

"I don't care, I tell you, except that it ought to be a long way off. I'm not joking, Kent; this is straight. A good long jaunt around the world would do you a barrel of good. Don't stop to think about it, just start, that's all. Will you?"

I laughed. The idea of my starting on a pleasure trip was ridiculous. If ever there was a home-loving and home-staying person it was I. The bare thought of leaving my comfort and my books and Hephzy made me shudder. I hadn't the least desire to see other countries and meet other people. I hated sleeping cars and railway trains and traveling acquaintances. So I laughed.

"Sorry, Jim," I said, "but I'm afraid I can't take your prescription."

"Why not?"

"For one reason because I don't want to."

"That's no reason at all. It doesn't make any difference what you want. Anything else?"

"Yes. I would no more wander about creation all alone than—"

"Take someone with you."

"Who? Will you go, yourself?"

He shook his head.

"I wish I could," he said, and I think he meant it. "I'd like nothing better. I'D keep you alive, you can bet on that. But I can't leave the literature works just now. I'll do my best to find someone who will, though. I know a lot of good fellows who travel—"

I held up my hand. "That's enough," I interrupted. "They can't travel with me. They wouldn't be good fellows long if they did."

He struck the chair arm with his fist.

"You're as near impossible as you can be, aren't you," he exclaimed. "Never mind; you're going to do as I tell you. I never gave you bad advice yet, now did I?"

"No—o. No, but—"

"I'm not giving it to you now. You'll go and you'll go in a hurry. I'll give you a week to think the idea over. At the end of that time if I don't hear from you I'll be down here again, and I'll worry you every minute until you'll go anywhere to get rid of me. Kent, you must do it. You aren't written out, as you call it, but you are rusting out, fast. If you don't get away and polish up you'll never do a thing worth while. You'll be another what's-his-name— Ase Tiddit; that's what you'll be. I can see it coming on. You're ossifying; you're narrowing; you're—"

I broke in here. I didn't like to be called narrow and I did not like to be paired with Asaph Tiddit, although our venerable town clerk is a good citizen and all right, in his way. But I had flattered myself that way was not mine.

"Stop it, Jim!" I ordered. "Don't blow off any more steam in this ridiculous fashion. If this is all you have to say to me, you may as well stop."

"Stop! I've only begun. I'll stop when you start, and not before. Will you go?"

"I can't, Jim. You know I can't."

"I know you can and I know you're going to. There!" rising and laying a hand on my shoulder, "it is time for ME to be starting. Kent, old man, I want you to promise me that you will do as I tell you. Will you?"

"I can't, Jim. I would if I could, but—"

"Will you promise me to think the idea over? Think it over carefully; don't think of anything else for the rest of the week? Will you promise me to do that?"

I hesitated. I was perfectly sure that all my thinking would but strengthen my determination to remain at home, but I did not like to appear too stubborn.

"Why, yes, Jim," I said, doubtfully, "I promise so much, if that is any satisfaction to you."

"All right. I'll give you until Friday to make up your mind. If I don't hear from you by that time I shall take it for granted that you have made it up in the wrong way and I'll be here on Saturday. I'll keep the process up week in and week out until you give in. That's MY promise. Come on. We must be moving."

He said good-by to Hephzy and we walked together to the station. His last words as we shook hands by the car steps were: "Remember—think. But don't you dare think of anything else." My answer was a dubious shake of the head. Then the train pulled out.

I believe that afternoon and evening to have been the "bluest" of all my blue periods, and I had had some blue ones prior to Jim's visit. I was dreadfully disappointed. Of course I should have realized that no advice or "prescription" could help me. As Campbell had said, "It was up to me;" I must help myself; but I had been trying to help myself for months and I had not succeeded. I had—foolishly, I admit—relied upon him to give me a new idea, a fresh inspiration, and he had not done it. I was disappointed and more discouraged than ever.

My state of mind may seem ridiculous. Perhaps it was. I was in good health, not very old—except in my feelings—and my stories, even the "Black Brig," had not been failures, by any means. But I am sure that every man or woman who writes, or paints, or does creative work of any kind, will understand and sympathize with me. I had "gone stale," that is the technical name for my disease, and to "go stale" is no joke. If you doubt it ask the writer or painter of your acquaintance. Ask him if he ever has felt that he could write or paint no more, and then ask him how he liked the feeling. The fact that he has written or painted a great deal since has no bearing on the matter. "Staleness" is purely a mental ailment, and the confident assurance of would-be doctors that its attacks are seldom fatal doesn't help the sufferer at the time. He knows he is dead, and that is no better, then, than being dead in earnest.

I knew I was dead, so far as my writing was concerned, and the advice to go away and bury myself in a strange country did not appeal to me. It might be true that I was already buried in Bayport, but that was my home cemetery, at all events. The more I thought of Jim Campbell's prescription the less I felt like taking it.

However, I kept on with the thinking; I had promised to do that. On Wednesday came a postcard from Jim, himself, demanding information. "When and where are you going?" he wrote. "Wire answer." I did not wire answer. I was not going anywhere.

I thrust the card into my pocket and, turning away from the frame of letter boxes, faced Captain Cyrus Whittaker, who, like myself, had come to Simmons's for his mail. He greeted me cordially.

"Hello, Kent," he hailed. "How are you?"

"About the same as usual, Captain," I answered, shortly.

"That's pretty fair, by the looks. You don't look too happy, though, come to notice it. What's the matter; got bad news?"

"No. I haven't any news, good or bad."

"That so? Then I'll give you some. Phoebe and I are going to start for California to-morrow."

"You are? To California? Why?"

"Oh, just for instance, that's all. Time's come when I have to go somewhere, and the Yosemite and the big trees look good to me. It's this way, Kent; I like Bayport, you know that. Nobody's more in love with this old town than I am; it's my home and I mean to live and die here, if I have luck. But it don't do for me to stay here all the time. If I do I begin to be no good, like a strawberry plant that's been kept in one place too long and has quit bearin'. The only thing to do with that plant is to transplant it and let it get nourishment in a new spot. Then you can move it back by and by and it's all right. Same way with me. Every once in a while I have to be transplanted so's to freshen up. My brains need somethin' besides post-office talk and sewin'-circle gossip to keep them from shrivelin'. I was commencin' to feel the shrivel, so it's California for Phoebe and me. Better come along, Kent. You're beginnin' to shrivel a little, ain't you?"

Was it as apparent as all that? I was indignant.

"Do I look it?" I demanded.

"No—o, but I ain't sure that you don't act it. No offence, you understand. Just a little ground bait to coax you to come on the California cruise along with Phoebe and me, that's all."

It was not likely that I should accept. Two are company and three a crowd, and if ever two were company Captain Cy and his wife were those two. I thanked him and declined, but I asked a question.

"You believe in travel as a restorative, you do?" I asked.

"Hey? I sartin do. Change your course once in awhile, same as you change your clothes. Wearin' the same suit and cruisin' in the same puddle all the time ain't healthy. You're too apt to get sick of the clothes and puddle both."

"But you don't believe in traveling alone, do you?"

"No," emphatically, "I don't, generally speakin.' If you go off by yourself you're too likely to keep thinkin' ABOUT yourself. Take somebody with you; somebody you're used to and know well and like, though. Travelin' with strangers is a little mite worse than travelin' alone. You want to be mighty sure of your shipmate."

I walked home. Hephzibah was in the sitting-room, reading and knitting a stocking, a stocking for me. She did not need to use her eyes for the knitting; I am quite sure she could have knit in her sleep.

"Hello, Hosy," she said, "been up to the office, have you? Any mail?"

"Nothing much. Humph! Still reading that Raymond and Whitcomb circular?"

"No, not that one. This is one I got last year. I've been sittin' here plannin' out just where I'd go and what I'd see if I could. It's the next best thing to really goin'."

I looked at her. All at once a new idea began to crystallize in my mind. It was a curious idea, a ridiculous idea, and yet—and yet it seemed—

"Hephzy," said I, suddenly, "would you really like to go abroad?"

"WOULD I? Hosy, how you talk! You know I've been crazy to go ever since I was a little girl. I don't know what makes me so. Perhaps it's the salt water in my blood. All our folks were sailors and ship captains. They went everywhere. I presume likely it takes more than one generation to kill off that sort of thing."

"And you really want to go?"

"Of course I do."

"Then why haven't you gone? You could afford to take a moderate-priced tour."

Hephzy laughed over her knitting.

"I guess," she said, "I haven't gone for the reason you haven't, Hosy. You could afford, it, too—you know you could. But how could I go and leave you? Why, I shouldn't sleep a minute wonderin' if you were wearin' clothes without holes in 'em and if you changed your flannels when the weather changed and ate what you ought to, and all that. You've been so—so sort of dependent on me and I've been so used to takin' care of you that I don't believe either of us would be happy anywhere without the other. I know certain sure I shouldn't."

I did not answer immediately. The idea, the amazing, ridiculous idea which had burst upon me suddenly began to lose something of its absurdity. Somehow it began to look like the answer to my riddle. I realized that my main objection to the Campbell prescription had been that I must take it alone or with strangers. And now—

"Hephzy," I demanded, "would you go away—on a trip abroad—with me?"

She put down the knitting.

"Hosy Knowles!" she exclaimed. "WHAT are you talkin' about?"

"But would you?"

"I presume likely I would, if I had the chance; but it isn't likely that—where are you goin'?"

I did not answer. I hurried out of the sitting-room and out of the house.

When I returned I found her still knitting. The circular lay on the floor at her feet. She regarded me anxiously.

"Hosy," she demanded, "where—"

I interrupted. "Hephzy," said I, "I have been to the station to send a telegram."

"A telegram? A TELEGRAM! For mercy sakes, who's dead?"

Telegrams in Bayport usually mean death or desperate illness. I laughed.

"No one is dead, Hephzy," I replied. "In fact it is barely possible that someone is coming to life. I telegraphed Mr. Campbell to engage passage for you and me on some steamer leaving for Europe next week."

Hephzibah turned pale. The partially knitted sock dropped beside the circular.

"Why—why—what—?" she gasped.

"On a steamer leaving next week," I repeated. "You want to travel, Hephzy. Jim says I must. So we'll travel together."

She did not believe I meant it, of course, and it took a long time to convince her. But when at last she began to believe—at least to the extent of believing that I had sent the telegram—her next remark was characteristic.

"But I—I can't go, Hosy," declared Hephzibah. "I CAN'T. Who—who would take care of the cat and the hens?"

CHAPTER IV
In Which Hephzy and I and the Plutonia Sail Together

The week which began that Wednesday afternoon seems, as I look back to it now, a bit of the remote past, instead of seven days of a year ago. Its happenings, important and wonderful as they were, seem trivial and tame compared with those which came afterward. And yet, at the time, that week was a season of wild excitement and delightful anticipation for Hephzibah, and of excitement not unmingled with doubts and misgivings for me. For us both it was a busy week, to put it mildly.

Once convinced that I meant what I said and that I was not "raving distracted," which I think was her first diagnosis of my case, Hephzy's practical mind began to unearth objections, first to her going at all and, second, to going on such short notice.

"I don't think I'd better, Hosy," she said. "You're awful good to ask me and I know you think you mean it, but I don't believe I ought to do it, even if I felt as if I could leave the house and everything alone. You see, I've lived here in Bayport so long that I'm old-fashioned and funny and countrified, I guess. You'd be ashamed of me."

I smiled. "When I am ashamed of you, Hephzy," I replied, "I shall be on my way to the insane asylum, not to Europe. You are much more likely to be ashamed of me."

"The idea! And you the pride of this town! The only author that ever lived in it—unless you call Joshua Snow an author, and he lived in the poorhouse and nobody but himself was proud of HIM."

Josh Snow was Bayport's Homer, its only native poet. He wrote the immortal ballad of the scallop industry, which begins:

"On a fine morning at break of day,
When the ice has all gone out of the bay,
And the sun is shining nice and it is like spring,
Then all hands start to go scallop-ING."

In order to get the fullest measure of music from this lyric gem you should put a strong emphasis on the final "ing." Joshua always did and the summer people never seemed to tire of hearing him recite it. There are eighteen more verses.

"I shall not be ashamed of you, Hephzy," I repeated. "You know it perfectly well. And I shall not go unless you go."

"But I can't go, Hosy. I couldn't leave the hens and the cat. They'd starve; you know they would."

"Susanna will look after them. I'll leave money for their provender. And I will pay Susanna for taking care of them. She has fallen in love with the cat; she'll be only too glad to adopt it."

"And I haven't got a single thing fit to wear."

"Neither have I. We will buy complete fit-outs in Boston or New York."

"But—"

There were innumerable "buts." I answered them as best I could. Also I reiterated my determination not to go unless she did. I told of Campbell's advice and laid strong emphasis on the fact that he had said travel was my only hope. Unless she wished me to die of despair she must agree to travel with me.

"And you have said over and over again that your one desire was to go abroad," I added, as a final clincher.

"I know it. I know I have. But—but now when it comes to really goin' I'm not so sure. Uncle Bedny Small was always declarin' in prayer-meetin' that he wanted to die so as to get to Heaven, but when he was taken down with influenza he made his folks call both doctors here in town and one from Harniss. I don't know whether I want to go or not, Hosy. I—I'm frightened, I guess."

Jim's answer to my telegram arrived the very next day.

"Have engaged two staterooms for ship sailing Wednesday the tenth," it read. "Hearty congratulations on your good sense. Who is your companion? Write particulars."

The telegram quashed the last of Hephzy's objections. The fares had been paid and she was certain they must be "dreadful expensive." All that money could not be wasted, so she accepted the inevitable and began preparations.

I did not write the "particulars" requested. I had a feeling that Campbell might consider my choice of a traveling companion a queer one and, although my mind was made up and his opinion could not change it, I thought it just as well to wait until our arrival in New York before telling him. So I wrote a brief note stating that my friend and I would reach New York on the morning of the tenth and that I would see him there. Also I asked, for my part, the name of the steamer he had selected.

His answer was as vague as mine. He congratulated me once more upon my decision, prophesied great things as the result of what he called my "foreign junket," and gave some valuable advice concerning the necessary outfit, clothes, trunks and the like. "Travel light," he wrote. "You can buy whatever else you may need on the other side. 'Phone as soon as you reach New York." But he did not tell me the name of the ship, nor for what port she was to sail.

So Hephzy and I were obliged to turn to the newspapers for information upon those more or less important subjects, and we speculated and guessed not a little. The New York dailies were not obtainable in Bayport except during the summer months and the Boston publications did not give the New York sailings. I wrote to a friend in Boston and he sent me the leading journals of the former city and, as soon as they arrived, Hephzy sat down upon the sitting-room carpet—which she had insisted upon having taken up to be packed away in moth balls—to look at the maritime advertisements. I am quite certain it was the only time she sat down, except at meals, that day.

I selected one of the papers and she another. We reached the same conclusion simultaneously.

"Why, it must be—" she began.

"The Princess Eulalie," I finished.

"It is the only one that sails on the tenth. There is one on the eleventh, though."

"Yes, but that one is the 'Plutonia,' one of the fastest and most expensive liners afloat. It isn't likely that Jim had booked us for the 'Plutonia.' She would scarcely be in our—in my class."

"Humph! I guess she isn't any too good for a famous man like you, Hosy. But I would look funny on her, I give in. I've read about her. She's always full of lords and ladies and millionaires and things. Just the sort of folks you write about. She'd be just the one for you."

I shook my head. "My lords and ladies are only paper dolls, Hephzy," I said, ruefully. "I should be as lost as you among the flesh and blood variety. No, the 'Princess Eulalie' must be ours. She runs to Amsterdam, though. Odd that Jim should send me to Holland."

Hephzy nodded and then offered a solution.

"I don't doubt he did it on purpose," she declared. "He knew neither you nor I was anxious to go to England. He knows we don't think much of the English, after our experience with that Morley brute."

"No, he doesn't know any such thing. I've never told him a word about Morley. And he doesn't know you're going, Hephzy. I've kept that as a—as a surprise for him."

"Well, never mind. I'd rather go to Amsterdam than England. It's nearer to France."

I was surprised. "Nearer to France?" I repeated. "What difference does that make? We don't know anyone in France."

Hephzibah was plainly shocked. "Why, Hosy!" she protested. "Have you forgotten Little Frank? He is in France somewhere, or he was at last accounts."

"Good Lord!" I groaned. Then I got up and went out. I had forgotten "Little Frank" and hoped that she had. If she was to flit about Europe seeing "Little Frank" on every corner I foresaw trouble. "Little Frank" was likely to be the bane of my existence.

We left Bayport on Monday morning. The house was cleaned and swept and scoured and moth-proofed from top to bottom. Every door was double-locked and every window nailed. Burglars are unknown in Bayport, but that didn't make any difference. "You can't be too careful," said Hephzy. I was of the opinion that you could.

The cat had been "farmed out" with Susanna's people and Susanna herself was to feed the hens twice a day, lock them in each night and let them out each morning. Their keeper had a carefully prepared schedule as to quantity and quality of food; Hephzy had prepared and furnished it.

"And don't you give 'em any fish," ordered Hephzy. "I ate a chicken once that had been fed on fish, and—my soul!"

There was quite an assemblage at the station to see us off. Captain Whittaker and his wife were not there, of course; they were near California by this time. But Mr. Partridge, the minister, was there and so was his wife; and Asaph Tidditt and Mr. and Mrs. Bailey Bangs and Captain Josiah Dimick and HIS wife, and several others. Oh, yes! and Angeline Phinney. Angeline was there, of course. If anything happened in Bayport and Angeline was not there to help it happen, then—I don't know what then; the experiment had never been tried in my lifetime.

Everyone said pleasant things to us. They really seemed sorry to have us leave Bayport, but for our sakes they expressed themselves as glad. It would be such a glorious trip; we would have so much to tell when we got back. Mr. Partridge said he should plan for me to give a little talk to the Sunday school upon my return. It would be a wonderful thing for the children. To my mind the most wonderful part of the idea was that he should take my consent for granted. *I* talk to the Sunday school! I, the Quahaug! My knees shook even at the thought.

Keturah Bangs hoped we would have a "lovely time." She declared that it had been the one ambition of her life to go sight-seeing. But she should never do it—no, no! Such things wasn't for her. If she had a husband like some women it might be, but not as 'twas. She had long ago given up hopin' to do anything but keep boarders, and she had to do that all by herself.

Bailey, her husband, grinned sheepishly but, for a wonder, he did not attempt defence. I gathered that Bailey was learning wisdom. It was time; he had attended his wife's academy a long while.

Captain Dimick brought a bag of apples, greenings, some he had kept in the cellar over winter. "Nice to eat on the cars," he told us. Everyone asked us to send postcards. Miss Phinney was especially solicitous.

"It'll be just lovely to know where you be and what you're doin'," she declared.

When the train had started and we had waved the last good-bys from the window Hephzibah expressed her opinion concerning Angeline's request.

"I send HER postcards!" she snapped. "I think I see myself doin' it! All she cares about 'em is so she can run from Dan to Beersheba showin' 'em to everybody and talkin' about how extravagant we are and wonderin' if we borrowed the money. But there! it won't make any difference. If I don't send 'em to her she'll read all I send to other folks. She and Rebecca Simmons are close as two peas in a pod and Becky reads everything that comes through her husband's post-office. All that aren't sealed, that is—yes, and some that are, I shouldn't wonder, if they're not sealed tight."

Her next remark was a surprising one.

"Hosy," she said, "how much they all think of you, don't they. Isn't it nice to know you're so popular."

I turned in the seat to stare at her.

"Popular!" I repeated. "Hephzy, I have a good deal of respect for your brain, generally speaking, but there are times when I think it shows signs of softening."

She did not resent my candor; she paid absolutely no attention to it.

"I don't mean popular with everybody, rag, tag and bobtail and all, like—well, Eben Salters," she went on. "But the folks that count all respect and like you, Hosy. I know they do."

Mr. Salters is our leading local statesman—since the departure of the Honorable Heman Atkins. He has filled every office in his native village and he has served one term as representative in the State House at Boston. He IS popular.

"It is marvelous how affection can be concealed," I observed, with sarcasm. Hephzy was back at me like a flash.

"Of course they don't tell you of it," she said. "If they did you'd probably tell 'em to their faces that they were fibbin' and not speak to 'em again. But they do like you, and I know it."

It was useless to carry the argument further. When Hephzy begins chanting my praises I find it easier to surrender—and change the subject.

In Boston we shopped. It seems to me that we did nothing else. I bought what I needed the very first day, clothes, hat, steamer coat and traveling cap included. It did not take me long; fortunately I am of the average height and shape and the salesmen found me easy to please. My shopping tour was ended by three o'clock and I spent the remainder of the afternoon at a bookseller's. There was a set of "Early English Poets" there, nineteen little, fat, chunky volumes, not new and shiny and grand, but middle-aged and shabby and comfortable, which appealed to me. The price, however, was high; I had the uneasy feeling that I ought not to afford it. Then the bookseller himself, who also was fat and comfortably shabby, and who had beguiled from me the information that I was about to travel, suggested that the "Poets" would make very pleasant reading en route.

"I have found," he said, beaming over his spectacles, "that a little book of this kind," patting one of the volumes, "which may be carried in the pocket, is a rare traveling companion. When you wish his society he is there, and when you tire of him you can shut him up. You can't do that with all traveling companions, you know. Ha! ha!"

He chuckled over his joke and I chuckled with him. Humor of that kind is expensive, for I bought the "English Poets" and ordered them sent to my hotel. It was not until they were delivered, an hour later, that I began to wonder what I should do with them. Our trunks were likely to be crowded and I could not carry all of the nineteen volumes in my pockets.

Kent Knowles | 53

Hephzibah, who had been shopping on her own hook, did not return until nearly seven. She returned weary and almost empty-handed.

"But didn't you buy ANYTHING?" I asked. "Where in the world have you been?"

She had been everywhere, so she said. This wasn't entirely true, but I gathered that she had visited about every department store in the city. She had found ever so many things she liked, but oh dear! they did cost so much.

"There was one traveling coat that I did want dreadfully," she said. "It was a dark brown, not too dark, but just light enough so it wouldn't show water spots. I've been out sailing enough times to know how your things get water-spotted. It fitted me real nice; there wouldn't have to be a thing done to it. But it cost thirty-one dollars! 'My soul!' says I, 'I can't afford THAT!' But they didn't have anything cheaper that wouldn't have made me look like one of those awful play-actin' girls that came to Bayport with the Uncle Tom's Cabin show. And I tried everywhere and nothin' pleased me so well."

"So you didn't buy the coat?"

"BUY it? My soul Hosy, didn't I tell you it cost—"

"I know. What else did you see that you didn't buy?"

"Hey? Oh, I saw a suit, a nice lady-like suit, and I tried it on. That fitted me, too, only the sleeves would have to be shortened. And it would have gone SO well with that coat. But the suit cost FORTY dollars. 'Good land!' I said, 'haven't you got ANYTHING for poor folks?' And you ought to have seen the look that girl gave me! And a hat—oh, yes, I saw a hat! It was—"

There was a great deal more. Summed up it amounted to something like this: All that suited her had been too high-priced and all that she considered within her means hadn't suited her at all. So she had bought practically nothing but a few non-essentials. And we were to leave for New York the following night and sail for Europe the day after.

"Hephzy," said I, "you will go shopping again to-morrow morning and I'll go with you."

Go we did, and we bought the coat and the hat and the suit and various other things. With each purchase Hephzy's groans and protests at my reckless extravagance grew louder. At last I had an inspiration.

"Hephzy," said I, "when we meet Little Frank over there in France, or wherever he may be, you will want him to be favorably impressed with your appearance, won't you? These things cost money of course, but we must think of Little Frank. He has never seen his American relatives and so much depends on a first impression."

Hephzy regarded me with suspicion. "Humph!" she sniffed, "that's the first time I ever knew you to give in that there WAS a Little Frank. All right, I sha'n't say any more, but I hope the foreign poorhouses are more comfortable than ours, that's all. If you make me keep on this way, I'll fetch up in one before the first month's over."

We left for New York on the five o'clock train. Packing those "Early English Poets" was a confounded nuisance. They had to be stuffed here, there and everywhere amid my wearing apparel and Hephzibah prophesied evil to come.

"Books are the worse things goin' to make creases," she declared. "They're all sharp edges."

I had to carry two of the volumes in my pockets, even then, at the very start. They might prove delightful traveling companions, as the bookman had said, but they were most uncomfortable things to sit on.

We reached the Grand Central station on time and went to a nearby hotel. I should have sent the heavier baggage directly to the steamer, but I was not sure—absolutely sure—which steamer it was to be. The "Princess Eulalie" almost certainly, but I did not dare take the risk.

Hephzy called to me from the room adjoining mine at twelve that night.

"Just think, Hosy!" she cried, "this is the last night either of us will spend on dry land."

"Heavens! I hope it won't be as bad as that," I retorted. "Holland is pretty wet, so they say, but we should be able to find some dry spots."

She did not laugh. "You know what I mean," she observed. "To-morrow night at twelve o'clock we shall be far out on the vasty deep."

"We shall be on the 'Princess Eulalie,'" I answered. "Go to sleep."

Neither of us spoke the truth. At twelve the following night we were neither "far out on the vasty deep" nor on the "Princess Eulalie."

My first move after breakfast was to telephone Campbell at his city home. He hailed me joyfully and ordered me to stay where I was, that is, at the hotel. He would be there in an hour, he said.

He was five minutes ahead of his promise. We shook hands heartily.

"You are going to take my prescription, after all," he crowed. "Didn't I tell you I was the only real doctor for sick authors? Bully for you! Wish I was going with you. Who is?"

"Come to my room and I'll show you," said I. "You may be surprised."

"See here! you haven't gone and dug up another fossilized bookworm like yourself, have you? If you have, I refuse—"

"Come and see."

We took the elevator to the fourth floor and walked to my room. I opened the door.

"Hephzy," said I, "here is someone you know."

Hephzy, who had been looking out of the window of her room, hurried in.

"Well, Mr. Campbell!" she exclaimed, holding out her hand, "how do you do? We got here all right, you see. But the way Hosy has been wastin' money, his and mine, buyin' things we didn't need, I began to think one spell we'd never get any further. Is it time to start for the steamer yet?"

Jim's face was worth looking at. He shook Hephzibah's hand mechanically, but he did not speak. Instead he looked at her and at me. I didn't speak either; I was having a thoroughly good time.

"Had we ought to start now?" repeated Hephzibah. "I'm all ready but puttin' on my things."

Jim came out of his trance. He dropped the hand and came to me.

"Are you—is she—" he stammered.

"Yes," said I. "Miss Cahoon is going with me. I wrote you I had selected a good traveling companion. I have, haven't I?"

"He would have it so, Mr. Campbell," put in Hephzy. "I said no and kept on sayin' it, but he vowed and declared he wouldn't go unless I did. I know you must think it's queer my taggin' along, but it isn't any queerer to you than it is to me."

Jim behaved very well, considering. He did not laugh. For a moment I thought he was going to; if he had I don't know what I should have done, said things for which I might have been sorry later on, probably. But he did not laugh. He didn't even express the tremendous surprise which he must have felt. Instead he shook hands again with both of us and said it was fine, bully, just the thing.

"To tell the truth, Miss Cahoon," he declared, "I have been rather fearful of this pet infant of ours. I didn't know what sort of helpless creature he might have coaxed into roaming loose with him in the wilds of Europe. I expected another babe in the woods and I was contemplating cabling the police to look out for them and shoo away the wolves. But he'll be all right now. Yes, indeed! he'll be looked out for now."

"Then you approve?" I asked.

He shot a side-long glance at me. "Approve!" he repeated. "I'm crazy about the whole business."

I judged he considered me crazy, hopelessly so. I did not care. I agreed with him in this—the whole business was insane and Hephzibah's going was the only sensible thing about it, so far.

His next question was concerning our baggage. I told him I had left it at the railway station because I was not sure where it should be sent.

"What time does the 'Princess Eulalie' sail?" I asked.

He looked at me oddly. "What?" he queried. "The 'Princess Eulalie'? Twelve o'clock, I believe, I'm not sure."

"You're not sure! And it is after nine now. It strikes me that—"

"Never mind what strikes you. So long as it isn't lightning you shouldn't complain. Have you the baggage checks? Give them to me."

I handed him the checks, obediently, and he stepped to the telephone and gave a number. A short conversation followed. Then he hung up the receiver.

"One of the men from the office will be here soon," he said. "He will attend to all your baggage, get it aboard the ship and see that it is put in your staterooms. Now, then, tell me all about it. What have you been doing since I saw you? When did you arrive? How did you happen to think of taking—er—Miss Cahoon with you? Tell me the whole."

I told him. Hephzy assisted, sitting on the edge of a rocking chair and asking me what time it was at intervals of ten minutes. She was decidedly fidgety. When she went to Boston she usually reached the station half an hour before train time, and to sit calmly in a hotel room, when the ship that was to take us to the ends of the earth was to sail in two hours, was a reckless gamble with Fate, to her mind.

The man from the office came and the baggage checks were turned over to him. So also were our bags and our umbrellas. Campbell stepped into the hall and the pair held a whispered conversation. Hephzy seized the opportunity to express to me her perturbation.

"My soul, Hosy!" she whispered. "Mr. Campbell's out of his head, ain't he? Here we are a sittin' and sittin' and time's goin' by. We'll be too late. Can't you make him hurry?"

I was almost as nervous as she was, but I would not have let our guardian know it for the world. If we lost a dozen steamers I shouldn't call his attention to the fact. I might be a "Babe in the Wood," but he should not have the satisfaction of hearing me whimper.

He came back to the room a moment later and began asking more questions. Our answers, particularly Hephzy's, seemed to please him a great deal. At some of them he laughed uproariously. At last he looked at his watch.

"Almost eleven," he observed. "I must be getting around to the office. Miss Cahoon will you excuse Kent and me for an hour or so? I have his letters of credit and the tickets in our safe and he had better come around with me and get them. If you have any last bits of shopping to do, now is your opportunity. Or you might wait here if you prefer. We will be back at half-past twelve and lunch together."

I started. Hephzy sprang from the chair.

"Half-past twelve!" I cried.

"Lunch together!" gasped Hephzy. "Why, Mr. Campbell! the 'Princess Eulalie' sails at noon. You said so yourself!"

Jim smiled. "I know I did," he replied, "but that is immaterial. You are not concerned with the 'Princess Eulalie.' Your passages are booked on the 'Plutonia' and she doesn't leave her dock until one o'clock to-morrow morning. We will meet here for lunch at twelve-thirty. Come, Kent."

I didn't attempt an answer. I am not exactly sure what I did. A few minutes later I walked out of that room with Campbell and I have a hazy recollection of leaving Hephzy seated in the rocker and of hearing her voice, as the door closed, repeating over and over:

"The 'Plutonia'! My soul and body! The 'Plutonia'! Me—ME on the 'Plutonia'!"

What I said and did afterwards doesn't make much difference. I know I called my publisher a number of disrespectful names not one of which he deserved.

"Confound you!" I cried. "You know I wouldn't have dreamed of taking a passage on a ship like that. She's a floating Waldorf, everyone says so. Dress and swagger society and—Oh, you idiot! I wanted quiet! I wanted to be alone! I wanted—"

Jim interrupted me.

"I know you did," he said. "But you're not going to have them. You've been alone too much. You need a change. If I know the 'Plutonia'—and I've crossed on her four times—you're going to have it."

He burst into a roar of laughter. We were in a cab, fortunately, or his behavior would have attracted attention. I could have choked him.

"You imbecile!" I cried. "I have a good mind to throw the whole thing up and go home to Bayport. By George, I will!"

He continued to chuckle.

"I see you doing it!" he observed. "How about your—what's her name?—Hephzibah? Going to tell her that it's all off, are you? Going to tell her that you will forfeit your passage money and hers? Why, man, haven't you a heart? If she was booked for Paradise instead of Paris she couldn't be any happier. Don't be foolish! Your trunks are on the 'Plutonia' and on the 'Plutonia' you'll be to-night. It's the best thing that can happen to you. I did it on purpose. You'll thank me come day."

I didn't thank him then.

We returned to the hotel at twelve-thirty, my pocket-book loaded with tickets and letters of credit and unfamiliar white paper notes bearing the name of the Bank of England. Hephzibah was still in the rocking chair. I am sure she had not left it.

We lunched in the hotel dining-room. Campbell ordered the luncheon and paid for it while Hephzibah exclaimed at his extravagance. She was too excited to eat much and too worried concerning the extent of her wardrobe to talk of less important matters.

"Oh dear, Hosy!" she wailed, "WHY didn't I buy another best dress. DO you suppose my black one will be good enough? All those lords and ladies and millionaires on the 'Plutonia'! Won't they think I'm dreadful poverty-stricken. I saw a dress I wanted awfully—in one of those Boston stores it was; but I didn't buy it because it was so dear. And I didn't tell you I wanted it because I knew if I did you'd buy it. You're so reckless with money. But now I wish I'd bought it myself. What WILL all those rich people think of me?"

"About what they think of me, Hephzy, I imagine," I answered, ruefully. "Jim here has put up a joke on us. He is the only one who is getting any fun out of it."

Jim, for a wonder, was serious. "Miss Cahoon," he declared, earnestly, "don't worry. I'm sure the black silk is all right; but if it wasn't it wouldn't make any difference. On the 'Plutonia' nobody notices other people's clothes. Most of them are too busy noticing their own. If Kent has his evening togs and you have the black silk you'll pass muster. You'll have a gorgeous time. I only wish I was going with you."

He repeated the wish several times during the afternoon. He insisted on taking us to a matinee and Hephzy's comments on the performance seemed to amuse him hugely. It had been eleven years, so she said, since she went to the theater.

"Unless you count 'Uncle Tom' or 'Ten Nights in a Barroom,' or some of those other plays that come to Bayport," she added. "I suppose I'm making a perfect fool of myself laughin' and cryin' over what's nothin' but make-believe, but I can't help it. Isn't it splendid, Hosy! I wonder what Father would say if he could know that his daughter was really travelin'—just goin' to Europe! He used to worry a good deal, in his last years, about me. Seemed to feel that he hadn't taken me around and done as much for me as he ought to in the days when he could. 'Twas just nonsense, his feelin' that way, and I told him so. But I wonder if he knows now how happy I am. I hope he does. My goodness! I can't realize it myself. Oh, there goes the curtain up again! Oh, ain't that pretty! I AM actin' ridiculous, I know, Mr. Campbell,' but you mustn't mind. Laugh at me all you want to; I sha'n't care a bit."

Jim didn't laugh—then. Neither did I. He and I looked at each other and I think the same thought was in both our minds. Good, kind, whole-souled, self-sacrificing Hephzibah! The last misgiving, the last doubt as to the wisdom of my choice of a traveling companion vanished from my thoughts. For the first time I was actually glad I was going, glad because of the happiness it would mean to her.

When we came out of the theater Campbell reached down in the crowd to shake my hand.

"Congratulations, old man," he whispered; "you did exactly the right thing. You surprised me, I admit, but you were dead right. She's a brick. But don't I wish I was going along! Oh my! oh my! to think of you two wandering about Europe together! If only I might be there to see and hear! Kent, keep a diary; for my sake, promise me you'll keep a diary. Put down everything she says and read it to me when you get home."

He left us soon afterward. He had given up the entire day to me and would, I know, have cheerfully given the evening as well, but I would not hear of it. A messenger from the office had brought him word of the presence in New York of a distinguished scientist who was preparing a manuscript for publication and the scientist had requested an interview that night. Campbell was very anxious to obtain that manuscript and I knew it. Therefore I insisted that he leave us. He was loathe to do so.

"I hate to, Kent," he declared. "I had set my heart on seeing you on board and seeing you safely started. But I do want to nail Scheinfeldt, I must admit. The book is one that he has been at work on for years and two other publishing houses are as anxious as ours to get it. To-night is my chance, and to-morrow may be too late."

"Then you must not miss the chance. You must go, and go now."

"I don't like to. Sure you've got everything you need? Your tickets and your letters of credit and all? Sure you have money enough to carry you across comfortably?"

"Yes, and more than enough, even on the 'Plutonia.'"

"Well, all right, then. When you reach London go to our English branch—you have the address, Camford Street, just off the Strand—and whatever help you may need they'll give you. I've cabled them instructions. Think you can get down to the ship all right?"

I laughed. "I think it fairly possible," I said. "If I lose my way, or Hephzy is kidnapped, I'll speak to the police or telephone you."

"The latter would be safer and much less expensive. Well, good-by, Kent. Remember now, you're going for a good time and you're to forget literature. Write often and keep in touch with me. Good-by, Miss Cahoon. Take care of this—er—clam of ours, won't you. Don't let anyone eat him on the half-shell, or anything like that."

Hephzy smiled. "They'd have to eat me first," she said, "and I'm pretty old and tough. I'll look after him, Mr. Campbell, don't you worry."

"I don't. Good luck to you both—and good-by."

A final handshake and he was gone. Hephzy looked after him.

"There!" she exclaimed; "I really begin to believe I'm goin'. Somehow I feel as if the last rope had been cast off. We've got to depend on ourselves now, Hosy, dear. Mercy! how silly I am talkin'. A body would think I was homesick before I started."

I did not answer, for I WAS homesick. We dined together at the hotel. There remained three long hours before it would be time for us to take the cab for the 'Plutonia's' wharf. I suggested another theater, but Hephzy, to my surprise, declined the invitation.

"If you don't mind, Hosy," she said, "I guess I'd rather stay right here in the room. I—I feel sort of solemn and as if I wanted to sit still and think. Perhaps it's just as well. After waitin' eleven years to go to one theater, maybe two in the same day would be more than I could stand."

So we sat together in the room at the hotel—sat and thought. The minutes dragged by. Outside beneath the windows, New York blazed and roared. I looked down at the hurrying little black manikins on the sidewalks, each, apparently, bound somewhere on business or pleasure of its own, and I wondered vaguely what that business or pleasure might be and why they hurried so. There were many single ones, of course, and occasionally groups of three or four, but couples were the most numerous. Husbands and wives, lovers and sweethearts, each with his or her life and interests bound up in the life and interests of the other. I envied them. Mine had been a solitary life, an unusual, abnormal kind of life. No one had shared its interests and ambitions with me, no one had spurred me on to higher endeavor, had loved with me and suffered with me, helping me through the shadows and laughing with me in the sunshine. No one, since Mother's death, except Hephzy and Hephzy's love and care and sacrifice, fine as they were, were different. I had missed something, I had missed a great deal, and now it was too late. Youth and high endeavor and ambition had gone by; I had left them behind. I was a solitary, queer, self-centered old bachelor, a "quahaug," as my fellow-Bayporters called me. And to ship a quahaug around the world is not likely to do the creature a great deal of good. If he lives through it he is likely to be shipped home again tougher and drier and more useless to the rest of creation than ever.

Hephzibah, too, had evidently been thinking, for she interrupted my dismal meditations with a long sigh. I started and turned toward her.

"What's the matter?" I asked.

"Oh, nothin'," was the solemn answer. "I was wonderin', that's all. Just wonderin' if he would talk English. It would be a terrible thing if he could speak nothin' but French or a foreign language and I couldn't understand him. But Ardelia was American and that brute of a Morley spoke plain enough, so I suppose—"

I judged it high time to interrupt.

"Come, Hephzy," said I. "It is half-past ten. We may as well start at once."

Broadway, seen through the cab windows, was bright enough, a blaze of flashing signs and illuminated shop windows. But —th street, at the foot of which the wharves of the Trans-Atlantic Steamship Company were located, was black and dismal. It was by no means deserted, however. Before and behind and beside us were other cabs and automobiles bound in the same direction. Hephzy peered out at them in amazement.

"Mercy on us, Hosy!" she exclaimed. "I never saw such a procession of carriages. They're as far ahead and as far back of us as you can see. It is like the biggest funeral that ever was, except that they don't crawl along the way a funeral does. I'm glad of that, anyhow. I wish I didn't FEEL so much as if I was goin' to be buried. I don't know why I do. I hope it isn't a presentiment."

If it was she forgot it a few minutes later. The cab stopped before a mammoth doorway in a long, low building and a person in uniform opened the door. The wide street was crowded with vehicles and from them were descending people attired as if for a party rather than an ocean voyage. I helped Hephzy to alight and, while I was paying the cab driver, she looked about her.

"Hosy! Hosy!" she whispered, seizing my arm tight, "we've made a mistake. This isn't the steamboat; this is—is a weddin' or somethin'. Look! look!"

I looked, looked at the silk hats, the opera cloaks, the jewels and those who wore them. For a moment I, too, was certain there must be a mistake. Then I looked upward and saw above the big doorway the flashing electric sign of the "Trans-Atlantic Navigation Company."

"No, Hephzy," said I; "I guess it is the right place. Come."

I gave her my arm—that is, she continued to clutch it with both hands—and we moved forward with the crowd, through the doorway, past a long, moving inclined plane up which bags, valises, bundles of golf sticks and all sorts of lighter baggage were gliding, and faced another and smaller door.

"Lift this way! This way to the lift!" bawled a voice.

"What's a lift?" whispered Hephzy, tremulously, "Hosy, what's a lift?"

"An elevator," I whispered in reply.

"But we can't go on board a steamboat in an elevator, can we? I never heard—"

I don't know what she never heard. The sentence was not finished. Into the lift we went. On either side of us were men in evening dress and directly in front was a large woman, hatless and opera-cloaked, with diamonds in her ears and a rustle of silk at every point of her persons. The car reeked with perfume.

The large woman wriggled uneasily.

"George," she said, in a loud whisper, "why do they crowd these lifts in this disgusting way? And WHY," with another wriggle, "do they permit PERSONS with packages to use them?"

As we emerged from the elevator Hephzy whispered again.

"She meant us, Hosy," she said. "I've got three of those books of yours in this bundle under my arm. I COULDN'T squeeze 'em into either of the valises. But she needn't have been so disagreeable about it, need she."

Still following the crowd, we passed through more wide doorways and into a huge loft where, through mammoth openings at our left, the cool air from the river blew upon our faces. Beyond these openings loomed an enormous something with rows of railed walks leading up its sides. Hephzibah and I, moving in a sort of bewildered dream, found ourselves ascending one of these walks. At its end was another doorway and, beyond, a great room, with more elevators and a mosaic floor, and mahogany and gilt and gorgeousness, and silk and broadcloth and satin.

Hephzy gasped and stopped short.

"It IS a mistake, Hosy!" she cried. "Where is the steamer?"

I smiled. I felt almost as "green" and bewildered as she, but I tried not to show my feelings.

"It is all right, Hephzy," I answered. "This is the steamer. I know it doesn't look like one, but it is. This is the 'Plutonia' and we are on board at last."

Two hours later we leaned together over the rail and watched the lights of New York grow fainter behind us.

Hephzibah drew a deep breath.

"It is so," she said. "It is really so. We ARE, aren't we, Hosy."

"We are," said I. "There is no doubt of it."

"I wonder what will happen to us before we see those lights again."

"I wonder."

"Do you think HE—Do you think Little Frank—"

"Hephzy," I interrupted, "if we are going to bed at all before morning, we had better start now."

"All right, Hosy. But you mustn't say 'go to bed.' Say 'turn in.' Everyone calls going to bed 'turning in' aboard a vessel."

CHAPTER V
In Which We View, and Even Mingle Slightly with, the Upper Classes

It is astonishing—the ease with which the human mind can accustom itself to the unfamiliar and hitherto strange. Nothing could have been more unfamiliar or strange to Hephzibah and me than an ocean voyage and the "Plutonia." And yet before three days of that voyage were at an end we were accustomed to both—to a degree. We had learned to do certain things and not to do others. Some pet illusions had been shattered, and new and, at first, surprising items of information had lost their newness and come to be accepted as everyday facts.

For example, we learned that people in real life actually wore monocles, something, which I, of course, had known to be true but which had seemed nevertheless an unreality, part of a stage play, a "dress-up" game for children and amateur actors. The "English swell" in the performances of the Bayport Dramatic Society always wore a single eyeglass, but he also wore Dundreary whiskers and clothes which would have won him admittance to the Home for Feeble-Minded Youth without the formality of an examination. His "English accent" was a combination of the East Bayport twang and an Irish brogue and he was a blithering idiot in appearance and behavior. No one in his senses could have accepted him as anything human and the eyeglass had been but a part of his unreal absurdity.

And yet, here on the "Plutonia," were at least a dozen men, men of dignity and manner, who sported monocles and acted as if they were used to them. The first evening before we left port, one or two were in evidence; the next afternoon, in the Lounge, there were more. The fact that they were on an English ship, bound for England, brought the monocles out of their concealment, as Hephzy said, "like hoptoads after the first spring thaw." Her amazed comments were unique.

"But what good are they, Hosy?" she demanded. "Can they see with 'em?"

"I suppose they can," I answered. "You can see better with your spectacles than you can without them."

"Humph! I can see better with two eyes than I can with one, as far as that goes. I don't believe they wear 'em for seein' at all. Take that man there," pointing to a long, lank Canadian in a yellow ulster, whom the irreverent smoking-room had already christened "The Duke of Labrador." "Look at him! He didn't wear a sign of one until this mornin'. If he needed it to see with he'd have worn it before, wouldn't he? Don't tell me! He wears it because he wants people to think he's a regular boarder at Windsor Castle. And he isn't; he comes from Toronto, and that's only a few miles from the United States. Ugh! You foolish thing!" as the "Duke of Labrador" strutted by our deck-chairs; "I suppose you think you're pretty, don't you? Well, you're not. You look for all the world like a lighthouse with one window in it and the lamp out."

I laughed. "Hephzy," said I, "every nation has its peculiarities and the monocle is an English national institution, like—well, like tea, for instance."

"Institution! Don't talk to me about institutions! I know the institution I'd put HIM in."

She didn't fancy the "Duke of Labrador." Neither did she fancy tea at breakfast and coffee at dinner. But she learned to accept the first. Two sessions with the "Plutonia's" breakfast coffee completed her education.

"Bring me tea," she said to our table steward on the third morning. "I've tried most every kind of coffee and lived through it, but I'm gettin' too old to keep on experimentin' with my health. Bring me tea and I'll try to forget what time it is."

We had tea at breakfast, therefore, and tea at four in the afternoon. Hephzibah and I learned to take it with the rest. She watched her fellow-passengers, however, and as usual had something to say concerning their behavior.

"Did you hear that, Hosy?" she whispered, as we sat together in the "Lounge," sipping tea and nibbling thin bread and butter and the inevitable plum cake. "Did you hear what that woman said about her husband?"

I had not heard, and said so.

"Well, judgin' by her actions, I thought her husband was lost and she was sure he had been washed overboard. 'Where is Edward?' she kept askin'. 'Poor Edward! What WILL he do? Where is he?' I was gettin' real anxious, and then it turned out that she was afraid that, if he didn't come soon, he'd miss his tea. My soul! Hosy, I've been thinkin' and do you know the conclusion I've come to?"

"No," I replied. "What is it?"

"Well, it sounds awfully irreverent, but I've come to the conclusion that the first part of the Genesis in the English scriptures must be different than ours. I'm sure they think that the earth was created in six days and, on the seventh, Adam and Eve had tea. I believe it for an absolute fact."

The pet illusion, the loss of which caused her the most severe shock, was that concerning the nobility. On the morning of our first day afloat the passenger lists were distributed. Hephzibah was early on deck. Fortunately neither she nor I were in the least discomfited by the motion of the ship, then or at any time. We proved to be good sailors; Hephzibah declared it was in the blood.

"For a Knowles or a Cahoon to be seasick," she announced, "would be a disgrace. Our men folks for four generations would turn over in their graves."

She was early on deck that first morning and, at breakfast she and I had the table to ourselves. She had the passenger list propped against the sugar bowl and was reading the names.

"My gracious, Hosy!" she exclaimed. "What, do you think! There are five 'Sirs' on board and one 'Lord'! Just think of it! Where do you suppose they are?"

"In their berths, probably, at this hour," I answered.

"Then I'm goin' to stay right here till they come out. I'm goin' to see 'em and know what they look like if I sit at this table all day."

I smiled. "I wouldn't do that, Hephzy," said I. "We can see them at lunch."

"Oh! O—Oh! And there's a Princess here! Princess B-e-r-g-e-n-s-t-e-i-n—Bergenstein. Princess Bergenstein. What do you suppose she's Princess of?"

"Princess of Jerusalem, I should imagine," I answered. "Oh, I see! You've skipped a line, Hephzy. Bergenstein belongs to another person. The Princess's name is Berkovitchky. Russian or Polish, perhaps."

"I don't care if she's Chinese; I mean to see her. I never expected to look at a live Princess in MY life."

We stopped in the hall at the entrance to the dining-saloon to examine the table chart. Hephzibah made careful notes of the tables at which the knights and the lord and the Princess were seated and their locations. At lunch she consulted the notes.

"The lord sits right behind us at that little table there," she said, excitedly. "That table for two is marked 'Lord and Lady Erskine.' Now we must watch when they come in."

A few minutes later a gray-haired little man, accompanied by a middle-aged woman entered the saloon and were seated at the small table by an obsequious steward. Hephzy gasped.

"Why—why, Hosy!" she exclaimed. "That isn't the lord, is it? THAT?"

"I suppose it must be," I answered. When our own Steward came I asked him.

"Yes, sir," he answered, with unction. "Yes, sir, that is Lord and Lady Erskine, sir, thank you, sir."

Hephzy stared at Lord and Lady Erskine. I gave our luncheon order, and the steward departed. Then her indignant disgust and disappointment burst forth.

"Well! well!" she exclaimed. "And that is a real live lord! That is! Why, Hosy, he's the livin' image of Asaph Tidditt back in Bayport. If Ase could afford clothes like that he might be his twin brother. Well! I guess that's enough. I don't want to see that Princess any more. Just as like as not she'd look like Susanna Wixon."

Her criticisms were not confined to passengers of other nationalities. Some of our own came in for comment quite as severe.

"Look at those girls at that table over there," she whispered. "The two in red, I mean. One of 'em has got a little flag pinned on her dress. What do you suppose that is for?"

I looked at the young ladies in red. They were vivacious damsels and their conversation and laughter were by no means subdued. A middle-aged man and woman and two young fellows were their table-mates and the group attracted a great deal of attention.

"What has she got that flag pinned on her for?" repeated Hephzy.

"She wishes everyone to know she's an American exportation, I suppose," I answered. "She is evidently proud of her country."

"Humph! Her country wouldn't be proud of her, if it had to listen to her the way we do. There's some exports it doesn't pay to advertise, I guess, and she and her sister are that kind. Every time they laugh I can see that Lady Erskine shrivel up like a sensitive plant. I hope she don't think all American girls are like those two."

"She probably does."

"Well, IF she does she's makin' a big mistake. I might as well believe all Englishmen were like this specimen comin' now, and I don't believe that, even if I do hail from Bayport."

The specimen was the "Duke of Labrador," who sauntered by, monocle in eye, hands in pockets and an elaborate affection of the "Oxford stoop" which he must have spent time and effort in acquiring. Hephzibah shook her head.

"I wish Toronto was further from home than it is," she declared. "But there! I shan't worry about him. I'll leave him for Lord Erskine and his wife to be ashamed of. He's their countryman, or he hopes he is. I've got enough to do bein' ashamed of those two American girls."

It may be gathered from these conversations that Hephzy and I had been so fortunate as to obtain a table by ourselves. This was not the case. There were four seats at our table and, according to the chart of the dining-saloon, one of them should be occupied by a "Miss Rutledge of New York" and the other by "A. Carleton Heathcroft of London." Miss Rutledge we had not seen at all. Our table steward informed us that the lady was "hindisposed" and confined to her room. She was an actress, he added. Hephzy, whose New England training had imbued her with the conviction that all people connected with the stage must be highly undesirable as acquaintances, was quite satisfied. "Of course I'm sorry she isn't well," she confided to me "but I'm awfully glad she won't be at our table. I shouldn't want to hurt her feelin's, but I couldn't talk to her as I would to an ordinary person. I COULDN'T! All I should be able to think of was what she wore, or didn't wear, when she was actin' her parts. I expect I'm old-fashioned, but when I think of those girls in the pictures outside that theater—the one we didn't go to—I—well—mercy!"

The "pictures" were the posters advertising a popular musical comedy which Campbell had at first suggested our witnessing the afternoon of our stay in New York. Hephzibah's shocked expression and my whispered advice had brought about a change of plans. We saw a perfectly respectable, though thrilling, melodrama instead. I might have relieved my relative's mind by assuring her that all actresses were not necessarily attired as "merry villagers," but the probable result of my assurance seemed scarcely worth the effort.

A. Carleton Heathcroft, Esquire, was not acquainted with the stage, in a professional way, at any rate. He was a slim and elegant gentleman, dressed with elaborate care, who appeared profoundly bored with life in general and our society in particular. He sported one of Hephzibah's detestations, a monocle, and spoke, when he spoke at all, with a languid drawl and what

I learned later was a Piccadilly accent. He favored us with his company during our first day afloat; after that we saw him amid the select group at that much sought—by some—center of shipboard prominence, "the Captain's table."

Oddly enough Hephzibah did not resent the Heathcroft condescension and single eyeglass as much as I had expected. She explained her feeling in this way.

"I know he's dreadfully high and mighty and all that," she said. "And the way he said 'Really?' when you and I spoke to him was enough to squelch even an Angelina Phinney. But I didn't care so much. Anybody, even a body as green as I am, can see that he actually IS somebody when he's at home, not a make-believe, like that Toronto man. And I'm glad for our waiter's sake that he's gone somewhere else. The poor thing bowed so low when he came in and was so terribly humble every time Mr. Heathcroft spoke to him. I should hate to feel I must say 'Thank you' when I was told that the food was 'rotten bad.' I never thought 'rotten' was a nice word, but all these English folks say it. I heard that pretty English girl over there tell her father that it was a 'jolly rotten mornin',' and she's as nice and sweet as she can be. Well, I'm learnin' fast, Hosy. I can see a woman smoke a cigarette now and not shiver—much. Old Bridget Doyle up in West Bayport, used to smoke a pipe and the whole town talked about it. She'd be right at home in that sittin'-room they call a 'Lounge' after dinner, wouldn't she?"

My acquaintance with A. Carleton Heathcroft, which appeared to have ended almost as soon as it began, was renewed in an odd way. I was in the "Smoke-Room" after dinner the third evening out, enjoying a cigar and idly listening to the bidding for pools on the ship's run, that time-honored custom which helps the traveling gentleman of sporting proclivities to kill time and lose money. On board the "Plutonia," with its unusually large quota of millionaires and personages, the bidding was lively and the prices paid for favored numbers high. Needless to say I was not one of the bidders. My interest was merely casual.

The auctioneer that evening was a famous comedian with an international reputation and his chatter, as he urged his hearers to higher bids, was clever and amusing. I was listening to it and smiling at the jokes when a voice at my elbow said:

"Five pounds."

I turned and saw that the speaker was Heathcroft. His monocle was in his eye, a cigarette was between his fingers and he looked as if he had been newly washed and ironed and pressed from head to foot. He nodded carelessly and I bowed in return.

"Five pounds," repeated Mr. Heathcroft.

The auctioneer acknowledged the bid and proceeded to urge his audience on to higher flights. The flights were made and my companion capped each with one more lofty. Eight, nine, ten pounds were bid. Heathcroft bid eleven. Someone at the opposite side of the room bid twelve. It seemed ridiculous to me. Possibly my face expressed my feeling; at any rate something caused the immaculate gentleman in the next chair to address me instead of the auctioneer.

"I say," he said, "that's running a bit high, isn't it?"

"It seems so to me," I replied. "The number is five hundred and eighty-six and I think we shall do better than that."

"Oh, do you! Really! And why do you think so, may I ask?"

"Because we are having a remarkably smooth sea and a favorable wind."

"Oh, but you forget the fog. There's quite a bit of fog about us now, isn't there."

I wish I could describe the Heathcroft manner of saying "Isn't there." I can't, however; there is no use trying.

"It will amount to nothing," I answered. "The glass is high and there is no indication of bad weather. Our run this noon was five hundred and ninety-one, you remember."

"Yes. But we did have extraordinarily good weather for that."

"Why, not particularly good. We slowed down about midnight. There was a real fog then and the glass was low. The second officer told me it dropped very suddenly and there was a heavy sea running. For an hour between twelve and one we were making not much more than half our usual speed."

"Really! That's interesting. May I ask if you and the second officer are friends?"

"Scarcely that. He and I exchanged a few words on deck this morning, that's all."

"But he told you about the fog and the—what is it—the glass, and all that. Fancy! that's extremely odd. I'm acquainted with the captain in a trifling sort of way; I sit at his table, I mean to say. And I assure you he doesn't tell us a word. And, by Jove, we cross-question him, too! Rather!"

I smiled. I could imagine the cross-questioning.

"I suppose the captain is obliged to be non-committal," I observed. "That's part of his job. The second officer meant to be, I have no doubt, but perhaps my remarks showed that I was really interested in ships and the sea. My father and grandfather, too, for that matter were seafaring men, both captains. That may have made the second officer more communicative. Not that he said anything of importance, of course."

Mr. Heathcroft seemed very interested. He actually removed his eyeglass.

"Oh!" he exclaimed. "You know something about it, then. I thought it was extraordinary, but now I see. And you think our run will be better than five hundred and eighty?"

"It should be, unless there is a remarkable change. This ship makes over six hundred, day after day, in good weather. She should do at least six hundred by to-morrow noon, unless there is a sudden change, as I said."

"But six hundred would be—it would be the high field, by Jove!"

"Anything over five hundred and ninety-four would be that. The numbers are very low to-night. Far too low, I should say."

Heathcroft was silent. The auctioneer, having forced the bid on number five hundred and eighty-six up to thirteen pounds ten, was imploring his hearers not to permit a certain winner to be sacrificed at this absurd figure.

"Fourteen pounds, gentlemen," he begged. "For the sake of the wife and children, for the honor of the star spangled banner and the union jack,—DON'T hesitate—don't even stammer—below fourteen pounds."

He looked in our direction as he said it. Mr. Heathcroft made no sign. He produced a gold cigarette box and extended it in my direction.

"Will you?" he inquired.

"No, thank you," I replied. "I will smoke a cigar, if you don't mind."

He did not appear to mind. He lighted his cigarette, readjusted his monocle, and stared stonily at the gesticulating auctioneer.

The bidding went on. One by one the numbers were sold until all were gone. Then the auctioneer announced that bids for the "high field," that is, any number above five hundred and ninety-four, were in order. My companion suddenly came to life.

"Ten pounds," he called.

I started. "For mercy sake, Mr. Heathcroft," I protested, "don't let anything I have said influence your bidding. I may be entirely wrong."

He turned and surveyed me through the eyeglass.

"You may wish to bid yourself," he drawled. "Careless of me. So sorry. Shall I withdraw the bid?"

"No, no. I'm not going to bid. I only—"

"Eleven pounds I am offered, gentlemen," shouted the auctioneer. "Eleven pounds! It would be like robbing an orphan asylum. Do I hear twelve?"

He heard twelve immediately—from Mr. Heathcroft.

Thirteen pounds were bid. Evidently others shared my opinion concerning the value of the "high field." Heathcroft promptly raised it to fourteen. I ventured another protest. So far as effect was concerned I might as well have been talking to one of the smoke-stacks. The bidding was lively and lengthy. At last the "high field" went to Mr. A. Carleton Heathcroft for twenty-one pounds, approximately one hundred and five dollars. I thought it time for me to make my escape. I was wondering where I should hide next day, when the run was announced.

"Greatly obliged to you, I'm sure," drawled the fortunate bidder. "Won't you join me in a whisky and soda or something?"

I declined the whisky and soda.

"Sorry," said Mr. Heathcroft. "Jolly grateful for putting me right, Mr.—er—"

"Knowles is my name," I said. He might have remembered it; I remembered his perfectly.

"Of course—Knowles. Thank you so much, Knowles. Thank you and the second officer. Nothing like having professional information—eh, what? Rather!"

There seemed to be no doubt in his mind that he was going to win. There was more than a doubt in mine. I told Hephzy of my experience when I joined her in the Lounge. My attempts to say "Really" and "Isn't it" and "Rather" in the Heathcroft manner and with the Heathcroft accent pleased her very much. As to the result of my unpremeditated "tip" she was quite indifferent.

"If he loses it will serve him good and right," she declared. "Gamblin's poor business and I sha'n't care if he does lose."

"I shall," I observed. "I feel responsible in a way and I shall be sorry."

"'SO sorry,' you mean, Hosy. That's what that blunderin' steward said when he stepped on my skirt and tore the gatherin' all loose. I told him he wasn't half as sorry as I was."

But at noon next day, when the observation was taken and the run posted on the bulletin board the figure was six hundred and two. My "tip" had been a good one after all and A. Carleton Heathcroft, Esquire, was richer by some seven hundred dollars, even after the expenses of treating the "smoke-room" and feeing the smoke-room steward had been deducted. I did not visit the smoke-room to share in the treat. I feared I might be expected to furnish more professional information. But that evening a bottle of vintage champagne was produced by our obsequious table steward. "With Mr. 'Eathcroft's compliments, sir, thank you, sir," announced the latter.

Hephzibah looked at the gilt-topped bottle.

"WHAT in the world will we do with it, Hosy?" she demanded.

"Why, drink it, I suppose," I answered. "It is the only thing we can do. We can't send it back."

"But you can't drink the whole of it, and I'm sure I sha'n't start in to be a drunkard at my age. I'll take the least little bit of a drop, just to see what it tastes like. I've read about champagne, just as I've read about lords and ladies, all my life, but I never expected to see either of 'em. Well there!" after a very small sip from the glass, "there's another pet idea gone to smash. A lord looks like Ase Tidditt, and champagne tastes like vinegar and soda. Tut! tut! tut! if I had to drink that sour stuff all my life I'd probably look like Asaph, too. No wonder that Erkskine man is such a shriveled-up thing."

I glanced toward the captain's table. Mr. Heathcroft raised his glass. I bowed and raised mine. The group at that table, the captain included, were looking in my direction. I judged that my smoke-room acquaintance had told them of my wonderful "tip." I imagined I could see the sarcastic smile upon the captain's face. I did not care for that kind of celebrity.

But the affair had one quite unexpected result. The next forenoon as Hephzibah and I were reclining in our deck-chairs the captain himself, florid-faced, gray-bearded, gold-laced and grand, halted before us.

"I believe your name is Knowles, sir," he said, raising his cap.

"It is," I replied. I wondered what in the world was coming next. Was he going to take me to task for talking with his second officer?

"Your home is in Bayport, Massachusetts, I see by the passenger list," he went on. "Is that Bayport on Cape Cod, may I ask?"

"Yes," I replied, more puzzled than ever.

"I once knew a Knowles from your town, sir. He was a seafaring man like myself. His name was Philander Knowles, and when I knew him he was commander of the bark 'Ranger.'"

"He was my father," I said.

Captain Stone extended his hand.

"Mr. Knowles," he declared, "this is a great pleasure, sir. I knew your father years ago when I was a young man, mate of one of our ships engaged in the Italian fruit trade. He was very kind to me at that time. I have never forgotten it. May I sit down?"

The chair next to ours happened to be unoccupied at the moment and he took it. I introduced Hephzibah and we chatted for some time. The captain appeared delighted to meet the son of his old acquaintance. Father and he had met in Messina—Father's ship was in the fruit trade also at that time— and something or other he had done to help young Stone had made a great impression on the latter. I don't know what the something was, whether it was monetary help or assistance in getting out of a serious scrape; Stone did not tell me and I didn't ask. But, at any rate, the pair had become very friendly there and at subsequent meetings in the Mediterranean ports. The captain asked all sorts of questions about Father, his life, his family and his death aboard the sinking "Monarch of the Seas." Hephzibah furnished most of the particulars. She remembered them well.

Captain Stone nodded solemnly.

"That is the way the master of a ship should die," he declared. "Your father, Mr. Knowles, was a man and he died like one. He was my first American acquaintance and he gave me a new idea of Yankees—if you'll excuse my calling them that, sir."

Hephzy had a comment to make.

"There are SOME pretty fair Yankees," she observed, drily. "ALL the good folks haven't moved back to England yet."

The captain solemnly assured her that he was certain of it.

"Though two of the best are on their way," I added, with a wink at Hephzy. This attempt at humor was entirely lost. Our companion said he presumed I referred to Mr. and Mrs. Van Hook, who sat next him at table.

"And that leads me to ask if Miss Cahoon and yourself will not join us," he went on. "I could easily arrange for two places."

I looked at Hephzy. Her face expressed decided disapproval and she shook her head.

"Thank you, Captain Stone," I said; "but we have a table to ourselves and are very comfortable. We should not think of troubling you to that extent."

He assured us it would not be a trouble, but a pleasure. We were firm in our refusal, however, and he ceased to urge. He declared his intention of seeing that our quarters were adequate, offered to accompany us through the engine-rooms and the working portions of the ship whenever we wished, ordered the deck steward, who was all but standing on his head in obsequious desire to oblige, to take good care of us, shook hands once more, and went away. Hephzibah drew a long breath.

"My goodness!" she exclaimed; "sit at HIS table! I guess not! There's another lord and his wife there, to say nothin' of the Van Hooks. I'd look pretty, in my Cape Cod clothes, perched up there, wouldn't I! A hen is all right in her place, but she don't belong in a peacock cage. And they drink champagne ALL the time there; I've watched 'em. No thank you, I'll stay in the henyard along with the everyday fowls."

"Odd that he should have known Father," I observed. "Well, I suppose the proper remark to make, under the circumstances, is that this is a small world. That is what nine-tenths of Bayport would say."

"It's what I say, too," declared Hephzy, with emphasis. "Well, it's awful encouraging for us, isn't it."

"Encouraging? What do you mean?"

"Why, I mean about Little Frank. It makes me feel surer than ever that we shall run across him."

I suppressed a groan. "Hephzy," said I, "why on earth should the fact that Captain Stone knew my father encourage you to believe that we shall meet a person we never knew at all?"

"Hosy, how you do talk! If you and I, just cruisin' this way across the broadside of creation, run across a man that knew Cousin Philander thirty-nine years ago, isn't it just as reasonable to suppose we'll meet a child who was born twenty-one years ago? I should say 'twas! Hosy, I've had a presentiment about this cruise of ours: We're SENT on it; that's what I think—we're sent. Oh, you can laugh! You'll see by and by. THEN you won't laugh."

"No, Hephzy," I admitted, resignedly, "I won't laugh then, I promise you. If I ever reach the stage where I see a Little Frank I promise you I sha'n't laugh. I'll believe diseases of the brain are contagious, like the measles, and I'll send for a doctor."

The captain met us again in the dining-room that evening. He came over to our table and chatted for some time. His visit caused quite a sensation. Shipboard society is a little world by itself and the ship's captain is the head of it. Persons who would, very likely, have passed Captain Stone on Fifth Avenue or Piccadilly without recognizing him now toadied to him as if he were a Czar, which, in a way, I suppose he is when afloat. His familiarity with us shed a sort of reflected glory upon Hephzy and me. Several of our fellow-passengers spoke to us that evening for the first time.

A. Carleton Heathcroft, Esquire, was not among the Lounge habitues; the smoke-room was his accustomed haunt. But the next forenoon as I leaned over the rail of the after promenade deck watching the antics of the "Stokers' Band" which was performing for the benefit of the second-class with an eye toward pennies and small silver from all classes, Heathcroft sauntered up and leaned beside me. We exchanged good-mornings. I thanked him for the wine.

"Quite unnecessary, Knowles," he said. "Least I could do, it seems to me. I pulled quite a tidy bit from that inside information of yours; I did really. Awfully obliged, and all that. You seem to have a wide acquaintance among the officers. That captain chap tells us he knew your father—the sailor one you told me of, you understand."

Having had but one father I understood perfectly. We chatted in a inconsequential way for a short time. In the course of our conversation I happened to mention that I wrote, professionally. To my surprise Heathcroft was impressed.

"Do you, really!" he exclaimed. "That's interesting, isn't it now! I have a cousin who writes. Don't know why she does it; she doesn't get her writings printed, but she keeps on. It is a habit of hers. Curious dissipation—eh, what? Does that—er—Miss—that companion of yours, write also?"

I laughed and informed him that writing was not one of Hephzibah's bad habits.

"Extraordinary woman, isn't she," he said. "I met her just now, walking about, and I happened to mention that I was taking the air. She said she wouldn't quarrel with me because of that. The more I took the better she would like it; she could spare about a gale and a quarter and not feel—What did she call it? Oh yes, 'scrimped.' What is 'scrimped,' may I ask?"

I explained the meaning of "scrimped." Heathcroft was much amused.

"It WAS blowing a bit strong up forward there," he declared. "That was a clever way of putting it, wasn't it?"

"She is a clever woman," I said, shortly.

Heathcroft did not enthuse.

"Oh," he said dubiously. "A relative of yours, I suppose."

"A cousin, that's all."

"One's relatives, particularly the feminine relatives, incline toward eccentricity as they grow older, don't you think. I have an aunt down in Sussex, who is queer. A good sort, too, no end of money, a big place and all that, but odd. She and I get on well together—I am her pet, I suppose I may say—but, by Jove, she has quarreled with everyone else in the family. I let her have her own way and it has convinced her that I am the only rational Heathcroft in existence. Do you golf, Knowles?"

"I attempt something in that line. I doubt if my efforts should be called golf."

"It is a rotten game when one is off form, isn't it. If you are down in Sussex and I chance to be there I should be glad to have you play an eighteen with me. Burglestone Bogs is the village. Anyone will direct you to the Manor. If I'm not there, introduce yourself to my aunt. Lady Kent Carey is the name. She'll be jolly glad to welcome you if you tell her you know me. I'm her sole interest in life, the greenhouses excepted, of course. Cultivating roses and rearing me are her hobbies."

I thought it improbable that the golfers of Burglestone Bogs would ever be put to shame by the brilliancy of my game. I thanked him, however. I was surprised at the invitation. I had been under the impression, derived from my reading, that the average Englishman required an acquaintance of several months before proffering hospitality. No doubt Mr. Heathcroft was not an average Englishman.

"Will you be in London long?" he asked. "I suppose not. You're probably off on a hurricane jaunt from one end of the Continent to the other. Two hours at Stratford, bowing before Shakespeare's tomb, a Derby through the cathedral towns, and then the Channel boat, eh? That's the American way, isn't it?"

"It is not our way," I replied. "We have no itinerary. I don't know where we may go or how long we shall stay."

Evidently I rose again in his estimation.

"Have you picked your hotel in London?" he inquired.

"No. I shall be glad of any help you may be kind enough to give along that line."

He reflected. "There's a decent little hotel in Mayfair," he said, after a moment. "A private sort of shop. I don't use it myself; generally put up at the club, I mean to say. But my aunt and my sisters do. They're quite mad about it. It is—Ah—Bancroft's—that's it, Bancroft's Hotel. I'll give you the address before I leave."

I thanked him again. He was certainly trying to be kind. No doubt the kindness was due to his sense of obligation engendered by what he called my "professional information," but it was kindness all the same.

The first bugle for luncheon sounded. Mr. Heathcroft turned to go.

"I'll see you again, Knowles," he said, "and give you the hotel street and number and all that. Hope you'll like it. If you shouldn't the Langham is not bad—quiet and old-fashioned, but really very fair. And if you care for something more public and—Ah—American, there are always the Savoy and the Cecil. Here is my card. If I can be of any service to you while you are in town drop me a line at my clubs, either of them. I must be toddling. By, by."

He "toddled" and I sought my room to prepare for luncheon.

Two days more and our voyage was at an end. We saw more of our friend the captain during those days and of Heathcroft as well. The former fulfilled his promise of showing us through the ship, and Hephzy and I, descending greasy iron stairways and twisting through narrow passages, saw great rooms full of mighty machinery, and a cavern where perspiring, grimy men, looking but half-human in the red light from the furnace mouths, toiled ceaselessly with pokers and shovels.

We stood at the forward end of the promenade deck at night, looking out into the blackness, and heard the clang of four bells from the shadows at the bow, the answering clang from the crow's-nest on the foremast, and the weird cry of "All's well" from the lookouts. This experience made a great impression on us both. Hephzy expressed my feeling exactly when she said in a hushed whisper:

"There, Hosy! for the first time I feel as if I really was on board a ship at sea. My father and your father and all our men-folks for ever so far back have heard that 'All's well'—yes, and called it, too, when they first went as sailors. Just think of it! Why Father was only sixteen when he shipped; just a boy, that's all. I've heard him say 'All's well' over and over again; 'twas a kind of byword with him. This whole thing seems like somethin' callin' to me out of the past and gone. Don't you feel it?"

I felt it, as she did. The black night, the quiet, the loneliness, the salt spray on our faces and the wash of the waves alongside, the high singsong wail from lookout to lookout—it WAS a voice from the past, the call of generations of sea-beaten, weather-worn, brave old Cape Codders to their descendants, reminding the latter of a dead and gone profession and of thousands of fine, old ships which had plowed the ocean in the days when "Plutonias" were unknown.

We attended the concert in the Lounge, and the ball on the promenade deck which followed. Mr. Heathcroft, who seemed to have made the acquaintance of most of the pretty girls on board, informed us in the intervals between a two-step and a tango, that he had been "dancing madly."

"You Americans are extraordinary people," he added. "Your dances are as extraordinary as your food. That Mrs. Van Hook, who sits near me at table, was indulging in—what do you call them?—oh, yes, griddle cakes— this morning. Begged me to try them. I declined. Horrid things they were. Round, like a—like a washing-flannel, and swimming in treacle. Frightful!"

"And that man," commented Hephzy, "eats cold toast and strawberry preserves for breakfast and washes 'em down with three cups of tea. And he calls nice hot pancakes frightful!"

At ten o'clock in the morning of the sixth day we sighted the Irish coast through the dripping haze which shrouded it and at four we dropped anchor abreast the breakwater of the little Welsh village which was to be our landing place. The sun was shining dimly by this time and the rounded hills and the mountains beyond them, the green slopes dotted with farms and checkered with hedges and stone walls, the gray stone fort with its white-washed barrack buildings, the spires and chimneys of the village in the hollow—all these combined to make a picture which was homelike and yet not like home, foreign and yet strangely familiar.

We leaned over the rail and watched the trunks and boxes and bags and bundles shoot down the slide into the baggage and mail-boat which lay alongside. Hephzy was nervous.

"They'll smash everything to pieces—they surely will!" she declared. "Either that or smash themselves, I don't know which is liable to happen first. Mercy on us! Did you see that? That box hit the man right in the back!"

"It didn't hurt him," I said, reassuringly. "It was nothing but a hat-box."

"Hurt HIM—no! But I guess likely it didn't do the hat much good. I thought baggage smashin' was an American institution, but they've got some experts over here. Oh, my soul and body! there goes MY trunk—end over end, of course. Well, I'm glad there's no eggs in it, anyway. Josiah Dimick always used to carry two dozen eggs to his daughter-in-law every time he went to Boston. He had 'em in a box once and put the box on the seat alongside of him and a big fat woman came and sat—Oh! that was your trunk, Hosy! Did you hear it hit? I expect every one of those 'English Poets' went from top to bottom then, right through all your clothes. Never mind, I suppose it's all part of travelin'."

Mr. Heathcroft, looking more English than ever in his natty top coat, and hat at the back of his head, sauntered up. He was, for him, almost enthusiastic.

"Looking at the water, were you?" he queried. "Glorious color, isn't it. One never sees a sea like that or a sky like that anywhere but here at home."

Hephzy looked at the sea and sky. It was plain that she wished to admire, for his sake, but her admiration was qualified.

"Don't you think if they were a little brighter and bluer they'd be prettier?" she asked.

Heathcroft stared at her through his monocle.

"Bluer?" he repeated. "My dear woman, there are no skies as blue as the English skies. They are quite celebrated—really."

He sauntered on again, evidently disgusted at our lack of appreciation.

"He must be color-blind," I observed. Hephzy was more charitable.

"I guess likely everybody's home things are best," she said. "I suppose this green-streaked water and those gray clouds do look bright and blue to him. We must make allowances, Hosy. He never saw an August mornin' at Bayport, with a northwest wind blowin' and the bay white and blue to the edge of all creation. That's been denied him. He means well, poor thing; he don't know any better."

An hour later we landed from the passenger tender at a stone pier covered with substantial stone buildings. Uniformed custom officers and uniformed policemen stood in line as we came up the gang-plank. Behind them, funny little locomotives attached to queer cars which appeared to be all doors, puffed and panted.

Hephzibah looked about her.

"Yes," she said, with conviction. "I'm believin' it more and more all the time. It is England, just like the pictures. How many times I've seen engines like that in pictures, and cars like that, too. I never thought I'd ride in 'em. My goodness me? Hephzibah Jane Cahoon, you're in England—YOU are! You needn't be afraid to turn over for fear of wakin' up, either. You're awake and alive and in England! Hosy," with a sudden burst of exuberance, "hold on to me tight. I'm just as likely to wave my hat and hurrah as I am to do anything. Hold on to me—tight."

We got through the perfunctory customs examination without trouble. Our tickets provided by Campbell, included those for the railway journey to London. I secured a first-class compartment at the booking-office and a guard conducted us to it and closed the door. Another short delay and then, with a whistle as queer and unfamiliar as its own appearance, the little locomotive began to pull our train out of the station.

Hephzy leaned back against the cushions with a sigh of supreme content.

"And now," said I, "for London. London! think of it, Hephzy!"

Hephzy shook her head.

"I'm thinkin' of it," she said. "London—the biggest city in the world! Who knows, Hosy? France is such a little ways off; probably Little Frank has been to London a hundred times. He may even be there now. Who knows? I shouldn't be surprised if we met him right in London. I sha'n't be surprised at anything anymore. I'm in England and on my way to London; that's surprise enough. NOTHIN' could be more wonderful than that."

CHAPTER VI
In Which We Are Received at Bancroft's Hotel and I Receive a Letter

It was late when we reached London, nearly eleven o'clock. The long train journey was a delight. During the few hours of daylight and dusk we peered through the car windows at the scenery flying past; at the villages, the green fields, the hedges, the neat, trim farms.

"Everything looks as if it has been swept and dusted," declared Hephzy. "There aren't any waste places at all. What do they do with their spare land?"

"They haven't any," I answered. "Land is too valuable to waste. There's another thatched roof. It looks like those in the pictures, doesn't it."

Hephzy nodded. "Just exactly," she said. "Everything looks like the pictures. I feel as if I'd seen it all before. If that engine didn't toot so much like a tin whistle I should almost think it was a picture. But it isn't—it isn't; it's real, and you and I are part of it."

We dined on the train. Night came and our window-pictures changed to glimpses of flashing lights interspersed with shadowy blotches of darkness. At length the lights became more and more frequent and began to string out in long lines marking suburban streets. Then the little locomotive tooted its tin whistle frantically and we rolled slowly under a great train shed— Paddington Station and London itself.

Amid the crowd on the platform Hephzy and I stood, two lone wanderers not exactly sure what we should do next. About us the busy crowd jostled and pushed. Relatives met relatives and fathers and mothers met sons and daughters returning home after long separations. No one met us, no one was interested in us at all, except the porters and the cabmen. I selected a red-faced chunky porter who was a decidedly able person, apparently capable of managing anything except the letter h. The acrobatics which he performed with that defenceless consonant were marvelous. I have said that I selected him; that he selected me would be nearer the truth.

Kent Knowles | 83

"Cab, sir. Yes, sir, thank you, sir," he said. "Leave that to me, sir. Will you 'ave a fourwheeler or a hordinary cab, sir?"

I wasn't exactly certain what a fourwheeler might be. I had read about them often enough, but I had never seen one pictured and properly labeled. For the matter of that, all the vehicles in sight appeared to have four wheels. So I said, at a venture, that I thought an ordinary cab would do.

"Yes, sir; 'ere you are, sir. Your boxes are in the luggage van, I suppose, sir."

I took it for granted he meant my trunks and those were in what I, in my ignorance, would have called a baggage car:

"Yes, sir," said the porter. "If the lidy will be good enough to wait 'ere, sir, you and I will go hafter the boxes, sir."

Cautioning Hephzy not to stir from her moorings on any account I followed my guide to the "luggage van." This crowded car disgorged our two steamer trunks and, my particular porter having corraled a fellow-craftsman to help him, the trunks were dragged to the waiting cab.

I found Hephzy waiting, outwardly calm, but inwardly excited.

"I saw one at last," she declared. "I'd about come to believe there wasn't such a thing, but there is; I just saw one."

"One—what?" I asked, puzzled.

"An Englishman with side-whiskers. They wasn't as big and long as those in the pictures, but they were side-whiskers. I feel better. When you've been brought up to believe every Englishman wore 'em, it was kind of humiliatin' not to see one single set."

I paid my porters—I learned afterward that, like most Americans, I had given them altogether too much—and we climbed into the cab with our bags. The "boxes," or trunks, were on the driver's seat and on the roof.

"Where to, sir?" asked the driver.

I hesitated. Even at this late date I had not made up my mind exactly "where to." My decision was a hasty one.

"Why—er—to—to Bancroft's Hotel," I said. "Blithe Street, just off Piccadilly."

I think the driver was somewhat astonished. Very few of his American passengers selected Bancroft's as a stopping place, I imagine. However, his answer was prompt.

"Yes, sir, thank you, sir," he said. The cab rolled out of the station.

"I suppose," said Hephzy, reflectively, "if you had told him or that porter man that they were everlastin' idiots they'd have thanked you just the same and called you 'sir' four times besides."

"No doubt they would."

"Yes, sir, I'm perfectly sure they would—thank you, sir. So this is London. It doesn't look such an awful lot different from Boston or New York so far."

But Bancroft's, when we reached it, was as unlike a Boston or New York hotel as anything could be. A short, quiet, eminently respectable street, leading from Piccadilly; a street fenced in, on both sides, by three-story, solid, eminently respectable houses of brick and stone. No signs, no street cars, no crowds, no glaring lights. Merely a gas lamp burning over the fanlight of a spotless white door, and the words "Bancroft's Hotel" in mosaic lettering set in a white stone slab in the pavement.

The cab pulled up before the white door and Hephzy and I looked out of the window. The same thought was in both our minds.

"This can't be the place," said I.

"This isn't a hotel, is it, Hosy?" asked Hephzy.

The white door opened and a brisk, red-cheeked English boy in uniform hastened to the cab. Before he reached it I had seen the lettering in the pavement and knew that, in spite of appearances, we had reached our destination.

"This is it, Hephzy," I said. "Come."

The boy opened the cab door and we alighted. Then in the doorway of "Bancroft's" appeared a stout, red-faced and very dignified person, also in uniform. This person wore short "mutton-chop" whiskers and had the air of a member of the Royal Family; that is to say, the air which a member of the Royal Family might be expected to have.

"Good evening, sir," said the personage, bowing respectfully. The bow was a triumph in itself; not too low, not abject in the least, not familiar; a bow which implied much, but promised nothing; a bow which seemed to demand references, but was far from repellant or bullying. Altogether a wonderful bow.

"Good evening," said I. "This is Bancroft's Hotel, is it not?"

"Yes, sir."

"I wish to secure rooms for this lady and myself, if possible."

"Yes, sir. This way, sir, if you please. Richard," this to the boy and in a tone entirely different—the tone of a commanding officer to a private—"see to the gentleman's luggage. This way, sir; thank you, sir."

I hesitated. "The cabman has not been paid," I stammered. I was a trifle overawed by the grandeur of the mutton-chops and the "sir."

"I will attend to that, sir. If you will be good enough to come in, sir."

We entered and found ourselves in a narrow hall, old-fashioned, homelike and as spotless as the white door. Two more uniforms bowed before us.

"Thank you, sir," said the member of the Royal Family. It was with difficulty that I repressed the desire to tell him he was quite welcome. His manner of thanking me seemed to imply that we had conferred a favor.

"I will speak to Mr. Jameson," he went on, with another bow. Then he left us.

"Is—is that Mr. Bancroft?" whispered Hephzy.

I shook my head. "It must be the Prince of Wales, at least," I whispered in return. "I infer that there is no Mr. Bancroft."

It developed that I was right. Mr. Jameson was the proprietor of the hotel, and Mr. Jameson was a pleasant, refined, quiet man of middle age. He appeared from somewhere or other, ascertained our wants, stated that he had a few vacant rooms and could accommodate us.

"Do you wish a sitting-room?" he asked.

I was not sure. I wanted comfort, that I knew, and I said so. I mentioned, as an afterthought, that Mr. Heathcroft had recommended Bancroft's to me.

The Heathcroft name seemed to settle everything. Mr. Jameson summoned the representative of royalty and spoke to him in a low tone. The representative—his name, I learned later, was Henry and he was butler and major-domo at Bancroft's—bowed once more. A few minutes later we were shown to an apartment on the second floor front, a room large, old-fashioned, furnished with easy-chairs, tables and a big, comfortable sofa. Sofa and easy-chairs were covered with figured, glazed chintz.

"Your sitting-room, sir," said Henry. "Your bedrooms open hoff it, sir. The chambermaid will 'ave them ready in a moment, sir. Richard and the porter will bring up your luggage and the boxes. Will you and the lady wish supper, sir? Thank you, sir. Very good, sir. Will you require a fire, sir?"

The room was a trifle chilly. There was a small iron grate at its end, and a coal fire ready to kindle. I answered that a fire might be enjoyable.

"Yes, sir," said Henry. "Himmediately, sir."

Soon Hephzy and I were drinking hot tea and eating bread and butter and plum cake before a snapping fire. George, the waiter, had brought us the tea and accessories and set the table; the chambermaid had prepared the bedrooms; Henry had supervised everything.

"Well," observed Hephzy, with a sigh of content, "I feel better satisfied every minute. When we were in the hack—cab, I mean—I couldn't realize we weren't ridin' through an American city. The houses and sidewalks and everything—what I could see of 'em—looked so much like Boston that I was sort of disappointed. I wanted it to be more different, some way. But this IS different. This may be a hotel—I suppose likely 'tis—but it don't seem like one, does it? If it wasn't for the Henry and that Richard and that—what's his name? George—and all the rest, I should think I was in Cap'n Cyrus Whittaker's settin-room back home. The furniture looks like Cap'n Cy's and the pictures look like those he has, and—and everything looks as stiff and starched and old-fashioned as can be. But the Cap'n never had a Henry. No, sirree, Henry don't belong on Cape Cod! Hosy," with a sudden burst of confidence, "it's a good thing I saw that Lord Erskine first. If I hadn't found out what a live lord looked like I'd have thought Henry was one sure. Do you really think it's right for me to call him by his Christian name? It seems sort of—sort of irreverent, somehow."

I wish it were possible for me to describe in detail our first days at Bancroft's. If it were not for the fact that so many really important events and happenings remain to be described—if it were not that the most momentous event of my life, the event that was the beginning of the great change in that life—if that event were not so close at hand, I should be tempted to linger upon those first few days. They were strange and wonderful and funny to Hephzibah and me. The strangeness and the wonder wore off gradually; the fun still sticks in my memory.

To have one's bedroom invaded at an early hour by a chambermaid who, apparently quite oblivious of the fact that the bed was still occupied by a male, proceeded to draw the curtains, bring the hot water and fill the tin tub for my bath, was astonishing and funny enough, Hephzibah's comments on the proceeding were funnier still.

"Do you mean to tell me," she demanded, "that that hussy was brazen enough to march right in here before you got up?"

"Yes," I said. "I am only thankful that I HADN'T got up."

"Well! I must say! Did she fetch the water in a garden waterin'-pot, same as she did to me?"

"Just the same."

"And did she pour it into that—that flat dishpan on the floor and tell you your 'bawth' was ready?"

"She did."

"Humph! Of all the—I hope she cleared out THEN?"

"She did."

"That's a mercy, anyhow. Did you take a bath in that dishpan?"

"I tried."

"Well, I didn't. I'd as soon try to bathe in a saucer. I'd have felt as if I'd needed a teaspoon to dip up the half pint of water and pour it over me. Don't these English folks have real bathtubs for grown-up people?"

I did not know, then. Later I learned that Bancroft's Hotel possessed several bathrooms, and that I might use one if I preferred. Being an American I did so prefer. Most of the guests, being English, preferred the "dishpans."

We learned to accept the early morning visits of the chambermaid as matters of course. We learned to order breakfast the night before and to eat it in our sitting-room. We tasted a "grilled sole" for the first time, and although Hephzy persisted in referring to it as "fried flatfish" we liked the taste. We became accustomed to being waited upon, to do next to nothing for ourselves, and I found that a valet who laid out my evening clothes, put the studs in my shirts, selected my neckties, and saw that my shoes were polished, was a rather convenient person to have about. Hephzy fumed a good deal at first; she declared that she felt ashamed, an able-bodied woman like her, to sit around with her hands folded and do nothing. She asked her maid a great many questions, and the answers she received explained some of her puzzles.

"Do you know what that poor thing gets a week?" she observed, referring to the maid. "Eight shillin's—two dollars a week, that's what she gets. And your valet man doesn't get any more. I can see now how Mr. Jameson can afford to keep so much help at the board he charges. I pay that Susanna Wixon thing at Bayport three dollars and she doesn't know enough to boil water without burnin' it on, scarcely. And Peters—why in the world do they call women by their last names?—Peters, she's the maid, says it's a real nice place and she's quite satisfied. Well, where ignorance is bliss it's foolish to be sensible, I suppose; but I wouldn't fetch and carry for the President's wife, to say nothin' of an everyday body like me, for two dollars a week."

We learned that the hotel dining-room was a "Coffee Room."

"Nobody with sense would take coffee there—not more'n once, they wouldn't," declared Hephzy. "I asked Peters why they didn't call it the 'Tea Room' and be done with it. She said because it was the Coffee Room. I suppose likely that was an answer, but I felt a good deal as if I'd come out of the same hole I went in at. She thanked me for askin' her, though; she never forgets that."

We became accustomed to addressing the lordly Henry by his Christian name and found him a most obliging person. He, like everyone else, had instantly recognized us as Americans, and, consequently, was condescendingly kind to strangers from a distant and barbarous country.

"What SORT of place do they think the States are?" asked Hephzy. "That's what they always call home—'the States'—and they seem to think it's about as big as a pocket handkerchief. That Henry asked me if the red Indians were numerous where we lived. I said no—as soon as I could say anything; I told him there was only one tribe of Red Men in town and they were white. I guess he thought I was crazy, but it don't make any difference. And Peters said she had a cousin in a place called Chicago and did I know him. What do you think of that?"

"What did you tell her?" I inquired.

"Hey? Oh, I told her that, bein' as Chicago was a thousand miles from Bayport, I hadn't had time to do much visitin' there. I told her the truth, but she didn't believe it. I could see she didn't. She thinks Chicago and San Francisco and New York and Boston are nests of wigwams in the same patch of woods and all hands that live there have been scalped at least once. SUCH ignorance!"

Henry, at my request, procured seats for us at one of the London theaters. There we saw a good play, splendidly acted, and Hephzy laughed and wept at the performance. As usual, however, she had a characteristic comment to make.

"Why do they call the front seats the 'stalls'?" she whispered to me between the acts. "Stalls! The idea! I'm no horse. Perhaps they call 'em that because folks are donkeys enough to pay two dollars and a half for the privilege of sittin' in 'em. Don't YOU be so extravagant again, Hosy."

One of the characters in the play was supposed to be an American gentleman, and his behavior and dress and speech stirred me to indignation. I asked the question which every American asks under similar circumstances.

"Why on earth," I demanded, "do they permit that fellow to make such a fool of himself? He yells and drawls and whines through his nose and wears clothes which would make an American cry. That last scene was supposed to be a reception and he wore an outing suit and no waistcoat. Do they suppose such a fellow would be tolerated in respectable society in the United States?"

And now it was Hephzy's turn to be philosophical.

"I guess likely the answer to that is simple enough," she said. "He's what they think an American ought to be, even if he isn't. If he behaved like a human bein' he wouldn't be the kind of American they expect on the stage. After all, he isn't any worse than the Englishmen we have in the Dramatic Society's plays at home. I haven't seen one of that kind since I got here; and I've given up expectin' to—unless you and I go to some crazy asylum—which isn't likely."

We rode on the tops of busses, we visited the Tower, and Westminster Abbey, and Saint Paul's. We saw the Horse Guard sentinels on duty in Whitehall, and watched the ceremony of guard changing at St. James's. Hephzy was impressed, in her own way, by the uniforms of the "Cold Streams."

"There!" she exclaimed, "I've seen 'em walk. Now I feel better. When they stood there, with those red jackets and with the fur hats on their heads, I couldn't make myself believe they hadn't been taken out of a box for children to play with. I wanted to get up close so as to see if their feet were glued to round pieces of wood like Noah's and Ham's and Japhet's in the Ark. But they aren't wood, they're alive. They're men, not toys. I'm glad I've seen 'em. THEY are satisfyin'. They make me more reconciled to a King with a Derby hat on."

She and I had stood in the crowd fringing the park mall and seen King George trot by on horseback. His Majesty's lack of crown and robes and scepter had been a great disappointment to Hephzy; I think she expected the crown at least.

I had, of course, visited the London office of my publishers, in Camford Street and had found Mr. Matthews, the manager, expecting me. Jim Campbell had cabled and written of my coming and Matthews' welcome was a warm one. He was kindness itself. All my financial responsibilities were to be shifted to his shoulders. I was to use the office as a bank, as a tourist agency, even as a guide's headquarters. He put his clerks at my disposal; they would conduct us on sight-seeing expeditions whenever and wherever we wished. He even made out a list of places in and about London which we, as strangers, should see.

His cordiality and thoughtfulness were appreciated. They made me feel less alone and less dependent upon my own resources. Campbell had arranged that all letters addressed to me in America should be forwarded to the Camford Street office, and Matthews insisted that I should write my own letters there. I began to make it a practice to drop in at the office almost every morning before starting on the day's round of sight-seeing.

Bancroft's Hotel also began to seem less strange and more homelike. Mr. Jameson, the proprietor, was a fine fellow—quiet, refined, and pleasant. He, too, tried to help us in every possible way. His wife, a sweet-faced Englishwoman, made Hephzy's acquaintance and Hephzy liked her extremely.

"She's as nice as she can be," declared Hephzy. "If it wasn't that she says 'Fancy!' and 'Really!' instead of 'My gracious!' and 'I want to know!' I should think I was talking to a Cape Codder, the best kind of one. She's got sense, too. SHE don't ask about 'red Indians' in Bayport."

Among the multitude of our new experiences we learned the value of a judicious "tip." We had learned something concerning tips on the "Plutonia"; Campbell had coached us concerning those, and we were provided with a schedule of rates—so much to the bedroom steward, so much to the stewardess, to the deck steward, to the "boots," and all the rest. But tipping in London we were obliged to adjust for ourselves, and the result of our education was surprising.

At Saint Paul's an elderly and impressively haughty person in a black robe showed us through the Crypt and delivered learned lectures before the tombs of Nelson and Wellington. His appearance and manner were somewhat awe-inspiring, especially to Hephzy, who asked me, in a whisper, if I thought likely he was a bishop or a canon or something. When the round was ended and we were leaving the Crypt she saw me put a hand in my pocket.

"Mercy sakes, Hosy," she whispered. "You aren't goin' to offer him money, are you? He'll be insulted. I'd as soon think of givin' Mr. Partridge, our minister, money for takin' us to the cemetery to see the first settlers' gravestones. Don't you do it. He'll throw it back at you. I'll be so ashamed."

But I had been watching our fellow-sight-seers as they filed out, and when our time came I dropped two shillings in the hand of the black-robed dignitary. The hand did not spurn the coins, which I—rather timidly, I confess—dropped into it. Instead it closed upon them tightly and the haughty lips thanked me, not profusely, not even smilingly, but thanked me, nevertheless.

At our visit to the Law Courts a similar experience awaited us. Another dignified and elderly person, who, judging by his appearance, should have been a judge at least, not only accepted the shilling I gave him, but bowed, smiled and offered to conduct us to the divorce court.

"A very interesting case there, sir, just now," he murmured, confidingly. "Very interesting and sensational indeed, sir. You and the lady will enjoy it, I'm sure, sir. All Americans do."

Hephzy was indignant.

"Well!" she exclaimed, as we emerged upon the Strand. "Well! I must say! What sort of folks does he think we are, I'd like to know. Divorce case! I'd be ashamed to hear one. And that old man bein' so wicked and ridiculous for twenty-five cents! Hosy, I do believe if you'd given him another shillin' he'd have introduced us to that man in the red robe and cotton wool wig— What did he call him?—Oh, yes, the Lord Chief Justice. And I suppose you'd have had to tip HIM, too."

The first two weeks of our stay in London came to an end. Our plans were still as indefinite as ever. How long we should stay, where we should go next, what we should do when we decided where that "next" was to be— all these questions we had not considered at all. I, for my part, was curiously uninterested in the future. I was enjoying myself in an idle, irresponsible way, and I could not seem to concentrate my thoughts upon a definite course of action. If I did permit myself to think I found my thoughts straying to my work and there they faced the same impassable wall. I felt no inclination to write; I was just as certain as ever that I should never write again. Thinking along this line only brought back the old feeling of despondency. So I refused to think and, taking Jim's advice, put work and responsibility from my mind. We would remain in London as long as we were contented there. When the spirit moved we would move with it—somewhere—either about England or to the Continent. I did not know which and I did not care; I did not seem to care much about anything.

Hephzy was perfectly happy. London to her was as wonderful as ever. She never tired of sight-seeing, and on occasions when I felt disinclined to leave the hotel she went out alone, shopping or wandering about the streets.

She scarcely mentioned "Little Frank" and I took care not to remind her of that mythical youth. I had expected her to see him on every street corner, to be brought face to face with unsuspecting young Englishmen and made to ask ridiculous questions which might lead to our being taken in charge as a pair of demented foreigners. But my forebodings were not realized. London was so huge and the crowds so great that even Hephzy's courage faltered. To select Little Frank from the multitude was a task too great, even for her, I imagine. At any rate, she did not make the attempt, and the belief that we were "sent" upon our pilgrimage for that express purpose she had not expressed since our evening on the train.

The third week passed. I was growing tired of trotting about. Not tired of London in particular. The gray, dingy, historic, wonderful old city was still fascinating. It is hard to conceive of an intelligent person's ever growing weary of the narrow streets with the familiar names—Fleet Street, Fetter Lane, Pudding Lane and all the rest—names as familiar to a reader of history or English fiction as that of his own town. To wander into an unknown street and to learn that it is Shoreditch, or to look up at an ancient building and discover it to be the Charterhouse, were ever fresh miracles to me, as I am sure they must be to every book-loving American. No, I was not tired of London. Had I come there under other circumstances I should have been as happy and content as Hephzy herself. But, now that the novelty was wearing off, I was beginning to think again, to think of myself—the very thing I had determined, and still meant, not to do.

One afternoon I drifted into the Camford Street office. Hephzy had left me at Piccadilly Circus and was now, it was safe to presume, enjoying a delightful sojourn amid the shops of Regent and Oxford Streets. When she returned she would have a half-dozen purchases to display, a two-and-six glove bargain from Robinson's, a bit of lace from Selfridge's, a knick-knack from Liberty's—"All so MUCH cheaper than you can get 'em in Boston, Hosy." She would have had a glorious time.

Matthews, the manager at Camford Street, was out, but Holton, the head clerk—I was learning to speak of him as a "clark"—was in.

"There are some American letters for you, sir," he said. "I was about to send them to your hotel."

He gave me the letters—four of them altogether—and I went into the private office to look them over. My first batch of mail from home; it gave me a small thrill to see two-cent stamps in the corners of the envelopes.

One of the letters was from Campbell. I opened it first of all. Jim wrote a rambling, good-humored letter, a mixture of business, news, advice and nonsense. "The Black Brig" had gone into another edition. Considering my opinion of such "slush" I should be ashamed to accept the royalties, but he would continue to give my account credit for them until I cabled to the contrary. He trusted we were behaving ourselves in a manner which would reflect credit upon our country. I was to be sure not to let Hephzy marry a title. And so on, for six pages. The letter was almost like a chat with Jim himself, and I read it with chuckles and a pang of homesickness.

One of the envelopes bore Hephzy's name and I, of course, did not open it. It was postmarked "Bayport" and I thought I recognized the handwriting as Susanna Wixon's. The third letter turned out to be not a letter at all, but a bill from Sylvanus Cahoon, who took care of our "lots" in the Bayport cemetery. It had been my intention to pay all bills before leaving home, but, somehow or other, Sylvanus's had been overlooked. I must send him a check at once.

The fourth and last envelope was stained and crumpled. It had traveled a long way. To my surprise I noticed that the stamp in the corner was English and the postmark "London." The address, moreover, was "Captain Barnabas Cahoon, Bayport, Massachusetts, U. S. A." The letter had obviously been mailed in London, had journeyed to Bayport, from there to New York, and had then been forwarded to London again. Someone, presumably Simmons, the postmaster, had written "Care Hosea Knowles" and my publisher's New York address in the lower corner. This had been scratched out and "28 Camford Street, London, England," added.

I looked at the envelope. Who in the world, or in England, could have written Captain Barnabas—Captain Barnabas Cahoon, my great-uncle, dead so many years? At first I was inclined to hand the letter, unopened, to Hephzy. She was Captain Barnabas's daughter and it belonged to her by right. But I knew Hephzy had no secrets from me and, besides, my curiosity was great. At length I yielded to it and tore open the envelope.

Inside was a sheet of thin foreign paper, both sides covered with writing. I read the first line.

"Captain Barnabas Cahoon.

"Sir:

"You are my nearest relative, my mother's father, and I—"

"I uttered an exclamation. Then I stepped to the door of the private office, made sure that it was shut, came back, sat down in the chair before the desk which Mr. Matthews had put at my disposal, and read the letter from beginning to end. This is what I read:

"Captain Barnabas Cahoon.

"Sir:

"You are my nearest relative, my mother's father, and I, therefore, address this letter to you. I know little concerning you. I do not know even that you are still living in Bayport, or that you are living at all. (N.B. In case Captain Cahoon is not living this letter is to be read and acted upon by his heirs, upon whose estate I have an equal claim.) My mother, Ardelia

Cahoon Morley, died in Liverpool in 1896. My father, Strickland Morley, died in Paris in December, 1908. I, as their only child, am their heir, and I am writing to you asking what I might demand—that is, a portion of the money which was my mother's and which you kept from her and from my father all these years. My father told me the whole story before he died, and he also told me that he had written you several times, but that his letters had been ignored. My father was an English gentleman and he was proud; that is why he did not take legal steps against you for the recovery of what was his by law in England OR ANY CIVILISED COUNTRY, one may presume. He would not STOOP to such measures even against those who, as you know well, so meanly and fraudulently deprived him and his of their inheritance. He is dead now. He died lacking the comforts and luxuries with which you might and SHOULD have provided him. His forbearance was wonderful and characteristic, but had I known of it sooner I should have insisted upon demanding from you the money which was his. I am now demanding it myself. Not BEGGING; that I wish THOROUGHLY understood. I am giving you the opportunity to make a partial restitution, that is all. It is what he would have wished, and his wish ALONE prevents my putting the whole matter in my solicitor's hands. If I do not hear from you within a reasonable time I shall know what to do. You may address me care Mrs. Briggs, 218 — — Street, London, England.

"Awaiting your reply, I am, sir,

"Yours,

"FRANCIS STRICKLAND MORLEY. "P. S.

"I am not to be considered under ANY circumstances a subject for charity. I am NOT begging. You, I am given to understand, are a wealthy man. I demand my share of that wealth—that is all."

I read this amazing epistle through once. Then, after rising and walking about the office to make sure that I was thoroughly awake, I sat down and read it again. There was no mistake. I had read it correctly. The writing was somewhat illegible in spots and the signature was blotted, but it was from Francis Strickland Morley. From "Little Frank!" I think my first and greatest sensation was of tremendous surprise that there really was a "Little Frank." Hephzy had been right. Once more I should have to take off my hat to Hephzy.

The surprise remained, but other sensations came to keep it company. The extraordinary fact of the letter's reaching me when and where it did, in London, the city from which it was written and where, doubtless, the writer still was. If I chose I might, perhaps, that very afternoon, meet and talk with Ardelia Cahoon's son, with "Little Frank" himself. I could scarcely realize it.

Hephzy had declared that our coming to London was the result of a special dispensation—we had been "sent" there. In the face of this miracle I was not disposed to contradict her.

The letter itself was more extraordinary than all else. It was that of a young person, of a hot-headed boy. But WHAT a boy he must be! What an unlicked, impudent, arrogant young cub! The boyishness was evident in every line, in the underscored words, the pitiful attempt at dignity and the silly veiled threats. He was so insistent upon the statement that he was not a beggar. And yet he could write a begging letter like this. He did not ask for charity, not he, he demanded it. Demanded it—he, the son of a thief, demanded, from those whom his father had robbed, his "rights." He should have his rights; I would see to that.

I was angry enough but, as I read the letter for the third time, the pitifulness of it became more apparent. I imagined Francis Strickland Morley to be the replica of the Strickland Morley whom I remembered, the useless, incompetent, inadequate son of a good-for-nothing father. No doubt the father was responsible for such a letter as this having been written. Doubtless he HAD told the boy all sorts of tales; perhaps he HAD declared himself to be the defrauded instead of the defrauder; he was quite capable of it. Possibly the youngster did believe he had a claim upon the wealthy relatives in that "uncivilized" country, America. The wealthy relatives! I thought of Captain Barnabas's last years, of Hephzibah's plucky fight against poverty, of my own lost opportunities, of the college course which I had been obliged to forego. My indignation returned. I would not go back at once to Hephzy with the letter. I would, myself, seek out the writer of that letter, and, if I found him, he and I would have a heart to heart talk which should disabuse his mind of a few illusions. We would have a full and complete understanding.

I hastily made a memorandum of the address, "Care Mrs. Briggs," thrust the letter back into the envelope, put it and my other mail into my pocket, and walked out into the main office. Holton, the clerk, looked up from his desk. Probably my feelings showed in my face, for he said:

"What is it, Mr. Knowles? No bad news, I trust, sir."

"No," I answered, shortly. "Where is — — Street? Is it far from here?"

It was rather far from there, in Camberwell, on the Surrey side of the river. I might take a bus at such a corner and change again at so and so. It sounded like a journey and I was impatient. I suggested that I might take a cab. Certainly I could do that. William, the boy, would call a cab at once.

William did so and I gave the driver the address from my memoranda. Through the Strand I was whirled, across Blackfriars Bridge and on through the intricate web of avenues and streets on the Surrey side. The locality did not impress me favorably. There was an abundance of "pubs" and of fried-fish shops where "jellied eels" seemed to be a viand much in demand.

— — Street, when I reached it, was dingy and third rate. Three-storied old brick houses, with shops on their first floors, predominated. Number 218 was one of these. The signs "Lodgings" over the tarnished bell-pull and the name "Briggs" on the plate beside it proved that I had located the house from which the letter had been sent.

I paid my cabman, dismissed him, and rang the bell. A slouchy maid-servant answered the ring.

"Is Mr. Francis Morley in?" I asked.

The maid looked at me.

"Wat, sir?" she said.

"Does Mr. Francis Morley live here?" I asked, raising my voice. "Is he in?"

The maid's face was as wooden as the door-post. Her mouth, already open, opened still wider and she continued to stare. A step sounded in the dark hall behind her and another voice said, sharply:

"'Oo is it, 'Arriet? And w'at does 'e want?"

The maid grinned. "'E wants to see MISTER Morley, ma'am," she said, with a giggle.

She was pushed aside and a red-faced woman, with thin lips and scowl, took her place.

"'OO do you want to see?" she demanded.

"Francis Morley. Does he live here?"

"'OO?"

"Francis Morley." My answer was sharp enough this time. I began to think I had invaded a colony of imbeciles—or owls; their conversation seemed limited to "oos."

"W'at do you want to see—to see Morley for?" demanded the red-faced female.

"On business. Is Mrs. Briggs in?"

"I'm Mrs. Briggs."

"Good! I'm glad of that. Now will you tell me if Mr. Morley is in?"

"There ain't no Mr. Morley. There's a—"

She was interrupted. From the hall, apparently from the top of the flight of stairs, another was heard, a feminine voice like the others, but unlike them—decidedly unlike.

"Who is it, Mrs. Briggs?" said this voice. "Does the gentleman wish to see me?"

"No, 'e don't," declared Mrs. Briggs, with emphasis. "'E wants to see Mister Morley and I'm telling 'im there ain't none such."

"But are you sure he doesn't mean Miss Morley? Ask him, please."

Before the Briggs woman could reply I spoke again.

"I want to see a Francis Morley," I repeated, loudly. "I have come here in answer to a letter. The letter gave this as his address. If he isn't here, will you be good enough to tell me where he is? I—"

There was another interruption, an exclamation from the darkness behind Mrs. Briggs and the maid.

"Oh!" said the third voice, with a little catch in it. "Who is it, please? Who is it? What is the person's name?"

Mrs. Briggs scowled at me.

"Wat's your name?" she snapped.

"My name is Knowles. I am an American relative of Mr. Morley's and I'm here in answer to a letter written by Mr. Morley himself."

There was a moment's silence. Then the third voice said:

"Ask—ask him to come up. Show him up, Mrs. Briggs, if you please."

Mrs. Briggs grunted and stepped aside. I entered the hall.

"First floor back," mumbled the landlady. "Straight as you go. You won't need any showin'."

I mounted the stairs. The landing at the top was dark, but the door at the rear was ajar. I knocked. A voice, the same voice I had heard before, bade me come in. I entered the room.

It was a dingy little room, sparely furnished, with a bed and two chairs, a dilapidated washstand and a battered bureau. I noticed these afterwards. Just then my attention was centered upon the occupant of the room, a young woman, scarcely more than a girl, dark-haired, dark-eyed, slender and graceful. She was standing by the bureau, resting one hand upon it, and gazing at me, with a strange expression, a curious compound of fright, surprise and defiance. She did not speak. I was embarrassed.

"I beg your pardon," I stammered. "I am afraid there is some mistake. I came here in answer to a letter written by a Francis Morley, who is—well, I suppose he is a distant relative of mine."

She stepped forward and closed the door by which I had entered. Then she turned and faced me.

"You are an American," she said.

"Yes, I am an American. I—"

She interrupted me.

"Do you—do you come from—from Bayport, Massachusetts?" she faltered.

I stared at her. "Why, yes," I admitted. "I do come from Bayport. How in the world did you—"

"Was the letter you speak of addressed to Captain Barnabas Cahoon?"

"Yes."

"Then—then there isn't any mistake. I wrote it."

I imagine that my mouth opened as wide as the maid's had done.

"You!" I exclaimed. "Why—why—it was written by Francis Morley—Francis Strickland Morley."

"I am Frances Strickland Morley."

I heard this, of course, but I did not comprehend it. I had been working along the lines of a fixed idea. Now that idea had been knocked into a cocked hat, and my intellect had been knocked with it.

"Why—why, no," I repeated, stupidly. "Francis Morley is the son of Strickland Morley."

"There was no son," impatiently. "I am Frances Morley, I tell you. I am Strickland Morley's daughter. I wrote that letter."

I sat down upon the nearest of the two chairs. I was obliged to sit. I could not stand and face the fact which, at least, even my benumbed brain was beginning to comprehend. The mistake was a simple one, merely the difference between an "i" and an "e" in a name, that was all. And yet that mistake—that slight difference between "Francis" and "Frances"—explained the amazing difference between the Little Frank of Hephzibah's fancy and the reality before me.

The real Little Frank was a girl.

CHAPTER VII
In Which a Dream Becomes a Reality

I said nothing immediately. I could not. It was "Little Frank" who resumed the conversation. "Who are you?" she asked.

"Who—I beg your pardon? I am rather upset, I'm afraid. I didn't expect—that is, I expected.... Well, I didn't expect THIS! What was it you asked me?"

"I asked you who you were."

"My name is Knowles—Kent Knowles. I am Captain Cahoon's grand-nephew."

"His grand-nephew. Then—Did Captain Cahoon send you to me?"

"Send me! I beg your pardon once more. No.... No. Captain Cahoon is dead. He has been dead nearly ten years. No one sent me."

"Then why did you come? You have my letter; you said so."

"Yes; I—I have your letter. I received it about an hour ago. It was forwarded to me—to my cousin and me—here in London."

"Here in London! Then you did not come to London in answer to that letter?"

"No. My cousin and I—"

"What cousin? What is his name?"

"His name? It isn't a—That is, the cousin is a woman. She is Miss Hephzibah Cahoon, your—your mother's half-sister. She is—Why, she is your aunt!"

It was a fact; Hephzibah was this young lady's aunt. I don't know why that seemed so impossible and ridiculous, but it did. The young lady herself seemed to find it so.

"My aunt?" she repeated. "I didn't know—But—but, why is my—my aunt here with you?"

"We are on a pleasure trip. We—I beg your pardon. What have I been thinking of? Don't stand. Please sit down."

She accepted the invitation. As she walked toward the chair it seemed to me that she staggered a little. I noticed then for the first time, how very slender she was, almost emaciated. There were dark hollows beneath her eyes and her face was as white as the bed-linen—No, I am wrong; it was whiter than Mrs. Briggs' bed-linen.

"Are you ill?" I asked involuntarily.

She did not answer. She seated herself in the chair and fixed her dark eyes upon me. They were large eyes and very dark. Hephzy said, when she first saw them, that they looked like "burnt holes in a blanket." Perhaps they did; that simile did not occur to me.

"You have read my letter?" she asked.

It was evident that I must have read the letter or I should not have learned where to find her, but I did not call attention to this. I said simply that I had read the letter.

"Then what do you propose?" she asked.

"Propose?"

"Yes," impatiently. "What proposition do you make me? If you have read the letter you must know what I mean. You must have come here for the purpose of saying something, of making some offer. What is it?"

I was speechless. I had come there to find an impudent young blackguard and tell him what I thought of him. That was as near a definite reason for my coming as any. If I had not acted upon impulse, if I had stopped to consider, it is quite likely that I should not have come at all. But the blackguard was—was—well, he was not and never had been. In his place was this white-faced, frail girl. I couldn't tell her what I thought of her. I didn't know what to think.

She waited for me to answer and, as I continued to play the dumb idiot, her impatience grew. Her brows—very dark brown they were, almost black against the pallor of her face—drew together and her foot began to pat the faded carpet. "I am waiting," she said.

I realized that I must say something, so I said the only thing which occurred to me. It was a question.

"Your father is dead?" I asked.

She nodded. "My letter told you that," she answered. "He died in Paris three years ago."

"And—and had he no relatives here in England?"

She hesitated before replying. "No near relatives whom he cared to recognize," she answered haughtily. "My father, Mr. Knowles was a gentleman and, having been most unjustly treated by his own family, as well as by OTHERS"—with a marked emphasis on the word—"he did not stoop, even in his illness and distress, to beg where he should have commanded."

"Oh! Oh, I see," I said, feebly.

"There is no reason why you should see. My father was the second son and—But this is quite irrelevant. You, an American, can scarcely be expected to understand English family customs. It is sufficient that, for reasons of his own, my father had for years been estranged from his own people."

The air with which this was delivered was quite overwhelming. If I had not known Strickland Morley, and a little of his history, I should have been crushed.

"Then you have been quite alone since his death?" I asked.

Again she hesitated. "For a time," she said, after a moment. "I lived with a married cousin of his in one of the London suburbs. Then I—But really, Mr. Knowles, I cannot see that my private affairs need interest you. As I understand it, this interview of ours is quite impersonal, in a sense. You understand, of course—you must understand—that in writing as I did I was not seeking the acquaintance of my mother's relatives. I do not desire their friendship. I am not asking them for anything. I am giving them the opportunity to do justice, to give me what is my own—my OWN. If you don't understand this I—I—Oh, you MUST understand it!"

She rose from the chair. Her eyes were flashing and she was trembling from head to foot. Again I realized how weak and frail she was.

"You must understand," she repeated. "You MUST!"

"Yes, yes," I said hastily. "I think I—I suppose I understand your feelings. But—"

"There are no buts. Don't pretend there are. Do you think for one instant that I am begging, asking you for HELP? YOU—of all the world!"

This seemed personal enough, in spite of her protestations.

"But you never met me before," I said, involuntarily.

"You never knew of my existence."

She stamped her foot. "I knew of my American relatives," she cried, scornfully. "I knew of them and their—Oh, I cannot say the word!"

"Your father told you—" I began. She burst out at me like a flame.

"My father," she declared, "was a brave, kind, noble man. Don't mention his name to me. I won't have you speak of him. If it were not for his forbearance and self-sacrifice you—all of you—would be—would be—Oh, don't speak of my father! Don't!"

To my amazement and utter discomfort she sank into the chair and burst into tears. I was completely demoralized.

"Don't, Miss Morley," I begged. "Please don't."

She continued to sob hysterically. To make matters worse sounds from behind the closed door led me to think that someone—presumably that confounded Mrs. Briggs—was listening at the keyhole.

"Don't, Miss Morley," I pleaded. "Don't!"

My pleas were unavailing. The young lady sobbed and sobbed. I fidgeted on the edge of my chair in an agony of mortified embarrassment. "Don'ts" were quite useless and I could think of nothing else to say except "Compose yourself" and that, somehow or other, was too ridiculously reminiscent of Mr. Pickwick and Mrs. Bardell. It was an idiotic situation for me to be in. Some men—men of experience with woman-kind—might have known how to handle it, but I had had no such experience. It was all my fault, of course; I should not have mentioned her father. But how was I to know that Strickland Morley was a persecuted saint? I should have called him everything but that.

At last I had an inspiration.

"You are ill," I said, rising. "I will call someone."

That had the desired effect. My newly found third—or was it fourth or fifth—cousin made a move in protest. She fought down her emotion, her sobs ceased, and she leaned back in her chair looking paler and weaker than ever. I should have pitied her if she had not been so superior and insultingly scornful in her manner toward me. I—Well, yes, I did pity her, even as it was.

"Don't," she said, in her turn. "Don't call anyone. I am not ill—not now."

"But you have been," I put in, I don't know why.

"I have not been well for some time. But I am not ill. I am quite strong enough to hear what you have to say."

This might have been satisfactory if I had had anything to say. I had not. She evidently expected me to express repentance for something or other and make some sort of proposition. I was not repentant and I had no proposition to make. But how was I to tell her that without bringing on another storm? Oh, if I had had time to consider. If I had not come alone. If Hephzy,—cool-headed, sensible Hephzy—were only with me.

"I—I—" I began. Then desperately: "I scarcely know what to say, Miss Morley," I faltered. "I came here, as I told you, expecting to find a—a—"

"What, pray?" with a haughty lift of the dark eyebrows. "What did you expect to find, may I ask?"

"Nothing—that is, I—Well, never mind that. I came on the spur of the moment, immediately after receiving your letter. I have had no time to think, to consult my—your aunt—"

"What has my—AUNT" with withering emphasis, "to do with it? Why should you consult her?"

"Well, she is your mother's nearest relative, I suppose. She is Captain Cahoon's daughter and at least as much interested as I. I must consult her, of course. But, frankly, Miss Morley, I think I ought to tell you that you are under a misapprehension. There are matters which you don't understand."

"I understand everything. I understand only too well. What do you mean by a misapprehension? Do you mean—do you dare to insinuate that my father did not tell me the truth?"

"Oh, no, no," I interrupted. That was exactly what I did mean, but I was not going to let the shade of the departed Strickland appear again until I was out of that room and house. "I am not insinuating anything."

"I am very glad to hear it. I wish you to know that I perfectly understand EVERYTHING."

That seemed to settle it; at any rate it settled me for the time. I took up my hat.

"Miss Morley," I said, "I can't discuss this matter further just now. I must consult my cousin first. She and I will call upon you to-morrow at any hour you may name."

She was disappointed; that was plain. I thought for the moment that she was going to break down again. But she did not; she controlled her feelings and faced me firmly and pluckily.

"At nine—no, at ten to-morrow, then," she said. "I shall expect your final answer then."

"Very well."

"You will come? Of course; I am forgetting. You said you would."

"We will be here at ten. Here is my address."

I gave her my card, scribbling the street and number of Bancroft's in pencil in the corner. She took the card.

"Thank you. Good afternoon," she said.

I said "Good afternoon" and opened the door. The hall outside was empty, but someone was descending the stairs in a great hurry. I descended also. At the top step I glanced once more into the room I had just left. Frances Strickland Morley—Little Frank—was seated in the chair, one hand before her eyes. Her attitude expressed complete weariness and utter collapse. She had said she was not sick, but she looked sick—she did indeed.

Harriet, the slouchy maid, was not in evidence, so I opened the street door for myself. As I reached the sidewalk—I suppose, as this was England, I should call it the "pavement"—I was accosted by Mrs. Briggs. She was out of breath; I am quite sure she had reached that pavement but the moment before.

"'Ow is she?" demanded Mrs. Briggs.

"Who?" I asked, not too politely.

"That Morley one. Is she goin' to be hill again?"

"How do I know? Has she been sick—ill, I mean?"

"Huh! Hill! 'Er? Now, now, sir! I give you my word she's been hill hever since she came 'ere. I thought one time she was goin' to die on my 'ands. And 'oo was to pay for 'er buryin', I'd like to know? That's w'at it is! 'Oo's goin' to pay for 'er buryin' and the food she eats; to say nothin' of 'er room money, and that's been owin' me for a matter of three weeks?"

"How should I know who is going to pay for it? She will, I suppose."

"She! W'at with? She ain't got a bob to bless 'erself with, she ain't. She's broke, stony broke. Honly for my kind 'eart she'd a been out on the street afore this. That and 'er tellin' me she was expectin' money from 'er rich friends in the States. You're from the States, ain't you, sir?"

"Yes. But do you mean to tell me that Miss Morley has no money of her own?"

"Of course I mean it. W'en she come 'ere she told me she was on the stage. A hopera singer, she said she was. She 'ad money then, enough to pay 'er way, she 'ad. She was expectin' to go with some troupe or other, but she never 'as. Oh, them stage people! Don't I know 'em? Ain't I 'ad experience of 'em? A woman as 'as let lodgin's as long as me? If it wasn't for them rich friends in the States I 'ave never put up with 'er the way I 'ave. You're from the States, ain't you, sir?"

"Yes, yes, I'm from the States. Now, see here, Mrs. Briggs; I'm coming back here to-morrow. If—Well, if Miss Morley needs anything, food or medicines or anything, in the meantime, you see that she has them. I'll pay you when I come."

Mrs. Briggs actually smiled. She would have patted my arm if I had not jerked it out of the way.

"You trust me, sir," she whispered, confidingly. "You trust my kind 'eart. I'll look after 'er like she was my own daughter."

I should have hated to trust even my worst enemy—if I had one—to Mrs. Briggs' "kind heart." I walked off in disgust. I found a cab at the next corner and, bidding the driver take me to Bancroft's, threw myself back on the cushions. This was a lovely mess! This was a beautiful climax to the first act—no, merely the prologue—of the drama of Hephzy's and my pilgrimage. What would Jim Campbell say to this? I was to be absolutely care-free; I was not to worry about myself or anyone else. That was the essential part of his famous "prescription." And now, here I was, with this impossible situation and more impossible young woman on my hands. If Little Frank had been a boy, a healthy boy, it would be bad enough. But Little Frank was a girl—a sick girl, without a penny. And a girl thoroughly convinced that she was the rightful heir to goodness knows how much wealth—wealth of which we, the uncivilized, unprincipled natives of an unprincipled, uncivilized country, had robbed her parents and herself. Little Frank had been a dream before; now he—she, I mean—was a nightmare; worse than that, for one wakes from a nightmare. And I was on my way to tell Hephzy!

Well, I told her. She was in our sitting-room when I reached the hotel and I told her the whole story. I began by reading the letter. Before she had recovered from the shock of the reading, I told her that I had actually met and talked with Little Frank; and while this astounding bit of news was, so to speak, soaking into her bewildered brain, I went on to impart the crowning item of information—namely, that Little Frank was Miss Frances. Then I sat back and awaited what might follow.

Her first coherent remark was one which I had not expected—and I had expected almost anything.

"Oh, Hosy," gasped Hephzy, "tell me—tell me before you say anything else. Does he—she, I mean—look like Ardelia?"

"Eh? What?" I stammered. "Look like—look like what?"

"Not what—who. Does she look like Ardelia? Like her mother? Oh, I HOPE she doesn't favor her father's side! I did so want our Little Frank to look like his—her—I CAN'T get used to it—like my poor Ardelia. Does she?"

"Goodness knows! I don't know who she looks like. I didn't notice."

"You didn't! I should have noticed that before anything else. What kind of a girl is she? Is she pretty?"

"I don't know. She isn't ugly, I should say. I wasn't particularly interested in her looks. The fact that she was at all was enough; I haven't gotten over that yet. What are we going to do with her? Or are we going to do anything? Those are the questions I should like to have answered. For heaven's sake, Hephzy, don't talk about her personal appearance. There she is and here are we. What are we going to do?"

Hephzy shook her head. "I don't know, Hosy," she admitted. "I don't know, I'm sure. This is—this is—Oh, didn't I tell you we were SENT—sent by Providence!"

I was silent. If we had been "sent," as she called it, I was far from certain that Providence was responsible. I was more inclined to place the responsibility in a totally different quarter.

"I think," she continued, "I think you'd better tell me the whole thing all over again, Hosy. Tell it slow and don't leave out a word. Tell me what sort of place she was in and what she said and how she looked, as near as you can remember. I'll try and pay attention; I'll try as hard as I can. It'll be a job. All I can think of now is that to-morrow mornin'—only to-morrow mornin'—I'm going to see Little Frank—Ardelia's Little Frank."

I complied with her request, giving every detail of my afternoon's experience. I reread the letter, and handed it to her, that she might read it herself. I described Mrs. Briggs and what I had seen of Mrs. Briggs' lodging-house. I described Miss Morley as best I could, dark eyes, dark hair and the look of weakness and frailty. I repeated our conversation word for word; I had forgotten nothing of that. Hephzy listened in silence. When I had finished she sighed.

"The poor thing," she said. "I do pity her so."

"Pity her!" I exclaimed. "Well, perhaps I pity her, too, in a way. But my pity and yours don't alter the situation. She doesn't want pity. She doesn't want help. She flew at me like a wildcat when I asked if she was ill. Her personal affairs, she says, are not ours; she doesn't want our acquaintance or our friendship. She has gotten some crazy notion in her head that you and I and Uncle Barnabas have cheated her out of an inheritance, and she wants that! Inheritance! Good Lord! A fine inheritance hers is! Daughter of the man who robbed us of everything we had."

"I know—I know. But SHE doesn't know, does she, Hosy. Her father must have told her—"

"He told her a barrel of lies, of course. What they were I can't imagine, but that fellow was capable of anything. Know! No, she doesn't know now, but she will have to know."

"Are you goin' to tell her, Hosy?"

I stared in amazement.

"Tell her!" I repeated. "What do you mean? You don't intend letting her think that WE are the thieves, do you? That's what she thinks now. Of course I shall tell her."

"It will be awful hard to tell. She worshipped her father, I guess. He was a dreadful fascinatin' man, when he wanted to be. He could make a body believe black was white. Poor Ardelia thought he was—"

"I can't help that. I'm not Ardelia."

"I know, but she is Ardelia's child. Hosy, if you are so set on tellin' her why didn't you tell her this afternoon? It would have been just as easy then as to-morrow."

This was a staggerer. A truthful answer would be so humiliating. I had not told Frances Morley that her father was a thief and a liar because I couldn't muster courage to do it. She had seemed so alone and friendless and ill. I lacked the pluck to face the situation. But I could not tell Hephzy this.

"Why didn't you tell her?" she repeated.

"Oh, bosh!" I exclaimed, impatiently. "This is nonsense and you know it, Hephzy. She'll have to be told and you and I must tell her. DON'T look at me like that. What else are we to do?"

Another shake of the head.

"I don't know. I can't decide any more than you can, Hosy. What do YOU think we should do?"

"I don't know."

With which unsatisfactory remark this particular conversation ended. I went to my room to dress for dinner. I had no appetite and dinner was not appealing; but I did not want to discuss Little Frank any longer. I mentally cursed Jim Campbell a good many times that evening and during the better part of a sleepless night. If it were not for him I should be in Bayport instead of London. From a distance of three thousand miles I could, without the least hesitancy, have told Strickland Morley's "heir" what to do.

Hephzy did not come down to dinner at all. From behind the door of her room she told me, in a peculiar tone, that she could not eat. I could not eat, either, but I made the pretence of doing so. The next morning, at breakfast in the sitting-room, we were a silent pair. I don't know what George, the waiter, thought of us.

At a quarter after nine I turned away from the window through which I had been moodily regarding the donkey cart of a flower huckster in the street below.

"You'd better get on your things," I said. "It is time for us to go."

Hephzy donned her hat and wrap. Then she came over to me.

"Don't be cross, Hosy," she pleaded. "I've been thinkin' it over all night long and I've come to the conclusion that you are probably right. She hasn't any real claim on us, of course; it's the other way around, if anything. You do just as you think best and I'll back you up."

"Then you agree that we should tell her the truth."

"Yes, if you think so. I'm goin' to leave it all in your hands. Whatever you do will be right. I'll trust you as I always have."

It was a big responsibility, it seemed to me. I did wish she had been more emphatic. However, I set my teeth and resolved upon a course of action. Pity and charity and all the rest of it I would not consider. Right was right, and justice was justice. I would end a disagreeable business as quickly as I could.

Mrs. Briggs' lodging-house, viewed from the outside, was no more inviting at ten in the morning than it had been at four in the afternoon. I expected Hephzy to make some comment upon the dirty steps and the still dirtier front door. She did neither. We stood together upon the steps and I rang the bell.

Mrs. Briggs herself opened the door. I think she had been watching from behind the curtains and had seen our cab draw up at the curb. She was in a state of great agitation, a combination of relieved anxiety, excitement and overdone politeness.

"Good mornin', sir," she said; "and good mornin', lady. I've been expectin' you, and so 'as she, poor dear. I thought one w'ile she was that hill she couldn't see you, but Lor' bless you, I've nursed 'er same as if she was my own daughter. I told you I would sir, now didn't I."

One word in this harangue caught my attention.

"Ill?" I repeated. "What do you mean? Is she worse than she was yesterday?"

Mrs. Briggs held up her hands. "Worse!" she cried. "Why, bless your 'art, sir, she was quite well yesterday. Quite 'erself, she was, when you come. But after you went away she seemed to go all to pieces like. W'en I went hup to 'er, to carry 'er 'er tea—She always 'as 'er tea; I've been a mother to 'er, I 'ave—she'll tell you so. W'en I went hup with the tea there she was in a faint. W'ite as if she was dead. My word, sir, I was frightened. And all night she's been tossin' about, a-cryin' out and—"

"Where is she now?" put in Hephzy, sharply.

"She's in 'er room ma'am. Dressed she is; she would dress, knowin' of your comin', though I told 'er she shouldn't. She's dressed, but she's lyin' down. She would 'ave tried to sit hup, but THAT I wouldn't 'ave, ma'am. 'Now, dearie,' I told 'er—"

But I would not hear any more. As for Hephzy she was in the dingy front hall already.

"Shall we go up?" I asked, impatiently.

"Of COURSE you're to go hup. She's a-waitin' for you. But sir—sir," she caught my sleeve; "if you think she's goin' to be ill and needin' the doctor, just pass the word to me. A doctor she shall 'ave, the best there is in London. All I ask you is to pay—"

I heard no more. Hephzy was on her way up the stairs and I followed. The door of the first floor back was closed. I rapped upon it.

"Come in," said the voice I remembered, but now it sounded weaker than before.

Hephzy looked at me. I nodded.

"You go first," I whispered. "You can call me when you are ready."

Hephzy opened the door and entered the room. I closed the door behind her.

Silence for what seemed a long, long time. Then the door opened again and Hephzy appeared. Her cheeks were wet with tears. She put her arms about my neck.

"Oh, Hosy," she whispered, "she's real sick. And—and—Oh, Hosy, how COULD you see her and not see! She's the very image of Ardelia. The very image! Come."

I followed her into the room. It was no brighter now, in the middle of a—for London—bright forenoon, than it had been on my previous visit. Just as dingy and forbidding and forlorn as ever. But now there was no defiant figure erect to meet me. The figure was lying upon the bed, and the pale cheeks of yesterday were flushed with fever. Miss Morley had looked far from well when I first saw her; now she looked very ill indeed.

She acknowledged my good-morning with a distant bow. Her illness had not quenched her spirit, that was plain. She attempted to rise, but Hephzy gently pushed her back upon the pillow.

"You stay right there," she urged. "Stay right there. We can talk just as well, and Mr. Knowles won't mind; will you, Hosy."

I stammered something or other. My errand, difficult as it had been from the first, now seemed impossible. I had come there to say certain things—I had made up my mind to say them; but how was I to say such things to a girl as ill as this one was. I would not have said them to Strickland Morley himself, under such circumstances.

"I—I am very sorry you are not well, Miss Morley," I faltered.

She thanked me, but there was no warmth in the thanks.

"I am not well," she said; "but that need make no difference. I presume you and this—this lady are prepared to make a definite proposition to me. I am well enough to hear it."

Hephzy and I looked at each other. I looked for help, but Hephzy's expression was not helpful at all. It might have meant anything—or nothing.

"Miss Morley," I began. "Miss Morley, I—I—"

"Well, sir?"

"Miss Morley, I—I don't know what to say to you."

She rose to a sitting posture. Hephzy again tried to restrain her, but this time she would not be restrained.

"Don't know what to say?" she repeated. "Don't know what to say? Then why did you come here?"

"I came—we came because—because I promised we would come."

"But WHY did you come?"

Hephzy leaned toward her.

"Please, please," she begged. "Don't get all excited like this. You mustn't. You'll make yourself sicker, you know. You must lie down and be quiet. Hosy—oh, please, Hosy, be careful."

Miss Morley paid no attention. She was regarding me with eyes which looked me through and through. Her thin hands clutched the bedclothes.

"WHY did you come?" she demanded. "My letter was plain enough, certainly. What I said yesterday was perfectly plain. I told you I did not wish your acquaintance or your friendship. Friendship—" with a blaze of scorn, "from YOU! I—I told you—I—"

"Hush! hush! please don't," begged Hephzy. "You mustn't. You're too weak and sick. Oh, Hosy, do be careful."

I was quite willing to be careful—if I had known how.

"I think," I said, "that this interview had better be postponed. Really, Miss Morley, you are not in a condition to—"

She sprang to her feet and stood there trembling.

"My condition has nothing to do with it," she cried. "Oh, CAN'T I make you understand! I am trying to be lenient, to be—to be—And you come here, you and this woman, and try to—to—You MUST understand! I don't want to know you. I don't want your pity! After your treatment of my mother and my father, I—I—I... Oh!"

She staggered, put her hands to her head, sank upon the bed, and then collapsed in a dead faint.

Hephzy was at her side in a moment. She knew what to do if I did not.

"Quick!" she cried, turning to me. "Send for the doctor; she has fainted. Hurry! And send that—that Briggs woman to me. Don't stand there like that. HURRY!"

I found the Briggs woman in the lower hall. From her I learned the name and address of the nearest physician, also the nearest public telephone. Mrs. Briggs went up to Hephzy and I hastened out to telephone.

Oh, those London telephones! After innumerable rings and "Hellos" from me, and "Are you theres" from Central, I, at last, was connected with the doctor's office and, by great good luck, with the doctor himself. He promised to come at once. In ten minutes I met him at the door and conducted him to the room above.

He was in that room a long time. Meanwhile, I waited in the hall, pacing up and down, trying to think my way through this maze. I had succeeded in thinking myself still deeper into it when the physician reappeared.

"How is she?" I asked.

"She is conscious again, but weak, of course. If she can be kept quiet and have proper care and nourishment and freedom from worry she will, probably, gain strength and health. There is nothing seriously wrong physically, so far as I can see."

I was glad to hear that and said so.

"Of course," he went on, "her nerves are completely unstrung. She seems to have been under a great mental strain and her surroundings are not—" He paused, and then added, "Is the young lady a relative of yours?"

"Ye—es, I suppose—She is a distant relative, yes."

"Humph! Has she no near relatives? Here in England, I mean. You and the lady with you are Americans, I judge."

I ignored the last sentence. I could not see that our being Americans concerned him.

"She has no near relatives in England, so far as I know," I answered. "Why do you ask?"

"Merely because—Well, to be frank, because if she had such relatives I should strongly recommend their taking charge of her. She is very weak and in a condition where she knight become seriously ill."

"I see. You mean that she should not remain here."

"I do mean that, decidedly. This," with a wave of the hand and a glance about the bare, dirty, dark hall, "is not—Well, she seems to be a young person of some refinement and—"

He did not finish the sentence, but I understood.

"I see," I interrupted. "And yet she is not seriously ill."

"Not now—no. Her weakness is due to mental strain and—well, to a lack of nutrition as much as anything."

"Lack of nutrition? You mean she hasn't had enough to eat!"

"Yes. Of course I can't be certain, but that would be my opinion if I were forced to give one. At all events, she should be taken from here as soon as possible."

I reflected. "A hospital?" I suggested.

"She might be taken to a hospital, of course. But she is scarcely ill enough for that. A good, comfortable home would be better. Somewhere where she might have quiet and rest. If she had relatives I should strongly urge her going to them. She should not be left to herself; I would not be responsible for the consequences if she were. A person in her condition might—might be capable of any rash act."

This was plain enough, but it did not make my course of action plainer to me.

"Is she well enough to be moved—now?" I asked.

"Yes. If she is not moved she is likely to be less well."

I paid him for the visit; he gave me a prescription—"To quiet the nerves," he explained—and went away. I was to send for him whenever his services were needed. Then I entered the room.

Hephzy and Mrs. Briggs were sitting beside the bed. The face upon the pillow looked whiter and more pitiful than ever. The dark eyes were closed.

Hephzy signaled me to silence. She rose and tiptoed over to me. I led her out into the hall.

"She's sort of dozin' now," she whispered. "The poor thing is worn out. What did the doctor say?"

I told her what the doctor had said.

"He's just right," she declared. "She's half starved, that's what's the matter with her. That and frettin' and worryin' have just about killed her. What are you goin' to do, Hosy?"

"How do I know!" I answered, impatiently. "I don't see exactly why we are called upon to do anything. Do you?"

"No—o, I—I don't know as we are called on. No—o. I—"

"Well, do you?"

"No. I know how you feel, Hosy. Considerin' how her father treated us, I won't blame you no matter what you do."

"Confound her father! I only wish it were he we had to deal with."

Hephzy was silent. I took a turn up and down the hall.

"The doctor says she should be taken away from here at once," I observed.

Hephzy nodded. "There's no doubt about that," she declared with emphasis. "I wouldn't trust a sick cat to that Briggs woman. She's a—well, she's what she is."

"I suggested a hospital, but he didn't approve," I went on. "He recommended some comfortable home with care and quiet and all the rest of it. Her relatives should look after her, he said. She hasn't any relatives that we know of, or any home to go to."

Again Hephzy was silent. I waited, growing momentarily more nervous and fretful. Of all impossible situations this was the most impossible. And to make it worse, Hephzy, the usually prompt, reliable Hephzy, was of no use at all.

"Do say something," I snapped. "What shall we do?"

"I don't know, Hosy, dear. Why!... Where are you going?"

"I'm going to the drug-store to get this prescription filled. I'll be back soon."

The drug-store—it was a "chemist's shop" of course—was at the corner. It was the chemist's telephone that I had used when I called the doctor. I gave the clerk the prescription and, while he was busy with it, I paced up and down the floor of the shop. At length I sat down before the telephone and demanded a number.

When I returned to the lodging-house I gave Hephzy the powders which the chemist's clerk had prepared.

"Is she any better?" I asked.

"She's just about the same."

"What does she say?"

"She's too weak and sick to say anything. I don't imagine she knows or cares what is happening to her."

"Is she strong enough to get downstairs to a cab, or to ride in one afterward?"

"I guess so. We could help her, you know. But, Hosy, what cab? What do you mean? What are you going to do?"

"I don't know what I'm going to do. I'm going to take her away from this hole. I must. I don't want to; there's no reason why I should and every reason why I shouldn't; but—Oh, well, confound it! I've got to. We CAN'T let her starve and die here."

"But where are you going to take her?"

"There's only one place to take her; that's to Bancroft's. I've 'phoned and engaged a room next to ours. She'll have to stay with us for the present. Oh, I don't like it any better than you do."

To my intense surprise, Hephzy threw her arms about my neck and hugged me.

"I knew you would, Hosy!" she sobbed. "I knew you would. I was dyin' to have you, but I wouldn't have asked for the world. You're the best man that ever lived. I knew you wouldn't leave poor Ardelia's little girl to—to—Oh, I'm so grateful. You're the best man in the world."

I freed myself from the embrace as soon as I could. I didn't feel like the best man in the world. I felt like a Quixotic fool.

Fortunately I was too busy for the next hour to think of my feelings. Hephzy went in to arrange for the transfer of the invalid to the cab and to collect and pack her most necessary belongings. I spent my time in a financial wrangle with Mrs. Briggs. The number of items which that woman wished included in her bill was surprising. Candles and soap—the bill itself was the sole evidence of soap's ever having made its appearance in that house—and washing and tea and food and goodness knows what. The total was amazing. I verified the addition, or, rather, corrected it, and then offered half of the sum demanded. This offer was received with protestations, tears and voluble demands to know if I 'ad the 'art to rob a lone widow who couldn't protect herself. Finally we compromised on a three-quarter basis and Mrs. Briggs receipted the bill. She said her kind disposition would be the undoing of her and she knew it. She was too silly and soft-'arted to let lodgings.

We had very little trouble in carrying or leading Little Frank to the cab. The effect of the doctor's powders—they must have contained some sort of opiate—was to render the girl only partially conscious of what was going on and we got her to and into the vehicle without difficulty. During the drive to Bancroft's she dozed on Hephzy's shoulder.

Her room—it was next to Hephzy's, with a connecting door—was ready and we led her up the stairs. Mr. and Mrs. Jameson were very kind and sympathetic. They asked surprisingly few questions.

"Poor young lady," said Mr. Jameson, when he and I were together in our sitting-room. "She is quite ill, isn't she."

"Yes," I admitted. "It is not a serious illness, however. She needs quiet and care more than anything else."

"Yes, sir. We will do our best to see that she has both. A relative of yours, sir, I think you said."

"A—a—my niece," I answered, on the spur of the moment. She was Hephzy's niece, of course. As a matter of fact, she was scarcely related to me. However, it seemed useless to explain.

"I didn't know you had English relatives, Mr. Knowles. I had been under the impression that you and Miss Cahoon were strangers here."

So had I, but I did not explain that, either. Mrs. Jameson joined us.

"She will sleep now, I think," she said. "She is quite quiet and peaceful. A near relative of yours, Mr. Knowles?"

"She is Mr. Knowles's niece," explained her husband.

"Oh, yes. A sweet girl she seems. And very pretty, isn't she."

I did not answer. Mr. Jameson and his wife turned to go.

"I presume you will wish to communicate with her people," said the former. "Shall I send you telegram forms?"

"Not now," I stammered. Telegrams! Her people! She had no people. We were her people. We had taken her in charge and were responsible. And how and when would that responsibility be shifted!

What on earth should we do with her?

Hephzy tiptoed in. Her expression was a curious one. She was very solemn, but not sad; the solemnity was not that of sorrow, but appeared to be a sort of spiritual uplift, a kind of reverent joy.

"She's asleep," she said, gravely; "she's asleep, Hosy."

There was precious little comfort in that.

"She'll wake up by and by," I said. "And then—what?"

"I don't know."

"Neither do I—now. But we shall have to know pretty soon."

"I suppose we shall, but I can't—I can't seem to think of anything that's ahead of us. All I can think is that my Little Frank—my Ardelia's Little Frank—is here, here with us, at last."

"And TO last, so far as I can see. Hephzy, for heaven's sake, do try to be sensible. Do you realize what this means? As soon as she is well enough to understand what has happened she will want to know what 'proposition' we have to make. And when we tell her we have none to make, she'll probably collapse again. And then—and then—what shall we do?"

"I don't know, Hosy. I declare I don't know."

I strode into my own room and slammed the door.

"Damn!" said I, with enthusiasm.

"What?" queried Hephzy, from the sitting-room. "What did you say, Hosy?"

I did not tell her.

CHAPTER VIII
In Which the Pilgrims Become Tenants

Two weeks later we left Bancroft's and went to Mayberry. Two weeks only, and yet in that two weeks all our plans—if our indefinite visions of irresponsible flitting about Great Britain and the continent might be called plans—had changed utterly. Our pilgrimage was, apparently, ended—it had become an indefinite stay. We were no longer pilgrims, but tenants, tenants in an English rectory, of all places in the world. I, the Cape Cod quahaug, had become an English country gentleman—or a country gentleman in England—for the summer, at least.

Little Frank—Miss Frances Morley—was responsible for the change, of course. Her sudden materialization and the freak of fortune which had thrown her, weak and ill, upon our hands, were responsible for everything. For how much more, how many other changes, she would be responsible the future only could answer. And the future would answer in its own good, or bad, time. My conundrum "What are we going to do with her?" was as much of a puzzle as ever. For my part I gave it up. Sufficient unto the day was the evil thereof—much more than sufficient.

For the first twenty-four hours following the arrival of "my niece" at Bancroft's Hotel the situation regarding that niece remained as it was. Miss Morley—or Frances—or Frank as Hephzy persisted in calling her—was too ill to care what had happened, or, at least, to speak of it. She spoke very little, was confined to her room and bed and slept the greater part of the time. The doctor whom I called, on Mr. Jameson's recommendation, confirmed his fellow practitioner's diagnosis; the young lady, he said, was suffering from general weakness and the effect of nervous strain. She needed absolute rest, care and quiet. There was no organic disease.

But on the morning of the second day she was much better and willing, even anxious to talk. She assailed Hephzy with questions and Hephzy, although she tried to avoid answering most, was obliged to answer some of them. She reported the interview to me during luncheon.

"She didn't seem to remember much about comin' here, or what happened before or afterward," said Hephzy. "But she wanted to know it all. I told her the best I could. 'You couldn't stay there,' I said. 'That Briggs hyena wasn't fit to take care of any human bein' and neither Hosy nor I could leave you in her hands. So we brought you here to the hotel where we're stoppin'.' She thought this over a spell and then she wanted to know whose idea bringin' her here was, yours or mine. I said 'twas yours, and just like you, too; you were the kindest-hearted man in the world, I said. Oh, you needn't look at me like that, Hosy. It's the plain truth, and you know it."

"Humph!" I grunted. "If the young lady were a mind-reader she might—well, never mind. What else did she say?"

"Oh, a good many things. Wanted to know if her bill at Mrs. Briggs' was paid. I said it was. She thought about that and then she gave me orders that you and I were to keep account of every cent—no, penny—we spent for her. She should insist upon that. If we had the idea that she was a subject of charity we were mistaken. She fairly withered me with a look from those big eyes of hers. Ardelia's eyes all over again! Or they would be if they were blue instead of brown. I remember—"

I cut short the reminiscence. I was in no mood to listen to the praises of any Morley.

"What answer did you make to that?" I asked.

"What could I say? I didn't want any more faintin' spells or hysterics, either. I said we weren't thinkin' of offerin' charity and if it would please her to have us run an expense book we'd do it, of course. She asked what the doctor said about her condition. I told her he said she must keep absolutely quiet and not fret about anything or she'd have an awful relapse. That was pretty strong but I meant it that way. Answerin' questions that haven't got any answer to 'em is too much of a strain for ME. You try it some time yourself and see."

"I have tried it, thank you. Well, is that all? Did she tell you anything about herself; where she has been or what she has been or what she has been doing since her precious father died?"

"No, not a word. I was dyin' to ask her, but I didn't. She says she wants to talk with the doctor next time he comes, that's all."

She did talk with the doctor, although not during his next call. Several days passed before he would permit her to talk with him. Meanwhile he and I had several talks. What he told me brought my conundrum no nearer its answer.

She was recovering rapidly, he said, but for weeks at least her delicate nervous organism must be handled with care. The slightest set-back would be disastrous. He asked if we intended remaining at Bancroft's indefinitely. I had no intentions—those I had had were wiped off my mental slate—so I said I did not know, our future plans were vague. He suggested a sojourn in the country, in some pleasant retired spot in the rural districts.

"An out-of-door life, walks, rides and sports of all sorts would do your niece a world of good, Mr. Knowles," he declared. "She needs just that. A very attractive young lady, sir, if you'll pardon my saying so," he went on. "Were her people Londoners, may I ask?"

He might ask but I had no intention of telling him. What I knew concerning my "niece's" people were things not usually told to strangers. I evaded the question.

"Has she had a recent bereavement?" he queried. "I hope you'll not think me merely idly inquisitive. I cannot understand how a young woman, normally healthy and well, should have been brought to such a strait. Our English girls, Mr. Knowles, do not suffer from nerves, as I am told your American young women so frequently do. Has your niece been in the States with you?"

I said she had not. Incidentally I informed him that American young women did NOT frequently suffer from nerves. He said "Really," but he did not believe me, I'm certain. He was a good fellow, and intelligent, but his ideas of "the States" had been gathered, largely, I think, from newspapers and novels. He was convinced that most Americans were confirmed neurotics and dyspeptics, just as Hephzy had believed all Englishmen wore side-whiskers.

I changed the conversation as soon as I could. I could tell him so little concerning my newly found "niece." I knew about as much concerning her life as he did. It is distinctly unpleasant to be uncle to someone you know nothing at all about. I devoutly wished I had not said she was my niece. I repeated that wish many times afterward.

Miss Morley's talk with the physician had definite results, surprising results. Following that talk she sent word by the doctor that she wished to see Hephzy and me. We went into her room. She was sitting in a chair by the window, and was wearing a rather pretty wrapper, or kimono, or whatever that sort of garment is called. At any rate, it was becoming. I was obliged to admit that the general opinion expressed by the Jamesons and Hephzy and the doctor—that she was pretty, was correct enough. She was pretty, but that did not help matters any.

She asked us—no, she commanded us to sit down. Her manner was decidedly business-like. She wasted no time in preliminaries, but came straight to the point, and that point was the one which I had dreaded. She asked us what decision we had reached concerning her.

"Have you decided what your offer is to be?" she asked.

I looked at Hephzy and she at me. Neither of us derived comfort from the exchange of looks. However, something must be done, or said, and I braced myself to say it.

"Miss Morley," I began, "before I answer that question I should like to ask you one. What do you expect us to do?"

She regarded me coldly. "I expect," she said, "that you and this—that you and Miss Cahoon will arrange to pay me the money which was my mother's and which my grandfather should have turned over to her while he lived."

Again I looked at Hephzy and again I braced myself for the scene which I was certain would follow.

"It is your impression then," I said, "that your mother had money of her own and that Captain Barnabas, your grandfather, kept that money for his own use."

"It is not an impression," haughtily; "I know it to be a fact."

"How do you know it?"

"My father told me so, during his last illness."

"Was—pardon me—was your father himself at the time? Was he—er—rational?"

"Rational! My father?"

"I mean—I mean was he himself—mentally? He was not delirious when he told you?"

"Delirious! Mr. Knowles, I am trying to be patient, but for the last time I warn you that I will not listen to insinuations against my father."

"I am not insinuating anything. I am seeking information. Were you and your father together a great deal? Did you know him well? Just what did he tell you?"

She hesitated before replying. When she spoke it was with an exaggerated air of patient toleration, as if she were addressing an unreasonable child.

"I will answer you," she said. "I will answer you because, so far, I have no fault to find with your behavior toward me. You and my—and my aunt have been as reasonable as I, perhaps, should expect, everything considered. Your bringing me here and providing for me was even kind, I suppose. So I will answer your questions. My father and I were not together a great deal. I attended a convent school in France and saw Father only at intervals. I supposed him to possess an independent income. It was only when he was—was unable to work," with a quiver in her voice, "that I learned how he lived. He had been obliged to depend upon his music, upon his violin playing, to earn money enough to keep us both alive. Then he told me of—of his life in America and how my mother and he had been—been cheated and defrauded by those who—who—Oh, DON'T ask me any more! Don't!"

"I must ask you. I must ask you to tell me this: How was he defrauded, as you call it?"

"I have told you, already. My mother's fortune—"

"But your mother had no fortune."

The anticipated scene was imminent. She sprang to her feet, but being too weak to stand, sank back again. Hephzy looked appealingly at me.

"Hosy," she cautioned; "Oh, Hosy, be careful! Think how sick she has been."

"I am thinking, Hephzy. I mean to be careful. But what I said is the truth, and you know it."

Hephzy would have replied, but Little Frank motioned her to be silent.

"Hush!" she commanded. "Mr. Knowles, what do you mean? My mother had money, a great deal of money. I don't know the exact sum, but my father said—You know it! You MUST know it. It was in my grandfather's care and—"

"Your grandfather had no money. He—well, he lost every dollar he had. He died as poor as a church rat."

Another interval of silence, during which I endured a piercing scrutiny from the dark eyes. Then Miss Morley's tone changed.

"Indeed!" she said, sarcastically. "You surprise me, Mr. Knowles. What became of the money, may I ask? I understand that my grandfather was a wealthy man."

"He was fairly well-to-do at one time, but he lost his money and died poor."

"How did he lose it?"

The question was a plain one and demanded a plain and satisfying answer. But how could I give that answer—then? Hephzy was shaking her head violently. I stammered and faltered and looked guilty, I have no doubt.

"Well?" said Miss Morley.

"He—he lost it, that is sufficient. You must take my word for it. Captain Cahoon died without a dollar of his own."

"When did he LOSE his wealth?" with sarcastic emphasis.

"Years ago. About the time your parents left the United States. There, there, Hephzy! I know. I'm doing my best."

"Indeed! When did he die?"

"Long ago—more than ten years ago."

"But my parents left America long before that. If my grandfather was penniless how did he manage to live all those years? What supported him?"

"Your aunt—Miss Cahoon here—had money in her own right."

"SHE had money and my mother had not. Yet both were Captain Cahoon's daughters. How did that happen?"

It seemed to me that it was Hephzy's time to play the target. I turned to her.

"Miss Cahoon will probably answer that herself," I observed, maliciously.

Hephzibah appeared more embarrassed than I.

"I—I—Oh, what difference does all this make?" she faltered. "Hosy has told you the truth, Frances. Really and truly he has. Father was poor as poverty when he died and all his last years, too. All his money had gone."

"Yes, so I have heard Mr. Knowles say. But how did it go?"

"In—in—well, it was invested in stocks and things and—and—"

"Do you mean that he speculated in shares?"

"Well, not—not—"

"I see. Oh, I see. Father told me a little concerning those speculations. He warned Captain Cahoon before he left the States, but his warnings were not heeded, I presume. And you wish me to believe that ALL the money was lost—my mother's and all. Is that what you mean?"

"Your mother HAD no money," I put in, desperately, "I have told you—"

"You have told me many things, Mr. Knowles. Even admitting that my grandfather lost his money, as you say, why should I suffer because of his folly? I am not asking for HIS money. I am demanding money that was my mother's and is now mine. That I expected from him and now I expect it from you, his heirs."

"But your mother had no—"

"I do not care to hear that again. I know she had money."

"But how do you know?"

"Because my father told me she had, and my father did not lie."

There we were again—just where we started. The doctor re-entered the room and insisted upon his patient's being left to herself. She must lie down and rest, he said. His manner was one of distinct disapproval. It was evident that he considered Hephzy and me disturbers of the peace; in fact he intimated as much when he joined us in the sitting-room in a few minutes.

"I am afraid I made a mistake in permitting the conference," he said. "The young lady seems much agitated, Mr. Knowles. If she is, complete nervous prostration may follow. She may be an invalid for months or even years. I strongly recommend her being taken into the country as soon as possible."

This speech and the manner in which it was made were impressive and alarming. The possibilities at which it hinted were more alarming still. We made no attempt to discuss family matters with Little Frank that day nor the next.

But on the day following, when I returned from my morning visit to Camford Street, I found Hephzy awaiting me in the sitting-room. She was very solemn.

"Hosy," she said, "sit down. I've got somethin' to tell you."

"About her?" I asked, apprehensively.

"Yes. She's just been talkin' to me."

"She has! I thought we agreed not to talk with her at all."

"We did, and I tried not to. But when I went in to see her just now she was waitin' for me. She had somethin' to say, she said, and she said it—Oh, my goodness, yes! she said it."

"What did she say? Has she sent for her lawyer—her solicitor, or whatever he is?"

"No, she hasn't done that. I don't know but I 'most wish she had. He wouldn't be any harder to talk to than she is. Hosy, she's made up her mind."

"Made up her mind! I thought HER mind was already made up."

"It was, but she's made it up again. That doctor has been talkin' to her and she's really frightened about her health, I think. Anyhow, she has decided that her principal business just now is to get well. She told me she had decided not to press her claim upon us for the present. If we wished to make an offer of what she calls restitution, she'll listen to it; but she judges we are not ready to make one."

"Humph! her judgment is correct so far."

"Yes, but that isn't all. While she is waitin' for that offer she expects us to take care of her. She has been thinkin', she says, and she has come to the conclusion that our providin' for her as we have done isn't charity— or needn't be considered as charity—at all. She is willin' to consider it a part of that precious restitution she's forever talkin' about. We are to take care of her, and pay her doctor's bills, and take her into the country as he recommends, and —"

I interrupted. "Great Scott!" I cried, "does she expect us to ADOPT her?"

"I don't know what she expects; I'm tryin' to tell you what she said. We're to do all this and keep a strict account of all it costs, and then when we are ready to make a—a proposition, as she calls it, this account can be subtracted from the money she thinks we've got that belongs to her."

"But there isn't any money belonging to her. I told her so, and so did you."

"I know, but we might tell her a thousand times and it wouldn't affect her father's tellin' her once. Oh, that Strickland Morley! If only —"

"Hush! hush, Hephzy... Well, by George! of all the- this thing has gone far enough. It has gone too far. We made a great mistake in bringing her here, in having anything to do with her at all—but we shan't go on making mistakes. We must stop where we are. She must be told the truth now—to-day."

"I know—I know, Hosy; but who'll tell her?"

"I will."

"She won't believe you."

"Then she must disbelieve. She can call in her solicitor and I'll make him believe."

Hephzy was silent. Her silence annoyed me.

"Why don't you say something?" I demanded. "You know what I say is plain common-sense."

"I suppose it is—I suppose 'tis. But, Hosy, if you start in tellin' her again you know what'll happen. The doctor said the least little thing would bring on nervous prostration. And if she has that, WHAT will become of her?"

It was my turn to hesitate.

"You couldn't—we couldn't turn her out into the street if she was nervous prostrated, could we," pleaded Hephzy. "After all, she's Ardelia's daughter and—"

"She's Strickland Morley's daughter. There is no doubt of that. Hereditary influence is plain enough in her case."

"I know, but she is Ardelia's daughter, too. I don't see how we can tell her, Hosy; not until she's well and strong again."

I was never more thoroughly angry in my life. My patience was exhausted.

"Look here, Hephzy," I cried: "what is it you are leading up to? You're not proposing—actually proposing that we adopt this girl, are you?"

"No—no—o. Not exactly that, of course. But we might take her into the country somewhere and—"

"Oh, DO be sensible! Do you realize what that would mean? We should have to give up our trip, stop sightseeing, stop everything we had planned to do, and turn ourselves into nurses running a sanitarium for the benefit of a girl whose father's rascality made your father a pauper. And, not only do this, but be treated by her as if—as if—"

"There, there, Hosy! I know what it will mean. I know what it would mean to you and I don't mean for you to do it. You've done enough and more than enough. But with me it's different. I could do it."

"You?"

"Yes. I've got some money of my own. I could find a nice, cheap, quiet boardin'-house in the country round here somewhere and she and I could go there and stay until she got well. You needn't go at all; you could go off travelin' by yourself and—"

"Hephzy, what are you talking about?"

"I mean it. I've thought it all out, Hosy. Ever since Ardelia and I had that last talk together and she whispered to me that—that—well, especially ever since I knew there was a Little Frank I've been thinkin' and plannin' about that Little Frank; you know I have. He—she isn't the kind of Little Frank I expected, but she's, my sister's baby and I can't—I CAN'T, turn her away to be sick and die. I can't do it. I shouldn't dare face Ardelia in—on the other side if I did. No, I guess it's my duty and I'm goin' to go on with it. But with you it's different. She isn't any real relation to you. You've done enough—and more than enough—as it is."

This was the climax. Of course I might have expected it, but of course I didn't. As soon as I recovered, or partially recovered, from my stupefaction I expostulated and scolded and argued. Hephzy was quiet but firm. She hated to part from me—she couldn't bear to think of it; but on the other hand she couldn't abandon her Ardelia's little girl. The interview ended by my walking out of the room and out of Bancroft's in disgust.

I did not return until late in the afternoon. I was in better humor then. Hephzy was still in the sitting-room; she looked as if she had been crying.

"Hosy," she said, as I entered, "I—I hope you don't think I'm too ungrateful. I'm not. Really I'm not. And I care as much for you as if you was my own boy. I can't leave you; I sha'n't. If you say for us to—"

I interrupted.

"Hephzy," I said, "I shan't say anything. I know perfectly well that you couldn't leave me any more than I could leave you. I have arranged with Matthews to set about house-hunting at once. As soon as rural England is ready for us, we shall be ready for it. After all, what difference does it make? I was ordered to get fresh experience. I might as well get it by becoming keeper of a sanitarium as any other way."

Hephzy looked at me. She rose from her chair.

"Hosy," she cried, "what—a sanitarium?"

"We'll keep it together," I said, smiling. "You and I and Little Frank. And it is likely to be a wonderful establishment."

Hephzy said—she said a great deal, principally concerning my generosity and goodness and kindness and self-sacrifice. I tried to shut off the flow, but it was not until I began to laugh that it ceased.

"Why!" cried Hephzy. "You're laughin'! What in the world? I don't see anything to laugh at."

"Don't you? I do. Oh, dear me! I—I, the Bayport quahaug to—Ho! ho! Hephzy, let me laugh. If there is any fun in this perfectly devilish situation let me enjoy it while I can."

And that is how and why I decided to become a country gentleman instead of a traveler. When I told Matthews of my intention he had been petrified with astonishment. I had written Campbell of that intention. I devoutly wished I might see his face when he read my letter.

For days and days Hephzy and I "house-hunted." We engaged a nurse to look after the future patient of the "sanitarium" while we did our best to look for the sanitarium itself. Mr. Matthews gave us the addresses of real estate agents and we journeyed from suburb to suburb and from seashore to hills. We saw several "semi-detached villas." The name "semi-detached villa" had an appealing sound, especially to Hephzy, but the villas themselves did not appeal. They turned out to be what we, in America, would have called "two-family houses."

"And I never did like the idea of livin' in a two-family house," declared Hephzy. "I've known plenty of real nice folks who did live in 'em, or one-half of one of 'em, but it usually happened that the folks in the other half was a dreadful mean set. They let their dog chase your cat and if your hens scratched up their flower garden they were real unlikely about it. I've heard Father tell about Cap'n Noah Doane and Cap'n Elkanah Howes who used to live in Bayport. They'd been chums all their lives and when they retired from the sea they thought 'twould be lovely to build a double house so's they would be right close together all the time. Well, they did it and they hadn't been settled more'n a month when they began quarrelin'. Cap'n Noah's wife wanted the house painted yellow and Mrs. Cap'n Elkanah, she wanted it green. They started the fuss and it ended by one-half bein' yellow and t'other half green—such an outrage you never saw—and a big fence down the middle of the front yard, and the two families not speakin', and law-suits and land knows what all. They wouldn't even go to the same church nor be buried in the same graveyard. No sir-ee! no two-family house for us if I can help it. We've got troubles enough inside the family without fightin' the neighbors."

"But think of the beautiful names," I observed. "Those names ought to appeal to your poetic soul, Hephzy. We haven't seen a villa yet, no matter how dingy, or small, that wasn't christened 'Rosemary Terrace' or 'Sunnylawn' or something. That last one—the shack with the broken windows—was labeled 'Broadview' and it faced an alley ending at a brick stable."

"I know it," she said. "If they'd called it 'Narrowview' or 'Cow Prospect' 'twould have been more fittin', I should say. But I think givin' names to homes is sort of pretty, just the same. We might call our house at home 'Writer's Rest.' A writer lives in it, you know."

"And he has rested more than he has written of late," I observed. "'Quahaug Stew' or 'The Tureen' would be better, I should say."

When we expressed disapproval of the semi-detached villas our real estate brokers flew to the other extremity and proceeded to show us "estates." These estates comprised acres of ground, mansions, game-keepers' and lodge-keepers' houses, and goodness knows what. Some, so the brokers were particular to inform us, were celebrated for their "shooting."

The villas were not good enough; the estates were altogether too good. We inspected but one and then declined to see more.

"Shootin'!" sniffed Hephzy. "I should feel like shootin' myself every time I paid the rent. I'd HAVE to do it the second time. 'Twould be a quicker end than starvin', 'and the first month would bring us to that."

We found one pleasant cottage in a suburb bearing the euphonious name of "Leatherhead"—that is, the village was named "Leatherhead"; the cottage was "Ash Clump." I teased Hephzy by referring to it as "Ash Dump," but it really was a pretty, roomy house, with gardens and flowers. For the matter of that, every cottage we visited, even the smallest, was bowered in flowers.

Hephzy's romantic spirit objected strongly to "Leatherhead," but I told her nothing could be more appropriate.

"This whole proposition—Beg pardon; I didn't mean to use that word; we've heard enough concerning 'propositions'—but really, Hephzy, 'Leatherhead' is very appropriate for us. If we weren't leather-headed and deserving of leather medals we should not be hunting houses at all. We should have left Little Frank and her affairs in a lawyer's hands and be enjoying ourselves as we intended. Leatherhead for the leather-heads; it's another dispensation of Providence."

"Ash Dump"—"Clump," I mean—was owned by a person named Cripps, Solomon Cripps. Mr. Cripps was a stout, mutton-chopped individual, strongly suggestive of Bancroft's "Henry." He was rather pompous and surly when I first knocked at the door of his residence, but when he learned we were house-hunting and had our eyes upon the "Clump," he became very polite indeed. "A 'eavenly spot," he declared it to be. "A beautiful neighborhood. Near the shops and not far from the Primitive Wesleyan chapel." He and Mrs. Cripps attended the chapel, he informed us.

I did not fancy Mr. Cripps; he was too—too something, I was not sure what. And Mrs. Cripps, whom we met later, was of a similar type. They, like everyone else, recognized us as Americans at once and they spoke highly of the "States."

"A very fine country, I am informed," said Mr. Cripps. "New, of course, but very fine indeed. Young men make money there. Much money—yes."

Mrs. Cripps wished to know if Americans were a religious people, as a rule. Religion, true spiritual religion was on the wane in England.

I gathered that she and her husband were doing their best to keep it up to the standard. I had read, in books by English writers, of the British middle-class Pharisee. I judged the Crippses to be Pharisees.

Hephzy's opinion was like mine.

"If ever there was a sanctimonious hypocrite it's that Mrs. Cripps," she declared. "And her husband ain't any better. They remind me of Deacon Hardy and his wife back home. He always passed the plate in church and she was head of the sewin' circle, but when it came to lettin' go of an extry cent for the minister's salary they had glue on their fingers. Father used to say that the Deacon passed the plate himself so nobody could see how little he put in it. They were the ones that always brought a stick of salt herrin' to the donation parties."

We didn't like the Crippses, but we did like "Ash Clump." We had almost decided to take it when our plans were quashed by the member of our party on whose account we had planned solely. Miss Morley flatly refused to go to Leatherhead.

"Don't ask ME why," said Hephzy, to whom the refusal had been made. "I don't know. All I know is that the very name 'Leatherhead' turned her whiter than she has been for a week. She just put that little foot of hers down and said no. I said 'Why not?' and she said 'Never mind.' So I guess we sha'n't be Leatherheaded—in that way—this summer."

I was angry and impatient, but when I tried to reason with the young lady I met a crushing refusal and a decided snub.

"I do not care," said Little Frank, calmly and coldly, "to explain my reasons. I have them, and that is sufficient. I shall not go to—that town or that place."

"But why?" I begged, restraining my desire to shake her.

"I have my reasons. You may go there, if you wish. That is your right. But I shall not. And before you go I shall insist upon a settlement of my claim."

The "claim" could neither be settled nor discussed; the doctor's warning was no less insistent although his patient was steadily improving. I faced the alternative of my compliance or her nervous prostration and I chose the former. My desire to shake her remained.

So "Ash Clump" was given up. Hephzy and I speculated much concerning Little Frank's aversion to Leatherhead.

"It must be," said Hephzy, "that she knows somebody there, or somethin' like that. That's likely, I suppose. You know we don't know much about her or what she's done since her father died, Hosy. I've tried to ask her but she won't tell. I wish we did know."

"I don't," I snarled. "I wish to heaven we had never known her at all."

Hephzy sighed. "It IS awful hard for you," she said. "And yet, if we had come to know her in another way you—we might have been glad. I—I think she could be as sweet as she is pretty to folks she didn't consider thieves—and Americans. She does hate Americans. That's her precious pa's doin's, I suppose likely."

The next afternoon we saw the advertisement in the Standard. George, the waiter, brought two of the London dailies to our room each day. The advertisement read as follows:

"To Let for the Summer Months—Furnished. A Rectory in Mayberry, Sussex. Ten rooms, servants' quarters, vegetable gardens, small fruit, tennis court, etc., etc. Water and gas laid on. Golf near by. Terms low. Rector—Mayberry, Sussex."

"I answered it, Hosy," said Hephzy.

"You did!"

"Yes. It sounded so nice I couldn't help it. It would be lovely to live in a rectory, wouldn't it."

"Lovely—and expensive," I answered. "I'm afraid a rectory with tennis courts and servants' quarters and all the rest of it will prove too grand for a pair of Bayporters like you and me. However, your answering the ad does no harm; it doesn't commit us to anything."

But when the answer to the answer came it was even more appealing than the advertisement itself. And the terms, although a trifle higher than we had planned to pay, were not entirely beyond our means. The rector—his name was Cole—urged us to visit Mayberry and see the place for ourselves. We were to take the train for Haddington on Hill where the trap would meet us. Mayberry was two miles from Haddington on Hill, it appeared.

We decided to go, but before writing of our intention, Hephzy consulted the most particular member of our party.

"It's no use doing anything until we ask her," she said. "She may be as down on Mayberry as she was on Leatherhead."

But she was not. She had no objections to Mayberry. So, after writing and making the necessary arrangements, we took the train one bright, sunny morning, and after a ride of an hour or more, alighted at Haddington on Hill.

Haddington on Hill was not on a hill at all, unless a knoll in the middle of a wide flat meadow be called that. There were no houses near the railway station, either rectories or any other sort. We were the only passengers to leave the train there.

The trap, however, was waiting. The horse which drew it was a black, plump little animal, and the driver was a neat English lad who touched his hat and assisted Hephzy to the back seat of the vehicle. I climbed up beside her.

The road wound over the knoll and away across the meadow. On either side were farm lands, fields of young grain, or pastures with flocks of sheep grazing contentedly. In the distance, in every direction, one caught glimpses of little villages with gray church towers rising amid the foliage. Each field and pasture was bordered with a hedge instead of a fence, and over all hung the soft, light blue haze which is so characteristic of good weather in England.

Birds which we took to be crows, but which we learned afterward were rooks, whirled and circled. As we turned a corner a smaller bird rose from the grass beside the road and soared upward, singing with all its little might until it was a fluttering speck against the sky. Hephzy watched it, her eyes shining.

"I believe," she cried, excitedly, "I do believe that is a skylark. Do you suppose it is?"

"A lark, yes, lady," said our driver.

"A lark, a real skylark! Just think of it, Hosy. I've heard a real lark. Well, Hephzibah Cahoon, you may never get into a book, but you're livin' among book things every day of your life. 'And singin' ever soars and soarin' ever singest.' I'd sing, too, if I knew how. You needn't be frightened—I sha'n't try."

The meadows ended at the foot of another hill, a real one this time. At our left, crowning the hill, a big house, a mansion with towers and turrets, rose above the trees. Hephzy whispered to me.

"You don't suppose THAT is the rectory, do you, Hosy?" she asked, in an awestricken tone.

"If it is we may as well go back to London," I answered. "But it isn't. Nothing lower in churchly rank than a bishop could keep up that establishment."

The driver settled our doubts for us.

"The Manor House, sir," he said, pointing with his whip. "The estate begins here, sir."

The "estate" was bordered by a high iron fence, stretching as far as we could see. Beside that fence we rode for some distance. Then another turn in the road and we entered the street of a little village, a village of picturesque little houses, brick or stone always—not a frame house among them. Many of the roofs were thatched. Flowers and climbing vines and little gardens everywhere. The village looked as if it had been there, just as it was, for centuries.

"This is Mayberry, sir," said our driver. "That is the rectory, next the church."

We could see the church tower and the roof, but the rectory was not yet visible to our eyes. We turned in between two of the houses, larger and more pretentious than the rest. The driver alighted and opened a big wooden gate. Before us was a driveway, shaded by great elms and bordered by rose hedges. At the end of the driveway was an old-fashioned, comfortable looking, brick house. Vines hid the most of the bricks. Flower beds covered its foundations. A gray-haired old gentleman stood in the doorway.

This was the rectory we had come to see and the gray-haired gentleman was the Reverend Mr. Cole, the rector.

"My soul!" whispered Hephzy, looking aghast at the spacious grounds, "we can never hire THIS. This is too expensive and grand for us, Hosy. Look at the grass to cut and the flowers to attend to, and the house to run. No wonder the servants have 'quarters.' My soul and body! I thought a rector was a kind of minister, and a rectory was a sort of parsonage, but I guess I'm off my course, as Father used to say. Either that or ministers' wages are higher than they are in Bayport. No, this place isn't for you and me, Hosy."

But it was. Before we left that rectory in the afternoon I had agreed to lease it until the middle of September, servants—there were five of them, groom and gardener included—horse and trap, tennis court, vegetable garden, fruit, flowers and all. It developed that the terms, which I had considered rather too high for my purse, included the servants' wages, vegetables from the garden, strawberries and other "small fruit"—everything. Even food for the horse was included in that all-embracing rent.

As Hephzy said, everything considered, the rent of Mayberry Rectory was lower than that of a fair-sized summer cottage at Bayport.

The Reverend Mr. Cole was a delightful gentleman. His wife was equally kind and agreeable. I think they were, at first, rather unpleasantly surprised to find that their prospective tenants were from the "States"; but Hephzy and I managed to behave as unlike savages as we could, and the Cole manner grew less and less reserved. Mr. Cole and his wife were planning to spend a long vacation in Switzerland and his "living," or parish, was to be left in charge of his two curates. There was a son at Oxford who was to join them on their vacation.

Mr. Cole and I walked about the grounds and visited the church, the yard of which, with its weather-beaten gravestones and fine old trees, adjoined the rectory on the western side, behind the tall hedge.

The church was built of stone, of course, and a portion of it was older than the Norman conquest. Before the altar steps were two ancient effigies of knights in armor, with crossed gauntlets and their feet supported by crouching lions. These old fellows were scratched and scarred and initialed. Upon one noble nose were the letters "A. H. N. 1694." I decided that vandalism was not a modern innovation.

While the rector and I were inspecting the church, Mrs. Cole and Hephzy were making a tour of the house. They met us at the door. Mrs. Cole's eyes were twinkling; I judged that she had found Hephzy amusing. If this was true it had not warped her judgment, however, for, a moment later when she and I were alone, she said:

"Your cousin, Miss Cahoon, is a good housekeeper, I imagine."

"She is all of that," I said, decidedly.

"Yes, she was very particular concerning the kitchen and scullery and the maids' rooms. Are all American housekeepers as particular?"

"Not all. Miss Cahoon is unique in many ways; but she is a remarkable woman in all."

"Yes. I am sure of it. And she has such a typical American accent, hasn't she."

We were to take possession on the following Monday. We lunched at the "Red Cow," the village inn, where the meal was served in the parlor and the landlord's daughter waited upon us. The plump black horse drew us to the railway station, and we took the train for London.

We have learned, by this time, that second, or even third-class travel was quite good enough for short journeys and that very few English people paid for first-class compartments. We were fortunate enough to have a second-class compartment to ourselves this time, and, when we were seated, Hephzy asked a question.

"Did you think to speak about the golf, Hosy?" she said. "You will want to play some, won't you?"

"Yes," said I. "I did ask about it. It seems that the golf course is a private one, on the big estate we passed on the way from the station. Permission is always given the rectory tenants."

"Oh! my gracious, isn't that grand! That estate isn't in Mayberry. The Mayberry bounds—that's what Mrs. Cole called them—and just this side. The estate is in the village of—of Burgleston Bogs. Burgleston Bogs—it's a funny name. Seem's if I'd heard it before."

"You have," said I, in surprise. "Burgleston Bogs is where that Heathcroft chap whom we met on the steamer visits occasionally. His aunt has a big place there. By George! you don't suppose that estate belongs to his aunt, do you?"

Hephzy gasped. "I wouldn't wonder," she cried. "I wouldn't wonder if it did. And his aunt was Lady Somebody, wasn't she. Maybe you'll meet him there. Goodness sakes! just think of your playin' golf with a Lady's nephew."

"I doubt if we need to think of it," I observed. "Mr. Carleton Heathcroft on board ship may be friendly with American plebeians, but on shore, and when visiting his aunt, he may be quite different. I fancy he and I will not play many holes together."

Hephzy laughed. "You 'fancy,'" she repeated. "You'll be sayin' 'My word' next. My! Hosy, you ARE gettin' English."

"Indeed I'm not!" I declared, with emphasis. "My experience with an English relative is sufficient of itself to prevent that. Miss Frances Morley and I are compatriots for the summer only."

CHAPTER IX
In Which We Make the Acquaintance of Mayberry and a Portion of Burgleston Bogs

We migrated to Mayberry the following Monday, as we had agreed to do. Miss Morley went with us, of course. I secured a first-class apartment for our party and the journey was a comfortable and quiet one. Our invalid was too weak to talk a great deal even if she had wished, which she apparently did not. Johnson, the groom, met us at Haddington on Hill and we drove to the rectory. There Miss Morley, very tired and worn out, was escorted to her room by Hephzy and Charlotte, the housemaid. She was perfectly willing to remain in that room, in fact she did not leave it for several days.

Meanwhile Hephzy and I were doing our best to become acquainted with our new and novel mode of life. Hephzy took charge of the household and was, in a way, quite in her element; in another way she was distinctly out of it.

"I did think I was gettin' used to bein' waited on, Hosy," she confided, "but it looks as if I'll have to begin all over again. Managin' one hired girl like Susanna was a job and I tell you I thought managin' three, same as we've got here, would be a staggerer. But it isn't. Somehow the kind of help over here don't seem to need managin'. They manage me more than I do them. There's Mrs. Wigham, the cook. Mrs. Cole told me she was a 'superior' person and I guess she is—at any rate, she's superior to me in some things. She knows what a 'gooseberry fool' is and I'm sure I don't. I felt like another kind of fool when she told me she was goin' to make one, as a 'sweet,' for dinner to-night. As nigh as I can make out it's a sort of gooseberry pie, but I should never have called a gooseberry pie a 'sweet'; a 'sour' would have been better, accordin' to my reckonin'. However, all desserts over here are 'sweets' and fruit is dessert. Then there's Charlotte, the housemaid, and Baker, the 'between-maid'—between upstairs and down, I suppose that means—and Grimmer, the gardener, and Johnson, the boy that takes care of the horse. Each one of 'em seems to know exactly what their own job is and just as exactly where it leaves off and t'other's job begins. I never saw such obligin' but independent folks in my life. As for my own job, that seems to be settin' still with my hands folded. Well, it's a brand new one and it's goin' to take me one spell to get used to it."

It seemed likely to be a "spell" before I became accustomed to my own "job," that of being a country gentleman with nothing to do but play the part. When I went out to walk about the rectory garden, Grimmer touched his hat. When, however, I ventured to pick a few flowers in that garden, his expression of shocked disapproval was so marked that I felt I must have made a dreadful mistake. I had, of course. Grimmer was in charge of those flowers and if I wished any picked I was expected to tell him to pick them. Picking them myself was equivalent to admitting that I was not accustomed to having a gardener in my employ, in other words that I was not a real gentleman at all. I might wait an hour for Johnson to return from some errand or other and harness the horse; but I must on no account save time by harnessing the animal myself. That sort of labor was not done by the "gentry." I should have lost caste with the servants a dozen times during my first few days in the rectory were it not for one saving grace; I was an American, and almost any peculiar thing was expected of an American.

When I strolled along the village street the male villagers, especially the older ones, touched their hats to me. The old women bowed or courtesied. Also they invariably paused, when I had passed, to stare after me. The group at the blacksmith shop—where the stone coping of the low wall was worn in hollows by the generations of idlers who had sat upon it, just as their descendants were sitting upon it now—turned, after I had passed, to stare. There would be a pause in the conversation, then an outburst of talk and laughter. They were talking about the "foreigner" of course, and laughing at him. At the tailor's, where I sent my clothes to be pressed, the tailor himself, a gray-haired, round-shouldered antique, ventured an opinion concerning those clothes. "That coat was not made in England, sir," he said. "We don't make 'em that way 'ere, sir. That's a bit foreign, that coat, sir."

Yes, I was a foreigner. It was hard to realize. In a way everything was so homelike; the people looked like people I had known at home, their faces were New England faces quite as much as they were old England. But their clothes were just a little different, and their ways were different, and a dry-goods store was a "draper's shop," and a drug-store was a "chemist's," and candies were "sweeties" and a public school was a "board school" and a boarding-school was a "public school." And I might be polite and pleasant to these people—persons out of my "class"—but I must not be too cordial, for if I did, in the eyes of these very people, I lost caste and they would despise me.

Yes, I was a foreigner; it was a queer feeling.

Coming from America and particularly from democratic Bayport, where everyone is as good as anyone else provided he behaves himself, the class distinction in Mayberry was strange at first. I do not mean that there was not independence there; there was, among the poorest as well as the richer element. Every male Mayberryite voted as he thought, I am sure; and was self-respecting and independent. He would have resented any infringement of his rights just as Englishmen have resented such infringements and fought against them since history began. But what I am trying to make plain is that political equality and social equality were by no means synonymous. A man was a man for 'a' that, but when he was a gentleman he was 'a' that' and more. And when he was possessed of a title he was revered because of that title, or the title itself was revered. The hatter in London where I purchased a new "bowler," had a row of shelves upon which were boxes containing, so I was told, the spare titles of eminent customers. And those hat-boxes were lettered like this: "The Right Hon. Col. Wainwright, V.C.," "His Grace the Duke of Leicester," "Sir George Tupman, K.C.B.," etc., etc. It was my first impression that the hatter was responsible for thus proclaiming his customers' titles, but one day I saw Richard, convoyed by Henry, reverently bearing a suitcase into Bancroft's Hotel. And that suitcase bore upon its side the inscription, in very large letters, "Lord Eustace Stairs." Then I realized that Lord Eustace, like the owners of the hat-boxes, recognizing the value of a title, advertised it accordingly.

I laughed when I saw the suitcase and the hat-boxes. When I told Hephzy about the latter she laughed, too.

"That's funny, isn't it," she said. "Suppose the folks that have their names on the mugs in the barber shop back home had 'em lettered 'Cap'n Elkanah Crowell,' 'Judge the Hon. Ezra Salters,' 'The Grand Exalted Sachem Order of Red Men George Kendrick.' How everybody would laugh, wouldn't they. Why they'd laugh Cap'n Elkanah and Ezra and Kendrick out of town."

So they would have done—in Bayport—but not in Mayberry or London. Titles and rank and class in England are established and accepted institutions, and are not laughed at, for where institutions of that kind are laughed at they soon cease to be. Hephzy summed it up pretty well when she said:

"After all, it all depends on what you've been brought up to, doesn't it, Hosy. Your coat don't look funny to you because you've always worn that kind of coat, but that tailor man thought 'twas funny because he never saw one made like it. And a lord takin' his lordship seriously seems funny to us, but it doesn't seem so to him or to the tailor. They've been brought up to it, same as you have to the coat."

On one point she and I had agreed before coming to Mayberry, that was that we must not expect calls from the neighbors or social intercourse with the people of Mayberry.

"They don't know anything about us," said I, "except that we are Americans, and that may or may not be a recommendation, according to the kind of Americans they have previously met. The Englishman, so all the books tell us, is reserved and distant at first. He requires a long acquaintance before admitting strangers to his home life and we shall probably have no opportunity to make that acquaintance. If we were to stay in Mayberry a year, and behaved ourselves, we might in time be accepted as desirable, but not during the first summer. So if they leave us to ourselves we must make the best of it."

Hephzy agreed thoroughly. "You're right," she said. "And, after all, it's just what would happen anywhere. You remember when that Portygee family came to Bayport and lived in the Solon Blodgett house. Nobody would have anything to do with 'em for a long time because they were foreigners, but they turned out to be real nice folks after all. We're foreigners here and you can't blame the Mayberry people for not takin' chances; it looks as if nobody in it ever had taken a chance, as if it had been just the way it is since Noah came out of the Ark. I never felt so new and shiny in my life as I do around this old rectory and this old town."

Which was all perfectly true and yet the fact remains that, "new and shiny" as we were, the Mayberry people—those of our "class"—began to call upon us almost immediately, to invite us to their homes, to show us little kindnesses, and to be whole-souled and hospitable and friendly as if we had known them and they us for years. It was one of the greatest surprises, and remains one of the most pleasant recollections, of my brief career as a resident in England, the kindly cordiality of these neighbors in Mayberry.

The first caller was Dr. Bayliss, who occupied "Jasmine Gables," the pretty house next door. He dropped in one morning, introduced himself, shook hands and chatted for an hour. That afternoon his wife called upon Hephzy. The next day I played a round of golf upon the private course on the Manor House grounds, the Burgleston Bogs grounds—with the doctor and his son, young Herbert Bayliss, just through Cambridge and the medical college at London. Young Bayliss was a pleasant, good-looking young chap and I liked him as I did his father. He was at present acting as his father's assistant in caring for the former's practice, a practice which embraced three or four villages and a ten-mile stretch of country.

Naturally I was interested in the Manor estate and its owner. The grounds were beautiful, three square miles in extent and cared for, so Bayliss, Senior, told me, by some hundred and fifty men, seventy of whom were gardeners. Of the Manor House itself I caught a glimpse, gray-turreted and huge, set at the end of lawns and flower beds, with fountains playing and statues gleaming white amid the foliage. I asked some questions concerning its owner. Yes, she was Lady Kent Carey and she had a nephew named Heathcroft. So there was a chance, after all, that I might again meet my ship acquaintance who abhorred "griddle cakes." I imagined he would be somewhat surprised at that meeting. It was an odd coincidence.

As for the game of golf, my part of it, the least said the better. Doctor Bayliss, who, it developed, was an enthusiast at the game, was kind enough to tell me I had a "topping" drive. I thanked him, but there was altogether too much "topping" connected with my play that forenoon to make my thanks enthusiastic. I determined to practice assiduously before attempting another match. Somehow I felt responsible for the golfing honor of my country.

Other callers came to the rectory. The two curates, their names were Judson and Worcester, visited us; young men, both of them, and good fellows, Worcester particularly. Although they wore clerical garb they were not in the least "preachy." Hephzy, although she liked them, expressed surprise.

"They didn't act a bit like ministers," she said. "They didn't ask us to come to meetin' nor hint at prayin' with the family or anything, yet they looked for all the while like two Methodist parsons, young ones. A curate is a kind of new-hatched rector, isn't he?"

"Not exactly," I answered. "He is only partially hatched. But, whatever you do, don't tell them they look like Methodists; they wouldn't consider it a compliment."

Hephzy was a Methodist herself and she resented the slur. "Well, I guess a Methodist is as good as an Episcopalian," she declared. "And they don't ACT like Methodists. Why, one of 'em smoked a pipe. Just imagine Mr. Partridge smokin' a pipe!"

Mr. Judson and I played eighteen holes of golf together. He played a little worse than I did and I felt better. The honor of Bayport's golf had been partially vindicated.

While all this was going on our patient remained, for the greater part of the time, in her room. She was improving steadily. Doctor Bayliss, whom I had asked to attend her, declared, as his London associates had done, that all she needed was rest, quiet and the good air and food which she was certain to get in Mayberry. He, too, like the physician at Bancroft's, seemed impressed by her appearance and manner. And he also asked similar embarrassing questions.

"Delightful young lady, Miss Morley," he observed. "One of our English girls, Knowles. She informs me that she IS English."

"Partly English," I could not help saying. "Her mother was an American."

"Oh, indeed! You know she didn't tell me that, now did she."

"Perhaps not."

"No, by Jove, she didn't. But she has lived all her life in England?"

"Yes—in England and France."

"Your niece, I think you said."

I had said it, unfortunately, and it could not be unsaid now without many explanations. So I nodded.

"She doesn't—er—behave like an American. She hasn't the American manner, I mean to say. Now Miss Cahoon has—er—she has—"

"Miss Cahoon's manner is American. So is mine; we ARE Americans, you see."

"Yes, yes, of course," hastily. "When are you and I to have the nine holes you promised, Knowles?"

One fine afternoon the invalid came downstairs. The "between-maid" had arranged chairs and the table on the lawn. We were to have tea there; we had tea every day, of course—were getting quite accustomed to it.

Frances—I may as well begin calling her that—looked in better health then than at any time since our meeting. She was becomingly, although simply gowned, and there was a dash of color in her cheeks. Hephzibah escorted her to the tea table. I rose to meet them.

"Frank- Frances, I mean—is goin' to join us to-day," said Hephzy. "She's beginnin' to look real well again, isn't she."

I said she was. Frances nodded to me and took one of the chairs, the most comfortable one. She appeared perfectly self-possessed, which I was sure I did not. I was embarrassed, of course. Each time I met the girl the impossible situation in which she had placed us became more impossible, to my mind. And the question, "What on earth shall we do with her?" more insistent.

Hephzy poured the tea. Frances, cup in hand, looked about her.

"This is rather a nice place, after all," she observed, "isn't it."

"It's a real lovely place," declared Hephzy with enthusiasm.

The young lady cast another appraising glance at our surroundings.

"Yes," she repeated, "it's a jolly old house and the grounds are not bad at all."

Her tone nettled me. Everything considered I thought she might have shown a little more enthusiasm.

"I infer that you expected something much worse," I observed.

"Oh, of course I didn't know what to expect. How should I? I had no hand in selecting it, you know."

"She's hardly seen it," put in Hephzy. "She was too sick when she came to notice much, I guess, and this is the first time she has been out doors."

"I am glad you approve," I observed, drily.

My sarcasm was wasted. Miss Morley said again that she did approve, of what she had seen, and added that we seemed to have chosen very well.

"I don't suppose," said Hephzy, complacently, "that there are many much prettier places in England than this one."

"Oh, indeed there are. But all England is beautiful, of course."

I thought of Mrs. Briggs' lodging-house, but I did not refer to it. Our guest—or my "niece"—or our ward—it was hard to classify her—changed the subject.

"Have you met any of the people about here?" she asked.

Hephzy burst into enthusiastic praise of the Baylisses and the curates and the Coles.

"They're all just as nice as they can be," she declared. "I never met nicer folks, at home or anywhere."

Frances nodded. "All English people are nice," she said.

Again I thought of Mrs. Briggs and again I kept my thoughts to myself. Hephzy went on rhapsodizing. I paid little attention until I heard her speak my name.

"And Hosy thinks so, too. Don't you, Hosy?" she said.

I answered yes, on the chance. Frances regarded me oddly.

"I thought—I understood that your name was Kent, Mr. Knowles," she said.

"It is."

"Then why does Miss Cahoon always—"

Hephzy interrupted. "Oh, I always call him Hosy," she explained. "It's a kind of pet name of mine. It's short for Hosea. His whole name is Hosea Kent Knowles, but 'most everybody but me does call him Kent. I don't think he likes Hosea very well."

Our companion looked very much as if she did not wonder at my dislike. Her eyes twinkled.

"Hosea," she repeated. "That is an odd name. The original Hosea was a prophet, wasn't he? Are you a prophet, Mr. Knowles?"

"Far from it," I answered, with decision. If I had been a prophet I should have been forewarned and, consequently, forearmed.

She smiled and against my will I was forced to admit that her smile was attractive; she was prettier than ever when she smiled.

"I remember now," she said; "all Americans have Scriptural names. I have read about them in books."

"Hosy writes books," said Hephzy, proudly. "That's his profession; he's an author."

"Oh, really, is he! How interesting!"

"Yes, he is. He has written ever so many books; haven't you, Hosy."

I didn't answer. My self and my "profession" were the last subjects I cared to discuss. The young lady's smile broadened.

"And where do you write your books, Mr. Knowles?" she asked. "In—er—Bayport?"

"Yes," I answered, shortly. "Hephzy, Miss Morley will have another cup of tea, I think."

"Oh, no, thank you. But tell me about your books, Mr. Knowles. Are they stories of Bayport?"

"No indeed!" Hephzy would do my talking for me, and I could not order her to be quiet. "No indeed!" she declared. "He writes about lords and ladies and counts and such. He hardly ever writes about everyday people like the ones in Bayport. You would like his books, Frances. You would enjoy readin' 'em, I know."

"I am sure I should. They must be delightful. I do hope you brought some with you, Mr. Knowles."

"He didn't, but I did. I'll lend you some, Frances. I'll lend you 'The Queen's Amulet.' That's a splendid story."

"I am sure it must be. So you write about queens, too, Mr. Knowles. I thought Americans scorned royalty. And what is his queen's name, Miss Cahoon? Is it Scriptural?"

"Oh, no indeed! Besides, all Americans' names aren't out of the Bible, any more than the names in England are. That man who wanted to let us his house in Copperhead—no, Leatherhead—funny I should forget THAT awful name—he was named Solomon—Solomon Cripps... Why, what is it?"

Miss Morley's smile and the mischievous twinkle had vanished. She looked startled, and even frightened, it seemed to me.

"What is it, Frances?" repeated Hephzy, anxiously.

"Nothing—nothing. Solomon—what was it? Solomon Cripps. That is an odd name. And you met this Mr.—er—Cripps?"

"Yes, we met him. He had a house he wanted to let us, and I guess we'd have taken it, too, only you seemed to hate the name of Leatherhead so. Don't you remember you did? I don't blame you. Of the things to call a pretty town that's about the worst."

"Yes, it is rather frightful. But this, Mr.—er—Cripps; was he as bad as his name? Did you talk with him?"

"Only about the house. Hosy and I didn't like him well enough to talk about anything else, except religion. He and his wife gave us to understand they were awful pious. I'm afraid we wouldn't have been churchy enough to suit them, anyway. Hosy, here, doesn't go to meetin' as often as he ought to."

"I am glad of it." The young lady's tone was emphatic and she looked as if she meant it. We were surprised.

"You're glad of it!" repeated Hephzy, in amazement. "Why?"

"Because I hate persons who go to church all the time and boast of it, who do all sorts of mean things, but preach, preach, preach continually. They are hypocritical and false and cruel. I HATE them."

She looked now as she had in the room at Mrs. Briggs's when I had questioned her concerning her father. I could not imagine the reason for this sudden squall from a clear sky. Hephzy drew a long breath.

"Well," she said, after a moment, "then Hosy and you ought to get along first-rate together. He's down on hypocrites and make-believe piety as bad as you are. The only time he and Mr. Partridge, our minister in Bayport, ever quarreled—'twasn't a real quarrel, but more of a disagreement—was over what sort of a place Heaven was. Mr. Partridge was certain sure that nobody but church members would be there, and Hosy said if some of the church members in Bayport were sure of a ticket, the other place had strong recommendations. 'Twas an awful thing to say, and I was almost as shocked as the minister was; that is I should have been if I hadn't known he didn't mean it."

Miss Morley regarded me with a new interest, or at least I thought she did.

"Did you mean it?" she asked.

I smiled. "Yes," I answered.

"Now, Hosy," cried Hephzy. "What a way that is to talk! What do you know about the hereafter?"

"Not much, but," remembering the old story, "I know Bayport. Humph! speaking of ministers, here is one now."

Judson, the curate, was approaching across the lawn. Hephzy hastily removed the lid of the teapot. "Yes," she said, with a sigh of relief, "there's enough tea left, though you mustn't have any more, Hosy. Mr. Judson always takes three cups."

Judson was introduced and, the "between-maid" having brought another chair, he joined our party. He accepted the first of the three cups and observed.

"I hope I haven't interrupted an important conversation. You appeared to be talking very earnestly."

I should have answered, but Hephzy's look of horrified expostulation warned me to be silent. Frances, although she must have seen the look, answered instead.

"We were discussing Heaven," she said, calmly. "Mr. Knowles doesn't approve of it."

Hephzy bounced on her chair. "Why!" she cried; "why, what a—why, WHAT will Mr. Judson think! Now, Frances, you know—"

"That was what you said, Mr. Knowles, wasn't it. You said if Paradise was exclusively for church members you preferred—well, another locality. That was what I understood you to say."

Mr. Judson looked at me. He was a very good and very orthodox and a very young man and his feelings showed in his face.

"I—I can scarcely think Mr. Knowles said that, Miss Morley," he protested. "You must have misunderstood him."

"Oh, but I didn't misunderstand. That was what he said."

Again Mr. Judson looked at me. It seemed time for me to say something.

"What I said, or meant to say, was that I doubted if the future life, the—er—pleasant part of it, was confined exclusively to—er—professed church members," I explained.

The curate's ruffled feelings were evidently not soothed by this explanation.

"But—but, Mr. Knowles," he stammered, "really, I—I am at a loss to understand your meaning. Surely you do not mean that—that—"

"Of course he didn't mean that," put in Hephzy. "What he said was that some of the ones who talk the loudest and oftenest in prayer-meetin' at our Methodist church in Bayport weren't as good as they pretended to be. And that's so, too."

Mr. Judson seemed relieved. "Oh," he exclaimed. "Oh, yes, I quite comprehend. Methodists—er—dissenters—that is quite different—quite."

"Mr. Judson knows that no one except communicants in the Church of England are certain of happiness," observed Frances, very gravely.

Our caller turned his attention to her. He was not a joker, but I think he was a trifle suspicious. The young lady met his gaze with one of serene simplicity and, although he reddened, he returned to the charge.

"I should—I should scarcely go as far as that, Miss Morley," he said. "But I understand Mr. Knowles to refer to—er—church members; and—er—dissenters—Methodists and others—are not—are not—"

"Well," broke in Hephzibah, with decision, "I'm a Methodist, myself, and I don't expect to go to perdition."

Judson's guns were spiked. He turned redder than ever and changed the subject to the weather.

The remainder of the conversation was confined for the most part to Frances and the curate. They discussed the village and the people in it and the church and its activities. At length Judson mentioned golf.

"Mr. Knowles and I are to have another round shortly, I trust," he said. "You owe me a revenge, you know, Mr. Knowles."

"Oh," exclaimed the young lady, in apparent surprise, "does Mr. Knowles play golf?"

"Not real golf," I observed.

"Oh, but he does," protested Mr. Judson, "he does. Rather! He plays a very good game indeed. He beat me quite badly the other day."

Which, according to my reckoning, was by no means a proof of extraordinary ability. Frances seemed amused, for some unexplained reason.

"I should never have thought it," she observed.

"Why not?" asked Judson.

"Oh, I don't know. Golf is a game, and Mr. Knowles doesn't look as if he played games. I should have expected nothing so frivolous from him."

"My golf is anything but frivolous," I said. "It's too seriously bad."

"Do you golf, Miss Morley, may I ask?" inquired the curate.

"I have occasionally, after a fashion. I am sure I should like to learn."

"I shall be delighted to teach you. It would be a great pleasure, really."

He looked as if it would be a pleasure. Frances smiled.

"Thank you so much," she said. "You and I and Mr. Knowles will have a threesome."

Judson's joy at her acceptance was tempered, it seemed to me.

"Oh, of course," he said. "It will be a great pleasure to have your uncle with us. A great pleasure, of course."

"My—uncle?"

"Why, yes—Mr. Knowles, you know. By the way, Miss Morley—excuse my mentioning it, but I notice you always address your uncle as Mr. Knowles. That seems a bit curious, if you'll pardon my saying so. A bit distant and—er—formal to our English habit. Do all nieces and nephews in your country do that? Is it an American custom?"

Hephzy and I looked at each other and my "niece" looked at both of us. I could feel the blood tingling in my cheeks and forehead.

"Is it an American custom?" repeated Mr. Judson.

"I don't know," with chilling deliberation. "I am NOT an American."

The curate said "Indeed!" and had the astonishing good sense not to say any more. Shortly afterward he said good-by.

"But I shall look forward to our threesome, Miss Morley," he declared. "I shall count upon it in the near future."

After his departure there was a most embarrassing interval of silence. Hephzy spoke first.

"Don't you think you had better go in now, Frances," she said. "Seems to me you had. It's the first time you've been out at all, you know."

The young lady rose. "I am going," she said. "I am going, if you and— my uncle—will excuse me."

That evening, after dinner, Hephzy joined me in the drawing-room. It was a beautiful summer evening, but every shade was drawn and every shutter tightly closed. We had, on our second evening in the rectory, suggested leaving them open, but the housemaid had shown such shocked surprise and disapproval that we had not pressed the point. By this time we had learned that "privacy" was another sacred and inviolable English custom. The rectory sat in its own ground, surrounded by high hedges; no one, without extraordinary pains, could spy upon its inmates, but, nevertheless, the privacy of those inmates must be guaranteed. So the shutters were closed and the shades drawn.

"Well?" said I to Hephzy.

"Well," said Hephzy, "it's better than I was afraid it was goin' to be. I explained that you told the folks at Bancroft's she was your niece because 'twas the handiest thing to tell 'em, and you HAD to tell 'em somethin'. And down here in Mayberry the same way. She understood, I guess; at any rate she didn't make any great objection. I thought at the last that she was laughin', but I guess she wasn't. Only what she said sounded funny."

"What did she say?"

"Why, she wanted to know if she should call you 'Uncle Hosea.' She supposed it should be that—'Uncle Hosy' sounded a little irreverent."

I did not answer. "Uncle Hosea!" a beautiful title, truly.

"She acted so different to-day, didn't she," observed Hephzy. "It's because she's gettin' well, I suppose. She was real full of fun, wasn't she."

"Confound her—yes," I snarled. "All the fun is on her side. Well, she should make the best of it while it lasts. When she learns the truth she may not find it so amusing."

Hephzy sighed. "Yes," she said, slowly, "I'm afraid that's so, poor thing. When—when are you goin' to tell her?"

"I don't know," I answered. "But pretty soon, that's certain."

CHAPTER X
In Which I Break All Previous
Resolutions and Make a New One

That afternoon tea on the lawn was the beginning of the great change in our life at the rectory. Prior to that Hephzy and I had, golfly speaking, been playing it as a twosome. Now it became a threesome, with other players added at frequent intervals. At luncheon next day our invalid, a real invalid no longer, joined us at table in the pleasant dining-room, the broad window of which opened upon the formal garden with the sundial in the center. She was in good spirits, and, as Hephzy confided to me afterward, was "gettin' a real nice appetite." In gaining this appetite she appeared to have lost some of her dignity and chilling condescension; at all events, she treated her American relatives as if she considered them human beings. She addressed most of her conversation to Hephzy, always speaking of and to her as "Miss Cahoon." She still addressed me as "Mr. Knowles," and I was duly thankful; I had feared being hailed as "Uncle Hosy."

After lunch Mr. Judson called again. He was passing, he explained, on his round of parish calls, and had dropped in casually. Mr. Worcester also came; his really was a casual stop, I think. He and his brother curate were very brotherly indeed, but I noticed an apparent reluctance on the part of each to leave before the other. They left together, but Mr. Judson again hinted at the promised golf game, and Mr. Worcester, having learned from Miss Morley that she played and sang, expressed great interest in music and begged permission to bring some "favorite songs," which he felt sure Miss Morley might like to run over.

Miss Morley herself was impartially gracious and affable to both the clerical gentlemen; she was looking forward to the golf, she said, and the songs she was certain would be jolly. Hephzy and I had very little to say, and no one seemed particularly anxious to hear that little.

The curates had scarcely disappeared down the driveway when Doctor Bayliss and his son strolled in from next door. Doctor Bayliss, Senior, was much pleased to find his patient up and about, and Herbert, the son, even more pleased to find her at all, I judge. Young Bayliss was evidently very favorably impressed with his new neighbor. He was a big, healthy, broad-shouldered fellow, a grown-up boy, whose laugh was a pleasure to hear, and who possessed the faculty, envied by me, the quahaug, of chatting entertainingly on all subjects from tennis and the new American dances to Lloyd-George and old-age pensions. Frances declared a strong aversion to the dances, principally because they were American, I suspected.

Doctor Bayliss, the old gentleman, then turned to me.

"What is the American opinion of the Liberal measures?" he asked.

"I should say," I answered, "that, so far as they are understood in America, opinion concerning them is divided, much as it is here."

"Really! But you haven't the Liberal and Conservative parties as we have, you know."

"We have liberals and conservatives, however, although our political parties are not so named."

"We call 'em Republicans and Democrats," explained Hephzy. "Hosy is a Republican," she added, proudly.

"I am not certain what I am," I observed. "I have voted a split ticket of late."

Young Bayliss asked a question.

"Are you a—what is it—Republican, Miss Morley?" he inquired.

Miss Morley's eyes dropped disdainfully.

"I am neither," she said. "My father was a Conservative, of course."

"Oh, I say! That's odd, isn't it. Your uncle here is—"

"Uncle Hosea, you mean?" sweetly. "Oh, Uncle Hosea is an American. I am English."

She did not add "Thank heaven," but she might as well. "Uncle Hosea" shuddered at the name. Young Bayliss grinned behind his blonde mustache. When he left, in company with his father, Hephzy invited him to "run in any time."

"We're next-door neighbors," she said, "so we mustn't be formal."

I was fairly certain that the invitation was superfluous. If I knew human nature at all I knew that Bayliss, Junior, did not intend to let formality stand in the way of frequent calls at the rectory.

My intuition was correct. The following afternoon he called again. So did Mr. Judson. Both calls were casual, of course. So was Mr. Worcester's that evening. He came to bring the "favorite songs" and was much surprised to find Miss Morley in the drawing-room. He said so.

Hephzy and I knew little of our relative's history. She had volunteered no particulars other than those given on the occasion of our first meeting, but we did know, because Mrs. Briggs had told us, that she had been a member of an opera troupe. This evening we heard her sing for the first time. She sang well; her voice was not a strong one, but it was clear and sweet and she knew how to use it. Worcester sang well also, and the little concert was very enjoyable.

It was the first of many. Almost every evening after dinner Frances sat down at the old-fashioned piano, with the candle brackets at each side of the music rack, and sang. Occasionally we were her only auditors, but more often one or both of the curates or Doctor and Mrs. Bayliss or Bayliss, Junior, dropped in. We made other acquaintances—Mrs. Griggson, the widow in "reduced circumstances," whose husband had been killed in the Boer war, and who occupied the little cottage next to the draper's shop; Mr. and Mrs. Samson, of Burgleston Bogs, friends of the Baylisses, and others. They were pleasant, kindly, unaffected people and we enjoyed their society.

Each day Frances gained in health and strength. The care-free, wholesome, out-of-door life at Mayberry seemed to suit her. She seemed to consider herself a member of the family now; at all events she did not speak of leaving nor hint at the prompt settlement of her preposterous "claim." Hephzy and I did not mention it, even to each other. Hephzy, I think, was quite satisfied with things as they were, and I, in spite of my threats and repeated declarations that the present state of affairs was ridiculous and could not last, put off telling "my niece" the truth. I, too, was growing more accustomed to the "threesome."

The cloud was always there, hanging over our heads and threatening a storm at any moment, but I was learning to forget it. The situation had its pleasant side; it was not all bad. For instance, meals in the pleasant dining-room, with Hephzy at one end of the table, I at the other, and Frances between us, were more social and chatty than they had been. To have the young lady come down to breakfast, her hair prettily arranged, her cheeks rosy with health, and her eyes shining with youth and the joy of life, was almost a tonic. I found myself taking more pains with my morning toilet, choosing my tie with greater care and being more careful concerning the condition of my boots. I even began to dress for dinner, a concession to English custom which was odd enough in one of my easy-going habits and Bayport rearing. I imagine that the immaculate appearance of young Bayliss, when he dropped in for the "sing" in the drawing-room, was responsible for the resurrection of my dinner coat. He did look so disgustingly young and handsome and at ease. I was conscious of each one of my thirty-eight years whenever I looked at him.

I was rejuvenating in other ways. It had been my custom at Bayport to retire to my study and my books each evening. Here, where callers were so frequent, I found it difficult to do this and, although the temptation was to sit quietly in a corner and let the others do the talking, I was not allowed to yield. The younger callers, particularly the masculine portion, would not have objected to my silence, I am sure, but "my niece" seemed to take mischievous pleasure in drawing the quahaug out of his shell. She had a disconcerting habit of asking me unexpected questions at times when my attention was wandering, and, if I happened to state a definite opinion, taking the opposite side with promptness. After a time I decided not to express opinions, but to agree with whatever was said as the simplest way of avoiding controversy and being left to myself.

This procedure should, it seemed to me, have satisfied her, but apparently it did not. On one occasion, Judson and Herbert Bayliss being present, the conversation turned to the subject of American athletic sports. The curate and Bayliss took the ground, the prevailing thought in England apparently, that all American games were not games, but fights in which the true sporting spirit was sacrificed to the desire to win at any cost. I had said nothing, keeping silent for two reasons. First, that I had given my views on the subject before, and, second, because argument from me was, in that company, fruitless effort. The simplest way to end discussion of a disagreeable topic was to pay no attention to it.

But I was not allowed to escape so easily. Bayliss asked me a question.

"Isn't it true, Mr. Knowles," he asked, "that the American football player wears a sort of armor to prevent his being killed?"

My thoughts had been drifting anywhere and everywhere. Just then they were centered about "my niece's" hands. She had very pretty hands and a most graceful way of using them. At the moment they were idly turning some sheets of music, but the way the slim fingers moved in and out between the pages was pretty and fascinating. Her foot, glimpsed beneath her skirt, was slender and graceful, too. She had an attractive trick of swinging it as she sat upon the piano stool.

Recalled from these and other pleasing observations by Bayliss's mention of my name, I looked up.

"I beg pardon?" said I.

Bayliss repeated his question.

"Oh, yes," said I, and looked down again at the foot.

"So I have been told," said the questioner, triumphantly. "And without that—er—armor many of the players would be killed, would they not?"

"What? Oh, yes; yes, of course."

"And many are killed or badly injured as it is?"

"Oh, yes."

"How many during a season, may I ask?"

"Eh? Oh—I don't know."

"A hundred?"

The foot was swinging more rapidly now. It was such a small foot. My own looked so enormous and clumsy and uncouth by comparison.

"A—oh, thousands," said I, at random. If the number were large enough to satisfy him he might cease to worry me.

"A beastly game," declared Judson, with conviction. "How can a civilized country countenance such brutality! Do you countenance it, Mr. Knowles?"

"Yes—er—that is, no."

"You agree, then, that it is brutal?"

"Certainly, certainly." Would the fellow never stop?

"Then—"

"Nonsense!" It was Frances who spoke and her tone was emphatic and impatient. We all looked at her; her cheeks were flushed and she appeared highly indignant. "Nonsense!" she said again. "He doesn't agree to any such thing. I've heard him say that American football was not as brutal as our fox-hunting and that fewer people were killed or injured. We play polo and we ride in steeplechases and the papers are full of accidents. I don't believe Americans are more brutal or less civilized in their sports than we are, not in the least."

Considering that she had at the beginning of the conversation apparently agreed with all that had been said, and, moreover, had often, in speaking to Hephzy and me, referred to the "States" as an uncivilized country, this declaration was astonishing. I was astonished for one. Hephzy clapped her hands.

"Of course they aren't," she declared. "Hosy—Mr. Knowles—didn't mean that they were, either."

Our callers looked at each other and Herbert Bayliss hastily changed the subject. After they had gone I ventured to thank my champion for coming to the rescue of my sporting countrymen. She flashed an indignant glance at me.

"Why do you say such things?" she demanded. "You know they weren't true."

"What was the use of saying anything else? They have read the accounts of football games which American penny-a-line correspondents send to the London papers and nothing I could say would change their convictions."

"It doesn't make any difference. You should say what you think. To sit there and let them—Oh, it is ridiculous!"

"My feelings were not hurt. Their ideas will broaden by and by, when they are as old as I am. They're young now."

This charitable remark seemed to have the effect of making her more indignant than ever.

"Nonsense!" she cried. "You speak as if you were an Old Testament patriarch."

Hephzy put in a word.

"Why, Frances," she said, "I thought you didn't like America."

"I don't. Of course I don't. But it makes me lose patience to have him sit there and agree to everything those boys say. Why didn't he answer them as he should? If I were an American no one—NO one should rag me about my country without getting as good as they gave."

I was amused. "What would you have me do?" I asked. "Rise and sing the 'Star Spangled Banner'?"

"I would have you speak your mind like a man. Not sit there like a—like a rabbit. And I wouldn't act and think like a Methusaleh until I was one."

It was quite evident that "my niece" was a young person of whims. The next time the "States" were mentioned and I ventured to speak in their defence, she calmly espoused the other side and "ragged" as mercilessly as the rest. I found myself continually on the defensive, and this state of affairs had one good effect at least—that of waking me up.

Toward Hephzy her manner was quite different. She now, especially when we three were alone, occasionally addressed her as "Auntie." And she would not permit "Auntie" to be made fun of. At the least hint of such a thing she snubbed the would-be humorist thoroughly. She and Hephzy were becoming really friendly. I felt certain she was beginning to like her—

to discern the real woman beneath the odd exterior. But when I expressed this thought to Hephzy herself she shook her head doubtfully.

"Sometimes I've almost thought so, Hosy," she said, "but only this mornin' when I said somethin' about her mother and how much she looked like her, she almost took my head off. And she's got her pa's picture right in the middle of her bureau. No, Hosy, she's nicer to us than she was at first because it's her nature to be nice. So long as she forgets who and what we are, or what her scamp of a father told her we were, she treats us like her own folks. But when she remembers we're receivers of stolen goods, livin' on money that belongs to her, then it's different. You can't blame her for that, I suppose. But—but how is it all goin' to end? *I* don't know."

I didn't know either.

"I had hoped," I said, "that, living with us as she does, she might come to know and understand us—to learn that we couldn't be the sort she has believed us to be. Then it seems to me we might tell her and she would listen to reason."

"I—I'm afraid we can't wait long. You see, there's another thing, Hosy. She needs clothes and—and lots of things. She realizes it. Yesterday she told me she must go up to London, shopping, pretty soon. She asked me to go with her. I put her off; said I was awful busy around the house just now, but she'll ask me again, and if I don't go she'll go by herself."

"Humph! I don't see how she can do much shopping. She hasn't a penny, so far as I know."

"You don't understand. She thinks she has got a good many pennies, or we've got 'em for her. She's just as liable to buy all creation and send us the bills."

I whistled. "Well," I said, decidedly, "when that happens we must put our foot down. Neither you nor I are millionaires, Hephzy, and she must understand that regardless of consequences."

"You mean you'll tell her—everything?"

"I shall have to. Why do you look at me like that? Are we to use common-sense or aren't we? Are we in a position to adopt a young woman of expensive tastes—actually adopt her? And not only that, but give her carte blanche—let her buy whatever she pleases and charge it to us?"

"I suppose not. But—"

"But what?"

"Well, I—I don't see how we can stop her buying whatever she pleases with what she thinks is her own money."

"I do. We can tell her she has no money. I shall do it. My mind is made up."

Hephzy said nothing, but her expression was one of doubt. I stalked off in a bad temper. Discussions of the kind always ended in just this way. However, I swore a solemn oath to keep my word this time. There were limits and they had been reached. Besides, as I had said, the situation was changed in one way; we no longer had an invalid to deal with. No, my mind was made up. True, this was at least the tenth time I had made it up, but this time I meant it.

The test came two days later and was the result of a call on the Samsons. The Samsons lived at Burgleston Bogs, and we drove to their house in the trap behind "Pet," the plump black horse. Mrs. Samson seemed very glad to see us, urged us to remain for tea, and invited us to attend a tennis tournament on their lawn the following week. She asked if Miss Morley played tennis. Frances said she had played, but not recently. She intended to practice, however, and would be delighted to witness the tournament, although, of course, she could not take part in it.

"Hosy—Mr. Knowles, I mean—plays tennis," observed Hephzy, seizing the opportunity, as usual, to speak a good word for me. "He used to play real well."

"Really!" exclaimed Mrs. Samson, "how interesting. If we had only known. No doubt Mr. Knowles would have liked to enter. I'm so sorry."

I hastened to protest. "My tennis is decidedly rusty," I said. "I shouldn't think of displaying it in public. In fact, I don't play at all now."

On the way home Frances was rather quiet. The next morning she announced that she intended going to Wrayton that afternoon. "Johnson will drive me over," she said. "I shall be glad if Auntie will go with me."

Wrayton was the county-seat, a good-sized town five miles from Mayberry. Hephzy declined the invitation. She had promised to "tea" with Mrs. Griggson that afternoon.

"Then I must go alone," said Frances. "That is unless—er—Uncle Hosea cares to go."

"Uncle Hosea" declined. The name of itself was sufficient to make him decline; besides Worcester and I were scheduled for golf.

"I shall go alone then," said "my niece," with decision. "Johnson will look after me."

But after luncheon, when I visited the stable to order Johnson to harness "Pet," I met with an unexpected difficulty. Johnson, it appeared, was ill, had been indisposed the day before and was now at home in bed. I hesitated. If this were Bayport I should have bade the gardener harness "Pet" or have harnessed him myself. But this was Mayberry, not Bayport.

The gardener, deprived of his assistant's help—Johnson worked about the garden when not driving—was not in good humor. I decided not to ask him to harness, but to risk a fall in the estimation of the servants by doing it myself.

The gardener watched me for a moment in shocked disapproval. Then he interfered.

"If you please, Mr. Knowles, sir," he said, "I'll 'arness, but I can't drive, sir. I am netting the gooseberries. Perhaps you might get a man from the Inn stables, unless you or the young lady might wish to drive yourselves."

I did not wish to drive, having the golf engagement; but when I walked to the Inn I found no driver available. So, rather than be disagreeable, I sent word to the curate that our match was postponed, and accepted the alternative.

Frances, rather to my surprise, seemed more pleased than otherwise to find that I was to be her coachman. Instead of occupying the rear seat she climbed to that beside me.

"Good-by, Auntie," she called to Hephzy, who was standing in the doorway. "Sorry you're not going. I'll take good care of Mr. Knowles— Uncle Hosea, I mean. I'll see that he behaves himself and," with a glance at my, I fear, not too radiant visage, "doesn't break any of his venerable bones."

The road, like all English roads which I traveled, was as firm and smooth as a table, the day was fine, the hedges were green and fragrant, the larks sang, and the flocks of sheep in the wayside pastures were picturesque as always. "Pet," who had led an easy life since we came to the rectory, was in high spirits and stepped along in lively fashion. My companion, too, was in good spirits and chatted and laughed as she had not done with me since I knew her.

Altogether it was a delightful ride. I found myself emerging from my shell and chatting and joking quite unlike the elderly quahaug I was supposed to be. We passed a party of young fellows on a walking tour, knapsacked and knickerbockered, and the admiring glances they passed at my passenger were flattering. They envied me, that was plain. Well, under different circumstances, I could conceive myself an object of envy. A dozen years younger, with the heart of youth and the comeliness of youth, I might have thought myself lucky to be driving along such a road with such a vision by my side. And, the best of it was, the vision treated me as if I really were her own age. I squared my shoulders and as Hephzy would have said, "perked up" amazingly.

We entered Wrayton and moved along the main street between the rows of ancient buildings, past the old stone church with its inevitable and always welcome gray, ivy-draped tower, to the quaint old square with the statue of William Pitt in its center. My companion, all at once, seemed to become aware of her surroundings.

"Why!" she exclaimed, "we are here, aren't we? Fancy! I expected a longer drive."

"So did I," I agreed. "We haven't hurried, either. Where has the time gone."

"I don't know. We have been so busy talking that I have thought of nothing else. Really, I didn't know you could be so entertaining—Uncle Hosea."

The detested title brought me to myself.

"We are here," I said, shortly. "And now where shall we go? Have you any stopping place in particular?"

She nodded.

"Yes," she said, "I want to stop now. Please pull up over there, in front of that shop with the cricket bats in the window."

The shop was what we, in America, would have called a "sporting-goods store." I piloted "Pet" to the curb and pulled up.

"I am going in," said Miss Morley. "Oh, don't trouble to help me. I can get down quite well."

She was down, springing from the step as lightly as a dandelion fluff before I could scramble down on the other side.

"I won't be long," she said, and went into the shop. I, not being invited, remained on the pavement. Two or three small boys appeared from somewhere and, scenting possible pennies, volunteered to hold the horse. I declined their services.

Five minutes passed, then ten. My passenger was still in the shop. I could not imagine what she was doing there. If it had been a shop of a different kind, and in view of Hephzy's recent statement concerning the buying of clothes, I might have been suspicious. But no clothes were on sale at that shop and, besides, it never occurred to me that she would buy anything of importance without mentioning her intention to me beforehand. I had taken it for granted that she would mention the subject and, when she did, I intended to be firm. But as the minutes went by my suspicions grew. She must be buying something—or contemplating buying, at least. But she had said nothing to me concerning money; HAD she money of her own after all? It might be possible that she had a very little, and was making some trifling purchase.

She reappeared in the doorway of the shop, followed by a very polite young man with a blonde mustache. The young man was bowing and smiling.

"Yes, miss," he said, "I'll have them wrapped immediately. They shall be ready when you return, miss. Thank you, miss."

Frances nodded acknowledgment of the thanks. Then she favored me with another nod and a most bewitching smile.

"That's over," she announced, "and now I'm going to the draper's for a moment. It is near here, you say?"

The young man bowed again.

"Yes, miss, on the next corner, next the chemist's."

She turned to me. "You may wait here, Mr. Knowles," she said. "I shall be back very soon."

She hurried away. I looked after her, and then, with all sorts of forebodings surging in my brain, strode into that "sporting-goods store."

The blond young man was at my elbow.

"Yes, sir," he said, ingratiatingly.

"Did—did that young lady make some purchases here?" I asked.

"Yes, sir. Here they are, sir."

There on the counter lay a tennis racket, a racket press and waterproof case, a pair of canvas tennis shoes and a jaunty white felt hat. I stared at the collection. The clerk took up the racket.

"Not a Slazenger," he observed, regretfully. "I did my best to persuade her to buy a Slazenger; that is the best racket we have. But she decided the Slazenger was a bit high in price, sir. However, sir, this one is not bad. A very fine racket for lady's use; very light and strong, sir, considering the cost—only sixteen and six, sir."

"Sixteen and six. Four dollars and—Did she pay for it?"

"Oh no, sir. She said you would do that, sir. The total is two pound eight and thruppence, sir. Shall I give you a bill, sir? Thank you, sir."

His thanks were wasted. I pushed him to one side and walked out of that shop. I could not answer; if I answered as I felt I might be sorry later. After all, it wasn't his fault. My business was not with him, but with her.

It was not the amount of the purchase that angered and alarmed me. Two pounds eight—twelve dollars—was not so much. If she had asked me, if she had said she desired the racket and the rest of it during the drive over, I think, feeling as I did during that drive, I should have bought them for her. But she had not asked; she had calmly bought them without consulting me at all. She had come to Wrayton for that very purpose. And then had told the clerk that I would pay.

The brazen presumption of it! I was merely a convenience, a sort of walking bank account, to be drawn upon as she saw fit, at her imperial will, if you please. It made no difference, to her mind, whether I liked it or not—whether I could afford it or not. I could, of course, afford this trifling sum, but this was only the beginning. If I permitted this there was no telling to what extent she might go on, buying and buying and buying. This was a precedent—that was what it was, a precedent; and a precedent once established... It should not be established. I had vowed to Hephzy that it should not. I would prove to this girl that I had a will of my own. The time had come.

One of the boys who had been so anxious to hold the horse was performing that entirely unnecessary duty.

"Stay here until I come back," I ordered and hurried to the draper's.

She was there standing before the counter, and an elderly man was displaying cloths—white flannels and serges they appeared to be. She was not in the least perturbed at my entrance.

"So you came, after all," she said. "I wondered if you would. Now you must help me. I don't know what your taste in tennis flannels may be, but I hope it is good. I shall have these made up at Mayberry, of course. My other frocks—and I need so many of them—I shall buy in London. Do you fancy this, now?"

I don't know whether I fancied it or not. I am quite sure I could not remember what it was if I were asked.

"Well?" she asked, after an instant. "Do you?"

"I—I don't know," I said. "May I ask you to step outside one moment. I—I have something I wish to say."

She regarded me curiously.

"Something you wish to say?" she repeated. "What is it?"

"I—I can't tell you here."

"Why not, pray?"

"Because I can't."

She looked at me still more intently. I was conscious of the salesman's regard also. My tone, I am sure, was anything but gracious, and I imagine I appeared as disgusted and embarrassed as I felt. She turned away.

"I think I will choose this one," she said, addressing the clerk. "You may give me five yards. Oh, yes; and I may as well take the same amount of the other. You may wrap it for me."

"Yes, miss, yes. Thank you, miss. Is there anything else?"

She hesitated. Then, after another sidelong glance at me, she said: "Yes, I believe there is. I wish to see some buttons, some braid, and—oh, ever so many things. Please show them to me."

"Yes, miss, certainly. This way, if you please."

She turned to me.

"Will you assist in the selection, Uncle Hosea?" she inquired, with suspicious sweetness. "I am sure your opinion will be invaluable. No? Then I must ask you to wait."

And wait I did, for I could do nothing else. That draper's shop was not the place for a scene, with a half-dozen clerks to enjoy it. I waited, fuming, while she wandered about, taking a great deal of time, and lingering over each purchase in a maddening manner. At last she seemed able to think of no more possibilities and strolled to where I was standing, followed by the salesman, whose hands were full.

"You may wrap these with the others," she said. "I have my trap here and will take them with me. The trap is here, isn't it—er—Uncle Hosea?"

"It is just above here," I answered, sulkily. "But—"

"But you will get it. Thank you so much."

The salesman noticed my hesitation, put his own interpretation upon it and hastened to oblige.

"I shall be glad to have the purchases carried there," he said. "Our boy will do it, miss. It will be no trouble."

Miss Morley thanked him so much. I was hoping she might leave the shop then, but she did not. The various packages were wrapped, handed to the boy, and she accompanied the latter to the door and showed him our equipage standing before the sporting-goods dealer's. Then she sauntered back.

"Thank you," she said, addressing the clerk. "That is all, I believe."

The clerk looked at her and at me.

"Yes, miss, thank you," he said, in return. "I—I—would you be wishing to pay at once, miss, or shall I—"

"Oh, this gentleman will pay. Do you wish to pay now—Uncle Hosea?"

Again I was stumped. The salesman was regarding me expectantly; the other clerks were near by; if I made a scene there—No, I could not do it. I would pay this time. But this should be the end.

Fortunately, I had money in my pocket—two five-pound notes and some silver. I paid the bill. Then, and at last, my niece led the way to the pavement. We walked together a few steps in silence. The sporting-goods shop was just ahead, and if ever I was determined not to do a thing that thing was to pay for the tennis racket and the rest.

"Frances," I began.

"Well—Mr. Knowles?" calmly.

"Frances, I have decided to speak with you frankly. You appear to take certain things for granted in your—your dealings with Miss Cahoon and myself, things which—which I cannot countenance or permit."

She had been walking slowly. Now she stopped short. I stopped, too, because she did.

"What do you mean?" she asked. "What things?"

She was looking me through and through. Again I hesitated, and my hesitation did not help matters.

"What do you mean?" she repeated. "What is it you cannot countenance or"—scornfully—"permit concerning me?"

"I—well, I cannot permit you to do as you have done to-day. You did not tell your aunt or me your purpose in coming to Wrayton. You did not tell us you were coming here to buy—to buy various things for yourself."

"Why should I tell you? They were for myself. Is it your idea that I should ask YOUR permission before buying what I choose?"

"Considering that you ask me to pay, I—"

"I most distinctly did NOT ask you. I TOLD you to pay. Certainly you will pay. Why not?"

"Why not?"

"Yes, why not. So this was what you wished to speak to me about. This was why you were so—so boorish and disagreeable in that shop. Tell me—was that the reason? Was that why you followed me there? Did you think—did you presume to think of preventing my buying what I pleased with my money?"

"If it had been your money I should not have presumed, certainly. If you had mentioned your intention to me beforehand I might even have paid for your purchases and said nothing. I should—I should have been glad to do so. I am not unreasonable."

"Indeed! Indeed! Do you mean that you would have condescended to make me a present of them? And was it your idea that I would accept presents from you?"

It was on the tip of my tongue to tell her that she had already accepted a good deal; but somehow the place, a public sidewalk, seemed hardly fitting for the discussion of weighty personal matters. Passers-by were regarding us curiously, and in the door of the draper's shop which we had just left I noticed the elderly clerk standing and looking in our direction. I temporized.

"You don't understand, Miss Morley," I said. "Neither your aunt nor I are wealthy. Surely, it is not too much to ask that you consult us before—before—"

She interrupted me. "I shall not consult you at all," she declared, fiercely. "Wealthy! Am I wealthy? Was my father wealthy? He should have been and so should I. Oh, WHAT do you mean? Are you trying to tell me that you cannot afford to pay for the few trifles I have bought this afternoon?"

"I can afford those, of course. But you don't understand."

"Understand? YOU do not understand. The agreement under which I came to Mayberry was that you were to provide for me. I consented to forego pressing my claim against you until—until you were ready to—to—Oh, but why should we go into this again? I thought—I thought you understood. I thought you understood and appreciated my forbearance. You seemed to understand and to be grateful and kind. I am all alone in the world. I haven't a friend. I have been almost happy for a little while. I was beginning to—"

She stopped. The dark eyes which had been flashing lightnings in my direction suddenly filled with tears. My heart smote me. After all, she did not understand. Another plea of that kind and I should have—Well, I'm not sure what I should have done. But the plea was not spoken.

"Oh, what a fool I am!" she cried, fiercely. "Mr. Knowles," pointing to the sporting-goods store, "I have made some purchases in that shop also. I expect you to pay for those as well. Will you or will you not?"

I was hesitating, weakly. She did not wait for me to reply.

"You WILL pay for them," she declared, "and you will pay for others that I may make. I shall buy what I please and do what I please with my money which you are keeping from me. You will pay or take the consequences."

That was enough. "I will not pay," I said, firmly, "under any such arrangement."

"You will NOT?"

"No, I will not."

She looked as if—Well, if she had been a man I should have expected a blow. Her breast heaved and her fingers clenched. Then she turned and walked toward the shop with the cricket bats in the window.

"Where are you going?" I asked.

"I am going to tell the man to send the things I have bought to Mayberry by carrier and I shall tell him to send the bill to you."

"If you do I shall tell him to do nothing of the kind. Miss Morley, I don't mean to be ungenerous or unreasonable, but—"

"Stop! Stop! Oh!" with a sobbing breath, "how I hate you!"

"I'm sorry. When I explain, as I mean to, you will understand, I think. If you will go back to the rectory with me now—"

"I shall not go back with you. I shall never speak to you again."

"Miss Morley, be reasonable. You must go back with me. There is no other way."

"I will not."

Here was more cheer in an already cheerful situation. She could not get to Mayberry that night unless she rode with me. She had no money to take her there or anywhere else. I could hardly carry her to the trap by main strength. And the curiosity of the passers-by was more marked than ever; two or three of them had stopped to watch us.

I don't know how it might have ended, but the end came in an unexpected manner.

"Why, Miss Morley," cried a voice from the street behind me. "Oh, I say, it IS you, isn't it. How do you do?"

I turned. A trim little motor car was standing there and Herbert Bayliss was at the wheel.

"Ah, Knowles, how do you do?" said Bayliss.

I acknowledged the greeting in an embarrassed fashion. I wondered how long he had been there and what he had heard. He alighted from the car and shook hands with us.

"Didn't see you, Knowles, at first," he said. "Saw Miss Morley here and thought she was alone. Was going to beg the privilege of taking her home in my car."

Miss Morley answered promptly. "You may have the privilege, Doctor Bayliss," she said. "I accept with pleasure."

Young Bayliss looked pleased, but rather puzzled.

"Thanks, awfully," he said. "But my car holds but two and your uncle—"

"Oh, he has the dogcart. It is quite all right, really. I should love the motor ride. May I get in?"

He helped her into the car. "Sure you don't mind, Knowles," he asked. "Sorry there's not more room; but you couldn't leave the horse, though, could you? Quite comfy, Miss Morley? Then we're off."

The car turned from the curb. I caught Miss Morley's eye for an instant; there was withering contempt in its look—also triumph.

Left alone, I walked to the trap, gave the horse-holding boy sixpence, climbed to the seat and took up the reins. "Pet" jogged lazily up the street. The ride over had been very, very pleasant; the homeward journey was likely to be anything but that.

To begin with, I was thoroughly dissatisfied with myself. I had bungled the affair dreadfully. This was not the time for explanations; I should not have attempted them. It would have been better, much better, to have accepted the inevitable as gracefully as I could, paid the bills, and then, after we reached home, have made the situation plain and "have put my foot down" once and for all. But I had not done that. I had lost my temper and acted like an eighteen-year-old boy instead of a middle-aged man.

She did not understand, of course. In her eyes I must have appeared stingy and mean and—and goodness knows what. The money I had refused to pay she did consider hers, of course. It was not hers, and some day she would know that it was not, but the town square at Wrayton was not the place in which to impart knowledge of that kind.

She was so young, too, and so charming—that is, she could be when she chose. And she had chosen to be so during our drive together. And I had enjoyed that drive; I had enjoyed nothing as thoroughly since our arrival in England. She had enjoyed it, too; she had said so.

Well, there would be no more enjoyment of that kind. This was the end, of course. And all because I had refused to pay for a tennis racket and a few other things. They were things she wanted—yes, needed, if she were to remain at the rectory. And, expecting to remain as she did, it was but natural that she should wish to play tennis and dress as did other young players of her sex. Her life had not been a pleasant one; after all, a little happiness added, even though it did cost me some money, was not much. And it must end soon. It seemed a pity to end it in order to save two pounds eight and threepence.

There is no use cataloguing all my thoughts. Some I have catalogued and the others were similar. The memory of her face and of the choke in her voice as she said she had been almost happy haunted me. My reason told me that, so far as principle and precedent went, I had acted rightly; but my conscience, which was quite unreasonable, told me I had acted like a boor. I stood it as long as I could, then I shouted at "Pet," who was jogging on, apparently half asleep.

"Whoa!" I shouted.

"Pet" stopped short in the middle of the road. I hesitated. The principle of the thing—

"Hang the principle!" said I, aloud. Then I turned the trap around and drove back to Wrayton. The blond young man in the sporting-goods store was evidently glad to see me. He must have seen me drive away and have judged that his sale was canceled. His judgment had been very near to right, but now I proved it wrong.

I paid for the racket and the press and the shoes and the rest. They were wrapped and ready.

"Thank you, sir," said the clerk. "I trust everything will be quite satisfactory. I'm sorry the young lady did not take the Slazenger, but the one she chose is not at all bad."

I was on my way to the door. I stopped and turned.

"Is the—the what is it—'Slazenger' so much better?" I asked.

"Oh, very much so, sir. Infinitely better, sir. Here it is; judge for yourself. The very best racket made. And only thirty-two shillings, sir."

It was a better racket, much better. And, after all, when one is hanging principle the execution may as well be complete.

"You may give me that one instead of the other," I said, and paid the difference.

On my arrival at the rectory Hephzy met me at the door. The between-maid took the packages from the trap. I entered the drawing-room and Hephzy followed me. She looked very grave.

"Frances is here, I suppose," I said.

"Yes, she came an hour ago. Doctor Bayliss, the younger one, brought her in his auto. She hardly spoke to me, Hosy, and went straight to her room. Hosy, what happened? What is the matter?"

"Nothing," said I, curtly. "Nothing unusual, that is. I made a fool of myself once more, that's all."

The between-maid knocked and entered. "Where would you wish the parcels, sir?" she asked.

"These are Miss Morley's. Take them to her room."

The maid retired to obey orders. Hephzy again turned to me.

"Now, Hosy, what is it?" she asked.

I told her the whole story. When I had finished Hephzy nodded understandingly. She did not say "I told you so," but if she had it would have been quite excusable.

"I think—I think, perhaps, I had better go up and see her," she said.

"All right. I have no objection."

"But she'll ask questions, of course. What shall I tell her?"

"Tell her I changed my mind. Tell her—oh, tell her anything you like. Don't bother me. I'm sick of the whole business."

She left me and I went into the Reverend Cole's study and closed the door. There were books enough there, but the majority of them were theological works or bulky volumes dealing with questions of religion. Most of my own books were in my room. These did not appeal to me; I was not religiously inclined just then.

So I sat dumbly in the rector's desk chair and looked out of the window. After a time there was a knock at the door.

"Come in," said I, expecting Hephzy. It was not Hephzy who came, however, but Miss Morley herself. And she closed the door behind her.

I did not speak. She walked over and stood beside me. I did not know what she was going to say and the expression did not help me to guess.

For a moment she did not say anything. Then:

"So you changed your mind," she said.

"Yes."

"Why?"

"I don't know."

"You don't know. Yet you changed it."

"Yes. Oh yes, I changed it."

"But why? Was it—was it because you were ashamed of yourself?"

"I guess so. As much that as anything."

"You realize that you treated me shamefully. You realize that?"

"Yes," wearily. "Yes, I realize everything."

"And you felt sorry, after I had gone, and so you changed your mind. Was that it?"

"Yes."

There was no use in attempting justification. For the absolute surrender I had made there was no justification. I might as well agree to everything.

"And you will never, never treat me in that way again?"

"No."

"And you realize that I was right and understand that I am to do as I please with my money?"

"Yes."

"And you beg my pardon?"

"Yes."

"Very well. Then I beg yours. I'm sorry, too."

Now I WAS surprised. I turned in my chair and looked at her.

"You beg my pardon?" I repeated. "For what?"

"Oh, for everything. I suppose I should have spoken to you before buying those things. You might not have been prepared to pay then and—and that would have been unpleasant for you. But—well, you see, I didn't think, and you were so queer and cross when you followed me to the draper's shop, that—that I—well, I was disagreeable, too. I am sorry."

"That's all right."

"Thank you. Is there anything else you wish to say?"

"No."

"You're sure?"

"Yes."

"Why did you buy the Slazenger racket instead of the other one?"

I had forgotten the "Slazenger" for the moment. She had caught me unawares.

"Oh—oh," I stammered, "well, it was a much better racket and—and, as you were buying one, it seemed foolish not to get the best."

"I know. I wanted the better one very much, but I thought it too expensive. I did not feel that I should spend so much money."

"That's all right. The difference wasn't so much and I made the change on my own responsibility. I—well, just consider that I bought the racket and you bought none."

She regarded me intently. "You mean that you bought it as a present for me?" she said slowly.

"Yes; yes, if you will accept it as such."

She was silent. I remembered perfectly well what she had said concerning presents from me and I wondered what I should do with that racket when she threw it back on my hands.

"Thank you," she said. "I will accept it. Thank you very much."

I was staggered, but I recovered sufficiently to tell her she was quite welcome.

She turned to go. Then she turned back.

"Doctor Bayliss asked me to play tennis with him tomorrow morning," she said. "May I?"

"May you? Why, of course you may, if you wish, I suppose. Why in the world do you ask my permission?"

"Oh, don't you wish me to ask? I inferred from what you said at Wrayton that you did wish me to ask permission concerning many things."

"I wished—I said—oh, don't be silly, please! Haven't we had silliness enough for one afternoon, Miss Morley."

"My Christian name is Frances. May I play tennis with Doctor Bayliss to-morrow morning, Uncle Hosea?"

"Of course you may. How could I prevent it, even if I wished, which I don't."

"Thank you, Uncle Hosea. Mr. Worcester is going to play also. We need a fourth. I can borrow another racket. Will you be my partner, Uncle Hosea?"

"*I?* Your partner?"

"Yes. You play tennis; Auntie says so. Will you play to-morrow morning as my partner?"

"But I play an atrocious game and—"

"So do I. We shall match beautifully. Thank you, Uncle Hosea."

Once more she turned to go, and again she turned.

"Is there anything else you wish me to do, Uncle Hosea?" she asked.

The repetition repeated was too much.

"Yes," I declared. "Stop calling me Uncle Hosea. I'm not your uncle."

"Oh, I know that; but you have told everyone that you were, haven't you?"

I had, unfortunately, so I could make no better reply than to state emphatically that I didn't like the title.

"Oh, very well," she said. "But 'Mr. Knowles' sounds so formal, don't you think. What shall I call you? Never mind, perhaps I can think while I am dressing for dinner. I will see you at dinner, won't I. Au revoir, and thank you again for the racket—Cousin Hosy."

"I'm not your cousin, either—at least not more than a nineteenth cousin. And if you begin calling me 'Hosy' I shall—I don't know what I shall do."

"Dear me, how particular you are! Well then, au revoir—Kent."

When Hephzy came to the study I was still seated in the rector's chair. She was brimful full of curiosity, I know, and ready to ask a dozen questions at once. But I headed off the first of the dozen.

"Hephzy," I observed, "I have made no less than fifty solemn resolutions since we met that girl—that Little Frank of yours. You've heard me make them, haven't you."

"Why, yes, I suppose I have. If you mean resolutions to tell her the truth about her father and put an end to the scrape we're in, I have, certain."

"Yes; well, I've made another one now. Never, no matter what happens, will I attempt to tell her a word concerning Strickland Morley or her 'inheritance' or anything else. Every time I've tried I've made a blessed idiot of myself and now I'm through. She can stay with us forever and run us into debt to her heart's desire—I don't care. If she ever learns the truth she sha'n't learn it from me. I'm incapable of telling it. I haven't the sand of a yellow dog and I'm not going to worry about it. I'm through, do you hear—through."

That was my newest resolution. It was a comfort to realize that THIS resolution I should probably stick to.

CHAPTER XI
In Which Complications Become More Complicated

And stick to it I did. From that day—the day of our drive to Wrayton—on through those wonderful summer days in which she and Hephzy and I were together at the rectory, not once did I attempt to remonstrate with my "niece" concerning her presumption in inflicting her presence upon us or in spending her money, as she thought it—our money as I knew it to be—as she saw fit. Having learned and relearned my lesson—namely, that I lacked the courage to tell her the truth I had so often declared must be told, having shifted the responsibility to Hephzy's shoulders, having admitted and proclaimed myself, in that respect at least, a yellow dog, I proceeded to take life as I found it, as yellow dogs are supposed to do.

And, having thus weakly rid myself of care and responsibility, I began to enjoy that life. To enjoy the freedom of it, and the novelty of the surroundings, and the friendship of the good people who were our neighbors. Yes, and to enjoy the home life, the afternoons on the tennis court or the golf course, the evenings in the drawing-room, the "teas" on the lawn—either our lawn or someone else's—the chats together across the dinner-table; to enjoy it all; and, more astonishing still, to accept the companionship of the young person who was responsible for our living in that way as a regular and understood part of that life.

Not that I understood the young person herself; no Bayport quahaug, who had shunned female companionship as I had for so long, could be expected to understand the whims and changing moods of a girl like Frances Morley. At times she charmed and attracted me, at others she tormented and irritated me. She argued with me one moment and disagreed the next. She laughed at Hephzy's and my American accent and idioms, but when Bayliss, Junior, or one of the curates ventured to criticize an "Americanism" she was quite as likely to declare that she thought it "jolly" and "so expressive." Against my will I was obliged to join in conversations, to take sides in arguments, to be present when callers came, to make calls. I, who had avoided the society of young people because, being no longer young, I felt out of place among them, was now dragged into such society every day and almost every evening. I did not want to be, but Little Frank seemed to find mischievous pleasure in keeping me there.

"It is good for you," she said, on one occasion, when I had sneaked off to my room and the company of the "British Poets." "Auntie says you started on your travels in order to find something new to write about. You'll never find it in those musty books; every poem in them is at least seventy years old. If you are going to write of England and my people you must know something about those that are alive."

"But, my dear young lady," I said, "I have no intention of writing of your people, as you call them."

"You write of knights and lords and ladies and queens. You do—or you did—and you certainly know nothing about THEM."

I was quite a bit ruffled. "Indeed!" said I. "You are quite sure of that, are you?"

"I am," decidedly. "I have read 'The Queen's Amulet' and no queen on earth—in England, surely—ever acted or spoke like that one. An American queen might, if there was such a thing."

She laughed and, provoked as I was, I could not help laughing with her. She had a most infectious laugh.

"My dear young lady—" I began again, but she interrupted me.

"Don't call me that," she protested. "You're not the Archbishop of Canterbury visiting a girl's school and making a speech. You asked me not to call you 'Uncle Hosea.' If you say 'dear young lady' to me again I shall address you publicly as 'dear old Nunky.' Don't be silly."

I laughed again. "But you ARE young," I said.

"Well, what of it. Perhaps neither of us likes to be reminded of our age. I'm sure you don't; I never saw anyone more sensitive on the subject. There! there! put away those silly old books and come down to the drawing-room. I'm going to sing. Mr. Worcester has brought in a lot of new music."

Reluctantly I closed the volume I had in my hand.

"Very well," I said; "I'll come if you wish. But I shall only be in the way, as I always am. Mr. Worcester didn't plead for my company, did he? Do you know I think he will bear up manfully if I don't appear."

She regarded me with disapproval.

"Don't be childish in your old age," she snapped, "Are you coming?"

I went, of course, and—it may have been by way of reward—she sang several old-fashioned, simple ballads which I had found in a dog's-eared portfolio in the music cabinet and which I liked because my mother used to sing them when I was a little chap. I had asked for them before and she had ignored the request.

This time she sang them and Hephzy, sitting beside me in the darkest corner reached over and laid a hand on mine.

"Her mother all over again," she whispered. "Ardelia used to sing those."

Next day, on the tennis court, she played with Herbert Bayliss against Worcester and me, and seemed to enjoy beating us six to one. The only regret she expressed was that she and her partner had not made it a "love set."

Altogether she was a decidedly vitalizing influence, an influence that was, I began to admit to myself, a good one for me. I needed to be kept alive and active, and here, in this wide-awake household, I couldn't be anything else. The future did not look as dull and hopeless as it had when I left Bayport. I even began to consider the possibilities of another novel, to hope that I might write one. Jim Campbell's "prescription," although working in quite a different way from that which he and I had planned, was working nevertheless.

Matthews, at the Camford Street office, was forwarding my letters and honoring my drafts with promptness. I received a note each week from Campbell. I had written him all particulars concerning Little Frank and our move to the rectory, and he professed to see in it only a huge joke.

"Tell your Miss Cahoon," he wrote, "that I am going to turn Spiritualist right away. I believe in dreams now, and presentiments and all sorts of things. I am trying to dream out a plot for a novel by you. Had a roof-garden supper the other night and that gave me a fine start, but I'll have to tackle another one before I get sufficient thrills to furnish forth one of your gems. Seriously though, old man, this whole thing will do you a world of good. Nothing short of an earthquake would have shaken you out of your Cape Cod dumps and it looks to me as if you and—what's her name—Hephzibah, had had the quake. What are you going to do with the Little Frank person in the end? Can't you marry her off to a wealthy Englishman? Or, if not that, why not marry her yourself? She'd turn a dead quahaug into a live lobster, I should imagine, if anyone could. Great idea! What?"

His "great idea" was received with the contempt it deserved. I tore up the letter and threw it into the waste basket.

But Hephzy herself spoke of matrimony and Little Frank soon after this. We were alone together; Frances had gone on a horseback ride with Herbert Bayliss and a female cousin who was spending the day at "Jasmine Gables."

"Hosy," said Hephzy, "do you realize the summer is half over? It's the middle of July now."

So it was, although it seemed scarcely possible.

"Yes," she went on. "Our lease of this place is up the first of October. We shall be startin' for home then, I presume likely, sha'n't we."

"I suppose so. We can't stay over here indefinitely. Life isn't all skittles and—and tea."

"That's so. I don't know what skittles are, but I know what tea is. Land sakes! I should say I did. They tell me the English national flower is a rose. It ought to be a tea-plant blossom, if there is such a thing. Hosy," with a sudden return to seriousness, "what are we goin' to do with—with HER when the time comes for us to go?"

"I don't know," I answered.

"Are you going to take her to America with us?"

"I don't know."

"Humph! Well, we'll have to know then."

"I suppose we shall; but," defiantly, "I'm not going to worry about it till the time comes."

"Humph! Well, you've changed, that's all I've got to say. 'Twan't so long ago that you did nothin' BUT worry. I never saw anybody change the way you have anyway."

"In what way?"

"In every way. You aren't like the same person you used to be. Why, through that last year of ours in Bayport I used to think sometimes you were older than I was—older in the way you thought and acted, I mean. Now you act as if you were twenty-one. Cavortin' around, playin' tennis and golf and everything! What has got into you?"

"I don't know. Jim Campbell's prescription is taking effect, I guess. He said the change of air and environment would do me good. I tell you, Hephzy, I have made up my mind to enjoy life while I can. I realize as well as you do that the trouble is bound to come, but I'm not going to let it trouble me beforehand. And I advise you to do the same."

"Well, I've been tryin' to, but sometimes I can't help wonderin' and dreadin'. Perhaps I'm havin' my dread for nothin'. It may be that, by the time we're ready to start for Bayport, Little Frank will be provided for."

"Provided for? What do you mean?"

"I mean provided for by somebody else. There's at least two candidates for the job: Don't you think so?"

"You mean—"

"I mean Mr. Worcester and Herbert Bayliss. That Worcester man is a gone case, or I'm no judge. He's keepin' company with Frances, or would, if she'd let him. 'Twould be funny if she married a curate, wouldn't it."

"Not very," I answered. "Married life on a curate's salary is not my idea of humor."

"I suppose likely that's so. And I can't imagine her a minister's wife, can you?"

I could not; nor, unless I was greatly mistaken, could the young lady herself. In fact, anything as serious as marriage was far from her thoughts at present, I judged. But Hephzy did not seem so sure.

"No," she went on, "I don't think the curate's got much chance. But young Doctor Bayliss is different. He's good-lookin' and smart and he's got prospects. I like him first-rate and I think Frances likes him, too. I shouldn't wonder if THAT affair came to somethin'. Wouldn't it be splendid if it did!"

I said that it would. And yet, even as I said it, I was conscious of a peculiar feeling of insincerity. I liked young Bayliss. He was all that Hephzy had said, and more. He would, doubtless, make a good husband for any girl. And his engagement to Frances Morley might make easier the explanation which was bound to come. I believed I could tell Herbert Bayliss the truth concerning the ridiculous "claim." A man would be susceptible to reason and proof; I could convince him. I should have welcomed the possibility, but, somehow or other, I did not. Somehow or other, the idea of her marrying anyone was repugnant to me. I did not like to think of it.

"Oh dear!" sighed Hephzy; "if only things were different. If only she knew all about her father and his rascality and was livin' with us because she wanted to—if that was the way of it, it would be so different. If you and I had really adopted her! If she only was your niece."

"Nonsense!" I snapped. "She isn't my niece."

"I know it. That's what makes your goodness to her seem so wonderful to me. You treat her as if you cared as much as I do. And of course you don't.

It isn't natural you should. She's my sister's child, and she's hardly any relation to you at all. You're awful good, Hosy. She's noticed it, too. I think she likes you now a lot better than she did; she as much as said so. She's beginning to understand you."

"Nonsense!" I said again. Understand me! I didn't understand myself. Nevertheless I was foolishly pleased to hear that she liked me. It was pleasant to be liked even by one who was destined to hate me later on.

"I hope she won't feel too hard against us," continued Hephzy. "I can't bear to think of her doin' that. She—she seems so near and dear to me now. We—I shall miss her dreadfully when it's all over."

I think she hoped that I might say that I should miss her, also. But I did not say anything of the kind.

I was resolved not to permit myself to miss her. Hadn't I been scheming and planning to get rid of her ever since she thrust herself upon us? To be sorry when she, at last, was gotten rid of would be too idiotic.

"Well," observed Hephzy, in conclusion, "perhaps she and Doctor Bayliss will make a match after all. We ought to help it all we can, I suppose."

This conversation had various effects upon me. One was to make me unaccountably "blue" for the rest of that day. Another was that I regarded the visits of Worcester and Herbert Bayliss with a different eye. I speculated foolishly concerning those visits and watched both young gentlemen more closely.

I did not have to watch the curate long. Suddenly he ceased calling at the rectory. Not altogether, of course, but he called only occasionally and his manner toward my "niece" was oddly formal and constrained. She was very kind to him, kinder than before, I thought, but there was a difference in their manner. Hephzy, of course, had an explanation ready.

"She's given him his clearance papers," was her way of expressing it. "She's told him that it's no use so far as he's concerned. Well, I never did think she cared for him. And that leaves the course clear for the doctor, doesn't it."

The doctor took advantage of the clear course. His calls and invitations for rides and tennis and golf were more frequent than ever. She must have understood; but, being a normal young woman, as well as a very, very pretty one, she was a bit of a coquette and kept the boy—for, after all, he was scarcely more than that—at arm's length and in a state of alternate hope and despair. I shared his varying moods. If he could not be sure of her feelings toward him, neither could I, and I found myself wondering, wondering constantly. It was foolish for me to wonder, of course. Why should I waste time in speculation on that subject? Why should I care whether she married or not? What difference did it make to me whom she married? I resolved not to think of her at all. And that resolution, like so many I had made, amounted to nothing, for I did think of her constantly.

And then to add a new complication to the already over-complicated situation, came A. Carleton Heathcroft, Esquire.

Frances and Herbert Bayliss were scheduled for nine holes of golf on the Manor House course that morning. I had had no intention of playing. My projected novel had reached the stage where, plot building completed, I had really begun the writing. The first chapter was finished and I had intended beginning the second one that day. But, just as I seated myself at the desk in the Reverend Cole's study, the young lady appeared and insisted that the twosome become a threesome, that I leave my "stupid old papers and pencils" and come for a round on the links. I protested, of course, but she was in one of her wilful moods that morning and declared that she would not play unless I did.

"It will do you good," she said. "You'll write all the better this afternoon. Now, come along."

"Is Doctor Bayliss as anxious for my company as you seem to be?" I asked maliciously.

She tossed her head. "Of course he is," she retorted. "Besides it doesn't make any difference whether he is or not. *I* want you to play, and that is enough."

"Humph! he may not agree with you."

"Then he can play by himself. It will do him good, too. He takes altogether too much for granted. Come! I am waiting."

So, after a few more fruitless protests, I reluctantly laid aside the paper and pencils, changed to golfing regalia and, with my bag of clubs on my shoulder, joined the two young people on the lawn.

Frances greeted me very cordially indeed. Her clubs—I had bought them myself on one of my trips to London: having once yielded, in the matter of the tennis outfit, I now bought various little things which I thought would please her—were carried by Herbert Bayliss, who, of course, also carried his own. His greeting was not as enthusiastic. He seemed rather glum and out of sorts. Frances addressed most of her conversation to me and I was inclined to think the pair had had some sort of disagreement, what Hephzy would have called a "lover's quarrel," perhaps.

We walked across the main street of Mayberry, through the lane past the cricket field, on by the path over the pastures, and entered the great gate of the Manor, the gate with the Carey arms emblazoned above it. Then a quarter of a mile over rolling hills, with rare shrubs and flowers everywhere, brought us to the top of the hill at the edge of the little wood which these English people persisted in calling a "forest." The first tee was there. You drove—if you were skillful or lucky—down the long slope to the green two hundred yards away. If you were neither skillful nor lucky you were quite as likely to drive into the long grass on either side of the fair green. Then you hunted for your ball and, having found it, wasted more or less labor and temper in pounding it out of the "rough."

At the first tee a man arrayed in the perfection of natty golfing togs was practicing his "swing." A caddy was carrying his bag. This of itself argued the swinger a person of privilege and consequence, for caddies on those links were strictly forbidden by the Lady of the Manor. Why they were forbidden she alone knew.

As we approached the tee the player turned to look at us. He was not a Mayberryite and yet there was something familiar in his appearance. He regarded us for a moment and then, dropping his driver, lounged toward me and extended his hand.

"Oh, I say!" he exclaimed. "It is you, isn't it! How do you do?"

"Why, Mr. Heathcroft!" I said. "This is a surprise."

We shook hands. He, apparently, was not at all surprised.

"Heard about your being here, Knowles," he drawled. "My aunt told me; that is, she said there were Americans at the rectory and when she mentioned the name I knew, of course, it must be you. Odd you should have located here, isn't it! Jolly glad to see you."

I said I was glad to see him. Then I introduced my companions.

"Bayliss and I have met before," observed Heathcroft. "Played a round with him in the tournament last year. How do, Bayliss? Don't think Miss Morley and I have met, though. Great pleasure, really. Are you a resident of Mayberry, Miss Morley?"

Frances said that she was a temporary resident.

"Ah! visiting here, I suppose?"

"Yes. Yes, I am visiting. I am living at the rectory, also."

"Miss Morley is Mr. Knowles's niece," explained Bayliss.

Heathcroft seemed surprised.

Kent Knowles | 179

"Indeed!" he drawled. "Didn't know you had a niece, Knowles. She wasn't with you on the ship, now was she."

"Miss Morley had been living in England—here and on the Continent," I answered. I could have kicked Bayliss for his officious explanation of kinship. Now I should have that ridiculous "uncle" business to contend with, in our acquaintance with Heathcroft as with the Baylisses and the rest. Frances, I am sure, read my thoughts, for the corners of her mouth twitched and she looked away over the course.

"Won't you ask Mr. Heathcroft to join our game—Uncle?" she said. She had dropped the hated "Hosea," I am happy to say, but in the presence of those outside the family she still addressed me as "Uncle." Of course she could not do otherwise without arousing comment, but I did not like it. Uncle! there was a venerable, antique quality in the term which I resented more and more each time I heard it. It emphasized the difference in our ages—and that difference needed no emphasis.

Heathcroft looked pleased at the invitation, but he hesitated in accepting it.

"Oh, I shouldn't do that, really," he declared. "I should be in the way, now shouldn't I."

Bayliss, to whom the remark was addressed, made no answer. I judged that he did not care for the honor of the Heathcroft company. But Frances, after a glance in his direction, answered for him.

"Oh, not in the least," she said. "A foursome is ever so much more sporting than a threesome. Mr. Heathcroft, you and I will play Doctor Bayliss and—Uncle. Shall we?"

Heathcroft declared himself delighted and honored. He looked the former. He had scarcely taken his eyes from Miss Morley since their introduction.

That match was hard fought. Our new acquaintance was a fair player and he played to win. Frances was learning to play and had a natural aptitude for the game. I played better than my usual form and I needed to, for Bayliss played wretchedly. He "dubbed" his approaches and missed easy putts. If he had kept his eye on the ball instead of on his opponents he might have done better, but that he would not do. He watched Heathcroft and Miss Morley continually, and the more he watched the less he seemed to like what he saw.

Perhaps he was not altogether to blame, everything considered. Frances was quite aware of the scrutiny and apparently enjoyed his discomfiture.

She—well, perhaps she did not precisely flirt with A. Carleton Heathcroft, but she was very, very agreeable to him and exulted over the winning of each hole without regard to the feelings of the losers. As for Heathcroft, himself, he was quite as agreeable to her, complimented her on her playing, insisted on his caddy's carrying her clubs, assisted her over the rough places on the course, and generally acted the gallant in a most polished manner. Bayliss and I were beaten three down.

Heathcroft walked with us as far as the lodge gate. Then he said good-by with evident reluctance.

"Thank you so much for the game, Miss Morley," he said. "Enjoyed it hugely. You play remarkably well, if you don't mind my saying so."

Frances was pleased. "Thank you," she answered. "I know it isn't true—that about my playing—but it is awfully nice of you to say it. I hope we may play together again. Are you staying here long?"

"Don't know, I'm sure. I am visiting my aunt and she will keep me as long as she can. Seems to think I have neglected her of late. Of course we must play again. By the way, Knowles, why don't you run over and meet Lady Carey? She'll be awfully pleased to meet any friends of mine. Bring Miss Morley with you. Perhaps she would care to see the greenhouses. They're quite worth looking over, really. Like to have you, too, Bayliss, of course."

Bayliss's thanks were not effusive. Frances, however, declared that she should love to see the greenhouses. For my part, common politeness demanded my asking Mr. Heathcroft to call at the rectory. He accepted the invitation at once and heartily.

He called the very next day and joined us at tea. The following afternoon we, Hephzy, Frances and I, visited the greenhouses. On this occasion we met, for the first time, the lady of the Manor herself. Lady Kent Carey was a stout, gray-haired person, of very decided manner and a mannish taste in dress. She was gracious and affable, although I suspected that much of her affability toward the American visitors was assumed because she wished to please her nephew. A. Carleton Heathcroft, Esquire, was plainly her ladyship's pride and pet. She called him "Carleton, dear," and "Carleton, dear" was, in his aunt's estimation, the model of everything desirable in man.

The greenhouses were spacious and the display of rare plants and flowers more varied and beautiful than any I had ever seen. We walked through the grounds surrounding the mansion, and viewed with becoming reverence the trees planted by various distinguished personages, His Royal

Highness the Prince of Wales, Her late Majesty Queen Victoria, Ex-President Carnot of France, and others. Hephzy whispered to me as we were standing before the Queen Victoria specimen:

"I don't believe Queen Victoria ever planted that in the world, do you, Hosy. She'd look pretty, a fleshy old lady like her, puffin' away diggin' holes with a spade, now would she!"

I hastily explained the probability that the hole was dug by someone else.

Hephzy nodded.

"I guess so," she added. "And the tree was put in by someone else and the dirt put back by the same one. Queen Victoria planted that tree the way Susanna Wixon said she broke my best platter, by not doin' a single thing to it. I could plant a whole grove that way and not get a bit tired."

Lady Carey bade us farewell at the fish-ponds and asked us to come again. Her nephew, however, accompanied us all the way home—that is, he accompanied Frances, while Hephzy and I made up the rear guard. The next day he dropped in for some tennis. Herbert Bayliss was there before him, so the tennis was abandoned, and a three-cornered chat on the lawn substituted. Heathcroft treated the young doctor with a polite condescension which would have irritated me exceedingly.

From then on, during the fortnight which followed, there was a great deal of Heathcroft in the rectory social circle. And when he was not there, it was fairly certain that he and Frances were together somewhere, golfing, walking or riding. Sometimes I accompanied them, sometimes Herbert Bayliss made one of the party. Frances' behavior to the young doctor was tantalizingly contradictory. At times she was very cordial and kind, at others almost cold and repellent. She kept the young fellow in a state of uncertainty most of the time. She treated Heathcroft much the same, but there was this difference between them—Heathcroft didn't seem to mind; her whims appeared to amuse rather than to annoy him. Bayliss, on the contrary, was either in the seventh heaven of bliss or the subcellar of despair. I sympathized with him, to an extent; the young lady's attitude toward me had an effect which, in my case, was ridiculous. My reason told me that I should not care at all whether she liked me or whether she didn't, whether I pleased or displeased her. But I did care, I couldn't help it, I cared altogether too much. A middle-aged quahaug should be phlegmatic and philosophical; I once had a reputation for both qualities, but I seemed to possess neither now.

I found myself speculating and wondering more than ever concerning the outcome of all this. Was there anything serious in the wind at all? Herbert Bayliss was in love with Frances Morley, that was obvious now. But was she in love with him? I doubted it. Did she care in the least for him? I did not know. She seemed to enjoy his society. I did not want her to fall in love with A. Carleton Heathcroft, certainly. Nor, to be perfectly honest, did I wish her to marry Bayliss, although I like him much better than I did Lady Carey's blasé nephew. Somehow, I didn't like the idea of her falling in love with anyone. The present state of affairs in our household was pleasant enough. We three were happy together. Why could not that happiness continue just as it was?

The answer was obvious: It could not continue. Each day that passed brought the inevitable end nearer. My determination to put the thought of that end from my mind and enjoy the present was shaken. In the solitude of the study, in the midst of my writing, after I had gone to my room for the night, I found my thoughts drifting toward the day in October when, our lease of the rectory ended, we must pack up and go somewhere. And when we went, would she go with us? Hardly. She would demand the promised "settlement," and then—What then? Explanations—quarrels—parting. A parting for all time. I had reached a point where, like Hephzy, I would have gladly suggested a real "adoption," the permanent addition to our family of Strickland Morley's daughter, but she would not consent to that. She was proud—very proud. And she idolized her father's memory. No, she would not remain under any such conditions—I knew it. And the certainty of that knowledge brought with it a pang which I could not analyze. A man of my age and temperament should not have such feelings.

Hephzy did not fancy Heathcroft. She had liked him well enough during our first acquaintance aboard the steamer, but now, when she knew him better, she did not fancy him. His lofty, condescending manner irritated her and, as he seemed to enjoy joking at her expense, the pair had some amusing set-tos. I will say this for Hephzy: In the most of these she gave at least as good as she received.

For example: we were sitting about the tea-table on the lawn, Hephzy, Frances, Doctor and Mrs. Bayliss, their son, and Heathcroft. The conversation had drifted to the subject of eatables, a topic suggested, doubtless, by the plum cake and cookies on the table. Mr. Heathcroft was amusing himself by poking fun at the American custom of serving cereals at breakfast.

"And the variety is amazing," he declared. "Oats and wheat and corn! My word! I felt like some sort of animal—a horse, by Jove! We feed our horses that sort of thing over here, Miss Cahoon."

Hephzy sniffed. "So do we," she admitted, "but we eat 'em ourselves, sometimes, when they're cooked as they ought to be. I think some breakfast foods are fine."

"Do you indeed? What an extraordinary taste! Do you eat hay as well, may I ask?"

"No, of course we don't."

"Why not? Why draw the line? I should think a bit of hay might be the—ah—the crowning tit-bit to a breakfasting American. Your horses and donkeys enjoy it quite as much as they do oats, don't they?"

"Don't know, I'm sure. I'm neither a horse nor a donkey, I hope."

"Yes. Oh, yes. But I assure you, Miss Morley, I had extraordinary experiences on the other side. I visited in a place called Milwaukee and my host there insisted on my trying a new cereal each morning. We did the oats and the corn and all the rest and, upon my word, I expected the hay. It was the only donkey food he didn't have in the house, and I don't see why he hadn't provided a supply of that."

"Perhaps he didn't know you were comin'," observed Hephzy, cheerfully. "Won't you have another cup, Mrs. Bayliss? Or a cooky or somethin'?"

The doctor's wife consented to the refilling of her cup.

"I suppose—what do you call them?—cereals, are an American custom," she said, evidently aware that her hostess's feelings were ruffled. "Every country has its customs, so travelers say. Even our own has some, doubtless, though I can't recall any at the moment."

Heathcroft stroked his mustache.

"Oh," he drawled, "we have some, possibly; but our breakfasts are not as queer as the American breakfasts. You mustn't mind my fun, Miss Cahoon, I hope you're not offended."

"Not a bit," was the calm reply. "We humans ARE animals, after all, I suppose, and some like one kind of food and some another. Donkeys like hay and pigs like sweets, and I don't know as I hadn't just as soon live in a stable as a sty. Do help yourself to the cake, Mr. Heathcroft."

No, our aristocratic acquaintance did not, as a general rule, come out ahead in these little encounters and I more than once was obliged to suppress a chuckle at my plucky relative's spirited retorts. Frances, too, seemed to appreciate and enjoy the Yankee victories. Her prejudice against America had, so far as outward expression went, almost disappeared. She was more likely to champion than criticize our ways and habits now.

But, in spite of all this, she seemed to enjoy the Heathcroft society. The two were together a great deal. The village people noticed the intimacy and comments reached my ears which were not intended for them. Hephzy and I had some discussions on the subject.

"You don't suppose he means anything serious, do you, Hosy?" she asked. "Or that she thinks he does?"

"I don't know," I answered. I didn't like the idea any better than she did.

"I hope not. Of course he's a big man around here. When his aunt dies he'll come in for the estate and the money, so everybody says. And if Frances should marry him she'd be—I don't know whether she'd be a 'Lady' or not, but she'd have an awful high place in society."

"I suppose she would. But I hope she won't do it."

"So do I, for poor young Doctor Bayliss's sake, if nothin' else. He's so good and so patient with it all. And he's just eaten up with jealousy; anybody can see that. I'm scared to death that he and this Heathcroft man will have some sort of—of a fight or somethin'. That would be awful, wouldn't it!"

I did not answer. My apprehensions were not on Herbert Bayliss's account. He could look out for himself. It was Frances' happiness I was thinking of.

"Hosy," said Hephzy, very seriously indeed, "there's somethin' else. I'm not sure that Mr. Heathcroft is serious at all. Somethin' Mrs. Bayliss said to me makes me feel a little mite anxious. She said Carleton Heathcroft was a great lady's man. She told me some things about him that—that—Well, I wish Frances wasn't so friendly with him, that's all."

I shrugged my shoulders, pretending more indifference than I felt.

"She's a sensible girl," said I. "She doesn't need a guardian."

"I know, but—but he's way up in society, Lady Carey's heir and all that. She can't help bein' flattered by his attentions to her. Any girl would be, especially an English girl that thinks as much of class and all that as they do over here and as she does. I wish I knew how she did feel toward him."

"Why don't you ask her?"

Hephzy shook her head. "I wouldn't dare," she said. "She'd take my head off. We're on awful thin ice, you and I, with her, as it is. She treats us real nicely now, but that's because we don't interfere. If I should try just once to tell her what she ought to do she'd flare up like a bonfire. And then do the other thing to show her independence."

"I suppose she would," I admitted, gloomily.

"I know she would. No, we mustn't say anything to her. But—but you might say somethin' to him, mightn't you. Just hint around and find out what he does mean by bein' with her so much. Couldn't you do that, Hosy?"

I smiled. "Possibly I could, but I sha'n't," I answered. "He would tell me to go to perdition, probably, and I shouldn't blame him."

"Why no, he wouldn't. He thinks you're her uncle, her guardian, you know. You'd have a right to do it."

I did not propose to exercise that right, and I said so, emphatically. And yet, before that week was ended, I did do what amounted to that very thing. The reason which led to this rash act on my part was a talk I had with Lady Kent Carey.

I met her ladyship on the putting green of the ninth hole of the golf course. I was playing a round alone. She came strolling over the green, dressed as mannishly as usual, but carrying a very feminine parasol, which by comparison with the rest of her get-up, looked as out of place as a silk hat on the head of a girl in a ball dress. She greeted me very affably, waited until I putted out, and then sat beside me on the bench under the big oak and chatted for some time.

The subject of her conversation was her nephew. She was, apparently, only too glad to talk about him at any time. He was her dead sister's child and practically the only relative she had. He seemed like a son to her. Such a charming fellow, wasn't he, now? And so considerate and kind to her. Everyone liked him; he was a great favorite.

"And he is very fond of you, Mr. Knowles," she said. "He enjoys your acquaintance so much. He says that there is a freshness and novelty about you Americans which is quite delightfully amusing. This Miss—ah—Cahoon—your cousin, I think she is—is a constant joy to him. He never tires of repeating her speeches. He does it very well, don't you think. He mimics the American accent wonderfully."

I agreed that the Heathcroft American accent was wonderful indeed. It was all that and more. Lady Carey went on.

"And this Miss Morley, your niece," she said, poking holes in the turf with the tip of her parasol, "she is a charming girl, isn't she. She and Carleton are quite friendly, really."

"Yes," I admitted, "they seem to be."

"Yes. Tell me about your niece, Mr. Knowles. Has she lived in England long? Who were her parents?"

I dodged the ticklish subject as best I could, told her that Frances' father was an Englishman, her mother an American, and that most of the young lady's life had been spent in France. I feared more searching questions, but she did not ask them.

"I see," she said, nodding, and was silent for a moment. Then she changed the subject, returning once more to her beloved Carleton.

"He's a dear boy," she declared. "I am planning great things for him. Some day he will have the estate here, of course. And I am hoping to get him the seat in Parliament when our party returns to power, as it is sure to do before long. He will marry then; in fact everything is arranged, so far as that goes. Of course there is no actual engagement as yet, but we all understand."

I had been rather bored, now I was interested.

"Indeed!" said I. "And may I ask who is the fortunate young lady?"

"A daughter of an old friend of ours in Warwickshire—a fine family, one of the oldest in England. She and Carleton have always been so fond of each other. Her parents and I have considered the affair settled for years. The young people will be so happy together."

Here was news. I offered congratulations.

"Thank you so much," she said. "It is pleasant to know that his future is provided for. Margaret will make him a good wife. She worships him. If anything should happen to—ah—disturb the arrangement her heart would break, I am sure. Of course nothing will happen. I should not permit it."

I made some comment, I don't remember what. She rose from the bench.

"I have been chatting about family affairs and matchmaking like a garrulous old woman, haven't I," she observed, smiling. "So silly of me. You have been charmingly kind to listen, Mr. Knowles. Forgive me, won't you. Carleton dear is my one interest in life and I talk of him on the least excuse, or without any. So sorry to have inflicted my garrulity upon you. I may count upon you entering our invitation golf tournament next month, may I not? Oh, do say yes. Thank you so much. Au revoir."

She moved off, as imposing and majestic as a frigate under full sail. I walked slowly toward home, thinking hard.

I should have been flattered, perhaps, at her taking me into confidence concerning her nephew's matrimonial projects. If I had believed the "garrulity," as she called it, to have been unintentional, I might have been flattered. But I did not so believe. I was pretty certain there was intention in it and that she expected Frances and Hephzy and me to take it as a warning.

Carleton dear was, in her eyes, altogether too friendly with the youngest tenant in Mayberry rectory. The "garrulity" was a notice to keep hands off.

I was not incensed at her; she amused me, rather. But with Heathcroft I was growing more incensed every moment. Engaged to be married, was he! He and this Warwickshire girl of "fine family" had been "so fond" of each other for years. Everything was understood, was it? Then what did he mean by his attentions to Frances, attentions which half of Mayberry was probably discussing at the moment? The more I considered his conduct the angrier I became. It was the worst time possible for a meeting with A. Carleton Heathcroft, and yet meet him I did at the loneliest and most secluded spot in the hedged lane leading to the lodge gate.

He greeted me cordially enough, if his languid drawl could be called cordial.

"Ah, Knowles," he said. "Been doing the round I see. A bit stupid by oneself, I should think. What? Miss Morley and I have been riding. Had a ripping canter together."

It was an unfortunate remark, just at that time. It had the effect of spurring my determination to the striking point. I would have it out with him then and there.

"Heathcroft," I said, bluntly, "I am not sure that I approve of Miss Morley's riding with you so often."

He regarded me with astonishment.

"You don't approve!" he repeated. "And why not? There's no danger. She rides extremely well."

"It's not a question of danger. It is one of proprieties, if I must put it that way. She is a young woman, hardly more than a girl, and she probably does not realize that being seen in your company so frequently is likely to cause comment and gossip. Her aunt and I realize it, however."

His expression of surprise was changing to one of languid amusement.

"Really!" he drawled. "By Jove! I say, Knowles, am I such a dangerously fascinating character? You flatter me."

"I don't know anything concerning your character. I do know that there is gossip. I am not accusing you of anything. I have no doubt you have been merely careless. Your intentions may have been—"

He interrupted me. "My intentions?" he repeated. "My dear fellow, I have no intentions. None whatever concerning your niece, if that is what you mean. She is a jolly pretty girl and jolly good company. I like her and she seems to like me. That is all, upon my word it is."

He was quite sincere, I was convinced of it. But I had gone too far to back out.

"Then you have been thoughtless—or careless," I said. "It seems to me that you should have considered her."

"Considered her! Oh, I say now! Why should I consider her pray?"

"Why shouldn't you? You are much older than she is and a man of the world besides. And you are engaged to be married, or so I am told."

His smile disappeared.

"Now who the devil told you that?" he demanded.

"I was told, by one who should know, that you were engaged, or what amounts to the same thing. It is true, isn't it?"

"Of course it's true! But—but—why, good God, man! you weren't under the impression that I was planning to marry your niece, were you? Oh, I say! that would be TOO good!"

He laughed heartily. He did not appear in the least annoyed or angry, but seemed to consider the whole affair a huge joke. I failed to see the joke, myself.

"Oh, no," he went on, before I could reply, "not that, I assure you. One can't afford luxuries of that kind, unless one is a luckier beggar than I am. Auntie is attending to all that sort of thing. She has me booked, you know, and I can't afford to play the high-spirited independent with her. I should say not! Rather!"

He laughed again.

"So you think I've been a bit too prevalent in your niece's neighborhood, do you?" he observed. "Sorry. I'd best keep off the lawn a bit, you mean to say, I suppose. Very well! I'll mind the notice boards, of course. Very glad you spoke. Possibly I have been a bit careless. No offence meant, Knowles, and none taken, I trust."

"No," I said, with some reluctance. "I'm glad you understand my—our position, and take my—my hint so well. I disliked to give it, but I thought it best that we have a clear understanding."

"Of course! Stern uncle and pretty niece, and all that sort of thing. You Americans are queer beggars. You don't strike me as the usual type of stern uncle at all, Knowles. Oh, by the way, does the niece know that uncle is putting up the notice boards?"

"Of course she doesn't," I replied, hastily.

His smile broadened. "I wonder what she'll say when she finds it out," he observed. "She has never struck me as being greatly in awe of her relatives. I should call HER independent, if I was asked. Well, farewell. You and I may have some golf together still, I presume? Good! By-by."

He sauntered on, his serene coolness and calm condescension apparently unruffled. I continued on my way also. But my serenity had vanished. I had the feeling that I had come off second-best in the encounter. I had made a fool of myself, I feared. And more than all, I wondered, as he did, what Frances Morley would say when she learned of my interference in her personal affairs.

I foresaw trouble—more trouble.

CHAPTER XII
In Which the Truth Is Told at Last

I said nothing to Hephzibah or Frances of my talk with Lady Carey or with Heathcroft. I was not proud of my share in the putting up of "the notice boards." I did not mention meeting either the titled aunt or the favored nephew. I kept quiet concerning them both and nervously awaited developments.

There were none immediately. That day and the next passed and nothing of importance happened. It did seem to me, however, that Frances was rather quiet during luncheon on the third day. She said very little and several times I found her regarding me with an odd expression. My guilty conscience smote me and I expected to be asked questions answering which would be difficult. But the questions were not asked—then. I went to my study and attempted to write; the attempt was a failure.

For an hour or so I stared hopelessly at the blank paper. I hadn't an idea in my head, apparently. At last I threw down the pencil and gave up the battle for the day. I was not in a writing mood. I lit my pipe, and, moving to the arm-chair by the window, sat there, looking out at the lawn and flower beds. No one was in sight except Grimmer, the gardener, who was trimming a hedge.

I sat there for some time, smoking and thinking. Hephzy dressed in her best, passed the window on her way to the gate. She was going for a call in the village and had asked me to accompany her, but I declined. I did not feel like calling.

My pipe, smoked out, I put in my pocket. If I could have gotten rid of my thoughts as easily I should have been happier, but that I could not do. They were strange thoughts, hopeless thoughts, ridiculous, unavailing thoughts. For me, Kent Knowles, quahaug, to permit myself to think in that way was worse than ridiculous; it was pitiful. This was a stern reality, this summer of mine in England, not a chapter in one of my romances. They ended happily; it was easy to make them end in that way. But this—this was no romance, or, if it was, I was but the comic relief in the story, the queer old bachelor who had made a fool of himself. That was what I was, an old fool. Well, I must stop being a fool before it was too late. No one knew I was such a fool. No one should know—now or ever.

And having reached this philosophical conclusion I proceeded to dream of dark eyes looking into mine across a breakfast table—our table; of a home in Bayport—our home; of someone always with me, to share my life, my hopes, to spur me on to a work worth while, to glory in my triumphs and comfort me in my reverses; to dream of what might have been if—if it were not absolutely impossible. Oh, fool, fool, fool!

A quick step sounded on the gravel walk outside the window. I knew the step, should have recognized it anywhere. She was walking rapidly toward the house, her head bent and her eyes fixed upon the path before her. Grimmer touched his hat and said "Good afternoon, miss," but she apparently did not hear him. She passed on and I heard her enter the hall. A moment later she knocked at the study door.

She entered the room in answer to my invitation and closed the door behind her. She was dressed in her golfing costume, a plain white shirtwaist—blouse, she would have called it—a short, dark skirt and stout boots. The light garden hat was set upon her dark hair and her cheeks were flushed from rapid walking. The hat and waist and skirt were extremely becoming. She was pretty—yes, beautiful—and young. I was far from beautiful and far from young. I make this obvious statement because it was my thought at the moment.

She did not apologize for interrupting me, as she usually did when she entered the study during my supposed working periods. This was strange, of itself, and my sense of guilt caused me to fear all sorts of things. But she smiled and answered my greeting pleasantly enough and, for the moment, I experienced relief. Perhaps, after all, she had not learned of my interview with Heathcroft.

"I have come to talk with you," she began. "May I sit down?"

"Certainly. Of course you may," I answered, smiling as cheerfully as I could. "Was it necessary to ask permission?"

She took a chair and I seated myself in the one from which I had just risen. For a moment she was silent. I ventured a remark.

"This begins very solemnly," I said. "Is the talk to be so very serious?"

She was serious enough and my apprehensions returned.

"I don't know," she answered. "I hope it may not be serious at all, Mr. Knowles."

I interrupted. "Mr. Knowles!" I repeated. "Whew! this IS a formal interview. I thought the 'Mr. Knowles' had been banished along with 'Uncle Hosea'."

She smiled slightly then. "Perhaps it has," she said. "I am just a little troubled—or puzzled—and I have come to you for advice."

"Advice?" I repeated. "I'm afraid my advice isn't worth much. What sort of advice do you want?"

"I wanted to know what I should do in regard to an invitation I have received to motor with Doctor Bayliss—Doctor Herbert Bayliss. He has asked me to go with him to Edgeboro to-morrow. Should I accept?"

I hesitated. Then: "Alone?" I asked.

"No. His cousin, Miss Tomlinson, will go also."

"I see no reason why you should not, if you wish to go."

"Thank you. But suppose it was alone?"

"Then—Well, I presume that would be all right, too. You have motored with him before, you know."

As a matter of fact, I couldn't see why she asked my opinion in such a matter. She had never asked it before. Her next remark was more puzzling still.

"You approve of Doctor Bayliss, don't you," she said. It did seem to me there was a hint of sarcasm in her tone.

"Yes—certainly," I answered. I did approve of young Bayliss, generally speaking; there was no sane reason why I should not have approved of him absolutely.

"And you trust me? You believe me capable of judging what is right or wrong?"

"Of course I do."

"If you didn't you would not presume to interfere in my personal affairs? You would not think of doing that, of course?"

"No—o," more slowly.

"Why do you hesitate? Of course you realize that you have no shadow of right to interfere. You know perfectly well why I consented to remain here for the present and why I have remained?"

"Yes, yes, I know that."

"And you wouldn't presume to interfere?"

"Doctor Herbert Bayliss is—"

She sprang to her feet. She was not smiling now.

"Stop!" she interrupted, sharply. "Stop! I did not come to discuss Doctor Bayliss. I have asked you a question. I ask you if you would presume to interfere in my personal affairs. Would you?"

"Why, no. That is, I—"

"You say that to me! YOU!"

"Frances, if you mean that I have interfered between you and the Doctor, I—"

She stamped her foot.

"Stop! Oh, stop!" she cried. "You know what I mean. What did you say to Mr. Heathcroft? Do you dare tell me you have not interfered there?"

It had come, the expected. Her smile and the asking for "advice" had been apparently but traps to catch me off my guard. I had been prepared for some such scene as this, but, in spite of my preparations, I hesitated and faltered. I must have looked like the meanest of pickpockets caught in the act.

"Frances," I stammered, "Frances—"

Her fury took my breath away.

"Don't call me Frances," she cried. "How dare you call me that?"

Perturbed as I was I couldn't resist making the obvious retort.

"You asked me to," I said.

"I asked you! Yes, I did. You had been kind to me, or I thought you had, and I—I was foolish. Oh, how I hate myself for doing it! But I was beginning to think you a gentleman. In spite of everything, I was beginning to—And now! Oh, at least I thought you wouldn't LIE to me."

I rose now.

"Frances—Miss Morley," I said, "do you realize what you are saying?"

"Realize it! Oh," with a scornful laugh, "I realize it quite well; you may be sure of that. Don't you like the word? What else do you call a denial of what we both know to be the truth. You did see Mr. Heathcroft. You did speak with him."

"Yes, I did."

"You did! You admit it!"

"I admit it. But did he tell you what I said?"

"He did not. Mr. Heathcroft IS a gentleman. He told me very little and that only in answer to my questions. I knew you and he met the other day. You did not mention it, but you were seen together, and when he did not come for the ride to which he had invited me I thought it strange. And his note to me was stranger still. I began to suspect then, and when we next met I asked him some questions. He told me next to nothing, but he is honorable and he does not LIE. I learned enough, quite enough."

I wondered if she had learned of the essential thing, of Heathcroft's engagement.

"Did he tell you why I objected to his intimacy with you?" I asked.

"He told me nothing! Nothing! The very fact that you had objected, as you call it, was sufficient. Object! YOU object to my doing as I please! YOU meddle with my affairs! And humiliate me in the eyes of my friends! I could—I could die of shame! I... And as if I did not know your reasons. As if they were not perfectly plain."

The real reason could not be plain to her. Heathcroft evidently had not told her of the Warwickshire heiress.

"I don't understand," I said, trying my hardest to speak calmly. "What reasons?"

"Must I tell you? Did you OBJECT to my friendship with Doctor Bayliss, pray?"

"Doctor Bayliss! Why, Doctor Bayliss is quite different. He is a fine young fellow, and—"

"Yes," with scornful sarcasm, "so it would appear. You and my aunt and he have the most evident of understandings. You need not praise him for my benefit. It is quite apparent how you both feel toward Doctor Bayliss. I am not blind. I have seen how you have thrown him in my company, and made opportunities for me to meet him. Oh, of course, I can see! I did not believe it at first. It was too absurd, too outrageously impertinent. I COULDN'T believe it. But now I know."

This was a little too much. The idea that I—I had been playing the matchmaker for Bayliss's benefit made me almost as angry as she was.

"Nonsense!" I declared. "Miss Morley, this is too ridiculous to go on. I did speak to Mr. Heathcroft. There was a reason, a good reason, for my doing so."

"I do not wish to hear your reason, as you call it. The fact that you did speak to him concerning me is enough. Mr. Knowles, this arrangement of ours, my living here with you, has gone on·too long. I should have known it was impossible in the beginning. But I did not know. I was alone—and ill—and I did need friends—I was SO alone. I had been through so much. I had struggled and suffered and—"

Again, as in our quarrel at Wrayton, she was on the verge of tears. And again that unreasonable conscience of mine smote me. I longed to—Well, to prove myself the fool I was.

But she did not give me the opportunity. Before I could speak or move she was on her way to the door.

"This ends it," she said. "I shall go away from here at once. I shall put the whole matter in my solicitor's hands. This is an end of forbearance and all the rest. I am going. You have made me hate you and despise you. I only hope that—that some day you will despise yourself as much. But you won't," scornfully. "You are not that sort."

The door closed. She was gone. Gone! And soon—the next day at the latest—she would have been gone for good. This WAS the end.

I walked many miles that day, how many I do not know. Dinner was waiting for me when I returned, but I could not eat. I rose from the table, went to the study and sat there, alone with my misery. I was torn with the wildest longings and desires. One, I think, was to kill Heathcroft forthwith. Another was to kill myself.

There came another knock at the door. This time I made no answer. I did not want to see anyone.

But the door opened, nevertheless, and Hephzy came in. She crossed the room and stood by my chair.

"What is it, Hosy?" she said, gently. "You must tell me all about it."

I made some answer, told her to go away and leave me, I think. If that was it she did not heed. She put her hand upon my shoulder.

"You must tell me, Hosy," she said. "What has happened? You and Frances have had some fallin' out, I know. She wouldn't come to dinner, either, and she won't see me. She's up in her room with the door shut. Tell me, Hosy; you and I have fought each other's battles for a good many years. You can't fight this one alone; I've got to do my share. Tell me, dearie, please."

And tell her I did. I did not mean to, and yet somehow the thought that she was there, so strong and quiet and big-hearted and sensible, was, if not a comfort to me, at least a marvelous help. I began by telling her a little and then went on to tell her all, of my talk with Lady Carey, my meeting with Heathcroft, the scene with Frances—everything, word for word.

When it was over she patted my shoulder.

"You did just right, Hosy," she said. "There was nothin' else you could do. I never liked that Heathcroft man. And to think of him, engaged to another girl, trottin' around with Frances the way he has. I'D like to talk with him. He'd get a piece of MY mind."

"He's all right enough," I admitted grudgingly. "He took my warning in a very good sort, I must say. He has never meant anything serious. It was just his way, that's all. He was amusing himself in her company, and doubtless thought she would be flattered with his aristocratic attentions."

"Humph! Well, I guess she wouldn't be if she'd known of that other girl. You didn't tell her that, you say."

"I couldn't. I think I should, perhaps, if she would have listened. I'm glad I didn't. It isn't a thing for me to tell her."

"I understand. But she ought to know it, just the same. And she ought to know how good you've been to her. Nobody could be better. She must know it. Whether she goes or whether she doesn't she must know that."

I seized her arm. "You mustn't tell her a word," I cried. "She mustn't know. It is better she should go. Better for her and for me—My God, yes! so much better for me."

I could feel the arm on my shoulder start. Hephzy bent down and looked into my face. I tried to avoid the scrutiny, but she looked and looked. Then she drew a long breath.

"Hosy!" she exclaimed. "Hosy!"

"Don't speak to me. Oh, Hephzy," with a bitter laugh, "did you ever dream there could be such a hopeless lunatic as I am! You needn't say it. I know the answer."

"Hosy! Hosy! you poor boy!"

She kissed me, soothing me as she had when I came home to our empty house at the time of my mother's death. That memory came back to me even then.

"Forgive me, Hephzy," I said. "I am ashamed of myself, of course. And don't worry. Nobody knows this but you and I, and nobody else shall. I'm going to behave and I'm going to be sensible. Just forget all this for my sake. I mean to forget it, too."

But Hephzy shook her head.

"It's all my fault," she said. "I'm to blame more than anybody else. It was me that brought her here in the first place and me that kept you from tellin' her the truth in the beginnin'. So it's me who must tell her now."

"Hephzy!"

"Oh, I don't mean the truth about—about what you and I have just said, Hosy. She'll never know that, perhaps. Certainly she'll never know it from me. But the rest of it she must know. This has gone far enough. She sha'n't go away from this house misjudgin' you, thinkin' you're a thief, as well as all the rest of it. That she sha'n't do. I shall see to that—now."

"Hephzy, I forbid you to—"

"You can't forbid me, Hosy. It's my duty, and I've been a silly, wicked old woman and shirked that duty long enough. Now don't worry any more. Go to your room, dearie, and lay down. If you get to sleep so much the better. Though I guess," with a sigh, "we sha'n't either of us sleep much this night."

Before I could prevent her she had left the room. I sprang after her, to call her back, to order her not to do the thing she had threatened. But, in the drawing-room, Charlotte, the housemaid, met me with an announcement.

"Doctor Bayliss—Doctor Herbert Bayliss—is here, sir," she said. "He has called to see you."

"To see me?" I repeated, trying hard to recover some measure of composure. "To see Miss Frances, you mean."

"No, sir. He says he wants to see you alone. He's in the hall now, sir."

He was; I could hear him. Certainly I never wished to see anyone less, but I could not refuse.

"Ask him to come into the study, Charlotte," said I.

The young doctor found me sitting in the chair by the desk. The long English twilight was almost over and the room was in deep shadow. Charlotte entered and lighted the lamp. I was strongly tempted to order her to desist, but I could scarcely ask my visitor to sit in the dark, however much I might prefer to do so. I compromised by moving to a seat farther from the lamp where my face would be less plainly visible. Then, Bayliss having, on my invitation, also taken a chair, I waited for him to state his business.

It was not easy to state, that was plain. Ordinarily Herbert Bayliss was cool and self-possessed. I had never before seen him as embarrassed as he seemed to be now. He fidgeted on the edge of the chair, crossed and recrossed his legs, and, finally, offered the original remark that it had been an extremely pleasant day. I admitted the fact and again there was an interval of silence. I should have helped him, I suppose. It was quite apparent that his was no casual call and, under ordinary circumstances, I should have been interested and curious. Now I did not care. If he would say his say and go away and leave me I should be grateful.

And, at last, he said it. His next speech was very much nearer the point.

"Mr. Knowles," he said, "I have called to—to see you concerning your niece, Miss Morley. I—I have come to ask your consent to my asking her to marry me."

I was not greatly surprised. I had vaguely suspected his purpose when he entered the room. I had long foreseen the likelihood of some such interview as this, had considered what I should say when the time came. But now it had come, I could say nothing. I sat in silence, looking at him.

Perhaps he thought I did not understand. At any rate he hastened to explain.

"I wish your permission to marry your niece," he repeated. "I have no doubt you are surprised. Perhaps you fancy I am a bit hasty. I suppose you do. But I—I care a great deal for her, Mr. Knowles. I will try to make her a good husband. Not that I am good enough for her, of course—no one could be that, you know; but I'll try and—and—"

He was very red in the face and floundered, amid his jerky sentences, like a newly-landed fish, but he stuck to it manfully. I could not help admiring the young fellow. He was so young and handsome and so honest and boyishly eager in his embarrassment. I admired him—yes, but I hated him, too, hated him for his youth and all that it meant, I was jealous—bitterly, wickedly jealous, and of all jealousy, hopeless, unreasonable jealousy is the worst, I imagine.

He went on to speak of his ambitions and prospects. He did not intend to remain always in Mayberry as his father's assistant, not he. He should remain for a time, of course, but then he intended to go back to London. There were opportunities there. A fellow with the right stuff in him could get on there. He had friends in the London hospitals and they had promised to put chances his way. He should not presume to marry Frances at once, of course. He would not be such a selfish goat as that. All he asked was that, my permission granted, she would be patient and wait a bit until he got on his feet, professionally he meant to say, and then—

I interrupted.

"One moment," said I, trying to appear calm and succeeding remarkably well, considering the turmoil in my brain; "just a moment, Bayliss, if you please. Have you spoken to Miss Morley yet? Do you know her feelings toward you?"

No, he had not. Of course he wouldn't do that until he and I had had our understanding. He had tried to be honorable and all that. But—but he thought she did not object to him. She—well, she had seemed to like him well enough. There had been times when he thought she—she—

"Well, you see, sir," he said, "she's a girl, of course, and a fellow never knows just what a girl is going to say or do. There are times when one is sure everything is quite right and then that it is all wrong. But I have hoped—I believe—She's such a ripping girl, you know. She would not flirt with a chap and—I don't mean flirt exactly, she isn't a flirt, of course—but—don't you think she likes me, now?"

"I have no reason to suppose she doesn't," I answered grudgingly. After all, he was acting very honorably; I could scarcely do less.

He seemed to find much comfort in my equivocal reply.

"Thanks, thanks awfully," he exclaimed. "I—I—by Jove, you know, I can't tell you how I like to hear you say that! I'm awfully grateful to you, Knowles, I am really. And you'll give me permission to speak to her?"

I smiled; it was not a happy smile, but there was a certain ironic humor in the situation. The idea of anyone's seeking my "permission" in any matter concerning Frances Morley. He noticed the smile and was, I think, inclined to be offended.

"Is it a joke?" he asked. "I say, now! it isn't a joke to me."

"Nor to me, I assure you," I answered, seriously. "If I gave that impression it was a mistaken one. I never felt less like joking."

He put his own interpretation on the last sentence. "I'm sorry," he said, quickly. "I beg your pardon. I understand, of course. You're very fond of her; no one could help being that, could they. And she is your niece."

I hesitated. I was minded to blurt out the fact that she was not my niece at all; that I had no authority over her in any way. But what would be the use? It would lead only to explanations and I did not wish to make explanations. I wanted to get through with the whole inane business and be left alone.

"But you haven't said yes, have you," he urged. "You will say it, won't you?"

I nodded. "You have my permission, so far as that goes," I answered.

He sprang to his feet and seized my hand.

"That's topping!" he cried, his face radiant. "I can't thank you enough."

"That's all right. But there is one thing more. Perhaps it isn't my affair, and you needn't answer unless you wish. Have you consulted your parents? How do they feel about your—your intentions?"

His expression changed. My question was answered before he spoke.

"No," he admitted, "I haven't told them yet. I—Well, you see, the Mater and Father have been making plans about my future, naturally. They have some silly ideas about a friend of the family that—Oh, she's a nice enough girl; I like her jolly well, but she isn't Miss Morley. Well, hardly! They'll take it quite well. By Jove!" excitedly, "they must. They've GOT to. Oh, they will. And they're very fond of—of Frances."

There seemed nothing more for me to say, nothing at that time, at any rate. I, too, rose. He shook my hand again.

"You've been a trump to me, Knowles," he declared. "I appreciate it, you know; I do indeed. I'm jolly grateful."

"You needn't be. It is all right. I—I suppose I should wish you luck and happiness. I do. Yes, why shouldn't you be happy, even if—"

"Even if—what? Oh, but you don't think she will turn me off, do you? You don't think that?"

"I've told you that I see no reason why she should."

"Thank you. Thank you so much. Is there anything else that you might wish to say to me?"

"Not now. Perhaps some day I—But not now. No, there's nothing else. Good night, Bayliss; good night and—and good luck."

"Good night. I—She's not in now, I suppose, is she?"

"She is in, but—Well, I scarcely think you had better see her to-night. She has gone to her room."

"Oh, I say! it's very early. She's not ill, is she?"

"No, but I think you had best not see her to-night."

He was disappointed, that was plain, but he yielded. He would have agreed, doubtless, with any opinion of mine just then.

"No doubt you're right," he said. "Good night. And thank you again."

He left the room. I did not accompany him to the door. Instead I returned to my chair. I did not occupy it long, I could not. I could not sit still. I rose and went out on the lawn. There, in the night mist, I paced up and down, up and down. I had longed to be alone; now that I was alone I was more miserable than ever.

Charlotte, the maid, called to me from the doorway.

"Would you wish the light in the study any longer, sir?" she asked.

"No," said I, curtly. "You may put it out."

"And shall I lock up, sir; all but this door, I mean?"

"Yes. Where is Miss Cahoon?"

"She's above, sir. With Miss Morley, I think, sir."

"Very well, Charlotte. That is all. Good night."

"Good night, sir."

She went into the house. The lamp in the study was extinguished. I continued my pacing up and down. Occasionally I glanced at the upper story of the rectory. There was a lighted window there, the window of Frances' room. She and Hephzy were together in that room. What was going on there? What had Hephzy said to her? What—Oh, WHAT would happen next?

Some time later—I don't know how much later it may have been—I heard someone calling me again.

"Hosy!" called Hephzy in a loud whisper; "Hosy, where are you?"

"Here I am," I answered.

She came to me across the lawn. I could not, of course, see her face, but her tone was very anxious.

"Hosy," she whispered, putting her hand on my arm, "what are you doin' out here all alone?"

I laughed. "I'm taking the air," I answered. "It is good for me. I am enjoying the glorious English air old Doctor Bayliss is always talking about. Fresh air and exercise—those will cure anything, so he says. Perhaps they will cure me. God knows I need curing."

"Sshh! shh, Hosy! Don't talk that way. I don't like to hear you. Out here bareheaded and in all this damp! You'll get your death."

"Will I? Well, that will be a complete cure, then."

"Hush! I tell you. Come in the house with me. I want to talk to you. Come!"

Still holding my arm she led me toward the house. I hung back.

"You have been up there with her?" I said, with a nod toward the lighted window of the room above. "What has happened? What have you said and done?"

"Hush! I'll tell you; I'll tell you all about it. Only come in now. I sha'n't feel safe until I get you inside. Oh, Hosy, DON'T act this way! Do you want to frighten me to death?"

That appeal had an effect. I was ashamed of myself.

"Forgive me, Hephzy," I said. "I'll try to be decent. You needn't worry about me. I'm a fool, of course, but now that I realize it I shall try to stop behaving like one. Come along; I'm ready."

In the drawing-room she closed the door.

"Shall I light the lamp?" she asked.

"No. Oh, for heaven's sake, can't you see that I'm crazy to know what you said to that girl and what she said to you? Tell me, and hurry up, will you!"

She did not resent my sudden burst of temper and impatience. Instead she put her arm about me.

"Sit down, Hosy," she pleaded. "Sit down and I'll tell you all about it. Do sit down."

I refused to sit.

"Tell me now," I commanded. "What did you say to her? You didn't— you didn't—"

"I did. I told her everything."

"EVERYTHING! You don't mean—"

"I mean everything. 'Twas time she knew it. I went to that room meanin' to tell her and I did. At first she didn't want to listen, didn't want to see me at all or even let me in. But I made her let me in and then she and I had it out."

"Hephzy!"

"Don't say it that way, Hosy. The good Lord knows I hate myself for doin' it, hated myself while I was doin' it, but it had to be done. Every word I spoke cut me as bad as it must have cut her. I kept thinkin', 'This is Little Frank I'm talkin' to. This is Ardelia's daughter I'm makin' miserable.' A dozen times I stopped and thought I couldn't go on, but every time I thought of you and what you'd put up with and been through, and I went on."

"Hephzy! you told her—"

"I said it was time she understood just the plain truth about her father and mother and grandfather and the money, and everything. She must know it, I said; things couldn't go on as they have been. I told it all. At first she wouldn't listen, said I was—well, everything that was mean and lyin' and bad. If she could she'd have put me out of her room, I presume likely, but I wouldn't go. And, of course, at first she wouldn't believe, but I made her believe."

"Made her believe! Made her believe her father was a thief! How could you do that! No one could."

"I did it. I don't know how exactly. I just went on tellin' it all straight from the beginnin', and pretty soon I could see she was commencin' to believe. And she believes now, Hosy; she does, I know it."

"Did she say so?"

"No, she didn't say anything, scarcely—not at the last. She didn't cry, either; I almost wish she had. Oh, Hosy, don't ask me any more questions than you have to. I can't bear to answer 'em."

She paused and turned away.

"How she must hate us!" I said, after a moment.

"Why, no—why, no, Hosy, I don't think she does; at least I'm tryin' to hope she doesn't. I softened it all I could. I told her why we took her with us in the first place; how we couldn't tell her the truth at first, or leave her, either, when she was so sick and alone. I told her why we brought her here, hopin' it would make her well and strong, and how, after she got that way, we put off tellin' her because it was such a dreadful hard thing to do. Hard! When I think of her sittin' there, white as a sheet, and lookin' at me with those big eyes of hers, her fingers twistin' and untwistin' in her lap—a way her mother used to have when she was troubled—and every word I spoke soundin' so cruel and—and—"

She paused once more. I did not speak. Soon she recovered and went on.

"I told her that I was tellin' her these things now because the misunderstandin's and all the rest had to stop and there was no use puttin' off any longer. I told her I loved her as if she was my very own and that this needn't make the least bit of difference unless she wanted it to. I said you felt just the same. I told her your speakin' to that Heathcroft man was only for her good and for no other reason. You'd learned that he was engaged to be married—"

"You told her that?" I interrupted, involuntarily. "What did she say?"

"Nothin', nothin' at all. I think she heard me and understood, but she didn't say anything. Just sat there, white and trembling and crushed, sort of, and looked and looked at me. I wanted to put my arms around her and ask her pardon and beg her to love me as I did her, but I didn't dare—I didn't dare. I did say that you and I would be only too glad to have her stay with us always, as one of the family, you know. If she'd only forget all the bad part that had gone and do that, I said—but she interrupted me. She said 'Forget!' and the way she said it made me sure she never would forget. And then—and then she asked me if I would please go away and leave her. Would I PLEASE not say any more now, but just leave her, only leave her alone. So I came away and—and that's all."

"That's all," I repeated. "It is enough, I should say. Oh, Hephzy, why did you do it? Why couldn't it have gone on as it has been going? Why did you do it?"

It was an unthinking, wicked speech. But Hephzy did not resent it. Her reply was as patient and kind as if she had been answering a child.

"I had to do it, Hosy," she said. "After our talk this evenin' there was only one thing to do. It had to be done—for your sake, if nothin' else—and so I did it. But—but—" with a choking sob, "it was SO hard to do! My Ardelia's baby!"

And at last, I am glad to say, I began to realize how very hard it had been for her. To understand what she had gone through for my sake and what a selfish brute I had been. I put my hands on her shoulders and kissed her almost reverently.

"Hephzy," said I, "you're a saint and a martyr and I am—what I am. Please forgive me."

"There isn't anything to forgive, Hosy. And," with a shake of the head, "I'm an awful poor kind of saint, I guess. They'd never put my image up in the churches over here—not if they knew how I felt this minute. And a saint from Cape Cod wouldn't be very welcome anyway, I'm afraid. I meant well, but that's a poor sort of recommendation. Oh, Hosy, you DO think I did for the best, don't you?"

"You did the only thing to be done," I answered, with decision. "You did what I lacked the courage to do. Of course it was best."

"You're awful good to say so, but I don't know. What'll come of it goodness knows. When I think of you and—and—"

"Don't think of me. I'm going to be a man if I can—a quahaug, if I can't. At least I'm not going to be what I have been for the last month."

"I know. But when I think of to-morrow and what she'll say to me, then, I—"

"You mustn't think. You must go to bed and so must I. To-morrow will take care of itself. Come. Let's both sleep and forget it."

Which was the very best of advice, but, like much good advice, impossible to follow. I did not sleep at all that night, nor did I forget. God help me! I was realizing that I never could forget.

At six o'clock I came downstairs, made a pretence at eating some biscuits and cheese which I found on the sideboard, scribbled a brief note to Hephzy stating that I had gone for a walk and should not be back to breakfast, and started out. The walk developed into a long one and I did not return to the rectory until nearly eleven in the forenoon. By that time I was in a better mood, more reconciled to the inevitable—or I thought I was. I believed I could play the man, could even see her married to Herbert Bayliss and still behave like a man. I vowed and revowed it. No one—no one but Hephzy and I should ever know what we knew.

Charlotte, the maid, seemed greatly relieved to see me. She hastened to the drawing-room.

"Here he is, Miss Cahoon," she said. "He's come back, ma'am. He's here."

"Of course I'm here, Charlotte," I said. "You didn't suppose I had run away, did you?... Why—why, Hephzy, what is the matter?"

For Hephzy was coming to meet me, her hands outstretched and on her face an expression which I did not understand—sorrow, agitation—yes, and pity—were in that expression, or so it seemed to me.

"Oh, Hosy!" she cried, "I'm so glad you've come. I wanted you so."

"Wanted me?" I repeated. "Why, what do you mean? Has anything happened?"

She nodded, solemnly.

"Yes," she said, "somethin' has happened. Somethin' we might have expected, perhaps, but—but—Hosy, read that."

I took what she handed me. It was a sheet of note paper, folded across, and with Hephzibah's name written upon one side. I recognized the writing and, with a sinking heart, unfolded it. Upon the other side was written in pencil this:

"I am going away. I could not stay, of course. When I think how I have stayed and how I have treated you both, who have been so very, very kind to me, I feel—I can't tell you how I feel. You must not think me ungrateful. You must not think of me at all. And you must not try to find me, even if you should wish to do such a thing. I have the money which I intended using for my new frocks and I shall use it to pay my expenses and my fare to the place I am going. It is your money, of course, and some day I shall send it to you. And someday, if I can, I shall repay all that you have spent on my account. But you must not follow me and you must not think of asking me to come back. That I shall never do. I do thank you for all that you have done for me, both of you. I cannot understand why you did it, but I shall always remember. Don't worry about me. I know what I am going to do and I shall not starve or be in want. Good-by. Please try to forget me.

"FRANCES MORLEY.

"Please tell Mr. Knowles that I am sorry for what I said to him this afternoon and so many times before. How he could have been so kind and patient I can't understand. I shall always remember it—always. Perhaps he may forgive me some day. I shall try and hope that he may."

I read to the end. Then, without speaking, I looked at Hephzy. Her eyes were brimming with tears.

"She has gone," she said, in answer to my unspoken question. "She must have gone some time in the night. The man at the inn stable drove her to the depot at Haddington on Hill. She took the early train for London. That is all we know."

CHAPTER XIII
In Which Hephzy and I Agree
to Live for Each Other

I shall condense the record of that day as much as possible. I should omit it altogether, if I could. We tried to trace her, of course. That is, I tried and Hephzy did not dissuade me, although she realized, I am sure, the hopelessness of the quest. Frances had left the rectory very early in the morning. The hostler at the inn had been much surprised to find her awaiting him when he came down to the yard at five o'clock. She was obliged to go to London, she said, and must take the very first train: Would he drive her to Haddington on Hill at once? He did so—probably she had offered him a great deal more than the regular fare—and she had taken the train.

Questioning the hostler, who was a surly, uncommunicative lout, resulted in my learning very little in addition to this. The young lady seemed about as usual, so far as he could see. She might 'ave been a bit nervous, impatient like, but he attributed that to her anxiety to make the train. Yes, she had a bag with her, but no other luggage. No, she didn't talk on the way to the station: Why should she? He wasn't the man to ask a lady questions about what wasn't his affair. She minded her own business and he minded his. No, he didn't know nothin' more about it. What was I a-pumpin' him for, anyway?

I gave up the "pumping" and hurried back to the rectory. There Hephzy told me a few additional facts. Frances had taken with her only the barest necessities, for the most part those which she had when she came to us. Her new frocks, those which she had bought with what she considered her money, she had left behind. All the presents which we had given her were in her room, or so we thought at the time. As she came, so she had gone, and the thought that she had gone, that I should never see her again, was driving me insane.

And like an insane man I must have behaved, at first. The things I did and said, and the way in which I treated Hephzy shame me now, as I remember them. I was going to London at once. I would find her and bring her back. I would seek help from the police, I would employ detectives, I would do anything—everything. She was almost without money; so far as I knew without friends. What would she do? What would become of her? I must find her. I must bring her back.

I stormed up and down the room, incoherently declaring my intentions and upbraiding Hephzy for not having sent the groom or the gardener to find me, for allowing all the precious time to elapse. Hephzy offered no excuse. She did not attempt justification. Instead she brought the railway time-table, gave orders that the horse be harnessed, helped me in every way. She would have prepared a meal for me with her own hands, would have fed me like a baby, if I had permitted it. One thing she did insist upon.

"You must rest a few minutes, Hosy," she said. "You must, or you'll be down sick. You haven't slept a wink all night. You haven't eaten anything to speak of since yesterday noon. You can't go this way. You must go to your room and rest a few minutes. Lie down and rest, if you can."

"Rest!"

"You must. The train doesn't leave Haddington for pretty nigh two hours, and we've got lots of time. I'll fetch you up some tea and toast or somethin' by and by and I'll be all ready to start when you are. Now go and lie down, Hosy dear, to please me."

I ignored the last sentence. "You will be ready?" I repeated. "Do you mean you're going with me?"

"Of course I am. It isn't likely I'll let you start off all alone, when you're in a state like this. Of course I'm goin' with you. Now go and lie down. You're so worn out, poor boy."

I must have had a glimmer of reason then, a trace of decency and unselfishness. For the first time I thought of her. I remembered that she, too, had loved Little Frank; that she, too, must be suffering.

"I am no more tired than you are," I said. "You have slept and eaten no more than I. You are the one who must rest. I sha'n't let you go with me."

"It isn't a question of lettin'. I shall go if you do, Hosy. And a woman don't need rest like a man. Please go upstairs and lie down, Hosy. Oh," with a sudden burst of feeling, "don't you see I've got about all I can bear as it is? I can't—I can't have YOU to worry about too."

My conscience smote me. "I'll go, Hephzy," said I. "I'll do whatever you wish; it is the least I can do."

She thanked me. Then she said, hesitatingly:

Kent Knowles | 209

"Here is—here is her letter, Hosy. You may like to read it again. Perhaps it may help you to decide what is best to do."

She handed me the letter. I took it and went to my room. There I read it again and again. And, as I read, the meaning of Hephzy's last sentence, that the letter might help me to decide what was best to do, began to force itself upon my overwrought brain. I began to understand what she had understood from the first, that my trip to London was hopeless, absolutely useless—yes, worse than useless.

"You must not try to find me... You must not follow me or think of asking me to come back. That I shall never do."

I was understanding, at last. I might go to London; I might even, through the help of the police, or by other means, find Frances Morley. But, having found her, what then? What claim had I upon her? What right had I to pursue her and force my presence upon her? I knew the shock she had undergone, the shattering of her belief in her father, the knowledge that she had—as she must feel—forced herself upon our kindness and charity. I knew how proud she was and how fiercely she had relented the slightest hint that she was in any way dependent upon us or under the least obligation to us. I knew all this and I was beginning to comprehend what her feelings toward us and toward herself must be—now.

I might find her—yes; but as for convincing her that she should return to Mayberry, to live with us as she had been doing, that was so clearly impossible as to seem ridiculous even to me. My following her, my hunting her down against her expressed wish, would almost surely make matters worse. She would probably refuse to see me. She would consider my following her a persecution and the result might be to drive her still further away. I must not do it, for her sake I must not. She had gone and, because I loved her, I must not follow her; I must not add to her misery. No, against my will I was forcing myself to realize that my duty was to make no attempt to see her again, but to face the situation as it was, to cover the running away with a lie, to pretend she had gone—gone somewhere or other with our permission and understanding; to protect her name from scandal and to conceal my own feelings from all the world. That was my duty; that was the situation I must face. But how could I face it!

That hour was the worst I have ever spent and I trust I may never be called upon to face such another. But, at last, I am glad to say, I had made up my mind, and when Hephzy came with the tea and toast I was measurably composed and ready to express my determination.

"Hephzy," said I, "I am not going to London. I have been thinking, and I'm not going."

Hephzy put down the tray she was carrying. She did seem surprised, but I am sure she was relieved.

"You're not goin'!" she exclaimed. "Why, Hosy!"

"No, I am not going. I've been crazy, Hephzy, I think, but I am fairly sane now. I have reached the conclusion that you reached sometime ago, I am certain. We have no right to follow her. Our finding her would only make it harder for her and no good could come of it. She went, of her own accord, and we must let her go."

"Let her go? And not try—"

"No. We have no right to try. You know it as well as I do. Now, be honest, won't you?"

Hephzy hesitated.

"Why," she faltered; "well, I—Oh, Hosy, I guess likely you're right. At first I was all for goin' after her right away and bringin' her back by main strength, if I had to. But the more I thought of it the more I—I—"

"Of course," I interrupted. "It is the only thing we can do. You must have been ashamed of me this morning. Well, I'll try and give you no cause to be ashamed again. That part of our lives is over. Now we'll start afresh."

Hephzy, after a long look at my face, covered her own with her hands and began to cry. I stepped to her side, but she recovered almost immediately.

"There! there!" she said, "don't mind me, Hosy. I've been holdin' that cry back for a long spell. Now I've had it and it's over and done with. After all, you and I have got each other left and we'll start fresh, just as you say. And the first thing is for you to eat that toast and drink that tea."

I smiled, or tried to smile.

"The first thing," I declared, "is for us to decide what story we shall tell young Bayliss and the rest of the people to account for her leaving so suddenly. I expect Herbert Bayliss here any moment. He came to see me about—about her last evening."

Hephzy nodded.

"I guessed as much," she said. "I knew he came and I guessed what 'twas about. Poor fellow, 'twill be dreadful hard for him, too. He was here this mornin' and I said Frances had been called away sudden and wouldn't be back to-day. And I said you would be away all day, too, Hosy. It was a fib, I guess, but I can't help it if it was. You mustn't see him now and you mustn't talk with me either. You must clear off that tray the first thing. We'll have our talk to-morrow, maybe. We'll—we'll see the course plainer then, perhaps. Now be a good boy and mind me. You ARE my boy, you know, and always will be, no matter how old and famous you get."

Herbert Bayliss called again that afternoon. I did not see him, but Hephzy did. The young fellow was frightfully disappointed at Frances' sudden departure and asked all sorts of questions as to when she would return, her London address and the like. Hephzy dodged the questions as best she could, but we both foresaw that soon he would have to be told some portion of the truth—not the whole truth; he need never know that, but something—and that something would be very hard to tell.

The servants, too, must not know or surmise what had happened or the reason for it. Hephzy had already given them some excuse, fabricated on the spur of the moment. They knew Miss Morley had gone away and might not return for some time. But we realized that upon our behavior depended a great deal and so we agreed to appear as much like our ordinary selves as possible.

It was a hard task. I shall never forget those first meals when we two were alone. We did not mention her name, but the shadow was always there—the vacant place at the table where she used to sit, the roses she had picked the morning before; and, afterward, in the drawing-room, the piano with her music upon the rack—the hundred and one little reminders that were like so many poisoned needles to aggravate my suffering and to remind me of the torture of the days to come. She had bade me forget her. Forget! I might forget when I was dead, but not before. If I could only die then and there it would seem so easy by comparison.

The next forenoon Hephzy and I had our talk. We discussed our future. Should we leave the rectory and England and go back to Bayport where we belonged? I was in favor of this, but Hephzy seemed reluctant. She, apparently, had some reason which made her wish to remain for a time, at least. At last the reason was disclosed.

"I supposed you'll laugh at me when I say it, Hosy," she said; "or at any rate you'll think I'm awful silly. But I know—I just KNOW that this isn't the end. We shall see her again, you and I. She'll come to us again or we'll go to her. I know it; somethin' inside me tells me so."

I shook my head.

"It's true," she went on. "You don't believe it, but it's true. It's a presentiment and you haven't believed in my presentiments before, but they've come true. Why, you didn't believe we'd ever find Little Frank at all, but we did. And do you suppose all that has happened so far has been just for nothin'? Indeed and indeed it hasn't. No, this isn't the end; it's only the beginnin'."

Her conviction was so strong that I hadn't the heart to contradict her. I said nothing.

"And that's why," she went on, "I don't like to have us leave here right away. She knows we're here, here in England, and if—if she ever should be in trouble and need our help she could find us here waitin' to give it. If we was away off on the Cape, way on the other side of the ocean, she couldn't reach us, or not until 'twas too late anyhow. That's why I'd like to stay here a while longer, Hosy. But," she hastened to add, "I wouldn't stay a minute if you really wanted to go."

I was silent for a moment. The temptation was to go, to get as far from the scene of my trouble as I could; but, after all, what did it matter? I could never flee from that trouble.

"All right, Hephzy," I said. "I'll stay, if it pleases you."

"Thank you, Hosy. It may be foolish, our stayin', but I don't believe it is. And—and there's somethin' else. I don't know whether I ought to tell you or not. I don't know whether it will make you feel better or worse. But I've heard you say that she must hate you. She doesn't—I know she doesn't. I've been lookin' over her things, those she left in her room. Everythin' we've given her or bought for her since she's been here, she left behind—every single thing except one. That little pin you bought for her in London the last time you was there and gave her to wear at the Samsons' lawn party, I can't find it anywhere. She must have taken it with her. Now why should she take that and leave all the rest?"

"Probably she forgot it," I said.

"Humph! Queer she should forget that and nothin' else. I don't believe she forgot it. *I* think she took it because you gave it to her and she wanted to keep it to remind her of you."

I dismissed the idea as absurd, but I found a ray of comfort in it which I should have been ashamed to confess. The idea that she wished to be reminded of me was foolish, but—but I was glad she had forgotten to leave the pin. It MIGHT remind her of me, even against her will.

A day or two later Herbert Bayliss and I had our delayed interview. He had called several times, but Hephzy had kept him out of my way. This time our meeting was in the main street of Mayberry, when dodging him was an impossibility. He hurried up to me and seized my hand.

"So you're back, Knowles," he said. "When did you return?"

For the moment I was at a loss to understand his meaning. I had forgotten Hephzy's "fib" concerning my going away. Fortunately he did not wait for an answer.

"Did Frances—did Miss Morley return with you?" he asked eagerly.

"No," said I.

His smile vanished.

"Oh!" he said, soberly. "She is still in London, then?"

"I—I presume she is."

"You presume—? Why, I say! don't you know?"

"I am not sure."

He seemed puzzled and troubled, but he was too well bred to ask why I was not sure. Instead he asked when she would return. I announced that I did not know that either.

"You don't know when she is coming back?" he repeated.

"No."

He regarded me keenly. There was a change in the tone of his next remark.

"You are not sure that she is in London and you don't know when she is coming back," he said, slowly. "Would you mind telling me why she left Mayberry so suddenly? She had not intended going; at least she did not mention her intention to me."

"She did not mention it to anyone," I answered. "It was a very sudden determination on her part."

He considered this.

"It would seem so," he said. "Knowles, you'll excuse my saying it, but this whole matter seems deucedly odd to me. There is something which I don't understand. You haven't answered my question. Under the circumstances, considering our talk the other evening, I think I have a right to ask it. Why did she leave so suddenly?"

I hesitated. Mayberry's principal thoroughfare was far from crowded, but it was scarcely the place for an interview like this.

"She had a reason for leaving," I answered, slowly. "I will tell you later, perhaps, what it was. Just now I cannot."

"You cannot!" he repeated. He was evidently struggling with his impatience and growing suspicious. "You cannot! But I think I have a right to know."

"I appreciate your feelings, but I cannot tell you now."

"Why not?"

"Because—Well, because I don't think it would be fair to her. She would not wish me to tell you."

"She would not wish it? Was it because of me she left?"

"No; not in the least."

"Was it—was it because of someone else? By Jove! it wasn't because of that Heathcroft cad? Don't tell me that! My God! she—she didn't—"

I interrupted. His suspicion angered me. I should have understood his feelings, should have realized that he had been and was disappointed and agitated and that my answers to his questions must have aroused all sorts of fears and forebodings in his mind. I should have pitied him, but just then I had little pity for others.

"She did nothing but what she considered right," I said sharply. "Her leaving had nothing to do with Heathcroft or with you. I doubt if she thought of either of you at all."

It was a brutal speech, and he took it like a man. I saw him turn pale and bite his lips, but when he next spoke it was in a calmer tone.

"I'm sorry," he said. "I was a silly ass even to think such a thing. But—but you see, Knowles, I—I—this means so much to me. I'm sorry, though. I ask her pardon and yours."

I was sorry, too. "Of course I didn't mean that, exactly," I said. "Her feelings toward you are of the kindest, I have no doubt, but her reason for leaving was a purely personal one. You were not concerned in it."

He reflected. He was far from satisfied, naturally, and his next speech showed it.

"It is extraordinary, all this," he said. "You are quite sure you don't know when she is coming back?"

"Quite."

"Would you mind giving me her London address?"

"I don't know it."

"You don't KNOW it! Oh, I say! that's damned nonsense! You don't know when she is coming back and you don't know her address! Do you mean you don't know where she has gone?"

"Yes."

"What—? Are you trying to tell me she is not coming back at all?"

"I am afraid not."

He was very pale. He seized my arm.

"What is all this?" he demanded, fiercely. "What has happened? Tell me; I want to know. Where is she? Why did she go? Tell me!"

"I can tell you nothing," I said, as calmly as I could. "She left us very suddenly and she is not coming back. Her reason for leaving I can't tell you, now. I don't know where she is and I have no right to try and find out. She has asked that no one follow her or interfere with her in any way. I respect her wish and I advise you, if you wish to remain her friend, to do the same, for the present, at least. That is all I can tell you."

He shook my arm savagely.

"By George!" he cried, "you must tell me. I'll make you! I—I—Do you think me a fool? Do you suppose I believe such rot as that? You tell me she has gone—has left Mayberry—and you don't know where she has gone and don't intend trying to find out. Why—"

"There, Bayliss! that is enough. This is not the place for us to quarrel. And there is no reason why we should quarrel at all. I have told you all that I can tell you now. Some day I may tell you more, but until then you must be patient, for her sake. Her leaving Mayberry had no connection with you whatever. You must be contented with that."

"Contented! Why, man, you're mad. She is your niece. You are her guardian and—"

"I am not her guardian. Neither is she my niece."

I had spoken involuntarily. Certainly I had not intended telling him that. The speech had the effect of causing him to drop my arm and step back. He stared at me blankly. No doubt he did think me crazy, then.

"I have no authority over her in any way," I went on. "She is Miss Cahoon's niece, but we are not her guardians. She has left our home of her own free will and neither I nor you nor anyone else shall follow her if I can help it. I am sorry to have deceived you. The deceit was unavoidable, or seemed to be. I am very, very sorry for you. That is all I can say now. Good morning."

I left him standing there in the street and walked away. He called after me, but I did not turn back. He would have followed me, of course, but when I did look back I saw that the landlord of the inn was trying to talk with him and was detaining him. I was glad that the landlord had appeared so opportunely. I had said too much already. I had bungled this interview as I had that with Heathcroft.

I told Hephzy all about it. She appeared to think that, after all, perhaps it was best.

"When you've got a toothache," she said, "you might as well go to the dentist's right off. The old thing will go on growlin' and grumblin' and it's always there to keep you in misery. You'd have had to tell him some time. Well, you've told him now, the worst of it, anyhow. The tooth's out; though," with a one-sided smile, "I must say you didn't give the poor chap any ether to help along."

"I'm afraid it isn't out," I said, truthfully. "He won't be satisfied with one operation."

"Then I'll be on hand to help with the next one. And, between us, I cal'late we can make that final. Poor boy! Well, he's young, that's one comfort. You get over things quicker when you're young."

I nodded. "That is true," I said, "but there is something else, Hephzy. You say I have acted for the best. Have I? I don't know. We know he cares for her, but—but does she—"

"Does she care for him, you mean? I don't think so, Hosy. For a spell I thought she did, but now I doubt it. I think—Well, never mind what I think. I think a lot of foolish things. My brain's softenin' up, I shouldn't wonder. It's a longshore brain, anyhow, and it needs the salt to keep it from spoilin'. I wish you and I could go clammin'. When you're diggin' clams you're too full of backache to worry about toothaches—or heartaches, either."

I expected a visit from young Bayliss that very evening, but he did not come to the rectory. Instead Doctor Bayliss, Senior, came and requested an interview with me. Hephzy announced the visitor.

"He acts pretty solemn, Hosy," she said. "I wouldn't wonder if his son had told him. I guess it's another toothache. Would you like to have me stay and help?"

I said I should be glad of her help. So, when the old gentleman was shown into the study, he found her there with me. The doctor was very grave and his usually ruddy, pleasant face was haggard and careworn. He took the chair which I offered him and, without preliminaries, began to speak of the subject which had brought him there.

It was as Hephzy had surmised. His son had told him everything, of his love for Frances, of his asking my permission to marry her, and of our talk before the inn.

"I am sure I don't need to tell you, Knowles," he said, "that all this has shaken the boy's mother and me dreadfully. We knew, of course, that the young people liked each other, were together a great deal, and all that. But we had not dreamed of any serious attachment between them."

Hephzy put in a word.

"We don't know as there has been any attachment between them," she said. "Your boy cared for her—we know that—but whether she cared for him or not we don't know."

Our visitor straightened in his chair. The idea that his son could love anyone and not be loved in return was plainly quite inconceivable.

"I think we may take that for granted, madame," he said. "The news was, as I say, a great shock to my wife and myself. Herbert is our only child and we had, naturally, planned somewhat concerning his future. The—the overthrow of our plans was and is a great grief and disappointment to us. Not, please understand, that we question your niece's worth or anything of that sort. She is a very attractive young woman and would doubtless make my son a good wife. But, if you will pardon my saying so, we know very little about her or her family. You are comparative strangers to us and although we have enjoyed your—ah—society and—ah—"

Hephzy interrupted.

"I beg your pardon for saying it, Doctor Bayliss," she said, "but you know as much about us as we do about you."

The doctor's composure was ruffled still more. He regarded Hephzy through his spectacles and then said, with dignity.

"Madame, I have resided in this vicinity for nearly forty years. I think my record and that of my family will bear inspection."

"I don't doubt it a bit. But, as far as that goes, I have lived in Bayport for fifty-odd years myself and our folks have lived there for a hundred and fifty. I'm not questionin' you or your family, Doctor Bayliss. If I had questioned 'em I could easily have looked up the record. All I'm sayin' is that I haven't thought of questionin', and I don't just see why you shouldn't take as much for granted as I have."

The old gentleman was a bit disconcerted. He cleared his throat and fidgeted in his seat.

"I do—I do, Miss Cahoon, of course," he said. "But—ah—Well, to return to the subject of my son and Miss Morley. The boy is dreadfully agitated, Mr. Knowles. He is quite mad about the girl and his mother and I are much concerned about him. We would—I assure you we would do anything and sacrifice anything for his sake. We like your niece, and, although, as I say, we had planned otherwise, nevertheless we will—provided all is as it should be—give our consent to—to the arrangement, for his sake."

I did not answer. The idea that marrying Frances Morley would entail a sacrifice upon anyone's part except hers angered me and I did not trust myself to speak. But Hephzy spoke for me.

"What do you mean by providin' everything is as it should be?" she asked.

"Why, I mean—I mean provided we learn that she is—is—That is,— Well, one naturally likes to know something concerning his prospective daughter-in-law's history, you know. That is to be expected, now isn't it."

Hephzy looked at me and I looked at her.

"Doctor," she said. "I wonder if your son told you about some things Hosy—Mr. Knowles, I mean—told him this mornin'. Did he tell you that?"

The doctor colored slightly. "Yes—yes, he did," he admitted. "He said he had a most extraordinary sort of interview with Mr. Knowles and was told by him some quite extraordinary things. Of course, we could scarcely believe that he had heard aright. There was some mistake, of course."

"There was no mistake, Doctor Bayliss," said I. "I told your son the truth, a very little of the truth."

"The truth! But it couldn't be true, you know, as Herbert reported it to me. He said Miss Morley had left Mayberry, had gone away for some unexplained reason, and was not coming back—that you did not know where she had gone, that she had asked not to be hindered or followed or something. And he said—My word! he even said you, Knowles, had declared yourself to be neither her uncle nor her guardian. THAT couldn't be true, now could it!"

Again Hephzy and I looked at each other. Without speaking we reached the same conclusion. Hephzy voiced that conclusion.

"I guess, Doctor Bayliss," she said, "that the time has come when you had better be told the whole truth, or as much of the whole truth about Frances as Hosy and I know. I'm goin' to tell it to you. It's a kind of long story, but I guess likely you ought to know it."

She began to tell that story, beginning at the very beginning, with Ardelia and Strickland Morley and continuing on, through the history of the latter's rascality and the fleeing of the pair from America, to our own pilgrimage, the finding of Little Frank and the astonishing happenings since.

"She's gone," she said. "She found out what sort of man her father really was and, bein' a high-spirited, proud girl—as proud and high-spirited as she is clever and pretty and good—she ran away and left us. We don't blame her, Hosy and I. We understand just how she feels and we've made up our minds to do as she asks and not try to follow her or try to bring her back to us against her will. We think the world of her. We haven't known her but a little while, but we've come—that is," with a sudden glance in my direction, "I've come to love her as if she was my own. It pretty nigh kills me to have her go. When I think of her strugglin' along tryin' to earn her own way by singin' and—and all, I have to hold myself by main strength to keep from goin' after her and beggin' her on my knees to come back. But I sha'n't do it, because she doesn't want me to. Of course I hope and believe that some day she will come back, but until she does and of her own accord, I'm goin' to wait. And, if your son really cares for her as much as we—as I do, he'll wait, too."

She paused and hastily dabbed at her eyes with her handkerchief. I turned in order that the Doctor might not see my face. It was an unnecessary precaution. Doctor Bayliss' mind was busy, apparently, with but one thought.

"An opera singer!" he exclaimed, under his breath. "An opera singer! Herbert to marry an opera singer! The granddaughter of a Yankee sailor and—and—"

"And the daughter of an English thief," put in Hephzy, sharply. "Maybe we'd better leave nationalities out, Doctor Bayliss. The Yankees have the best end of it, 'cordin' to my notion."

He paid no attention to this.

He was greatly upset. "It is impossible!" he declared. "Absolutely impossible! Why haven't we known of this before? Why did not Herbert know of it? Mr. Knowles, I must say that—that you have been most unthinking in this matter."

"I have been thinking of her," I answered, curtly. "It was and is her secret and we rely upon you to keep it as such. We trust to your honor to tell no one, not even your son."

"My son! Herbert? Why I must tell him! I must tell my wife."

"You may tell your wife. And your son as much as you think necessary. Further than that it must not go."

"Of course, of course. I understand. But an opera singer!"

"She isn't a real opera singer," said Hephzy. "That is, not one of those great ones. And she told me once that she realized now that she never could be. She has a real sweet voice, a beautiful voice, but it isn't powerful enough to make her a place in the big companies. She tried and tried, she said, but all the managers said the same thing."

"Hephzy," I said, "when did she tell you this? I didn't know of it."

"I know you didn't, Hosy. She told me one day when we were alone. It was the only time she ever spoke of herself and she didn't say much then. She spoke about her livin' with her relatives here in England and what awful, mean, hard people they were. She didn't say who they were nor where they lived, but she did say she ran away from them to go on the stage as a singer and what trials and troubles she went through afterward. She told me that much and then she seemed sorry that she had. She made me promise not to tell anyone, not even you. I haven't, until now."

Doctor Bayliss was sitting with a hand to his forehead.

"A provincial opera singer," he repeated. "Oh, impossible! Quite impossible!"

"It may seem impossible to you," I couldn't help observing, "but I question if it will seem so to your son. I doubt if her being an opera singer will make much difference to him."

The doctor groaned. "The boy is mad about her, quite mad," he admitted.

I was sorry for him. Perhaps if I were in his position I might feel as he did.

"I will say this," I said: "In no way, so far as I know, has Miss Morley given your son encouragement. He told me himself that he had never spoken to her of his feelings and we have no reason to think that she regards him as anything more than a friend. She left no message for him when she went away."

He seemed to find some ground for hope in this. He rose from the chair and extended his hand.

"Knowles," he said, "if I have said anything to hurt your feelings or those of Miss Cahoon I am very sorry. I trust it will make no difference in our friendship. My wife and I respect and like you both and I think I understand how deeply you must feel the loss of your—of Miss Morley. I hope she—I hope you may be reunited some day. No doubt you will be. As for Herbert—he is our son and if you ever have a son of your own, Mr. Knowles, you may appreciate his mother's feelings and mine. We have planned and—and—Even now I should not stand in the way of his happiness if—if I believed happiness could come of it. But such marriages are never happy. And," with a sudden burst of hope, "as you say, she may not be aware of his attachment. The boy is young. He may forget."

"Yes," said I, with a sigh. "He IS young, and he may forget."

After he had gone Hephzy turned to me.

"If I hadn't understood that old man's feelin's," she declared, "I'd have given him one talkin' to. The idea of his speakin' as if Frances wouldn't be a wife anybody, a lord or anybody else, might be proud of! But he didn't know. He's been brought up that way, and he doesn't know. And, of course, his son IS the only person on earth to him. Well, that's over! We haven't got to worry about them any more. We'll begin to live for each other now, Hosy, same as we used to do. And we'll wait for the rest. It'll come and come right for all of us. Just you see."

CHAPTER XIV
In Which I Play Golf and Cross the Channel

And so we began "to live for each other again," Hephzy and I. This meant, of course, that Hephzy forgot herself entirely and spent the greater part of her time trying to find ways to make my living more comfortable, just as she had always done. And I—well, I did my best to appear, if not happy, at least reasonably calm and companionable. It was a hard job for both of us; certainly my part of it was hard enough.

Appearances had to be considered and so we invented a tale of a visit to relatives in another part of England to account for the unannounced departure of Miss Morley. This excuse served with the neighbors and friends not in the secret and, for the benefit of the servants, Hephzy elaborated the deceit by pretending eagerness at the arrival of the mails and by certain vague remarks at table concerning letters she was writing.

"I AM writing 'em, too, Hosy," she said. "I write to her every few days. Of course I don't mail the letters, but it sort of squares things with my conscience to really write after talking so much about it. As for her visitin' relatives—well, she's got relatives somewhere in England, we know that much, and she MAY be visitin' 'em. At any rate I try to think she is. Oh, dear, I 'most wish I'd had more experience in tellin' lies; then I wouldn't have to invent so many extra ones to make me believe those I told at the beginnin'. I wish I'd been brought up a book agent or a weather prophet or somethin' like that; then I'd have been in trainin'."

Without any definite agreement we had fallen into the habit of not mentioning the name of Little Frank, even when we were alone together. In consequence, on these occasions, there would be long intervals of silence suddenly broken by Hephzy's bursting out with a surmise concerning what was happening in Bayport, whether they had painted the public library building yet, or how Susanna was getting on with the cat and hens. She had received three letters from Miss Wixon and, as news bearers, they were far from satisfactory.

"That girl makes me so provoked," sniffed Hephzy, dropping the most recent letter in her lap with a gesture of disgust. "She says she's got a cold in the head and she's scared to death for fear it'll get 'set onto her,' whatever that is. Two pages of this letter is nothin' but cold in the head and t'other two is about a new hat she's goin' to have and she don't know whether to trim it with roses or forget-me-nots. If she trimmed it with cabbage 'twould match her head better'n anything else. I declare! she ought to be thankful she's got a cold in a head like hers; it must be comfortin' to know there's SOMETHIN' there. You've got a letter, too, Hosy. Who is it from?"

"From Campbell," I answered, wearily. "He wants to know how the novel is getting on, of course."

"Humph! Well, you write him that it's gettin' on the way a squid gets ahead—by goin' backwards. Don't let him pester you one bit, Hosy. You write that novel just as fast or slow as you feel like. He told you to take a vacation, anyway."

I smiled. Mine was a delightful vacation.

The summer dragged on. The days passed. Pleasant days they were, so far as the weather was concerned. I spent them somehow, walking, riding, golfing, reading. I gave up trying to work; the half-written novel remained half written. I could not concentrate my thoughts upon it and I lacked the courage to force myself to try. I wrote Campbell that he must be patient, I was doing the best I could. He answered by telling me not to worry, to enjoy myself. "Why do you stay there in England?" he wrote. "I ordered you to travel, not to plant yourself in one place and die of dry rot. A British oyster is mighty little improvement on a Cape Cod quahaug. You have been in that rectory about long enough. Go to Monte Carlo for change. You'll find it there—or lose it."

It may have been good advice—or bad—according to the way in which it was understood, but, good or bad, it didn't appeal to me. I had no desire to travel, unless it were to travel back to Bayport, where I belonged. I felt no interest in Monte Carlo—for the matter of that, I felt no interest in Mayberry or anywhere else. I was not interested in anything or anybody—except one, and that one had gone out of my life. Night after night I went to sleep determining to forget and morning after morning I awoke only to remember, and with the same dull, hopeless heartache and longing.

July passed, August was half gone. Still we remained at the rectory. Our lease was up on the first of October. The Coles would return then and we should be obliged to go elsewhere, whether we wished to or not. Hephzy, although she did not say much about it, was willing to go, I think. Her "presentiment" had remained only a presentiment so far; no word came from Little Frank. We had heard or learned nothing concerning her or her whereabouts.

Our neighbors and friends in Mayberry were as kind and neighborly as ever. For the first few days after our interview with Doctor Bayliss, Senior, Hephzy and I saw nothing of him or his family. Then the doctor called again. He seemed in better spirits. His son had yielded to his parents' entreaties and had departed for a walking tour through the Black Forest with some friends.

"The invitation came at exactly the right time," said the old gentleman. "Herbert was ready to go anywhere or do anything. The poor boy was in the depths and when his mother and I urged him to accept he did so. We are hoping that when he returns he will have forgotten, or, if not that, at least be more reconciled."

Heathcroft came and went at various times during the summer. I met him on the golf course and he was condescendingly friendly as ever. Our talk concerning Frances, which had brought such momentous consequences to her and to Hephzy and to me, had, apparently, not disturbed him in the least. He greeted me blandly and cheerfully, asked how we all were, said he had been given to understand that "my charming little niece" was no longer with us, and proceeded to beat me two down in eighteen holes. I played several times with him afterward and, under different circumstances, should have enjoyed doing so, for we were pretty evenly matched.

His aunt, the Lady of the Manor, I also met. She went out of her way to be as sweetly gracious as possible. I presume she inferred from Frances' departure that I had taken her hint and had removed the disturbing influence from her nephew's primrose-bordered path. At each of our meetings she spoke of the "invitation golf tournament," several times postponed and now to be played within a fortnight. She insisted that I must take part in it. At last, having done everything except decline absolutely, I finally consented to enter the tournament. It is not easy to refuse to obey an imperial decree and Lady Carey was Empress of Mayberry.

After accepting I returned to the rectory to find that Hephzy also had received an invitation. Not to play golf, of course; her invitation was of a totally different kind.

"What do you think, Hosy!" she cried. "I've got a letter and you can't guess who it's from."

"From Susanna?" I ventured.

"Susanna! You don't suppose I'd be as excited as all this over a letter from Susanna Wixon, do you? No indeed! I've got a letter from Mrs. Hepton, who had the Nickerson cottage last summer. She and her husband are in Paris and they want us to meet 'em there in a couple of weeks and go for a short trip through Switzerland. They got our address from Mr. Campbell before they left home. Mrs. Hepton writes that they're countin' on our company. They're goin' to Lake Lucerne and to Mont Blanc and everywhere. Wouldn't it be splendid!"

The Heptons had been summer neighbors of ours on the Cape for several seasons. They were friends of Jim Campbell's and had first come to Bayport on his recommendation. I liked them very well, and, oddly enough, for I was not popular with the summer colony, they had seemed to like me.

"It was very kind of them to think of us," I said. "Campbell shouldn't have given them our address, of course, but their invitation was well meant. You must write them at once. Make our refusal as polite as possible."

Hephzy seemed disappointed, I thought.

"Then you think I'd better say no?" she observed.

"Why, of course. You weren't thinking of accepting, were you?"

"Well, I didn't know. I'm not sure that our goin' wouldn't be the right thing. I've been considerin' for some time, Hosy, and I've about come to the conclusion that stayin' here is bad for you. Maybe it's bad for both of us. Perhaps a change would do us both good."

I was astonished. "Humph!" I exclaimed; "this is a change of heart, Hephzy. A while ago, when I suggested going back to Bayport, you wouldn't hear of it. You wanted to stay here and—and wait."

"I know I did. And I've been waitin', but nothin' has come of it. I've still got my presentiment, Hosy. I believe just as strong as I ever did that some time or other she and you and I will be together again. But stayin' here and seein' nobody but each other and broodin' don't do us any good. It's doin' you harm; that's plain enough. You don't write and you don't eat—that is, not much—and you're gettin' bluer and more thin and peaked every day. You have just got to go away from here, no matter whether I do or not. And I've reached the point where I'm willin' to go, too. Not for good, maybe. We'll come back here again. Our lease isn't up until October and we can leave the servants here and give them our address to have mail forwarded. If—if she—that is, if a letter or—or anything—SHOULD come we could hurry right back. The Heptons are real nice folks; you always liked 'em, Hosy. And you always wanted to see Switzerland; you used to say so. Why don't we say yes and go along?"

I did not answer. I believed I understood the reason for Campbell's giving our address to the Heptons; also the reason for the invitation. Jim was very anxious to have me leave Mayberry; he believed travel and change of scene were what I needed. Doubtless he had put the Heptons up to asking us to join them on their trip. It was merely an addition to his precious prescription.

"Why don't we go?" urged Hephzy.

"Not much!" I answered, decidedly. "I should be poor company on a pleasure trip like that. But you might go, Hephzy. There is no reason in the world why you shouldn't go. I'll stay here until you return. Go, by all means, and enjoy yourself."

Hephzy shook her head.

"I'd do a lot of enjoyin' without you, wouldn't I," she observed. "While I was lookin' at the scenery I'd be wonderin' what you had for breakfast. Every mite of rain would set me to thinkin' of your gettin' your feet wet and when I laid eyes on a snow peak I'd wonder if you had blankets enough on your bed. I'd be like that yellow cat we used to have back in the time when Father was alive. That cat had kittens and Father had 'em all drowned but one. After that you never saw the cat anywhere unless the kitten was there, too. She wouldn't eat unless it were with her and between bites she'd sit down on it so it couldn't run off. She lugged it around in her mouth until Father used to vow he'd have eyelet holes punched in the scruff of its neck for her teeth to fit into and make it easier for both of 'em. It died, finally; she wore it out, I guess likely. Then she adopted a chicken and started luggin' that around. She had the habit, you see. I'm a good deal like her, Hosy. I've took care of you so long that I've got the habit. No, I shouldn't go unless you did."

No amount of urging moved her, so we dropped the subject.

The morning of the golf tournament was clear and fine. I shouldered my bag of clubs and walked through the lane toward the first tee. I never felt less like playing or more inclined to feign illness and remain at home. But I had promised Lady Carey and the promise must be kept.

There was a group of people, players and guests, awaiting me at the tee. Her ladyship was there, of course; so also was her nephew, Mr. Carleton Heathcroft, whom I had not seen for some time. Heathcroft was in conversation with a young fellow who, when he turned in my direction, I recognized as Herbert Bayliss. I was surprised to see him; I had not heard of his return from the Black Forest trip.

Lady Carey was affable and gracious, also very important and busy. She welcomed me absent-mindedly, introduced me to several of her guests, ladies and gentlemen from London down for the week-end, and then bustled away to confer with Mr. Handliss, steward of the estate, concerning the arrangements for the tournament. I felt a touch on my arm and, turning, found Doctor Bayliss standing beside me. He was smiling and in apparent good humor.

"The boy is back, Knowles," he said. "Have you seen him?"

"Yes," said I, "I have seen him, although we haven't met yet. I was surprised to find him here. When did he return?"

"Only yesterday. His mother and I were surprised also. We hadn't expected him so soon. He's looking very fit, don't you think?"

"Very." I had not noticed that young Bayliss was looking either more or less fit than usual, but I answered as I did because the old gentleman seemed so very anxious that I should. He was evidently gratified. "Yes," he said, "he's looking very fit indeed. I think his trip has benefited him hugely. And I think—Yes, I think he is beginning to forget his—that is to say, I believe he does not dwell upon the—the recent happenings as he did. I think he is forgetting; I really think he is."

"Indeed," said I. It struck me that, if Herbert Bayliss was forgetting, his memory must be remarkably short. I imagined that his father's wish was parent to the thought.

"He has—ah—scarcely mentioned our—our young friend's name since his return," went on the doctor. "He did ask if you had heard—ah—by the way, Knowles, you haven't heard, have you?"

"No."

"Dear me! dear me! That's very odd, now isn't it?"

He did not say he was sorry. If he had said it I should not have believed him. If ever anything was plain it was that the longer we remained without news of Frances Morley the better pleased Herbert Bayliss's parents would be.

"But I say, Knowles," he added, "you and he must meet, you know. He doesn't hold any ill-feeling or—or resentment toward you. Really he doesn't. Herbert! Oh, I say, Herbert! Come here, will you."

Young Bayliss turned. The doctor whispered in my ear.

"Perhaps it would be just as well not to refer to—to—You understand me, Knowles. Better let sleeping dogs lie, eh? Oh, Herbert, here is Knowles waiting to shake hands with you."

We shook hands. The shake, on his part, was cordial enough, perhaps, but not too cordial. It struck me that young Bayliss was neither as "fit" nor as forgetful as his fond parents wished to believe. He looked rather worn and nervous, it seemed to me. I asked him about his tramping trip and we chatted for a few moments. Then Bayliss, Senior, was called by Lady Carey and Handliss to join the discussion concerning the tournament rules and the young man and I were left alone together.

"Knowles," he asked, the moment after his father's departure, "have you heard anything? Anything concerning—her?"

"No."

"You're sure? You're not—"

"I am quite sure. We haven't heard nor do we expect to."

He looked away across the course and I heard him draw a long breath.

"It's deucedly odd, this," he said. "How she could disappear so entirely I don't understand. And you have no idea where she may be?"

"No."

"But—but, confound it, man, aren't you trying to find her?"

"No."

"You're not! Why not?"

"You know why not as well as I. She left us of her own free will and her parting request was that we should not follow her. That is sufficient for us. Pardon me, but I think it should be for all her friends."

He was silent for a moment. Then his teeth snapped together.

"I'll find her," he declared, fiercely. "I'll find her some day."

"In spite of her request?"

"Yes. In spite of the devil."

He turned on his heel and walked off. Mr. Handliss stepped to the first tee, clapped his hands to attract attention and began a little speech.

The tournament, he said, was about to begin. Play would be, owing to the length and difficulty of the course, but eighteen holes instead of the usual thirty-six. This meant that each pair of contestants would play the nine holes twice. Handicaps had been fixed as equitably as possible according to each player's previous record, and players having similar handicaps were to play against each other. A light lunch and refreshments would be served after the first round had been completed by all. Prizes would be distributed by her ladyship when the final round was finished. Her ladyship bade us all welcome and was gratified by our acceptance of her invitation. He would now proceed to read the names of those who were to play against each other, stating handicaps and the like. He read accordingly, and I learned that my opponent was to be Mr. Heathcroft, each of us having a handicap of two.

Considering everything I thought my particular handicap a stiff one. Heathcroft had been in the habit of beating me in two out of three of our matches. However, I determined to play my best. Being the only outlander on the course I couldn't help feeling that the sporting reputation of Yankeeland rested, for this day at least, upon my shoulders.

The players were sent off in pairs, the less skilled first. Heathcroft and I were next to the last. A London attorney by the name of Jaynes and a Wrayton divine named Wilson followed us. Their rating was one plus and, judging by the conversation of the "gallery," they were looked upon as winners of the first and second prizes respectively. The Reverend Mr. Wilson was called, behind his back, "the sporting curate." In gorgeous tweeds and a shepherd's plaid cap he looked the part.

The first nine went to me. An usually long drive and a lucky putt on the eighth gave me the round by one. I played with care and tried my hardest to keep my mind on the game. Heathcroft was, as always, calm and careful, but between tees he was pleased to be chatty and affable.

"And how is the aunt with the odd name, Knowles?" he inquired. "Does she still devour her—er—washing flannels and treacle for breakfast?"

"She does when she cares to," I replied. "She is an independent lady, as I think you know."

"My word! I believe you. And how are the literary labors progressing? I had my bookselling fellow look up a novel of yours the other day. Began it that same night, by Jove! It was quite interesting, really. I should have finished it, I think, but some of the chaps at the club telephoned me to join them for a bit of bridge and of course that ended literature for the time. My respected aunt tells me I'm quite dotty on bridge. She foresees a gambler's end for me, stony broke, languishing in dungeons and all that sort of thing. I am to die of starvation, I think. Is it starvation gamblers die of? 'Pon my soul, I should say most of those I know would be more likely to die of thirst. Rather!"

Later on he asked another question.

"And how is the pretty niece, Knowles?" he inquired. "When is she coming back to the monastery or the nunnery or rectory, or whatever it is?"

"I don't know," I replied, curtly.

"Oh, I say! Isn't she coming at all? That would be a calamity, now wouldn't it? Not to me in particular. I should mind your notice boards, of course. But if I were condemned, as you are, to spend a summer among the feminine beauties of Mayberry, a face like hers would be like a whisky and soda in a thirsty land, as a chap I know is fond of saying. Oh, and by the way, speaking of your niece, I had a curious experience in Paris a week ago. Most extraordinary thing. For the moment I began to believe I really was going dotty, as Auntie fears. I... Your drive, Knowles. I'll tell you the story later."

He did not tell it during that round, forgot it probably. I did not remind him. The longer he kept clear of the subject of my "niece" the more satisfied I was. We lunched in the pavilion by the first tee. There were sandwiches and biscuits—crackers, of course—and cakes and sweets galore. Also thirst-quenching materials sufficient to satisfy even the gamblers of Mr. Heathcroft's acquaintance. The "sporting curate," behind a huge Scotch and soda, was relating his mishaps in approaching the seventh hole for the benefit of his brother churchmen, Messrs. Judson and Worcester. Lady Carey was dilating upon her pet subject, the talents and virtues of "Carleton, dear," for the benefit of the London attorney, who was pretending to listen with the respectful interest due blood and title, but who was thinking of something else, I am sure. "Carleton, dear," himself, was chatting languidly with young Bayliss. The latter seemed greatly interested. There was a curious expression on his face. I was surprised to see him so cordial to Heathcroft; I knew he did not like Lady Carey's nephew.

The second and final round of the tournament began. For six holes Heathcroft and I broke even. The seventh he won, making us square for the match so far and, with an equal number of strokes. The eighth we halved. All depended on the ninth. Halving there would mean a drawn match between us and a drawing for choice of prizes, provided we were in the prize-winning class. A win for either of us meant the match itself.

Heathcroft, in spite of the close play, was as bland and unconcerned as ever. I tried to appear likewise. As a matter of fact, I wanted to win. Not because of the possible prize, I cared little for that, but for the pleasure of winning against him. We drove from the ninth tee, each got a long brassy shot which put us on the edge of the green, and then strolled up the hill together.

"I say, Knowles," he observed; "I haven't finished telling you of my Paris experience, have I. Odd coincidence, by Jove! I was telling young Bayliss about it just now and he thought it odd, too. I was—some other chaps and I drifted into the Abbey over in Paris a week or so ago and while we were there a girl came out and sang. She was an extremely pretty girl, you understand, but that wasn't the extraordinary part of it. She was the image—my word! the very picture of your niece, Miss Morley. It quite staggered me for the moment. Upon my soul I thought it was she! She sang extremely well, but not for long. I tried to get near her—meant to speak to her, you know, but she had gone before I reached her. Eh! What did you say?"

I had not said anything—at least I think I had not. He misinterpreted my silence.

"Oh, you mustn't be offended," he said, laughing. "Of course I knew it wasn't she—that is, I should have known it if I hadn't been so staggered by the resemblance. It was amazing, that resemblance. The face, the voice—everything was like hers. I was so dotty about it that I even hunted up one of the chaps in charge and asked him who the girl was. He said she was an Austrian—Mademoiselle Juno or Junotte or something. That ended it, of course. I was a fool to imagine anything else, of course. But you would have been a bit staggered if you had seen her. And she didn't look Austrian, either. She looked English or American—rather! I say, I hope I haven't hurt your feelings, old chap. I apologize to you and Miss Morley, you understand. I couldn't help telling you; it was extraordinary now, wasn't it."

I made some answer. He rattled on about that sort of thing making one believe in the Prisoner of Zenda stuff, doubles and all that. We reached the green. My ball lay nearest the pin and it was his putt. He made it, a beauty, the ball halting just at the edge of the cup. My putt was wild. He holed out on the next shot. It took me two and I had to concentrate my thought by main strength even then. The hole and match were his.

He was very decent about it, proclaimed himself lucky, declared I had, generally speaking, played much the better game and should have won easily. I paid little attention to what he said although I did, of course, congratulate him and laughed at the idea that luck had anything to do with the result. I no longer cared about the match or the tournament in general or anything connected with them. His story of the girl who was singing in Paris was what I was interested in now. I wanted him to tell me more, to give me particulars. I wanted to ask him a dozen questions; and, yet, excited as I was, I realized that those questions must be asked carefully. His suspicions must not be aroused.

Before I could ask the first of the dozen Mr. Handliss bustled over to us to learn the result of our play and to announce that the distribution of prizes would take place in a few moments; also that Lady Carey wished to speak with her nephew. The latter sauntered off to join the group by the pavilion and my opportunity for questioning had gone, for the time.

Of the distribution of prizes, with its accompanying ceremony, I seem to recall very little. Lady Carey made a little speech, I remember that, but just what she said I have forgotten. "Much pleasure in rewarding skill," "Dear old Scottish game," "English sportsmanship," "Race not to the swift"—I must have been splashed with these drops from the fountain of oratory, for they stick in my memory. Then, in turn, the winners were called up to select their prizes. Wilson, the London attorney, headed the list; the sporting curate came next; Heathcroft next; and then I. It had not occurred to me that I should win a prize. In fact I had not thought anything about it. My thoughts were far from the golf course just then. They were in Paris, in a cathedral—Heathcroft had called it an abbey, but cathedral he must have meant—where a girl who looked like Frances Morley was singing.

However, when Mr. Handliss called my name I answered and stepped forward. Her Ladyship said something or other about "our cousin from across the sea" and "Anglo-Saxon blood" and her especial pleasure in awarding the prize. I stammered thanks, rather incoherently expressed they were, I fear, selected the first article that came to hand—it happened to be a cigarette case; I never smoke cigarettes—and retired to the outer circle. The other winners—Herbert Bayliss and Worcester among them—selected their prizes and then Mr. Wilson, winner of the tournament, speaking in behalf of us all, thanked the hostess for her kindness and hospitality.

Her gracious invitation to play upon the Manor-House course Mr. Wilson mentioned feelingly. Also the gracious condescension in presenting the prizes with her own hand. They would be cherished, not only for their own sake, but for that of the donor. He begged the liberty of proposing her ladyship's health.

The "liberty" was, apparently, expected, for Mr. Handliss had full glasses ready and waiting. The health was drunk. Lady Carey drank ours in return, and the ceremony was over.

I tried in vain to get another word with Heathcroft. He was in conversation with his aunt and several of the feminine friends and, although I waited for some time, I, at last, gave up the attempt and walked home. The Reverend Judson would have accompanied me, but I avoided him. I did not wish to listen to Mayberry gossip; I wanted to be alone.

Heathcroft's tale had made a great impression upon me—a most unreasonable impression, unwarranted by the scant facts as he related them. The girl whom he had seen resembled Frances—yes; but she was an Austrian, her name was not Morley. And resemblances were common enough. That

Frances should be singing in a Paris church was most improbable; but, so far as that went, the fact of A. Carleton Heathcroft's attending a church service I should, ordinarily, have considered improbable. Improbable things did happen. Suppose the girl he had seen was Frances. My heart leaped at the thought.

But even supposing it was she, what difference did it make—to me? None, of course. She had asked us not to follow her, to make no attempt to find her. I had preached compliance with her wish to Hephzy, to Doctor Bayliss—yes, to Herbert Bayliss that very afternoon. But Herbert Bayliss was sworn to find her, in spite of me, in spite of the Evil One. And Heathcroft had told young Bayliss the same story he had told me. HE would not be deterred by scruples; her wish would not prevent his going to Paris in search of her.

I reached the rectory, to be welcomed by Hephzy with questions concerning the outcome of the tournament and triumphant gloatings over my perfectly useless prize. I did not tell her of Heathcroft's story. I merely said I had met that gentleman and that Herbert Bayliss had returned to Mayberry. And I asked a question.

"Hephzy," I asked, "when do the Heptons leave Paris for their trip through Switzerland?"

Hephzy considered. "Let me see," she said. "Today is the eighteenth, isn't it. They start on the twenty-second; that's four days from now."

"Of course you have written them that we cannot accept their invitation to go along?"

She hesitated. "Why, no," she admitted, "I haven't. That is, I have written 'em, but I haven't posted the letter. Humph! did you notice that 'posted'? Shows what livin' in a different place'll do even to as settled a body as I am. In Bayport I should have said 'mailed' the letter, same as anybody else. I must be careful or I'll go back home and call the expressman a 'carrier' and a pie a 'tart' and a cracker a 'biscuit.' Land sakes! I remember readin' how David Copperfield's aunt always used to eat biscuits soaked in port wine before she went to bed. I used to think 'twas dreadful dissipated business and that the old lady must have been ready for bed by the time she got through. You see I always had riz biscuits in mind. A cracker's different; crackers don't soak up much. We'd ought to be careful how we judge folks, hadn't we, Hosy."

"Yes," said I, absently. "So you haven't posted the letter to the Heptons. Why not?"

"Well—well, to tell you the truth, Hosy, I was kind of hopin' you might change your mind and decide to go, after all. I wish you would; 'twould do you good. And," wistfully, "Switzerland must be lovely. But there! I know just how you feel, you poor boy. I'll mail the letter to-night."

"Give it to me," said I. "I'll—I'll see to it."

Hephzy handed me the letter. I put it in my pocket, but I did not post it that evening. A plan—or the possible beginning of a plan—was forming in my mind.

That night was another of my bad ones. The little sleep I had was filled with dreams, dreams from which I awoke to toss restlessly. I rose and walked the floor, calling myself a fool, a silly old fool, over and over again. But when morning came my plan, a ridiculous, wild plan from which, even if it succeeded—which was most unlikely—nothing but added trouble and despair could possibly come, my plan was nearer its ultimate formation.

At eleven o'clock that forenoon I walked up the marble steps of the Manor House and rang the bell. The butler, an exalted personage in livery, answered my ring. Mr. Heathcroft? No, sir. Mr. Heathcroft had left for London by the morning train. Her ladyship was in her boudoir. She did not see anyone in the morning, sir. I had no wish to see her ladyship, but Heathcroft's departure was a distinct disappointment. I thanked the butler and, remembering that even cathedral ushers accepted tips, slipped a shilling into his hand. His dignity thawed at the silver touch, and he expressed regret at Mr. Heathcroft's absence.

"You're not the only gentleman who has been here to see him this morning, sir," he said. "Doctor Bayliss, the younger one, called about an hour ago. He seemed quite as sorry to find him gone as you are, sir."

I think that settled it. When I again entered the rectory my mind was made up. The decision was foolish, insane, even dishonorable perhaps, but the decision was made.

"Hephzy," said I, "I have changed my mind. Travel may do me good. I have telegraphed the Heptons that we will join them in Paris on the evening of the twenty-first. After that—Well, we'll see."

Hephzy's delight was as great as her surprise. She said I was a dear, unselfish boy. Considering what I intended doing I felt decidedly mean; but I did not tell her what that intention was.

We took the two-twenty train from Charing Cross on the afternoon of the twenty-first. The servants had been left in charge of the rectory. We would return in a fortnight, so we told them.

It was a beautiful day, bright and sunshiny, but, after smoky, grimy London had been left behind and we were whizzing through the Kentish countryside, between the hop fields and the pastures where the sheep were feeding, we noticed that a stiff breeze was blowing. Further on, as we wound amid the downs near Folkestone, the bending trees and shrubs proved that the breeze was a miniature gale. And when we came in sight of the Channel, it was thickly sprinkled with whitecaps from beach to horizon.

"I imagine we shall have a rather rough passage, Hephzy," said I.

Hephzy's attention was otherwise engaged.

"Why do they call a hill a 'down' over here?" she asked. "I should think an 'up' would be better. What did you say, Hosy? A rough passage? I guess that won't bother you and me much. This little mite of water can't seem very much stirred up to folks who have sailed clear across the Atlantic Ocean. But there! I mustn't put on airs. I used to think Cape Cod Bay was about all the water there was. Travelin' does make such a difference in a person's ideas. Do you remember the Englishwoman at Bancroft's who told me that she supposed the Thames must remind us of our own Mississippi?"

"So that's the famous English Channel, is it," she observed, a moment later. "How wide is it, Hosy?"

"About twenty miles at the narrowest point, I believe," I said.

"Twenty miles! About as far as Bayport to Provincetown. Well, I don't know whether any of your ancestors or mine came over with William the Conquerer or not, but if they did, they didn't have far to come. I cal'late I'll be contented with having my folks cross in the Mayflower. They came three thousand miles anyway."

She was inclined to regard the Channel rather contemptuously just then. A half hour later she was more respectful.

The steamer was awaiting us at the pier. As the throng of passengers filed up the gang-plank she suddenly squeezed my arm.

"Look! Hosy!" she cried. "Look! Isn't that him?"

I looked where she was pointing.

"Him? Who?" I asked.

"Look! There he goes now. No, he's gone. I can't see him any more. And yet I was almost certain 'twas him."

"Who?" I asked again. "Did you see someone you knew?"

"I thought I did, but I guess I was mistaken. He's just got home; he wouldn't be startin' off again so soon. No, it couldn't have been him, but I did think—"

I stopped short. "Who did you think you saw?" I demanded.

"I thought I saw Doctor Herbert Bayliss goin' up those stairs to the steamboat. It looked like him enough to be his twin brother, if he had one."

I did not answer. I looked about as we stepped aboard the boat, but if young Bayliss was there he was not in sight. Hephzy rattled on excitedly.

"You can't tell much by seein' folks's backs," she declared. "I remember one time your cousin Hezekiah Knowles—You don't remember him, Hosy; he died when you was little—One time Cousin Hezzy was up to Boston with his wife and they was shoppin' in one of the big stores. That is, Martha Ann—the wife—was shoppin' and he was taggin' along and complainin', same as men generally do. He was kind of nearsighted, Hezzy was, and when Martha was fightin' to get a place in front of a bargain counter he stayed astern and kept his eyes fixed on a hat she was wearin'. 'Twas a new hat with blue and yellow flowers on it. Hezzy always said, when he told the yarn afterward, that he never once figured that there could be another hat like that one. I saw it myself and, if I'd been in his place, I'd have HOPED there wasn't anyway. Well, he followed that hat from one counter to another and, at last, he stepped up and said, 'Look here, dearie,' he says—They hadn't been married very long, not long enough to get out of the mushy stage—'Look here, dearie,' he says, 'hadn't we better be gettin' on home? You'll tire those little feet of yours all out trottin' around this way.' And when the hat turned around there was a face under it as black as a crow. He'd been followin' a darkey woman for ten minutes. She thought he was makin' fun of her feet and was awful mad, and when Martha came along and found who he'd taken for her she was madder still. Hezzy said, 'I couldn't help it, Martha. Nobody could. I never saw two craft look more alike from twenty foot astern. And she wears that hat just the way you do.' That didn't help matters any, of course, and—Why, Hosy, where are you goin'? Why don't you say somethin'? Hadn't we better sit down? All the good seats will be gone if we don't."

I had been struggling through the crowd, trying my best to get a glimpse of the man she had thought to be Herbert Bayliss. If it was he then my suspicions were confirmed. Heathcroft's story of the girl who sang in Paris had impressed him as it had me and he was on his way to see for himself. But the man, whoever he might be, had disappeared.

"How the wind does blow," said Hephzy. "What are the people doin' with those black tarpaulins?"

Sailors in uniform were passing among the seated passengers distributing large squares of black waterproof canvas. I watched the use to which the tarpaulins were put and I understood. I beckoned to the nearest sailor and rented two of the canvases for use during the voyage.

"How much?" I asked.

"One franc each," said the man, curtly.

I had visited the money-changers near the Charing Cross station and was prepared. Hephzy's eyes opened.

"A franc," she repeated. "That's French money, isn't it. Is he a Frenchman?"

"Yes," said I. "This is a French boat, I think."

She watched the sailor for a moment. Then she sighed.

"And he's a Frenchman," she said. "I thought Frenchmen wore mustaches and goatees and were awful polite. He was about as polite as a pig. And all he needs is a hand-organ and a monkey to be an Italian. A body couldn't tell the difference without specs. What did you get those tarpaulins for, Hosy?"

I covered our traveling bags with one of the tarpaulins, as I saw our fellow-passengers doing, and the other I tucked about Hephzy, enveloping her from her waist down.

"I don't need that," she protested. "It isn't cold and it isn't rainin', either. I tell you I don't need it, Hosy. Don't tuck me in any more. I feel as if I was goin' to France in a baby carriage, not a steamboat. And what are they passin' round those—those tin dippers for?"

"They may be useful later on," I said, watching the seas leap and foam against the stone breakwater. "You'll probably understand later, Hephzy."

She understood. The breakwater was scarcely passed when our boat, which had seemed so large and steady and substantial, began to manifest a desire to stand on both ends at once and to roll like a log in a rapid. The sun was shining brightly overhead, the verandas of the hotels along the beach were crowded with gaily dressed people, the surf fringing that beach was dotted with bathers, everything on shore wore a look of holiday and joy—and yet out here, on the edge of the Channel, there was anything but calm and anything but joy.

How that blessed boat did toss and rock and dip and leap and pitch! And how the spray began to fly as we pushed farther and farther from land! It came over the bows in sheets; it swept before the wind in showers, in torrents. Hephzy hastily removed her hat and thrust it beneath the tarpaulin. I turned up the collar of my steamer coat and slid as far down into that collar as I could.

"My soul!" exclaimed Hephzy, the salt water running down her face. "My soul and body!"

"I agree with you," said I.

On we went, over the waves or through them. Our fellow-passengers curled up beneath their tarpaulins, smiled stoically or groaned dismally, according to their dispositions—or digestions. A huge wave—the upper third of it, at least—swept across the deck and spilled a gallon or two of cold water upon us. A sturdy, red-faced Englishman, sitting next me, grinned cheerfully and observed:

"Trickles down one's neck a bit, doesn't it, sir."

I agreed that it did. Hephzy, huddled under the lee of my shoulder, sputtered.

"Trickles!" she whispered. "My heavens and earth! If this is a trickle then Noah's flood couldn't have been more than a splash. Trickles! There's a Niagara Falls back of both of my ears this minute."

Another passenger, also English, but gray-haired and elderly, came tacking down the deck, bound somewhere or other. His was a zig-zag transit. He dove for the rail, caught it, steadied himself, took a fresh start, swooped to the row of chairs by the deck house, carromed from them, and, in company with a barrel or two of flying brine, came head first into my lap. I expected profanity and temper. I did get a little of the former.

"This damned French boat!" he observed, rising with difficulty. "She absolutely WON'T be still."

"The sea is pretty rough."

"Oh, the sea is all right. A bit damp, that's all. It's the blessed boat. Foreigners are such wretched sailors."

He was off on another tack. Hephzy watched him wonderingly.

"A bit damp," she repeated. "Yes, I shouldn't wonder if 'twas. I suppose likely he wouldn't call it wet if he fell overboard."

"Not on this side of the Channel," I answered. "This side is English water, therefore it is all right."

A few minutes later Hephzy spoke again.

"Look at those poor women," she said.

Opposite us were two English ladies, middle-aged, wretchedly ill and so wet that the feathers on their hats hung down in strings.

"Just like drowned cats' tails," observed Hephzy. "Ain't it awful! And they're too miserable to care. You poor thing," she said, leaning forward and addressing the nearest, "can't I fix you so you're more comfortable?"

The woman addressed looked up and tried her best to smile.

"Oh, no, thank you," she said, weakly but cheerfully. "We're doing quite well. It will soon be over."

Hephzy shook her head.

"Did you hear that, Hosy?" she whispered. "I declare! if it wasn't off already, and that's a mercy, I'd take off my hat to England and the English people. Not a whimper, not a complaint, just sit still and soak and tumble around and grin and say it's 'a bit damp.' Whenever I read about the grumblin', fault-findin' Englishman I'll think of the folks on this boat. It may be patriotism or it may be the race pride and reserve we hear so much about—but, whatever it is, it's fine. They've all got it, men and women and children. I presume likely the boy that stood on the burnin' deck would have said 'twas a bit sultry, and that's all.... What is it, Hosy?"

I had uttered an exclamation. A young man had just reeled by us on his way forward. His cap was pulled down over his eyes and his coat collar was turned up, but I recognized him. He was Herbert Bayliss.

We were three hours crossing from Folkestone to Boulogne, instead of the usual scant two. We entered the harbor, where the great crucifix on the hill above the town attracted Hephzy's attention and the French signs over the doors of hotels and shops by the quay made her realize, so she said, that we really were in a foreign country.

"Somehow England never did seem so very foreign," she said. "And the Mayberry folks were so nice and homey and kind I've come to think of 'em as, not just neighbors, but friends. But this—THIS is foreign enough, goodness knows! Let go of my arm!" to the smiling, gesticulating porter who was proffering his services. "DON'T wave your hands like that; you make me dizzy. Keep 'em still, man! I could understand you just as well if they was tied. Hosy, you'll have to be skipper from now on. Now I KNOW Cape Cod is three thousand miles off."

We got through the customs without trouble, found our places in the train, and the train, after backing and fussing and fidgeting and tooting in a manner thoroughly French, rolled out of the station.

We ate our dinner, and a very good dinner it was, in the dining-car. Hephzy, having asked me to translate the heading "Compagnie Internationale des Wagon Lits" on the bill of fare, declared she couldn't see why a dining-car should be called a "wagon bed." "There's enough to eat to put you to sleep," she declared, "but you couldn't stay asleep any more than you could in the nail factory up to Tremont. I never heard such a rattlin' and slambangin' in my life."

We whizzed through the French country, catching glimpses of little towns, with red-roofed cottages clustered about the inevitable church and chateau, until night came and looking out of the window was no longer profitable. At nine, or thereabouts, we alighted from the train at Paris.

In the cab, on the way to the hotel where we were to meet the Heptons, Hephzy talked incessantly.

"Paris!" she said, over and over again. "Paris! where they had the Three Musketeers and Notre Dame and Henry of Navarre and Saint Bartholomew and Napoleon and the guillotine and Innocents Abroad and—and everything. Paris! And I'm in it!"

At the door of the hotel Mr. Hepton met us.

Before we retired that night I told Hephzy what I had deferred telling until then, namely, that I did not intend leaving for Switzerland with her and with the Heptons the following day. I did not tell her my real reason for staying; I had invented a reason and told her that instead.

"I want to be alone here in Paris for a few days," I said. "I think I may find some material here which will help me with my novel. You and the Heptons must go, just as you have planned, and I will join you at Lucerne or Interlaken."

Hephzy stared at me.

"I sha'n't stir one step without you," she declared. "If I'd known you had such an idea as that in your head I—"

"You wouldn't have come," I interrupted. "I know that; that's why I didn't tell you. Of course you will go and of course you will leave me here. We will be separated only two or three days. I'll ask Hepton to give me an itinerary of the trip and I will wire when and where I will join you. You must go, Hephzy; I insist upon it."

In spite of my insisting Hephzy still declared she should not go. It was nearly midnight before she gave in.

"And if you DON'T come in three days at the longest," she said, "you'll find me back here huntin' you up. I mean that, Hosy, so you'd better understand it. And now," rising from her chair, "I'm goin' to see about the things you're to wear while we're separated. If I don't you're liable to keep on wet stockin's and shoes and things all the time and forget to change 'em.

You needn't say you won't, for I know you too well. Mercy sakes! do you suppose I've taken care of you all these years and DON'T know?"

The next forenoon I said good-by to her and the Heptons at the railway station. Hephzy's last words to me were these:

"Remember," she said, "if you do get caught in the rain, there's dry things in the lower tray of your trunk. Collars and neckties and shirts are in the upper tray. I've hung your dress suit in the closet in case you want it, though that isn't likely. And be careful what you eat, and don't smoke too much, and—Yes, Mr. Hepton, I'm comin'—and don't spend ALL your money in book-stores; you'll need some of it in Switzerland. And—Oh, dear, Hosy! do be a good boy. I know you're always good, but, from all I've heard, this Paris is an awful place and—good-by. Good-by. In Lucerne in two days or Interlaken in three. It's got to be that, or back I come, remember. I HATE to leave you all alone amongst these jabberin' foreigners. I'm glad you can jabber, too, that's one comfort. If it was me, all I could do would be to holler United States language at 'em, and if they didn't understand that, just holler louder. I—Yes, Mr. Hepton, I AM comin' now. Good-by, Hosy, dear."

The train rolled out of the station. I watched it go. Then I turned and walked to the street. So far my scheme had worked well. I was alone in Paris as I had planned to be. And now—and now to find where a girl sang, a girl who looked like Frances Morley.

CHAPTER XV
In Which I Learn that All Abbeys Are Not Churches

And that, now that I really stopped to consider it, began to appear more and more of a task. Paris must be full of churches; to visit each of them in turn would take weeks at least. Hephzy had given me three days. I must join her at Interlaken in three days or there would be trouble. And how was I to make even the most superficial search in three days?

Of course I had realized something of this before. Even in the state of mind which Heathcroft's story had left me, I had realized that my errand in Paris was a difficult one. I realized that I had set out on the wildest of wild goose chases and that, even in the improbable event of the singer's being Frances, my finding her was most unlikely. The chances of success were a hundred to one against me. But I was in the mood to take the hundredth chance. I should have taken it if the odds were higher still. My plan—if it could be called a plan—was first of all to buy a Paris Baedeker and look over the list of churches. This I did, and, back in the hotel room, I consulted that list. It staggered me. There were churches enough—there were far too many. Cathedrals and chapels and churches galore—Catholic and Protestant. But there was no church calling itself an abbey. I closed the Baedeker, lit a cigar, and settled myself for further reflection.

The girl was singing somewhere and she called herself Mademoiselle Juno or Junotte, so Heathcroft had said. So much I knew and that was all. It was very, very little. But Herbert Bayliss had come to Paris, I believed, because of what Heathcroft had told him. Did he know more than I? It was possible. At any rate he had come. I had seen him on the steamer, and I believed he had seen and recognized me. Of course he might not be in Paris now; he might have gone elsewhere. I did not believe it, however. I believed he had crossed the Channel on the same errand as I. There was a possible chance. I might, if the other means proved profitless, discover at which hotel Bayliss was staying and question him. He might tell me nothing, even if he knew, but I could keep him in sight, I could follow him and discover where he went. It would be dishonorable, perhaps, but I was desperate and doggedly regardless of scruples. I was set upon one thing—to find her, to see her and speak with her again.

Shadowing Bayliss, however, I set aside as a last resort. Before that I would search on my own hook. And, tossing aside the useless Baedeker, I tried to think of someone whose advice might be of value. At last, I resolved to question the concierge of the hotel. Concierges, I knew, were the ever present helps of travelers in trouble. They knew everything, spoke all languages, and expected to be asked all sorts of unreasonable questions.

The concierge at my hotel was a transcendant specimen of his talented class. His name and title was Monsieur Louis—at least that is what I had heard the other guests call him. And the questions which he had been called upon to answer, in my hearing, ranged in subject from the hour of closing the Luxemburg galleries to that of opening the Bal Tabarin, with various interruptions during which he settled squabbles over cab fares, took orders for theater and opera tickets, and explained why fruit at the tables of the Cafe des Ambassadeurs was so very expensive.

Monsieur Louis received me politely, listened, with every appearance of interest, to my tale of a young lady, a relative, who was singing at one of the Paris churches and whose name was Juno or Junotte, but, when I had finished, reluctantly shook his head. There were many, many churches in Paris—yes, and, at some of them, young ladies sang; but these were, for the most part, the Protestant churches. At the larger churches, the Catholic churches, most of the singers were men or boys. He could recall none where a lady of that name sang. Monsieur had not been told the name of the church?

"The person who told me referred to it as an abbey," I said.

Louis raised his shoulders. "I am sorry, Monsieur," he said, "but there is no abbey, where ladies sing, in Paris. It is, alas, regrettable, but it is so."

He announced it as he might have broken to me the news of the death of a friend. Incidentally, having heard a few sentences of my French, he spoke in English, very good English.

"I will, however, make inquiries, Monsieur," he went on. "Possibly I may discover something which will be of help to Monsieur in his difficulty." In the meantime there was to be a parade of troops at the Champ de Mars at four, and the evening performance at the Folies Bergeres was unusually good and English and American gentlemen always enjoyed it. It would give him pleasure to book a place for me.

I thanked him but I declined the offer, so far as the Folies were concerned. I did ask him, however, to give me the name of a few churches at which ladies sang. This he did and I set out to find them, in a cab which whizzed through the Paris streets as if the driver was bent upon suicide and manslaughter.

I visited four places of worship that afternoon and two more that evening. Those in charge—for I attended no services—knew nothing of Mademoiselle Junotte or Juno. I retired at ten, somewhat discouraged, but stubbornly determined to keep on, for my three days at least.

The next morning I consulted Baedeker again, this time for the list of hotels, a list which I found quite as lengthy as that of the churches. Then I once more sought the help of Monsieur Louis. Could he tell me a few of the hotels where English visitors were most likely to stay.

He could do more than that, apparently. Would I be so good as to inform him if the lady or gentleman—being Parisian he put the lady first—whom I wished to find had recently arrived in Paris. I told him that the gentleman had arrived the same evening as I. Whereupon he produced a list of guests at all the prominent hotels. Herbert Bayliss was registered at the Continental.

To the Continental I went and made inquiries of the concierge there. Mr. Bayliss was there, he was in his room, so the concierge believed. He would be pleased to ascertain. Would I give my name? I declined to give the name, saying that I did not wish to disturb Mr. Bayliss. If he was in his room I would wait until he came down. He was in his room, had not yet breakfasted, although it was nearly ten in the forenoon. I sat down in a chair from which I could command a good view of the elevators, and waited.

The concierge strolled over and chatted. Was I a friend of Mr. Bayliss? Ah, a charming young gentleman, was he not. This was not his first visit to Paris, no indeed; he came frequently—though not as frequently of late—and he invariably stayed at the Continental. He had been out late the evening before, which doubtless explained his non-appearance. Ah, he was breakfasting now; had ordered his "cafe complete." Doubtless he would be down very soon? Would I wish to send up my name now?

Again I declined, to the polite astonishment of the concierge, who evidently considered me a queer sort of a friend. He was called to his desk by a guest, who wished to ask questions, of course, and I waited where I was. At a quarter to eleven Herbert Bayliss emerged from the elevator.

His appearance almost shocked me. Out late the night before! He looked as if he had been out all night for many nights. He was pale and solemn. I stepped forward to greet him and the start he gave when he saw me was evidence of the state of his nerves. I had never thought of him as possessing any nerves.

"Eh? Why, Knowles!" he exclaimed.

"Good morning, Bayliss," said I.

We both were embarrassed, he more than I, for I had expected to see him and he had not expected to see me. I made a move to shake hands but he did not respond. His manner toward me was formal and, I thought, colder than it had been at our meeting the day of the golf tournament.

"I called," I said, "to see you, Bayliss. If you are not engaged I should like to talk with you for a few moments."

His answer was a question.

"How did you know I was here?" he asked.

"I saw your name in the list of recent arrivals at the Continental," I answered.

"I mean how did you know I was in Paris?"

"I didn't know. I thought I caught a glimpse of you on the boat. I was almost sure it was you, but you did not appear to recognize me and I had no opportunity to speak then."

He did not speak at once, he did not even attempt denial of having seen and recognized me during the Channel crossing. He regarded me intently and, I thought, suspiciously.

"Who sent you here?" he asked, suddenly.

"Sent me! No one sent me. I don't understand you."

"Why did you follow me?"

"Follow you?"

"Yes. Why did you follow me to Paris? No one knew I was coming here, not even my own people. They think I am—Well, they don't know that I am here."

His speech and his manner were decidedly irritating. I had made a firm resolve to keep my temper, no matter what the result of this interview might be, but I could not help answering rather sharply.

"I had no intention of following you—here or anywhere else," I said. "Your action and whereabouts, generally speaking, are of no particular interest to me. I did not follow you to Paris, Doctor Bayliss."

He reddened and hesitated. Then he led the way to a divan in a retired corner of the lobby and motioned to me to be seated. There he sat down beside me and waited for me to speak. I, in turn, waited for him to speak.

At last he spoke.

"I'm sorry, Knowles," he said. "I am not myself today. I've had a devil of a night and I feel like a beast this morning. I should probably have insulted my own father, had he appeared suddenly, as you did. Of course I should have known you did not follow me to Paris. But—but why did you come?"

I hesitated now. "I came," I said, "to—to—Well, to be perfectly honest with you, I came because of something I heard concerning—concerning—"

He interrupted me. "Then Heathcroft did tell you!" he exclaimed. "I thought as much."

"He told you, I know. He said he did."

"Yes. He did. My God, man, isn't it awful! Have you seen her?"

His manner convinced me that he had seen her. In my eagerness I forgot to be careful.

"No," I answered, breathlessly; "I have not seen her. Where is she?"

He turned and stared at me.

"Don't you know where she is?" he asked, slowly.

"I know nothing. I have been told that she—or someone very like her—is singing in a Paris church. Heathcroft told me that and then we were interrupted. I—What is the matter?"

He was staring at me more oddly than ever. There was the strangest expression on his face.

"In a church!" he repeated. "Heathcroft told you—"

"He told me that he had seen a girl, whose resemblance to Miss Morley was so striking as to be marvelous, singing in a Paris church. He called it an abbey, but of course it couldn't be that. Do you know anything more definite? What did he tell you?"

He did not answer.

"In a church!" he said again. "You thought—Oh, good heavens!"

He began to laugh. It was not a pleasant laugh to hear. Moreover, it angered me.

"This may be very humorous," I said, brusquely. "Perhaps it is—to you. But—Bayliss, you know more of this than I. I am certain now that you do. I want you to tell me what you know. Is that girl Frances Morley? Have you seen her? Where is she?"

He had stopped laughing. Now he seemed to be considering.

"Then you did come over here to find her," he said, more slowly still. "You were following her, why?"

"WHY?"

"Yes, why. She is nothing to you. You told my father that. You told me that she was not your niece. You told Father that you had no claim upon her whatever and that she had asked you not to try to trace her or to learn where she was. You said all that and preached about respecting her wish and all that sort of thing. And yet you are here now trying to find her."

The only answer I could make to this was a rather childish retort.

"And so are you," I said.

His fists clinched.

"I!" he cried, fiercely. "I! Did *I* ever say she was nothing to me? Did *I* ever tell anyone I should not try to find her? I told you, only the other day, that I would find her in spite of the devil. I meant it. Knowles, I don't understand you. When I came to you thinking you her uncle and guardian, and asked your permission to ask her to marry me, you gave that permission. You did. You didn't tell me that she was nothing to you. I don't understand you at all. You told my father a lot of rot—"

"I told your father the truth. And, when I told you that she had left no message for you, that was the truth also. I have no reason to believe she cares for you—"

"And none to think that she doesn't. At all events she did not tell ME not to follow her. She did tell you. Why are you following her?"

It was a question I could not answer—to him. That reason no one should know. And yet what excuse could I give, after all my protestations?

"I—I feel that I have the right, everything considered," I stammered. "She is not my niece, but she is Miss Cahoon's."

"And she ran away from both of you, asking, as a last request, that you both make no attempt to learn where she was. The whole affair is beyond understanding. What the truth may be—"

"Are you hinting that I have lied to you?"

"I am not hinting at anything. All I can say is that it is deuced queer, all of it. And I sha'n't say more."

"Will you tell me—"

"I shall tell you nothing. That would be her wish, according to your own statement and I will respect that wish, if you don't."

I rose to my feet. There was little use in an open quarrel between us and I was by far the older man. Yes, and his position was infinitely stronger than mine, as he understood it. But I never was more strongly tempted. He knew where she was. He had seen her. The thought was maddening.

He had risen also and was facing me defiantly.

"Good morning, Doctor Bayliss," said I, and walked away. I turned as I reached the entrance of the hotel and looked back. He was still standing there, staring at me.

That afternoon I spent in my room. There is little use describing my feelings. That she was in Paris I was sure now. That Bayliss had seen her I was equally sure. But why had he spoken and looked as he did when I first spoke of Heathcroft's story? What had he meant by saying something or other was "awful?" And why had he seemed so astonished, why had he laughed in that strange way when I had said she was singing in a church?

That evening I sought Monsieur Louis, the concierge, once more.

"Is there any building here in Paris," I asked, "a building in which people sing, which is called an abbey? One that is not a church or an abbey, but is called that?"

Louis looked at me in an odd way. He seemed a bit embarrassed, an embarrassment I should not have expected from him.

"Monsieur asks the question," he said, smiling. "It was in my mind last night, the thought, but Monsieur asked for a church. There is a place called L'Abbaye and there young women sing, but—" he hesitated, shrugged and then added, "but L'Abbaye is not a church. No, it is not that."

"What is it?" I asked.

"A restaurant, Monsieur. A cafe chantant at Montmartre."

Montmartre at ten that evening was just beginning to awaken. At the hour when respectable Paris, home-loving, domestic Paris, the Paris of which the tourist sees so little, is thinking of retiring, Montmartre—or that section of it in which L'Abbaye is situated—begins to open its eyes. At ten-thirty, as my cab buzzed into the square and pulled up at the curb, the electric signs were blazing, the sidewalks were, if not yet crowded, at least well filled, and the sounds of music from the open windows of The Dead Rat and the other cafes with the cheerful names were mingling with noises of the street.

Monsieur Louis had given me my sailing orders, so to speak. He had told me that arriving at L'Abbaye before ten-thirty was quite useless. Midnight was the accepted hour, he said; prior to that I would find it rather dull, triste. But after that—Ah, Monsieur would, at least, be entertained.

"But of course Monsieur does not expect to find the young lady of whom he is in search there," he said. "A relative is she not?"

Remembering that I had, when I first mentioned the object of my quest to him, referred to her as a relative, I nodded.

He smiled and shrugged.

"A relative of Monsieur's would scarcely be found singing at L'Abbaye," he said. "But it is a most interesting place, entertaining and chic. Many English and American gentlemen sup there after the theater."

I smiled and intimated that the desire to pass a pleasant evening was my sole reason for visiting the place. He was certain I would be pleased.

The doorway of L'Abbaye was not deserted, even at the "triste" hour of ten-thirty. Other cabs were drawn up at the curb and, upon the stairs leading to the upper floors, were several gaily dressed couples bound, as I had proclaimed myself to be, in search of supper and entertainment. I had, acting upon the concierge's hint, arrayed myself in my evening clothes and I handed my silk hat, purchased in London—where, as Hephzy said, "a man without a tall hat is like a rooster without tail feathers"—to a polite and busy attendant. Then a personage with a very straight beard and a very curly mustache, ushered me into the main dining-room.

"Monsieur would wish seats for how many?" he asked, in French.

"For myself only," I answered, also in French. His next remark was in English. I was beginning to notice that when I addressed a Parisian in his native language, he usually answered in mine. This may have been because of a desire to please me, or in self-defence; I am inclined to think the latter.

"Ah, for one only. This way, Monsieur."

I was given a seat at one end of a long table, and in a corner. There were plenty of small tables yet unoccupied, but my guide was apparently reserving these for couples or quartettes; at any rate he did not offer one to me. I took the seat indicated.

"I shall wish to remain here for some time?" I said. "Probably the entire—" I hesitated; considering the hour I scarcely knew whether to say "evening" or "morning." At last I said "night" as a compromise.

The bearded person seemed doubtful.

"There will be a great demand later," he said. "To oblige Monsieur is of course our desire, but.... Ah, merci, Monsieur, I will see that Monsieur is not disturbed."

The reason for his change of heart was the universal one in restaurants. He put the reason in his pocket and summoned a waiter to take my order.

I gave the order, a modest one, which dropped me a mile or two in the waiter's estimation. However, after a glance at my fellow-diners at nearby tables, I achieved a partial uplift by ordering a bottle of extremely expensive wine. I had had the idea that, being in France, the home of champagne, that beverage would be cheap or, at least, moderately priced. But in L'Abbaye the idea seemed to be erroneous.

The wine was brought immediately; the supper was somewhat delayed. I did not care. I had not come there to eat—or to drink, either, for that matter. I had come—I scarcely knew why I had come. That Frances Morley would be singing in a place like this I did not believe. This was the sort of "abbey" that A. Carleton Heathcroft would be most likely to visit, that was true, but that he had seen her here was most improbable. The coincidence of the "abbey" name would not have brought me there, of itself. Herbert Bayliss had given me to understand, although he had not said it, that she was not singing in a church and he had found the idea of her being where she was "awful." It was because of what he had said that I had come, as a sort of last chance, a forlorn hope. Of course she would not be here, a hired singer in a Paris night restaurant; that was impossible.

How impossible it was likely to be I realized more fully during the next hour. There was nothing particularly "awful" about L'Abbaye of itself—at first, nor, perhaps, even later; at least the awfulness was well covered. The program of entertainment was awful enough, if deadly mediocrity is awful. A big darkey, dressed in a suit which reminded me of the "end man" at an old-time minstrel show, sang "My Alabama Coon," accompanying himself, more or less intimately, on the banjo. I could have heard the same thing, better done, at a ten cent theater in the States, where this chap had doubtless served an apprenticeship. However, the audience, which was growing larger every minute, seemed to find the bellowing enjoyable and applauded loudly. Then a feminine person did a Castilian dance between the tables. I was ready to declare a second war with Spain when she had finished. Then there was an orchestral interval, during which the tables filled.

The impossibility of Frances singing in a place like this became more certain each minute, to my mind. I called the waiter.

"Does Mademoiselle Juno sing here this evening?" I asked, in my lame French.

He shook his head. "Non, Monsieur," he answered, absently, and hastened on with the bottle he was carrying.

Apparently that settled it. I might as well go. Then I decided to remain a little longer. After all, I was there, and I, or Heathcroft, might have misunderstood the name. I would stay for a while.

The long table at which I sat was now occupied from end to end. There were several couples, male and female, and a number of unattached young ladies, well-dressed, pretty for the most part, and vivacious and inclined to be companionable. They chatted with their neighbors and would have chatted with me if I had been in the mood. For the matter of that everyone talked with everyone else, in French or English, good, bad and indifferent, and there was much laughter and gaiety. L'Abbaye was wide awake by this time.

The bearded personage who had shown me to my seat, appeared, followed by a dozen attendants bearing paper parasols and bags containing little celluloid balls, red, white, and blue. They were distributed among the feminine guests. The parasols, it developed, were to be waved and the balls to be thrown. You were supposed to catch as many as were thrown at you and throw them back. It was wonderful fun—or would have been for children—and very, very amusing—after the second bottle.

For my part I found it very stupid. As I have said at least once in this history I am not what is called a "good mixer" and in an assemblage like this I was as out of place as a piece of ice on a hot stove. Worse than that, for the ice would have melted and I congealed the more. My bottle of champagne remained almost untouched and when a celluloid ball bounced on the top of my head I did not scream "Whoopee! Bullseye!" as my American neighbors did or "Voila! Touche!" like the French. There were plenty of Americans and English there, and they seemed to be having a good time, but their good time was incomprehensible to me. This was "gay Paris," of course, but somehow the gaiety seemed forced and artificial and silly, except to the proprietors of L'Abbaye. If I had been getting the price for food and liquids which they received I might, perhaps, have been gay.

The young Frenchman at my right was gay enough. He had early discovered my nationality and did his best to be entertaining. When a performer from the Olympia, the music hall on the Boulevard des Italiens, sang a distressing love ballad in a series of shrieks like those of a circular saw in a lumber mill, this person shouted his "Bravos" with the rest and then, waving his hands before my face, called for, "De cheer Americain! One, two, tree—Heep! Heep! Heep! Oo—ray-y-y!" I did not join in "the cheer Americain," but I did burst out laughing, a proceeding which caused the young lady at my left to pat my arm and nod delighted approval. She evidently thought I was becoming gay and lighthearted at last. She was never more mistaken.

It was nearly two o'clock and I had had quite enough of L'Abbaye. I had not enjoyed myself—had not expected to, so far as that went. I hope I am not a prig, and, whatever I am or am not, priggishness had no part in my feelings then. Under ordinary circumstances I should not have enjoyed myself in a place like that. Mine is not the temperament—I shouldn't know how. I must have appeared the most solemn ass in creation, and if I had come there with the idea of amusement, I should have felt like one. As it was, my feeling was not disgust, but unreasonable disappointment. Certainly I did not wish— now that I had seen L'Abbaye—to find Frances Morley there; but just as certainly I was disappointed.

I called for my bill, paid it, and stood up. I gave one look about the crowded, noisy place, and then I started violently and sat down again. I had seen Herbert Bayliss. He had, apparently, just entered and a waiter was finding a seat for him at a table some distance away and on the opposite side of the great room.

There was no doubt about it; it was he. My heart gave a bound that almost choked me and all sorts of possibilities surged through my brain. He had come to Paris to find her, he had found her—in our conversation he had intimated as much. And now, he was here at the "Abbey." Why? Was it here that he had found her? Was she singing here after all?

Bayliss glanced in my direction and I sank lower in my chair. I did not wish him to see me. Fortunately the lady opposite waved her paper parasol just then and I went into eclipse, so far as he was concerned. When the eclipse was over he was looking elsewhere.

The black-bearded Frenchman, who seemed to be, if not one of the proprietors, at least one of the managers of L'Abbaye, appeared in the clear space at the center of the room between the tables and waved his hands. He was either much excited or wished to seem so. He shouted something in French which I could not understand. There was a buzz of interest all about me; then the place grew still—or stiller. Something was going to happen, that was evident. I leaned toward my voluble neighbor, the French gentleman who had called for "de cheer Americain."

"What is it?" I asked. "What is the matter?"

He ignored, or did not hear, my question. The bearded person was still waving his hands. The orchestra burst into a sort of triumphal march and then into the open space between the tables came—Frances Morley.

She was dressed in a simple evening gown, she was not painted or powdered to the extent that women who had sung before her had been, her hair was simply dressed. She looked thinner than she had when I last saw her, but otherwise she was unchanged. In that place, amid the lights and the riot of color, the silks and satins and jewels, the flushed faces of the crowd, she stood and bowed, a white rose in a bed of tiger lilies, and the crowd rose and shouted at her.

The orchestra broke off its triumphal march and the leader stood up, his violin at his shoulder. He played a bar or two and she began to sing.

She sang a simple, almost childish, love song in French. There was nothing sensational about it, nothing risque, certainly nothing which should have appealed to the frequenters of L'Abbaye. And her voice, although sweet and clear and pure, was not extraordinary. And yet, when she had finished, there was a perfect storm of "Bravos." Parasols waved, flowers were thrown, and a roar of applause lasted for minutes. Why this should have been is a puzzle to me even now. Perhaps it was because of her clean, girlish beauty; perhaps because it was so unexpected and so different; perhaps because of the mystery concerning her. I don't know. Then I did not ask. I sat in my chair at the table, trembling from head to foot, and looking at her. I had never expected to see her again and now she was before my eyes—here in this place.

She sang again; this time a jolly little ballad of soldiers and glory and the victory of the Tri-Color. And again she swept them off their feet. She bowed and smiled in answer to their applause and, motioning to the orchestra leader, began without accompaniment, "Loch Lomond," in English. It was one of the songs I had asked her to sing at the rectory, one I had found in the music cabinet, one that her mother and mine had sung years before.

> *"Ye'll take the high road*
> *And I'll take the low road,*
> *And I'll be in Scotland afore ye—"*

I was on my feet. I have no remembrance of having risen, but I was standing, leaning across the table, looking at her. There were cries of "Sit down" in English and other cries in French. There were tugs at my coat tails.

> *"But me and my true love*
> *Shall never meet again,*
> *By the bonny, bonny banks*
> *Of Loch—"*

She saw me. The song stopped. I saw her turn white, so white that the rouge on her cheeks looked like fever spots. She looked at me and I at her. Then she raised her hand to her throat, turned and almost ran from the room.

I should have followed her, then and there, I think. I was on my way around the end of the table, regardless of masculine boots and feminine skirts. But a stout Englishman got in my way and detained me and the crowd was so dense that I could not push through it. It was an excited crowd, too. For a moment there had been a surprised silence, but now everyone was exclaiming and talking in his or her native language.

"Oh, I say! What happened? What made her do that?" demanded the stout Englishman. Then he politely requested me to get off his foot.

The bearded manager—or proprietor—was waving his hands once more and begging attention and silence. He got both, in a measure. Then he made his announcement.

He begged ten thousand pardons, but Mademoiselle Guinot—That was it, Guinot, not Juno or Junotte—had been seized with a most regrettable illness. She had been unable to continue her performance. It was not serious, but she could sing no more that evening. To-morrow evening—ah, yes. Most certainly. But to-night—no. Monsieur Hairee Opkins, the most famous Engleesh comedy artiste would now entertain the patrons of L'Abbaye. He begged, he entreated attention for Monsieur Opkins.

I did not wait for "Monsieur Hairee." I forced my way to the door. As I passed out I cast a glance in the direction of young Bayliss. He was on his feet, loudly shouting for a waiter and his bill. I had so much start, at all events.

Through the waiters and uniformed attendants I elbowed. Another man with a beard—he looked enough like the other to be his brother, and perhaps he was—got in my way at last. A million or more pardons, but Monsieur could not go in that direction. The exit was there, pointing.

As patiently and carefully as I could, considering my agitation, I explained that I did not wish to find the exit. I was a friend, a—yes, a—er—relative of the young lady who had just sung and who had been taken ill. I wanted to go to her.

Another million pardons, but that was impossible. I did not understand, Mademoiselle was—well, she did not see gentlemen. She was—with the most expressive of shrugs—peculiar. She desired no friends. It was—ah—quite impossible.

I found my pocketbook and pressed my card into his hand. Would he give Mademoiselle my card? Would he tell her that I must see her, if only for a minute? Just give her the card and tell her that.

He shook his head, smiling but firm. I could have punched him for the smile, but instead I took other measures. I reached into my pocket, found some gold pieces—I have no idea how many or of what denomination—and squeezed them in the hand with the card. He still smiled and shook his head, but his firmness was shaken.

"I will give the card," he said, "but I warn Monsieur it is quite useless. She will not see him."

The waiter with whom I had seen Herbert Bayliss in altercation was hurrying by me. I caught his arm.

"Pardon, Monsieur," he protested, "but I must go. The gentleman yonder desires his bill."

"Don't give it to him," I whispered, trying hard to think of the French words. "Don't give it to him yet. Keep him where he is for a time."

I backed the demand with another gold piece, the last in my pocket. The waiter seemed surprised.

"Not give the bill?" he repeated.

"No, not yet." I did my best to look wicked and knowing—"He and I wish to meet the same young lady and I prefer to be first."

That was sufficient—in Paris. The waiter bowed low.

"Rest in peace, Monsieur," he said. "The gentleman shall wait."

I waited also, for what seemed a long time. Then the bearded one reappeared. He looked surprised but pleased.

"Bon, Monsieur," he whispered, patting my arm. "She will see you. You are to wait at the private door. I will conduct you there. It is most unusual. Monsieur is a most fortunate gentleman."

At the door, at the foot of a narrow staircase—decidedly lacking in the white and gold of the other, the public one—I waited, for another age. The staircase was lighted by one sickly gas jet and the street outside was dark and dirty. I waited on the narrow sidewalk, listening to the roar of nocturnal Montmartre around the corner, to the beating of my own heart, and for her footstep on the stairs.

At last I heard it. The door opened and she came out. She wore a cloak over her street costume and her hat was one that she had bought in London with my money. She wore a veil and I could not see her face.

I seized her hands with both of mine.

"Frances!" I cried, chokingly. "Oh, Frances!"

She withdrew her hands. When she spoke her tone was quiet but very firm.

"Why did you come here?" she asked.

"Why did I come? Why—"

"Yes. Why did you come? Was it to find me? Did you know I was here?"

"I did not know. I had heard—"

"Did Doctor Bayliss tell you?"

I hesitated. So she HAD seen Bayliss and spoken with him.

"No," I answered, after a moment, "he did not tell me, exactly. But I had heard that someone who resembled you was singing here in Paris."

"And you followed me. In spite of my letter begging you, for my sake, not to try to find me. Did you get that letter?"

"Yes, I got it."

"Then why did you do it? Oh, WHY did you?"

For the first time there was a break in her voice. We were standing before the door. The street, it was little more than an alley, was almost deserted, but I felt it was not the place for explanations. I wanted to get her away from there, as far from that dreadful "Abbey" as possible. I took her arm.

"Come," I said, "I will tell you as we go. Come with me now."

She freed her arm.

"I am not coming with you," she said. "Why did you come here?"

"I came—I came—Why did YOU come? Why did you leave us as you did? Without a word!"

She turned and faced me.

"You know why I left you," she said. "You know. You knew all the time. And yet you let me believe—You let me think—I lived upon your money—I—I—Oh, don't speak of it! Go away! please go away and leave me."

"I am not going away—without you. I came to get you to go back with me. You don't understand. Your aunt and I want you to come with us. We want you to come and live with us again. We—"

She interrupted. I doubt if she had comprehended more than the first few words of what I was saying.

"Please go away," she begged. "I know I owe you money, so much money. I shall pay it. I mean to pay it all. At first I could not. I could not earn it. I tried. Oh, I tried SO hard! In London I tried and tried, but all the companies were filled, it was late in the season and I—no one would have me. Then I got this chance through an agency. I am succeeding here. I am earning the money at last. I am saving—I have saved—And now you come to—Oh, PLEASE go and leave me!"

Her firmness had gone. She was on the verge of tears. I tried to take her hands again, but she would not permit it.

"I shall not go," I persisted, as gently as I could. "Or when I go you must go with me. You don't understand."

"But I do understand. My aunt—Miss Cahoon told me. I understand it all. Oh, if I had only understood at first."

"But you don't understand—now. Your aunt and I knew the truth from the beginning. That made no difference. We were glad to have you with us. We want you to come back. You are our relative—"

"I am not. I am not really related to you in any way. You know I am not."

"You are related to Miss Cahoon. You are her sister's daughter. She wants you to come. She wants you to live with us again, just as you did before."

"She wants that! She—But it was your money that paid for the very clothes I wore. Your money—not hers; she said so."

"That doesn't make any difference. She wants you and—"

I was about to add "and so do I," but she did not permit me to finish the sentence. She interrupted again, and there was a change in her tone.

"Stop! Oh, stop!" she cried. "She wanted me and—and so you—Did you think I would consent? To live upon your charity?"

"There is no charity about it."

"There is. You know there is. And you believed that I—knowing what I know—that my father—my own father—"

"Hush! hush! That is all past and done with."

"It may be for you, but not for me. Mr. Knowles, your opinion of me must be a very poor one. Or your desire to please your aunt as great as your—your charity to me. I thank you both, but I shall stay here. You must go and you must not try to see me again."

There was firmness enough in this speech; altogether too much. But I was as firm as she was.

"I shall not go," I reiterated. "I shall not leave you—in a place like this. It isn't a fit place for you to be in. You know it is not. Good heavens! you MUST know it?"

"I know what the place is," she said quietly.

"You know! And yet you stay here! Why? You can't like it!"

It was a foolish speech, and I blurted it without thought. She did not answer. Instead she began to walk toward the corner. I followed her.

"I beg your pardon," I stammered, contritely. "I did not mean that, of course. But I cannot think of your singing night after night in such a place— before those men and women. It isn't right; it isn't—you shall not do it."

She answered without halting in her walk.

"I shall do it," she said. "They pay me well, very well, and I—I need the money. When I have earned and saved what I need I shall give it up, of course. As for liking the work—Like it! Oh, how can you!"

"I beg your pardon. Forgive me. I ought to be shot for saying that. I know you can't like it. But you must not stay here. You must come with me."

"No, Mr. Knowles, I am not coming with you. And you must leave me and never come back. My sole reason for seeing you to-night was to tell you that. But—" she hesitated and then said, with quiet emphasis, "you may tell my aunt not to worry about me. In spite of my singing in a cafe chantant I shall keep my self-respect. I shall not be—like those others. And when I have paid my debt—I can't pay my father's; I wish I could—I shall send you the money. When I do that you will know that I have resigned my present position and am trying to find a more respectable one. Good-by."

We had reached the corner. Beyond was the square, with its lights and its crowds of people and vehicles. I seized her arm.

"It shall not be good-by," I cried, desperately. "I shall not let you go."

"You must."

"I sha'n't. I shall come here night after night until you consent to come back to Mayberry."

She stopped then. But when she spoke her tone was firmer than ever.

"Then you will force me to give it up," she said. "Before I came here I was very close to—There were days when I had little or nothing to eat, and, with no prospects, no hope, I—if you don't leave me, Mr. Knowles, if you do come here night after night, as you say, you may force me to that again. You can, of course, if you choose; I can't prevent you. But I shall NOT go back to Mayberry. Now, will you say good-by?"

She meant it. If I persisted in my determination she would do as she said; I was sure of it.

"I am sure my aunt would not wish you to continue to see me, against my will," she went on. "If she cares for me at all she would not wish that. You have done your best to please her. I—I thank you both. Good-by."

What could I do, or say?

"Good-by," I faltered.

She turned and started across the square. A flying cab shut her from my view. And then I realized what was happening, realized it and realized, too, what it meant. She should not go; I would not let her leave me nor would I leave her. I sprang after her.

The square was thronged with cabs and motor cars. The Abbey and The Dead Rat and all the rest were emptying their patrons into the street. Paris traffic regulations are lax and uncertain. I dodged between a limousine and a hansom and caught a glimpse of her just as she reached the opposite sidewalk.

"Frances!" I called. "Frances!"

She turned and saw me. Then I heard my own name shouted from the sidewalk I had just left.

"Knowles! Knowles!"

I looked over my shoulder. Herbert Bayliss was at the curb. He was shaking a hand, it may have been a fist, in my direction.

"Knowles!" he shouted. "Stop! I want to see you."

I did not reply. Instead I ran on. I saw her face among the crowd and upon it was a curious expression, of fear, of frantic entreaty.

"Kent! Kent!" she cried. "Oh, be careful! KENT!"

There was a roar, a shout; I have a jumbled recollection of being thrown into the air, and rolling over and over upon the stones of the street. And there my recollections end, for the time.

CHAPTER XVI
In Which I Take My Turn at Playing the Invalid

Not for a very long time. They begin again—those recollections—a few minutes later, break off once more, and then return and break off alternately, over and over again.

The first thing I remember, after my whirligig flight over the Paris pavement, is a crowd of faces above me and someone pawing at my collar and holding my wrist. This someone, a man, a stranger, said in French:

"He is not dead, Mademoiselle."

And then a voice, a voice that I seemed to recognize, said:

"You are sure, Doctor? You are sure? Oh, thank God!"

I tried to turn my head toward the last speaker—whom I decided, for some unexplainable reason, must be Hephzy—and to tell her that of course I wasn't dead, and then all faded away and there was another blank.

The next interval of remembrance begins with a sense of pain, a throbbing, savage pain, in my head and chest principally, and a wish that the buzzing in my ears would stop. It did not stop, on the contrary it grew louder and there was a squeak and rumble and rattle along with it. A head—particularly a head bumped as hard as mine had been—might be expected to buzz, but it should not rattle, or squeak either. Gradually I began to understand that the rattle and squeak were external and I was in some sort of vehicle, a sleeping car apparently, for I seemed to be lying down. I tried to rise and ask a question and a hand was laid on my forehead and a voice—the voice which I had decided was Hephzy's—said, gently:

"Lie still. You mustn't move. Lie still, please. We shall be there soon."

Where "there" might be I had no idea and it was too much trouble to ask, so I drifted off again.

Next I was being lifted out of the car; men were lifting me—or trying to. And, being wider awake by this time, I protested.

"Here! What are you doing?" I asked. "I am all right. Let go of me. Let go, I tell you."

Again the voice—it sounded less and less like Hephzy's—saying:

"Don't! Please don't! You mustn't move."

But I kept on moving, although moving was a decidedly uncomfortable process.

"What are they doing to me?" I asked. "Where am I? Hephzy, where am I?"

"You are at the hospital. You have been hurt and we are taking you to the hospital. Lie still and they will carry you in."

That woke me more thoroughly.

"Nonsense!" I said, as forcefully as I could. "Nonsense! I'm not badly hurt. I am all right now. I don't want to go to a hospital. I won't go there. Take me to the hotel. I am all right, I tell you."

The man's voice—the doctor's, I learned afterward—broke in, ordering me to be quiet. But I refused to be quiet. I was not going to be taken to any hospital.

"I am all right," I declared. "Or I shall be in a little while. Take me to my hotel. I will be looked after, there. Hephzy will look after me."

The doctor continued to protest—in French—and I to affirm—in English. Also I tried to stand. At length my declarations of independence seemed to have some effect, for they ceased trying to lift me. A dialogue in French followed. I heard it with growing impatience.

"Hephzy," I said, fretfully. "Hephzy, make them take me to my hotel. I insist upon it."

"Which hotel is it? Kent—Kent, answer me. What is the name of the hotel?"

I gave the name; goodness knows how I remembered it. There was more argument, and, after a time, the rattle and buzz and squeak began again. The next thing I remember distinctly is being carried to my room and hearing the voice of Monsieur Louis in excited questioning and command.

After that my recollections are clearer. But it was broad daylight when I became my normal self and realized thoroughly where I was. I was in my room at the hotel, the sunlight was streaming in at the window and Hephzy—I still supposed it was Hephzy—was sitting by that window. And for the first time it occurred to me that she should not have been there; by all that was right and proper she should be waiting for me in Interlaken.

"Hephzy," I said, weakly, "when did you get here?"

The figure at the window rose and came to the bedside. It was not Hephzy. With a thrill I realized who it was.

"Frances!" I cried. "Frances! Why—what—"

"Hush! You mustn't talk. You mustn't. You must be quiet and keep perfectly still. The doctor said so."

"But what happened? How did I get here? What—?"

"Hush! There was an accident; you were hurt. We brought you here in a carriage. Don't you remember?"

What I remembered was provokingly little.

"I seem to remember something," I said. "Something about a hospital. Someone was going to take me to a hospital and I wouldn't go. Hephzy— No, it couldn't have been Hephzy. Was it—was it you?"

"Yes. We were taking you to the hospital. We did take you there, but as they were taking you from the ambulance you—"

"Ambulance! Was I in an ambulance? What happened to me? What sort of an accident was it?"

"Please don't try to talk. You must not talk."

"I won't if you tell me that. What happened?"

"Don't you remember? I left you and crossed the street. You followed me and then—and then you stopped. And then—Oh, don't ask me! Don't!"

"I know. Now I do remember. It was that big motor car. I saw it coming. But who brought me here? You—I remember you; I thought you were Hephzy. And there was someone else."

"Yes, the doctor—the doctor they called—and Doctor Bayliss."

"Doctor Bayliss! Herbert Bayliss, do you mean? Yes, I saw him at the 'Abbey'—and afterward. Did he come here with me?"

"Yes. He was very kind. I don't know what I should have done if it had not been for him. Now you MUST not speak another word."

I did not, for a few moments. I lay there, feebly trying to think, and looking at her. I was grateful to young Bayliss, of course, but I wished— even then I wished someone else and not he had helped me. I did not like to be under obligations to him. I liked him, too; he was a good fellow and I had always liked him, but I did not like THAT.

She rose from the chair by the bed and walked across the room.

"Don't go," I said.

She came back almost immediately.

"It is time for your medicine," she said.

I took the medicine. She turned away once more.

"Don't go," I repeated.

"I am not going. Not for the present."

I was quite contented with the present. The future had no charms just then. I lay there, looking at her. She was paler and thinner than she had been when she left Mayberry, almost as pale and thin as when I first met her in the back room of Mrs. Briggs' lodging house. And there was another change, a subtle, undefinable change in her manner and appearance that puzzled me. Then I realized what it was; she had grown older, more mature. In Mayberry she had been an extraordinarily pretty girl. Now she was a beautiful woman. These last weeks had worked the change. And I began to understand what she had undergone during those weeks.

"Have you been with me ever since it happened—since I was hurt?" I asked, suddenly.

"Yes, of course."

"All night?"

She smiled. "There was very little of the night left," she answered.

"But you have had no rest at all. You must be worn out."

"Oh, no; I am used to it. My—" with a slight pause before the word—"work of late has accustomed me to resting in the daytime. And I shall rest by and by, when my aunt—when Miss Cahoon comes."

"Miss Cahoon? Hephzy? Have you sent for her?"

My tone of surprise startled her, I think. She looked at me.

"Sent for her?" she repeated. "Isn't she here—in Paris?"

"She is in Interlaken, at the Victoria. Didn't the concierge tell you?"

"He told us she was not here, at this hotel, at present. He said she had gone away with some friends. But we took it for granted she was in Paris. I told them I would stay until she came. I—"

I interrupted.

"Stay until she comes!" I repeated. "Stay—! Why you can't do that! You can't! You must not!"

"Hush! hush! Remember you are ill. Think of yourself!"

"Of myself! I am thinking of you. You mustn't stay here—with me. What will they think? What—"

"Hush! hush, please. Think! It makes no difference what they think. If I had cared what people thought I should not be singing at—Hush! you must not excite yourself in this way."

But I refused to hush.

"You must not!" I cried. "You shall not! Why did you do it? They could have found a nurse, if one was needed. Bayliss—"

"Doctor Bayliss does not know. If he did I should not care. As for the others—" she colored, slightly,

"Well, I told the concierge that you were my uncle. It was only a white lie; you used to say you were, you know."

"Say! Oh, Frances, for your own sake, please—"

"Hush! Do you suppose," her cheeks reddened and her eyes flashed as I had seen them flash before, "do you suppose I would go away and leave you now? Now, when you are hurt and ill and—and—after all that you have done! After I treated you as I did! Oh, let me do something! Let me do a little, the veriest little in return. I—Oh, stop! stop! What are you doing?"

I suppose I was trying to sit up; I remember raising myself on my elbow. Then came the pain again, the throbbing in my head and the agonizing pain in my side. And after that there is another long interval in my recollections.

For a week—of course I did not know it was a week then—my memories consist only of a series of flashes like the memory of the hours immediately following the accident. I remember people talking, but not what they said; I remember her voice, or I think I do, and the touch of her hand on my forehead. And afterward, other voices, Hephzy's in particular. But when I came to myself, weak and shaky, but to remain myself for good and all, Hephzy—the real Hephzy—was in the room with me.

Even then they would not let me ask questions. Another day dragged by before I was permitted to do that. Then Hephzy told me I had a cracked rib and a variety of assorted bruises, that I had suffered slight concussion of the brain, and that my immediate job was to behave myself and get well.

"Land sakes!" she exclaimed, "there was a time when I thought you never was goin' to get well. Hour after hour I've set here and listened to your gabblin' away about everything under the sun and nothin' in particular, as crazy as a kitten in a patch of catnip, and thought and thought, what should I do, what SHOULD I do. And now I KNOW what I'm goin' to do. I'm goin' to keep you in that bed till you're strong and well enough to get out of it, if I have to sit on you to hold you down. And I'm no hummin'-bird when it comes to perchin', either."

She had received the telegram which Frances sent and had come from Interlaken post haste.

"And I don't know," she declared, "which part of that telegram upset me most—what there was in it or the name signed at the bottom of it. HER name! I couldn't believe my eyes. I didn't stop to believe 'em long. I just came. And then I found you like this."

"Was she here?" I asked.

"Who—Frances! My, yes, she was here. So pale and tired lookin' that I thought she was goin' to collapse. But she wouldn't give in to it. She told me all about how it happened and what the doctor said and everything. I didn't pay much attention to it then. All I could think of was you. Oh, Hosy! my poor boy! I—I—"

"There! there!" I broke in, gently. "I'm all right now, or I'm going to be. You will have the quahaug on your hands for a while longer. But," returning to the subject which interested me most, "what else did she tell you? Did she tell you how I met her—and where?"

"Why, yes. She's singin' somewhere—she didn't say where exactly, but it is in some kind of opera-house, I judged. There's a perfectly beautiful opera-house a little ways from here on the Avenue de L'Opera, right by the Boulevard des Italiens, though there's precious few Italians there, far's I can see. And why an opera is a l'opera I—"

"Wait a moment, Hephzy. Did she tell you of our meeting? And how I found her?"

"Why, not so dreadful much, Hosy. She's acted kind of queer about that, seemed to me. She said you went to this opera-house, wherever it was, and saw her there. Then you and she were crossin' the road and one of these dreadful French automobiles—the way they let the things tear round is a disgrace—ran into you. I declare! It almost made ME sick to hear about it. And to think of me away off amongst those mountains, enjoyin' myself and not knowin' a thing! Oh, it makes me ashamed to look in the glass. I NEVER ought to have left you alone, and I knew it. It's a judgment on me, what's happened is."

"Or on me, I should rather say," I added. Frances had not told Hephzy of L'Abbaye, that was evident. Well, I would keep silence also.

"Where is she now?" I asked. I asked it with as much indifference as I could assume, but Hephzy smiled and patted my hand.

"Oh, she comes every day to ask about you," she said. "And Doctor Bayliss comes too. He's been real kind."

"Bayliss!" I exclaimed. "Is he with—Does he come here?"

"Yes, he comes real often, mostly about the time she does. He hasn't been here for two days now, though. Hosy, do you suppose he has spoken to her about—about what he spoke to you?"

"I don't know," I answered, curtly. Then I changed the subject.

"Has she said anything to you about coming back to Mayberry?" I asked. "Have you told her how we feel toward her?"

Hephzy's manner changed. "Yes," she said, reluctantly, "I've told her. I've told her everything."

"Not everything? Hephzy, you haven't told her—"

"No, no. Of course I didn't tell her THAT. You know I wouldn't, Hosy. But I told her that her money havin' turned out to be our money didn't make a mite of difference. I told her how much we come to think of her and how we wanted her to come with us and be the same as she had always been. I begged her to come. I said everything I could say."

"And she said?"

"She said no, Hosy. She wouldn't consider it at all. She asked me not to talk about it. It was settled, she said. She must go her way and we ours and we must forget her. She was more grateful than she could tell—she most cried when she said that—but she won't come back and if I asked her again she declared she should have to go away for good."

"I know. That is what she said to me."

"Yes. I can't make it out exactly. It's her pride, I suppose. Her mother was just as proud. Oh, dear! When I saw her here for the first time, after I raced back from Interlaken, I thought—I almost hoped—but I guess it can't be."

I did not answer. I knew only too well that it could not be.

"Does she seem happy?" I asked.

"Why, no; I don't think she is happy. There are times, especially when you began to get better, when she seemed happier, but the last few times she was here she was—well, different."

"How different?"

"It's hard to tell you. She looked sort of worn and sad and discouraged. Hosy, what sort of a place is it she is singin' in?"

"Why do you ask that?"

"Oh, I don't know. Some things you said when you were out of your head made me wonder. That, and some talk I overheard her and Doctor Bayliss havin' one time when they were in the other room—my room—together. I had stepped out for a minute and when I came back, I came in this door instead of the other. They were in the other room talkin' and he was beggin' her not to stay somewhere any more. It wasn't a fit place for her to be, he said; her reputation would be ruined. She cut him short by sayin' that her reputation was her own and that she should do as she thought best, or somethin' like that. Then I coughed, so they would know I was around, and they commenced talkin' of somethin' else. But it set me thinkin' and when you said—"

She paused. "What did I say?" I asked.

"Why, 'twas when she and I were here. You had been quiet for a while and all at once you broke out—delirious you was—beggin' somebody or other not to do somethin'. For your sake, for their own sake, they mustn't do it. 'Twas awful to hear you. A mixed-up jumble about Abbie, whoever she is—not much, by the way you went on about her—and please, please, please, for the Lord's sake, give it up. I tried to quiet you, but you wouldn't be quieted. And finally you said: 'Frances! Oh, Frances! don't! Say that you won't any more.' I gave you your sleepin' drops then; I thought 'twas time. I was afraid you'd say somethin' that you wouldn't want her to hear. You understand, don't you, Hosy?"

"I understand. Thank you, Hephzy."

"Yes. Well, I didn't understand and I asked her if she did. She said no, but she was dreadfully upset and I think she did understand, in spite of her sayin' it. What sort of a place is it, this opera-house where she sings?"

I dodged the question as best I could. I doubt if Hephzy's suspicions were allayed, but she did not press the subject. Instead she told me I had talked enough for that afternoon and must rest.

That evening I saw Bayliss for the first time since the accident. He congratulated me on my recovery and I thanked him for his help in bringing me to the hotel. He waved my thanks aside.

"Quite unnecessary, thanking me," he said, shortly. "I couldn't do anything else, of course. Well, I must be going. Glad you're feeling more fit, Knowles, I'm sure."

"And you?" I asked. "How are you?"

"I? Oh, I'm fit enough, I suppose. Good-by."

He didn't look fit. He looked more haggard and worn and moody than ever. And his manner was absent and distrait. Hephzy noticed it; there were few things she did not notice.

"Either that boy's meals don't agree with him," she announced, "or somethin's weighin' on his mind. He looks as if he'd lost his last friend. Hosy, do you suppose he's spoken to—to her about what he spoke of to you?"

"I don't know. I suppose he has. He was only too anxious to speak, there in Mayberry."

"Humph! Well, IF he has, then—Hosy, sometimes I think this, all this pilgrimage of ours—that's what you used to call it, a pilgrimage—is goin' to turn out right, after all. Don't it remind you of a book, this last part of it?"

"A dismal sort of book," I said, gloomily.

"Well, I don't know. Here are you, the hero, and here's she, the heroine. And the hero is sick and the heroine comes to take care of him—she WAS takin' care of you afore I came, you know; and she falls in love with him and—"

"Yes," I observed, sarcastically. "She always does—in books. But in those books the hero is not a middle-aged quahaug. Suppose we stick to real life and possibilities, Hephzy."

Hephzy was unconvinced. "I don't care," she said. "She ought to even if she doesn't. I fell in love with you long ago, Hosy. And she DID bring you here after you were hurt and took care of you."

"Hush! hush!" I broke in. "She took care of me, as you call it, because she thought it was her duty. She thinks she is under great obligation to us because we did not pitch her into the street when we first met her. She insists that she owes us money and gratitude. Her kindness to me and her care are part payment of the debt. She told me so, herself."

"But—"

"There aren't any 'buts.' You mustn't be an idiot because I have been one, Hephzy. We agreed not to speak of that again. Don't remind me of it."

Hephzy sighed. "All right," she said. "I suppose you are right, Hosy. But—but how is all this goin' to end? She won't go with us. Are we goin' to leave her here alone?"

I was silent. The same question was in my mind, but I had answered it. I was NOT going to leave her there alone. And yet—

"If I was sure," mused Hephzy, "that she was in love with Herbert Bayliss, then 'twould be all right, I suppose. They would get married and it would be all right—or near right—wouldn't it, Hosy."

I said nothing.

The next morning I saw her. She came to inquire for me and Hephzy brought her into my room for a stay of a minute or two. She seemed glad to find me so much improved in health and well on the road to recovery. I tried to thank her for her care of me, for her sending for Hephzy and all the rest of it, but she would not listen. She chatted about Paris and the French people, about Monsieur Louis, the concierge, and joked with Hephzy about that gentleman's admiration for "the wonderful American lady," meaning Hephzy herself.

"He calls you 'Madame Cay-hoo-on,'" she said, "and he thinks you a miracle of decision and management. I think he is almost afraid of you, I really do."

Hephzy smiled, grimly. "He'd better be," she declared. "The way everybody was flyin' around when I first got here after comin' from Interlaken, and the way the help jabbered and hunched up their shoulders when I asked questions made me so fidgety I couldn't keep still. I wanted an egg for breakfast, that first mornin' and when the waiter brought it, it was in the shell, the way they eat eggs over here. I can't eat 'em that way—I'm no weasel—and I told the waiter I wanted an egg cup. Nigh as I could make out from his pigeon English he was tellin' me there was a cup there. Well, there was, one of those little, two-for-a-cent contraptions, just big enough to stick one end of the egg into. 'I want a big one,' says I. 'We, Madame,' says he, and off he trotted. When he came back he brought me a big EGG, a duck's egg, I guess 'twas. Then I scolded and he jabbered some more and by and by he went and fetched this Monsieur Louis man. He could speak English, thank goodness, and he was real nice, in his French way. He begged my pardon for the waiter's stupidness, said he was a new hand, and the like of that, and went on apologizin' and bowin' and smilin' till I almost had a fit.

"'For mercy sakes!' I says, 'don't say any more about it. If that last egg hadn't been boiled 'twould have hatched out an—an ostrich, or somethin' or other, by this time. And it's stone cold, of course. Have this—this jumpin'-jack of yours bring me a hot egg—a hen's egg—opened, in a cup big enough to see without spectacles, and tell him to bring some cream with the coffee. At any rate, if there isn't any cream, have him bring some real milk instead of this watery stuff. I might wash clothes with that, for I declare I think there's bluin' in it, but I sha'n't drink it; I'd be afraid of swallowin' a fish by accident. And do hurry!'

"He went away then, hurryin' accordin' to orders, and ever since then he's been bobbin' up to ask if 'Madame finds everything satisfactory.' I suppose likely I shouldn't have spoken as I did, he means well—it isn't his fault, or the waiter's either, that they can't talk without wavin' their hands as if they were givin' three cheers—but I was terribly nervous that mornin' and I barked like a tied-up dog. Oh dear, Hosy! if ever I missed you and your help it's in this blessed country."

Frances laughed at all this; she seemed just then to be in high spirits; but I thought, or imagined, that her high spirits were assumed for our benefit. At the first hint of questioning concerning her own life, where she lodged or what her plans might be, she rose and announced that she must go.

Each morning of that week she came, remaining but a short time, and always refusing to speak of herself or her plans. Hephzy and I, finding that a reference to those plans meant the abrupt termination of the call, ceased trying to question. And we did not mention our life at the rectory, either; that, too, she seemed unwilling to discuss. Once, when I spoke of our drive to Wrayton, she began a reply, stopped in the middle of a sentence, and then left the room.

Hephzy hastened after her. She returned alone.

"She was cryin', Hosy," she said. "She said she wasn't, but she was. The poor thing! she's unhappy and I know it; she's miserable. But she's so proud she won't own it and, although I'm dyin' to put my arms around her and comfort her, I know if I did she'd go away and never come back. Do you notice she hasn't called me 'Auntie' once. And she always used to—at the rectory. I'm afraid—I'm afraid she's just as determined as she was when she ran away, never to live with us again. What SHALL we do?"

I did not know and I did not dare to think. I was as certain that these visits would cease very soon as I was that they were the only things which made my life bearable. How I did look forward to them! And while she was there, with us, how short the time seemed and how it dragged when she had gone. The worst thing possible for me, this seeing her and being with her; I knew it. I knew it perfectly well. But, knowing it, and realizing that it could not last and that it was but the prelude to a worse loneliness which was sure to come, made no difference. I dreaded to be well again, fearing that would mean the end of those visits.

But I was getting well and rapidly. I sat up for longer and longer periods each day. I began to read my letters now, instead of having Hephzy read them to me, letters from Matthews at the London office and from Jim Campbell at home. Matthews had cabled Jim of the accident and later that I was recovering. So Jim wrote, professing to find material gain in the affair.

"Great stuff," he wrote. "Two chapters at least. The hero, pursuing the villain through the streets of Paris at midnight, is run down by an auto driven by said villain. 'Ah ha!' says the villain: 'Now will you be good?' or words to that effect. 'Desmond,' says the hero, unflinchingly, as they extract the cobble-stones from his cuticle, 'you triumph for the moment, but beware! there will be something doing later on.' See? If it wasn't for the cracked rib and the rest I should be almost glad it happened. All you need is the beautiful heroine nursing you to recovery. Can't you find her?"

He did not know that I had found her, or that the hoped-for novel was less likely to be finished than ever.

Hephzy was now able to leave me occasionally, to take the walks which I insisted upon. She had some queer experiences in these walks.

"Lost again to-day, Hosy," she said, cheerfully, removing her bonnet. "I went cruisin' through the streets over to the south'ard and they were so narrow and so crooked—to say nothin' of bein' dirty and smelly—that I thought I never should get out. Of course I could have hired a hack and let it bring me to the hotel but I wouldn't do that. I was set on findin' my own way. I'd walked in and I was goin' to walk out, that was all there was to it. 'Twasn't the first time I'd been lost in this Paris place and I've got a system of my own. When I get to the square 'Place delay Concorde,' they call it, I know where I am. And 'Concorde' is enough like Concord, Mass., to make me remember the name. So I walk up to a nice appearin' Frenchman with a tall hat and whiskers—I didn't know there was so many chin whiskers outside of East Harniss, or some other back number place—and I say, 'Pardon, Monseer. Place delay Concorde?' Just like that with a question mark after it. After I say it two or three times he begins to get a floatin' sniff of what I'm drivin' at and says he: 'Place delay Concorde? Oh, we, we, we, Madame!' Then a whole string of jabber and arm wavin', with some countin' in the middle of it. Now I've learned 'one, two, three' in French and I know he means for me to keep on for two or three more streets in the way he's pointin'. So I keep on, and, when I get there, I go through the whole rigamarole with another Frenchman. About the third session and I'm back on the Concord Place. THERE I am all right. No, I don't propose to stay lost long. My father and grandfather and all my men folks spent their lives cruisin' through crooked passages and crowded shoals and I guess I've inherited some of the knack."

At last I was strong enough to take a short outing in Hephzy's company. I returned to the hotel, where Hephzy left me. She was going to do a little shopping by herself. I went to my room and sat down to rest. A bell boy—at least that is what we should have called him in the States—knocked at the door.

"A lady to see Monsieur," he said.

The lady was Frances.

She entered the room and I rose to greet her.

"Why, you are alone!" she exclaimed. "Where is Miss Cahoon?"

"She is out, on a shopping expedition," I explained. "She will be back soon. I have been out too. We have been driving together. What do you think of that!"

She seemed pleased at the news but when I urged her to sit and wait for Hephzy's return she hesitated. Her hesitation, however, was only momentary. She took the chair by the window and we chatted together, of my newly-gained strength, of Hephzy's adventures as a pathfinder in Paris, of the weather, of a dozen inconsequential things. I found it difficult to sustain my part in the conversation. There was so much of real importance which I wanted to say. I wanted to ask her about herself, where she lodged, if she was still singing at L'Abbaye, what her plans for the future might be. And I did not dare.

My remarks became more and more disjointed and she, too, seemed uneasy and absent-minded. At length there was an interval of silence. She broke that silence.

"I suppose," she said, "you will be going back to Mayberry soon."

"Back to Mayberry?" I repeated.

"Yes. You and Miss Cahoon will go back there, of course, now that you are strong enough to travel. She told me that the American friends with whom you and she were to visit Switzerland had changed their plans and were going on to Italy. She said that she had written them that your proposed Continental trip was abandoned."

"Yes. Yes, that was given up, of course."

"Then you will go back to England, will you not?"

"I don't know. We have made no plans as yet."

"But you will go back. Miss Cahoon said you would. And, when your lease of the rectory expires, you will sail for America."

"I don't know."

"But you must know," with a momentary impatience. "Surely you don't intend to remain here in Paris."

"I don't know that, either. I haven't considered what I shall do. It depends—that is—"

I did not finish the sentence. I had said more than I intended and it was high time I stopped. But I had said too much, as it was. She asked more questions.

"Upon what does it depend?" she asked.

"Oh, nothing. I did not mean that it depended upon anything in particular. I—"

"You must have meant something. Tell me—answer me truthfully, please: Does it depend upon me?"

Of course that was just what it did depend upon. And suddenly I determined to tell her so.

"Frances," I demanded, "are you still there—at that place?"

"At L'Abbaye. Yes."

"You sing there every night?"

"Yes."

"Why do you do it? You know—"

"I know everything. But you know, too. I told you I sang there because I must earn my living in some way and that seems to be the only place where I can earn it. They pay me well there, and the people—the proprietors—are considerate and kind, in their way."

"But it isn't a fit place for you. And you don't like it; I know you don't."

"No," quietly. "I don't like it."

"Then don't do it. Give it up."

"If I give it up what shall I do?"

"You know. Come back with us and live with us as you did before. I want you; Hephzy is crazy to have you. We—she has missed you dreadfully. She grieves for you and worries about you. We offer you a home and—"

She interrupted. "Please don't," she said. "I have told you that that is impossible. It is. I shall never go back to Mayberry."

"But why? Your aunt—"

"Don't! My aunt is very kind—she has been so kind that I cannot bear to speak of her. Her kindness and—and yours are the few pleasant memories that I have—of this last dreadful year. To please you both I would do anything—anything—except—"

"Don't make any exceptions. Come with us. If not to Mayberry, then somewhere else. Come to America with us."

"No."

"Frances—"

"Don't! My mind is made up. Please don't speak of that again."

Again I realized the finality in her tone. The same finality was in mine as I answered.

"Then I shall stay here," I declared. "I shall not leave you alone, without friends or a protector of any kind, to sing night after night in that place. I shall not do it. I shall stay here as long as you do."

She was silent. I wondered what was coming next. I expected her to say, as she had said before, that I was forcing her to give up her one opportunity. I expected reproaches and was doggedly prepared to meet them. But she did not reproach me. She said nothing; instead she seemed to be thinking, to be making up her mind.

"Don't do it, Frances," I pleaded. "Don't sing there any longer. Give it up. You don't like the work; it isn't fit work for you. Give it up."

She rose from her chair and standing by the window looked out into the street. Suddenly she turned and looked at me.

"Would it please you if I gave up singing at L'Abbaye?" she asked quietly. "You know it would."

"And if I did would you and Miss Cahoon go back to England—at once?"

Here was another question, one that I found very hard to answer. I tried to temporize.

"We want you to come with us," I said, earnestly. "We want you. Hephzy—"

"Oh, don't, don't, don't! Why will you persist? Can't you understand that you hurt me? I am trying to believe I have some self-respect left, even after all that has happened. And you—What CAN you think of me! No, I tell you! NO!"

"But for Hephzy's sake. She is your only relative."

She looked at me oddly. And when she spoke her answer surprised me.

"You are mistaken," she said. "I have other—relatives. Good-by, Mr. Knowles."

She was on her way to the door.

"But, Frances," I cried, "you are not going. Wait. Hephzy will be here any moment. Don't go."

She shook her head.

"I must go," she said. At the door she turned and looked back.

"Good-by," she said, again. "Good-by, Kent."

She had gone and when I reached the door she had turned the corner of the corridor.

When Hephzy came I told her of the visit and what had taken place.

"That's queer," said Hephzy. "I can't think what she meant. I don't know of any other relatives she's got except Strickland Morley's tribe. And they threw him overboard long, long ago. I can't understand who she meant; can you, Hosy?"

I had been thinking.

"Wasn't there someone else—some English cousins of hers with whom she lived for a time after her father's death? Didn't she tell you about them?"

Hephzy nodded vigorously. "That's so," she declared. "There was. And she did live with 'em, too. She never told me their names or where they lived, but I know she despised and hated 'em. She gave me to understand that. And she ran away from 'em, too, just as she did from us. I don't see why she should have meant them. I don't believe she did. Perhaps she'll tell us more next time she comes. That'll be tomorrow, most likely."

I hoped that it might be to-morrow, but I was fearful. The way in which she had said good-by made me so. Her look, her manner, seemed to imply more than a good-by for a day. And, though this I did not tell Hephzy, she had called me "Kent" for the first time since the happy days at the rectory. I feared—all sorts of things.

She did not come on the morrow, or the following day, or the day after that. Another week passed and she did not come, nor had we received any word from her. By that time Hephzy was as anxious and fretful as I. And, when I proposed going in search of her, Hephzy, for a wonder, considering how very, very careful she was of my precious health, did not say no.

"You're pretty close to bein' as well as ever you was, Hosy," she said. "And I know how terribly worried you are. If you do go out at night you may be sick again, but if you don't go and lay awake frettin' and frettin' about her I KNOW you'll be sick. So perhaps you'd better do it. Shall I— Sha'n't I go with you?"

"I think you had better not," I said.

"Well, perhaps you're right. You never would tell me much about this opera-house, or whatever 'tis, but I shouldn't wonder if, bein' a Yankee,

I'd guessed considerable. Go, Hosy, and bring her back if you can. Find her anyhow. There! there run along. The hack's down at the door waitin'. Is your head feelin' all right? You're sure? And you haven't any pain? And you'll keep wrapped up? All right? Good-by, dearie. Hurry back! Do hurry back, for my sake. And I hope—Oh, I do hope you'll bring no bad news."

L'Abbaye, at eight-thirty in the evening was a deserted place compared to what it had been when I visited it at midnight. The waiters and attendants were there, of course, and a few early bird patrons, but not many. The bearded proprietors, or managers, were flying about, and I caught one of them in the middle of a flight.

He did not recognize me at first, but when I stated my errand, he did. Out went his hands and up went his shoulders.

"The Mademoiselle," he said. "Ah, yes! You are her friend, Monsieur; I remember perfectly. Oh, no, no, no! she is not here any more. She has left us. She sings no longer at L'Abbaye. We are desolate; we are inconsolable. We pleaded, but she was firm. She has gone. Where? Ah, Monsieur, so many ask that; but alas! we do not know."

"But you do know where she lives," I urged. "You must know her home address. Give me that. It is of the greatest importance that I see her at once."

At first he declared that he did not know her address, the address where she lodged. I persisted and, at last, he admitted that he did know it, but that he was bound by the most solemn promise to reveal it to no one.

"It was her wish, Monsieur. It was a part of the agreement under which she sang for us. No one should know who she was or where she lived. And I—I am an honorable man, Monsieur. I have promised and—" the business of shoulders and hands again—"my pledged word to a lady, how shall it be broken?"

I found a way to break it, nevertheless. A trio of gold pieces and the statement that I was her uncle did the trick. An uncle! Ah, that was different. And, Mademoiselle had consented to see me when I came before, that was true. She had seen the young English gentleman also—but we two only. Was the young English Monsieur—"the Doctor Baylees"—was he a relative also?

I did not answer that question. It was not his business and, beside, I did not wish to speak of Herbert Bayliss.

The address which the manager of L'Abbaye gave me, penciled on a card, was a number in a street in Montmartre, and not far away. I might easily have walked there, I was quite strong enough for walking now, but I preferred a cab. Paris motor cabs, as I knew from experience, moved rapidly. This one bore me to my destination in a few minutes.

A stout middle-aged French woman answered my ring. But her answer to my inquiries was most unsatisfactory. And, worse than all, I was certain she was telling me the truth.

The Mademoiselle was no longer there, she said. She had given up her room three days ago and had gone away. Where? That, alas, was a question. She had told no one. She had gone and she was not coming back. Was it not a pity, a great pity! Such a beautiful Mademoiselle! such an artiste! who sang so sweetly! Ah, the success she had made. And such a good young lady, too! Not like the others—oh, no, no, no! No one was to know she lodged there; she would see no one. Ah, a good girl, Monsieur, if ever one lived.

"Did she—did she go alone?" I asked.

The stout lady hesitated. Was Monsieur a very close friend? Perhaps a relative?

"An uncle," I said, telling the old lie once more.

Ah, an uncle! It was all right then. No, Mademoiselle had not gone alone. A young gentleman, a young English gentleman had gone with her, or, at least, had brought the cab in which she went and had driven off in it with her. A young English gentleman with a yellow mustache. Perhaps I knew him.

I recognized the description. She had left the house with Herbert Bayliss. What did that mean? Had she said yes to him? Were they married? I dreaded to know, but know I must.

And, as the one possible chance of settling the question, I bade my cab driver take me to the Hotel Continental. There, at the desk, I asked if Doctor Bayliss was still in the hotel. They said he was. I think I must have appeared strange or the gasp of relief with which I received the news was audible, for the concierge asked me if I was ill. I said no, and then he told me that Bayliss was planning to leave the next day, but was just then in his room. Did I wish to see him? I said I did and gave them my card.

He came down soon afterward. I had not seen him for a fortnight, for his calls had ceased even before Frances' last visit. Hephzy had said that, in her opinion, his meals must be disagreeing with him. Judging by his appearance his digestion was still very much impaired. He was in evening dress, of course; being an English gentleman he would have dressed for his own execution, if it was scheduled to take place after six o'clock. But his tie was carelessly arranged, his shirt bosom was slightly crumpled and there was a general "don't care" look about his raiment which was, for him, most unusual. And he was very solemn. I decided at once, whatever might have happened, it was not what I surmised. He was neither a happy bridegroom nor a prospective one.

"Good evening, Bayliss," said I, and extended my hand.

"Good evening, Knowles," he said, but he kept his own hands in his pockets. And he did not ask me to be seated.

"Well?" he said, after a moment.

"I came to you," I began—mine was a delicate errand and hard to state—"I came to you to ask if you could tell me where Miss Morley has gone. She has left L'Abbaye and has given up her room at her lodgings. She has gone—somewhere. Do you know where she is?"

It was quite evident that he did know. I could see it in his face. He did not answer, however. Instead he glanced about uneasily and then, turning, led the way toward a small reception room adjoining the lobby. This room was, save for ourselves, unoccupied.

"We can be more private here," he explained, briefly. "What did you ask?"

"I asked if you knew where Miss Morley had gone and where she was at the present time?"

He hesitated, pulling at his mustache, and frowning. "I don't see why you should ask me that?" he said, after a moment.

"But I do ask it. Do you know where she is?"

Another pause. "Well, if I did," he said, stiffly, "I see no reason why I should tell you. To be perfectly frank, and as I have said to you before, I don't consider myself bound to tell you anything concerning her."

His manner was most offensive. Again, as at the time I came to him at that very hotel on a similar errand, after my arrival in Paris, I found it hard to keep my temper.

"Don't misunderstand me," I said, as calmly as I could. "I am not pretending now to have a claim upon Miss Morley. I am not asking you to tell me just where she is, if you don't wish to tell. And it is not for my sake—that is, not primarily for that—that I am anxious about her. It is for hers. I wish you might tell me this: Is she safe? Is she among friends? Is she—is she quite safe and in a respectable place and likely to be happy? Will you tell me that?"

He hesitated again. "She is quite safe," he said, after a moment. "And she is among friends, or I suppose they are friends. As to her being happy—well, you ought to know that better than I, it seems to me."

I was puzzled. "*I* ought to know?" I repeated. "I ought to know whether she is happy or not? I don't understand."

He looked at me intently. "Don't you?" he asked. "You are certain you don't? Humph! Well, if I were in your place I would jolly well find out; you may be sure of that."

"What are you driving at, Bayliss? I tell you I don't know what you mean."

He did not answer. He was frowning and kicking the corner of a rug with his foot.

"I don't understand what you mean," I repeated. "You are saying too much or too little for my comprehension."

"I've said too much," he muttered. "At all events, I have said all I shall say. Was there any other subject you wished to see me about, Knowles? If not I must be going. I'm rather busy this evening."

"There was no subject but that one. And you will tell me nothing more concerning Miss Morley?"

"No."

"Good night," I said, and turned away. Then I turned back.

"Bayliss," said I, "I think perhaps I had better say this: I have only the kindest feelings toward you. You may have misunderstood my attitude in all this. I have said nothing to prejudice her—Miss Morley against you. I never shall. You care for her, I know. If she cares for you that is enough, so far as I am concerned. Her happiness is my sole wish. I want you to consider me your friend—and hers."

Once more I extended my hand. For an instant I thought he was going to take it, but he did not.

"No," he said, sullenly. "I won't shake hands with you. Why should I? You don't mean what you say. At least I don't think you do. I—I—By Jove! you can't!"

"But I do," I said, patiently.

"You can't! Look here! you say I care for her. God knows I do! But you—suppose you knew where she was, what would you do? Would you go to her?"

I had been considering this very thing, during my ride to the lodgings and on the way to the hotel; and I had reached a conclusion.

"No," I answered, slowly. "I think I should not. I know she does not wish me to follow her. I suppose she went away to avoid me. If I were convinced that she was among friends, in a respectable place, and quite safe, I should try to respect her wish. I think I should not follow her there."

He stared at me, wide-eyed.

"You wouldn't!" he repeated. "You wouldn't! And you—Oh, I say! And you talked of her happiness!"

"It is her happiness I am thinking of. If it were my own I should—"

"What?"

"Nothing, nothing. She will be happier if I do not follow her, I suppose. That is enough for me."

He regarded me with the same intent stare.

"Knowles," he said, suddenly, "she is at the home of a relative of hers— Cripps is the name—in Leatherhead, England. There! I have told you. Why I should be such a fool I don't know. And now you will go there, I suppose. What?"

"No," I answered. "No. I thank you for telling me, Bayliss, but it shall make no difference. I will respect her wish. I will not go there."

"You won't!"

"No, I will not trouble her again."

To my surprise he laughed. It was not a pleasant laugh, there was more sarcasm than mirth in it, or so it seemed, but why he should laugh at all I could not understand.

"Knowles," he said, "you're a good fellow, but—"

"But what?" I asked, stiffly.

"You're no end of a silly ass in some ways. Good night."

He turned on his heel and walked off.

CHAPTER XVII
In Which I, as Well as Mr. Solomon Cripps, Am Surprised

"And to think," cried Hephzy, for at least the fifth time since I told her, "that those Crippses are her people, the cousins she lived with after her pa's death! No wonder she was surprised when I told her how you and I went to Leatherhead and looked at their 'Ash Dump'—'Ash Chump,' I mean. And we came just as near hirin' it, too; we would have hired it if she hadn't put her foot down and said she wouldn't go there. A good many queer things have happened on this pilgrimage of ours, Hosy, but I do believe our goin' straight to those Crippses, of all the folks in England, is about the strangest. Seems as if we was sent there with a purpose, don't it?"

"It is a strange coincidence," I admitted.

"It's more'n that. And her goin' back to them is queerer still. She hates 'em, I know she does. She as much as said so, not mention' their names, of course. Why did she do it?"

I knew why she had done it, or I believed I did.

"She did it to please you and me, Hephzy," I said. "And to get rid of us. She said she would do anything to please us, and she knew I did not want her to remain here in Paris. I told her I should stay here as long as she did, or at least as long as she sang at—at the place where she was singing. And she asked if, provided she gave up singing there, you and I would go back to England—or America?"

"Yes, I know; you told me that, Hosy. But you said you didn't promise to do it."

"I didn't promise anything. I couldn't promise not to follow her. I didn't believe I could keep the promise. But I sha'n't follow her, Hephzy. I shall not go to Leatherhead."

Hephzy was silent for a moment. Then she said: "Why not?"

"You know why. That night when I first met her, the night after you had gone to Lucerne, she told me that if I persisted in following her and trying to see her I would force her to give up the only means of earning a living she had been able to find. Well, I have forced her to do that. She has been obliged to run away once more in order to get rid of us. I am not going to persecute her further. I am going to try and be unselfish and decent, if I can. Now that we know she is safe and among friends—"

"Friends! A healthy lot of friends they are—that Solomon Cripps and his wife! If ever I ran afoul of a sanctimonious pair of hypocrites they're the pair. Oh, they were sweet and buttery enough to us, I give in, but that was because they thought we was goin' to hire their Dump or Chump, or whatever 'twas. I'll bet they could be hard as nails to anybody they had under their thumbs. Whenever I see a woman or a man with a mouth that shuts up like a crack in a plate, the way theirs do, it takes more than Scriptur' texts from that mouth to make me believe it won't bite when it has the chance. Safe! poor Little Frank may be safe enough at Leatherhead, but I'll bet she's miserable. WHAT made her go there?"

"Because she had no other place to go, I suppose," I said. "And there, among her relatives, she thought she would be free from our persecution."

"There's some things worse than persecution," Hephzy declared; "and, so far as that goes, there are different kinds of persecution. But what makes those Crippses willin' to take her in and look after her is what I can't understand. They MAY be generous and forgivin' and kind, but, if they are, then I miss my guess. The whole business is awful queer. Tell me all about your talk with Doctor Bayliss, Hosy. What did he say? And how did he look when he said it?"

I told her, repeating our conversation word for word, as near as I could remember it. She listened intently and when I had finished there was an odd expression on her face.

"Humph!" she exclaimed. "He seemed surprised to think you weren't goin' to Leatherhead, you say?"

"Yes. At least I thought he was surprised. He knew I had chased her from Mayberry to Paris and was there at the hotel trying to learn from him where she was. And he knows you are her aunt. I suppose he thought it strange that we were not going to follow her any further."

"Maybe so... maybe so. But why did he call you a—what was it?—a silly donkey?"

"Because I am one, I imagine," I answered, bitterly. "It's my natural state. I was born one."

"Humph! Well, 'twould take more than that boy's word to make me believe it. No there's something!—I wish I could see that young fellow myself. He's at the Continental Hotel, you say?"

"Yes; but he leaves to-morrow. There, Hephzy, that's enough. Don't talk about it. Change the subject. I am ready to go back to England—yes, or America either, whenever you say the word. The sooner the better for me."

Hephzy obediently changed the subject and we decided to leave Paris the following afternoon. We would go back to the rectory, of course, and leave there for home as soon as the necessary arrangements could be made. Hephzy agreed to everything, she offered no objections, in fact it seemed to me that she was paying very little attention. Her lack of interest—yes, and apparent lack of sympathy, for I knew she must know what my decision meant to me—hurt and irritated me.

I rose.

"Good night," I said, curtly. "I'm going to bed."

"That's right, Hosy. You ought to go. You'll be sick again if you sit up any longer. Good night, dearie."

"And you?" I asked. "What are you going to do?"

"I'm going to set up a spell longer. I want to think."

"I don't. I wish I might never think again. Or dream, either. I am awake at last. God knows I wish I wasn't!"

She moved toward me. There was the same odd expression on her face and a queer, excited look in her eyes.

"Perhaps you aren't really awake, Hosy," she said, gently. "Perhaps this is the final dream and when you do wake you'll find—"

"Oh, bosh!" I interrupted. "Don't tell me you have another presentiment. If you have keep it to yourself. Good night."

I was weak from my recent illness and I had been under a great nervous strain all that evening. These are my only excuses and they are poor ones. I spoke and acted abominably and I was sorry for it afterward. I have told Hephzy so a good many times since, but I think she understood without my telling her.

"Well," she said, quietly, "dreams are somethin', after all. It's somethin' to have had dreams. I sha'n't forget mine. Good night, Hosy."

The next morning after breakfast she announced that she had an errand or two to do. She would run out and do them, she said, but she would be gone only a little while. She was gone nearly two hours during which I paced the floor or sat by the window looking out. The crowded boulevard was below me, but I did not see it. All I saw was a future as desolate and blank as the Bayport flats at low tide, and I, a quahaug on those flats, doomed to live, or exist, forever and ever and ever, with nothing to live for.

Hephzy, when she did return to the hotel, was surprisingly chatty and good-humored. She talked, talked, talked all the time, about nothing in particular, laughed a good deal, and flew about, packing our belongings and humming to herself. She acted more like the Hephzy of old than she had for weeks. There was an air of suppressed excitement about her which I could not understand. I attributed it to the fact of our leaving for America in the near future and her good humor irritated me. My spirits were lower than ever.

"You seem to be remarkably happy," I observed, fretfully.

"What makes you think so, Hosy? Because I was singin'? Father used to say my singin' was the most doleful noise he ever heard, except a fog-horn on a lee shore. I'm glad if you think it's a proof of happiness: I'm much obliged for the compliment."

"Well, you are happy, or you are trying to appear so. If you are pretending for my benefit, don't. I'M not happy."

"I know, Hosy; I know. Well, perhaps you—"

She didn't finish the sentence.

"Perhaps what?"

"Oh, nothin', nothin'. How many shirts did you bring with you? is this all?"

She sang no more, probably because she saw that the "fog-horn" annoyed me, but her manner was just as strange and her nervous energy as pronounced. I began to doubt if my surmise, that her excitement and exaltation were due to the anticipation of an early return to Bayport, was a correct one. I began to thing there must be some other course and to speculate concerning it. And I, too, grew a bit excited.

"Hephzy," I said, suddenly, "where did you go when you went out this morning? What sort of 'errands' were those of yours?"

She was folding my ties, her back toward me, and she answered without turning.

"Oh, I had some odds and ends of things to do," she said. "This plaid necktie of yours is gettin' pretty shabby, Hosy. I guess you can't wear it again. There! I mustn't stop to talk. I've got my own things to pack."

She hurried to her own room and I asked no more questions just then. But I was more suspicious than ever. I remembered a question of hers the previous evening and I believed.... But, if she had gone to the Continental and seen Herbert Bayliss, what could he have told her to make her happy?

We took the train for Calais and crossed the Channel to Dover. This time the eccentric strip of water was as calm as a pond at sunset. No jumpy, white-capped billows, no flying spray, no seasick passengers. Tarpaulins were a drag on the market.

"I wouldn't believe," declared Hephzy, "that this lookin'-glass was the same as that churned-up tub of suds we slopped through before. It doesn't trickle down one's neck now, does it, Hosy. A 'nahsty' cross-in' comin' and a smooth one comin' back. I wonder if that's a sign."

"Oh, don't talk about signs, Hephzy," I pleaded, wearily. "You'll begin to dream again, I suppose, pretty soon."

"No, I won't. I think you and I have stopped dreamin', Hosy. Maybe we're just wakin' up, same as I told you."

"What do you mean by that?"

"Mean? Oh, I guess I didn't mean anything. Good-by, old France! You're a lovely country and a lively one, but I sha'n't cry at sayin' good-by to you this time. And there's England dead ahead. Won't it seem good to be where they talk instead of jabber! I sha'n't have to navigate by the 'one-two-three' chart over there."

Dover, a flying trip through the customs, the train again, an English dinner in an English restaurant car—not a "wagon bed," as Hephzy said, exultantly—and then London.

We took a cab to the hotel, not Bancroft's this time, but a modern downtown hostelry where there were at least as many Americans as English. In our rooms I would have cross-questioned Hephzy, but she would not be questioned, declaring that she was tired and sleepy. I was tired, also, but not sleepy. I was almost as excited as she seemed to be by this time. I was sure she had learned something that morning in Paris, something which pleased her greatly. What that something might be I could not imagine; but I believed she had learned it from Herbert Bayliss.

And the next morning, after breakfast, she announced that she had arranged for a cab and we must start for the station at once. I said nothing then, but when the cab pulled up before a railway station, a station which was not our accustomed one but another, I said a great deal.

"What in the world, Hephzy!" I exclaimed. "We can't go to Mayberry from here."

"Hush, hush, Hosy. Wait a minute—wait till I've paid the driver. Yes, I'm doin' it myself. I'm skipper on this cruise. You're an invalid, didn't you know it. Invalids have to obey orders."

The cabman paid, she took my arm and led me into the station.

"And now, Hosy," she said, "let me tell you. We aren't goin' to Mayberry—not yet. We're going to Leatherhead."

"To Leatherhead!" I repeated. "To Leatherhead! To—her? We certainly will do no such thing."

"Yes, we will, Hosy," quietly. "I haven't said anything about it before, but I've made up my mind. It's our duty to see her just once more, once more before—before we say good-by for good. It's our duty."

"Duty! Our duty is to let her alone, to leave her in peace, as she asked us."

"How do you know she is in peace? Suppose she isn't. Suppose she's miserable and unhappy. Isn't it our duty to find out? I think it is?"

I looked her full in the face. "Hephzy," I said, sharply, "you know something about her, something that I don't know. What is it?"

"I don't know as I know anything, Hosy. I can't say that I do. But—"

"You saw Herbert Bayliss yesterday. That was the 'errand' you went upon yesterday morning in Paris. Wasn't it?"

She was very much taken aback. She has told me since that she had no idea I suspected the truth.

"Wasn't it?" I repeated.

"Why—why, yes, it was, Hosy. I did go to see him, there at his hotel. When you told me how he acted and what he said to you I thought 'twas awfully funny, and the more I thought it over the funnier it seemed. So I made up my mind to see him and talk with him myself. And I did."

"What did he tell you?" I asked.

"He told me—he told me—Well, he didn't tell me so much, maybe, but he gave me to understand a whole lot. She's gone to those Crippses, Hosy, just as I suspicioned, not because she likes 'em—she hates 'em—or because she wanted to go, but because she thought 'twould please us if she did. It doesn't please us; it doesn't please me, anyway. She sha'n't be miserable for our sake, not without a word from us. No, we must go there and see her and—and tell her once more just how we feel about it. It's our duty to go and we must. And," with decision, "we're goin' now."

She had poured out this explanation breathlessly, hurrying as if fearful that I might interrupt and ask more questions. I asked one of them the moment she paused.

"We knew all that before," I said. "That is, we were practically sure she had left Paris to get rid of us and had gone to her cousins, the Crippses, because of her half-promise to me not to sing at places like the Abbey again. We knew all that. And she asked me to promise that we would not follow her. I didn't promise, but that makes no difference. Was that all Bayliss told you?"

Hephzy was still embarrassed and confused, though she answered promptly enough.

"He told me he knew she didn't want to go to—to those Leatherheaded folks," she declared. "We guessed she didn't, but we didn't know it for sure. And he said we ought to go to her. He said that."

"But why did he say it? Our going will not alter her determination to stay and our seeing her again will only make it harder for her."

"No, it won't—no it won't," hastily. "Besides I want to see that Cripps man and have a talk with him, myself. I want to know why a man like him—I'm pretty well along in years; I've met folks and bargained and dealt with 'em all my grown-up life and I KNOW he isn't the kind to do things for nothin' for ANYBODY—I want to know why he and his wife are so generous to her. There's somethin' behind it."

"There's something behind you, Hephzy. Some other reason that you haven't told me. Was that all Bayliss said?"

She hesitated. "Yes," she said, after a moment, "that's all, all I can tell you now, anyway. But I want you to go with me to that Ash Dump and see her once more."

"I shall not, Hephzy."

"Well, then I'll have to go by myself. And if you don't go, too, I think you'll be awfully sorry. I think you will. Oh, Hosy," pleadingly, "please go with me. I don't ask you to do many things, now do I? I do ask you to do this."

I shook my head.

"I would do almost anything for your sake, Hephzy," I began.

"But this isn't for my sake. It's for hers. For hers. I'm sure—I'm ALMOST sure you and she will both be glad you did it."

I could not understand it at all. I had never seen her more earnest. She was not the one to ask unreasonable things and yet where her sister's child was concerned she could be obstinate enough—I knew that.

"I shall go whether you do or not," she said, as I stood looking at her.

"You mean that, Hephzy?"

"I surely do. I'm goin' to see her this very forenoon. And I do hope you'll go with me."

I reflected. If she went alone it would be almost as hard for Frances as if I went with her. And the temptation was very strong. The desire to see her once more, only once....

"I'll go, Hephzy," I said. I didn't mean to say it; the words seemed to come of themselves.

"You will! Oh, I'm so glad! I'm so glad! And I think—I think you'll be glad, too, Hosy. I'm hopin' you will."

"I'll go," I said. "But this is the last time you and I must trouble her. I'll go—not because of any reason you have given me, Hephzy, but because I believe there must be some other and stronger reason, which you haven't told me."

Hephzy drew a long breath. She seemed to be struggling between a desire to tell me more—whatever that more might be—and a determination not to tell.

"Maybe there is, Hosy," she said, slowly. "Maybe there is. I—I—Well, there! I must go and buy the tickets. You sit down and wait. I'm skipper of this craft to-day, you know. I'm in command on this voyage."

Leatherhead looked exactly as it had on our previous visit. "Ash Clump," the villa which the Crippses had been so anxious for us to hire, was still untenanted, or looked to be. We walked on until we reached the Cripps home and entered the Cripps gate. I rang the bell and the maid answered the ring.

In answer to our inquiries she told us that Mr. Cripps was not in. He and Mrs. Cripps had gone to chapel. I remembered then that the day was Sunday. I had actually forgotten it.

"Is Miss Morley in?" asked Hephzy.

The maid shook her head.

"No, ma'am," she said. "Miss Morley ain't in, either. I think she's gone to chapel, too. I ain't sure, ma'am, but I think she 'as. She's not in."

She asked if we would leave cards. Hephzy said no.

"It's 'most noon," she said. "They'll be back pretty soon. We'll wait. No, we won't come in. We'll wait out here, I guess."

There was a rustic seat on the lawn near the house and Hephzy seated herself upon it. I walked up and down. I was in a state of what Hephzy would have called "nerves." I had determined to be very calm when I met her, to show no emotion, to be very calm and cool, no matter what happened. But this waiting was hard. I grew more nervous every minute.

"I'm going to stroll about, Hephzy," I said. "About the garden and grounds. I sha'n't go far and I'll return soon. I shall be within call. Send one of the servants for me if she—if the Crippses come before I get back."

Hephzy did not urge me to remain. Nor did she offer to accompany me. As usual she seemed to read my thoughts and understand them.

"All right, Hosy," she said. "You go and have your walk. I'll wait here. But don't be long, will you."

I promised not to be long. The Cripps gardens and grounds were not extensive, but they were well kept even if the beds were geometrically ugly and the color masses jarring and in bad taste. The birds sang, the breeze stirred the leaves and petals, and there was a Sunday quiet, the restful hush of an English Sunday, everywhere.

I strolled on along the paths, through the gap in the hedge dividing the kitchen garden from the purely ornamental section, past the stables, until I emerged from the shrubbery at the top of a little hill. There was a pleasant view from this hill, the customary view of hedged fields and meadows, flocks of sheep and groups of grazing cattle, and over all the soft blue haze and misty sky.

I paused. And then close beside me, I heard a startled exclamation.

I turned. In a nook of the shrubbery was another rustic seat. Rising from that seat and gazing at me with a look of amazed incredulity, was—Frances Morley.

I did not speak. I could not, for the moment. She spoke first.

"You!" she exclaimed. "You—here!"

And still I did not speak. Where was the calm with which I was to meet her? Where were the carefully planned sentences which were to explain how I had come and why? I don't know where they were; I seemed to know only that she was there, that I was alone with her as I had never thought or meant to be again, and that if I spoke I should say things far different from those I had intended.

She was recovering from her surprise. She came toward me.

"What are you doing here?" she asked. "Why did you come?"

I stammered a word or two, some incoherences to the effect that I had not expected to find her there, that I had been told she was at church. She shook her head, impatiently.

"I mean why did you come here—to Leatherhead?" she asked. "Why did you come? Did you know—"

I interrupted her. If ever I was to explain, or attempt to explain, I realized that it must be at that moment. She might listen to me then, before she had had time to think. Later I knew she would not.

"I knew you were here," I broke in, quickly. "I—we—your aunt knew and we came."

"But HOW did you know? Who told you?"

"The—we learned," I answered. "And we came."

It was a poor explanation—or none at all. She seemed to think it so. And yet she seemed more hurt than offended.

"You came—yes," she said. "And you knew that I left Paris because— Oh, you knew that! I asked you not to follow me. You promised you would not."

I was ashamed, thoroughly ashamed and disgusted with myself for yielding to Hephzy's entreaties.

"No, no," I protested, "I did not promise. I did not promise, Frances."

"But you know I did not wish you to do it. I did not wish you to follow me to Paris, but you did it. I told you you would force me to give up my only means of earning money. You did force me to give it up. I gave it up to please you, for your sake, and now—"

"Did you?" I cried, eagerly. "Did you give it up for my sake, Frances? Did you?"

"You know I did. You must know it. And now that I have done it, now that I have given up my opportunity and my—my self-respect and my one chance and come here to this—to this place, you—you—Oh, how could you! Wasn't I unhappy enough before? And unhappy enough now? Oh, how could you!"

I was more ashamed than ever. I tried desperately to justify my action.

"But that was it," I persisted. "Don't you see? It was your happiness, the thought that you were unhappy which brought me here. I know—you told your aunt how unhappy you had been when you were with these people before. I know how much you disliked them. That was why I came. To ask you to give this up as you did the other. To come with us and BE happy. I want you to come, Frances. Think! Think how much I must want you."

And, for the moment I thought this appeal had some effect. It seemed to me that her resolution was shaken, that she was wavering.

"You—you really want me?" she repeated.

"Yes. Yes, I can't tell you—I must not tell you how much I want you. And your aunt—she wants you to come. She is here, too. She will tell you."

Her manner changed once more. The tone in which she spoke was different. There were no signs of the wavering which I had noticed—or hoped I noticed.

"No," she said. "No. I shall not see my aunt. And I must not talk with you any longer. I asked you not to follow me here. You did it, in spite of my asking. Now, unless you wish to drive me away from here, as you did from Paris, you will leave me and not try to see me again. Oh, don't you see—CAN'T you see how miserable you are making me? And yet you talk of my happiness!"

"But you aren't happy here. ARE you happy?"

"I am happy enough. Yes, I am happy."

"I don't believe it. Are these Crippses kind to you?"

"Yes."

I didn't believe that, either, but I did not say so. Instead I said what I had determined to say, the same thing that I should have said before, in Mayberry and in Paris—if I could have mustered the courage and decency to say it.

"Frances," I said, "there is something else, something which may have a bearing on your happiness, or may not, I don't know. The night before you left us, at Mayberry, Herbert Bayliss came to me and asked my permission to marry you, if you were willing. He thought you were my niece—then. I said that—I said that, although of course I had no shadow of authority over you, I did care for your happiness. I cared for that a great deal. If you loved him I should certainly—"

"I see," she broke in, scornfully. "I see. He told you I was here. That is why you came. Did he send you to me to say—what you are trying to say?"

"Oh, no, no! You are mistaken. You wrong him, Frances. He did not do that. He's not that sort. He's a good fellow, an honorable man. And he does care for you. I know it. He cares greatly. He would, I am sure, make you a good husband, and if you care for him, he would do his best to make you happy, I—"

Again she interrupted. "One moment," she said, "Let me understand. Are you urging me to marry Herbert Bayliss?"

"No. I am not urging you, of course. But if you do care for him—"

"I do not."

"Oh, you don't love him?"

I wonder if there was relief in my tone. There should not have been, of course, but I fear there was.

"No, I do not—love him. He is a gentleman and I like him well enough, but not in that way. Please don't say any more."

"Very well. I only meant—Tell me this, if you will: Is there someone you do care for?"

She did not answer. I had offended her again. She had cause to be offended. What business was it of mine?

"I beg your pardon," I said, humbly. "I should not have asked that. I have no right to ask it. But if there is someone for whom you care in that way and he cares for you, it—"

"Oh, don't, don't! He doesn't."

"Then there is someone?"

She was silent. I tried to speak like a man, like the man I was pretending to be.

"I am glad to know it," I said. "If you care for him he must care for you. He cannot help it. I am sure you will be happy by and by. I can leave you here now with more—with less reluctance. I—"

I could not trust myself to go on, although I tried to do so. She answered, without looking at me.

"Yes," she said, "you can leave me now. I am safe and—and happy. Good-by."

I took her hand.

Kent Knowles | 293

"Good-by," I said. "Forgive me for coming. I shall not trouble you again. This time I promise. You may not wish to write us, but we shall write you. And I—I hope you won't forget us."

It was a lame conclusion and trite enough. She must have thought so.

"I shall not forget you," she said, simply. "And I will try to write occasionally. Yes, I will try. Now please go. Good-by."

I went, without looking back. I strode along the paths, scarcely noticing where I was going. As I neared the corner of the house I heard voices, loud voices. One of them, though it was not as loud as the others, was Hephzy's.

"I knew it," she was saying, as I turned the corner. "I knew it. I knew there was some reason, some mean selfish reason why you were willin' to take that girl under your wing. I knew it wasn't kind-heartedness and relationship. I knew it."

It was Solomon Cripps who answered. Mr. and Mrs. Cripps, arrayed in their Sabbath black and white, were standing by the door of their villa. Hephzy was standing before them. Her face was set and determined and she looked highly indignant. Mr. Cripps' face was red and frowning and he gesticulated with a red hand, which clasped a Testament. His English was by no means as pure and undefiled as when he had endeavored to persuade us into hiring "Ash Clump."

"Look 'ere," he snarled. "Don't you talk to me like that. Don't you suppose I know what I'm doing. You Yankees may be clever at your tricks, but you can't trick me. Don't I know about the money you stole from 'er father? Don't I, eh? You can tell 'er your lies about it being stolen by someone else, but I can see a 'ole through a millstone. You can't trick me, I tell you. They're giving that girl a good 'ome and care and all that, but we're goin' to see she 'as 'er rights. You've filled 'er silly 'ead with your stories. You've made 'er think you're all that's good and—"

I was at hand by this time.

"What's all this, Hephzy?" I asked.

Before Hephzy could reply Mrs. Cripps spoke.

"It's him!" she cried, seizing her husband's arm with one hand and pointing at me with the other. "It's him," she cried, venomously. "He's here, too."

The sight of me appeared to upset what little self-control Mr. Cripps had left.

"You!" he shouted, "I might 'ave known you were 'ere. You're the one that's done it. You're responsible. Filling her silly 'ead with lies about your goodness and all that. Making her fall in love with you and—"

I sprang forward.

"WHAT?" I cried. "What are you saying?"

Hephzy was frightened.

"Hosy," she cried, "don't look so. Don't! You frighten me."

I scarcely heard her.

"WHAT did you say?" I demanded, addressing Cripps, who shrank back, rather alarmed apparently. "Why, you scoundrel! What do you mean by saying that? Speak up! What do you mean by it?"

If Mr. Cripps was alarmed his wife was not. She stepped forward and faced me defiantly.

"He means just what he says," she declared, her shrill voice quivering with vindictive spite. "And you know what he means perfectly well. You ought to be ashamed of yourself, a man as old as you and she an innocent young girl! You've hypnotized her—that is what you've done, hypnotized her. All those ridiculous stories about her having no money she believes because you told them to her. She would believe the moon was made of green cheese if you said so. She's mad about you—the poor little fool! She won't hear a word against you—says you're the best, noblest man in the world! You! Why she won't even deny that she's in love with you; she was brazen enough to tell me she was proud of it. Oh.... Stop! Where are you going? Solomon, stop him!"

Solomon did not stop me. I am very glad he didn't try. No one could have stopped me then. I was on my way back along the garden path, and if I did not keep to that path, but plunged ruthlessly through flower beds and shrubbery I did not care, nor do I care now.

She was sitting on the rustic seat where I had left her. There were tears on her cheeks. She had heard me coming—a deaf person would have heard that—and she rose as I burst into view.

"What is it?" she cried, in alarm. "Oh, what is it?"

At the sight of her I paused. I had not meant to pause; I had intended to take her in my arms, to ask her if what I had just heard was true, to make her answer me. But now, as she stood there before me, so young, so girlish, so beautiful, the hopeless idiocy of the thing struck me with overwhelming force. It WAS idiocy. It couldn't be true.

"What is it?" she repeated. "Oh, Kent! what is the matter? Why did you come back? What has happened?"

I stepped forward. True or false I must know. I must know then and there. It was now or never for me.

"Frances," I stammered, "I came back because—I—I have just heard—Frances, you told me you loved someone—not Bayliss, but someone else. Who is that someone?"

She had been pale. My sudden and unexpected appearance had frightened her. Now as we faced each other, as I stood looking down into her face, I saw the color rise and spread over that face from throat to brow.

"Who is it?" I repeated.

She drew back.

"I—I can't tell you," she faltered. "You mustn't ask me."

"But I do ask. You must tell me, Frances—Frances, it isn't—it can't be that you love ME. Do you?"

She drew back still further. If there had been a way of escape I think she would have taken it. But there was none. The thick shrubbery was behind her and I was between her and the path. And I would not let her pass.

"Oh, Frances, do you?" I repeated. "I never meant to ask you. I never meant that you should know. I am so much older, and so—so unworthy—it has seemed so hopeless and ridiculous. But I love you, Frances, I have loved you from the very beginning, although at first I didn't realize it. I—If you do—if you can—I—I—"

I faltered, hesitated, and stopped. She did not answer for a moment, a long, long moment. Then:

"Mr. Knowles," she said, "you surprise me. I didn't suspect—I didn't think—"

I sighed. I had had my answer. Of course it was idiotic. I should have known; I did know.

"I see," I said. "I understand. Forgive me, please. I was a fool to even think of such a thing. I didn't think it. I didn't dare until—until just now. Then I was told—your cousin said—I might have known he didn't mean what he said. But he said it and—and—"

"What did he say? Mr. Cripps, do you mean? What did he say?"

"He said—he said you—you cared for me—in that way. Of course you don't—you can't. I know better. But for the moment I dared to hope. I was crazy, of course. Forgive me, Frances."

She looked up and then down again.

"There is nothing to forgive," she said.

"Yes, there is. There is a great deal. An old—"

"Hush! hush, please. Don't speak like that. I—I thank you. I—you mustn't suppose I am not grateful. I know you pity me. I know how generous you are. But your pity—"

"It isn't pity. I should pity myself, if that were all. I love you Frances, and I shall always love you. I am not ashamed of it. I shall have that love to comfort me till I die. I am ashamed of having told you, of troubling you again, that is all."

I was turning away, but I heard her step beside me and felt her hand upon my sleeve. I turned back again. She was looking me full in the face now and her eyes were shining.

"What Mr. Cripps said was true," she said.

I could not believe it. I did not believe it even then.

"True!" I repeated. "No, no! You don't mean—"

"I do mean it. I told him that I loved you."

I don't know what more she would have said. I did not wait to hear. She was in my arms at last and all England was whirling about me like a top.

"But you can't!" I found myself saying over and over. I must have said other things before, but I don't remember them. "You can't! it is impossible. You! marry an old fossil like me! Oh, Frances, are you sure? Are you sure?"

"Yes, Kent," softly, "I am sure."

"But you can't love me. You are sure that your—You have no reason to be grateful to me, but you have said you were, you know. You are sure you are not doing this because—"

"I am sure. It is not because I am grateful."

"But, my dear—think! Think what it means, I am—"

"I know what you are," tenderly. "No one knows as well. But, Kent— Kent, are YOU sure? It isn't pity for me?"

I think I convinced her that it was not pity. I know I tried. And I was still trying when the sound of steps and voices on the other side of the shrubbery caused us—or caused her; I doubt if I should have heard anything except her voice just then—to start and exclaim:

"Someone is coming! Don't, dear, don't! Someone is coming."

It was the Crippses who were coming, of course. Mr. and Mrs. Cripps and Hephzy. They would have come sooner, I learned afterwards, but Hephzy had prevented it.

Solomon's red face was redder still when he saw us together. And Mrs. Cripps' mouth looked more like "a crack in a plate" than ever.

"So!" she exclaimed. "Here's where you are! I thought as much. And you—you brazen creature!"

I objected strongly to "brazen creature" as a term applied to my future wife. I intended saying so, but Mr. Cripps got ahead of me.

"You get off my grounds," he blurted, waving his fist. "You get out of 'ere now or I'll 'ave you put off. Do you 'ear?"

I should have answered him as he deserved to be answered, but Frances would not let me.

"Don't, Kent," she whispered. "Don't quarrel with him, please. He is going, Mr. Cripps. We are going—now."

Mrs. Cripps fairly shrieked. "WE are going?" she repeated. "Do you mean you are going with him?"

Hephzy joined in, but in a quite different tone.

"You are goin'?" she said, joyfully. "Oh, Frances, are you comin' with us?"

It was my turn now and I rejoiced in the prospect. An entire brigade of Crippses would not have daunted me then. I should have enjoyed defying them all.

"Yes," said I, "she is coming with us, Hephzy. Mr. Cripps, will you be good enough to stand out of the way? Come, Frances."

It is not worth while repeating what Mr. and Mrs. Cripps said. They said a good deal, threatened all sorts of things, lawsuits among the rest. Hephzy fired the last guns for our side.

"Yes, yes," she retorted, impatiently. "I know you're goin' to sue. Go ahead and sue and prosecute yourselves to death, if you want to. The lawyers'll get their fees out of you, and that's some comfort—though I shouldn't wonder if THEY had to sue to get even that. And I tell you this: If you don't send Little Frank's—Miss Morley's trunks to Mayberry inside of two days we'll come and get 'em and we'll come with the sheriff and the police."

Mrs. Cripps, standing by the gate, fell back upon her last line of intrenchments, the line of piety.

"And to think," she declared, with upturned eyes, "that this is the 'oly Sabbath! Never mind, Solomon. The Lord will punish 'em. I shall pray to Him not to curse them too hard."

Hephzy's retort was to the point.

"I wouldn't," she said. "If I had been doin' what you two have been up to, pretendin' to care for a young girl and offerin' to give her a home, and all the time doin' it just because I thought I could squeeze money out of her, I shouldn't trouble the Lord much. I wouldn't take the risk of callin' His attention to me."

CHAPTER XVIII
In Which the Pilgrimage Ends Where It Began

We did not go to Mayberry that day. We went to London and to the hotel; not Bancroft's, but the hotel where Hephzy and I had stayed the previous night. It was Frances' wish that we should not go to Bancroft's.

"I don't think that I could go there, Kent," she whispered to me, on the train. "Mr. and Mrs Jameson were very kind, and I liked them so much, but—but they would ask questions; they wouldn't understand. It would be hard to make them understand. Don't you see, Kent?"

I saw perfectly. Considering that the Jamesons believed Miss Morley to be my niece, it would indeed be hard to make them understand. I was not inclined to try. I had had quite enough of the uncle and niece business.

So we went to the other hotel and if the clerk was surprised to see us again so soon he said nothing about it. Perhaps he was not surprised. It must take a good deal to surprise a hotel clerk.

On the train, in our compartment—a first-class compartment, you may be sure; I would have hired the whole train if it had been necessary; there was nothing too good or too expensive for us that afternoon—on the train, discussing the ride to London, Hephzy did most of the talking. I was too happy to talk much and Frances, sitting in her corner and pretending to look out of the window, was silent also. I should have been fearful that she was not happy, that she was already repenting her rashness in promising to marry the Bayport "quahaug," but occasionally she looked at me, and, whenever she did, the wireless message our eyes exchanged, sent that quahaug aloft on a flight through paradise. A flying clam is an unusual specimen, I admit, but no other quahaug in this wide, wide world had an excuse like mine for developing wings.

Hephzy did not appear to notice our silence. She chatted and laughed continuously. We had not told her our secret—the great secret—and if she suspected it she kept her suspicions to herself. Her chatter was a curious mixture: triumph over the detached Crippses; joy because, after all, "Little Frank" had consented to come with us, to live with us again; and triumph over me because her dreams and presentiments had come true.

"I told you, Hosy," she kept saying. "I told you! I said it would all come out in the end. He wouldn't believe it, Frances. He said I was an old lunatic and—"

"I didn't say anything of the kind," I broke in.

"You said what amounted to that and I don't know as I blame you. But I knew—I just KNEW he and I had been 'sent' on this course and that we—all three of us—would make the right port in the end. And we have—we have, haven't we, Frances?"

"Yes," said Frances, simply. "We have, Auntie—"

"There! do you hear that, Hosy? Isn't it good to hear her call me 'Auntie' again! Now I'm satisfied; or" —with a momentary hesitation—"pretty nearly satisfied, anyway."

"Oh, then you're not quite satisfied, after all," I observed. "What more do you want?"

"I want just one thing more; just one, that's all."

I believed I know what that one thing was, but I asked her. She shot a look at me, a look of indignant meaning.

"Never mind," she said, decidedly. "That's my affair. Oh, Ho!" with a reminiscent chuckle, "how that Cripps woman did glare at me when I said 'twas pretty risky her callin' the Almighty's attention to their doin's. I hope it did her good. Maybe she'll think of it next time she goes to chapel. But I suppose she won't. All such folks care for is money. They wouldn't be so anxious to get to Heaven if they hadn't read about the golden streets."

That evening, at the hotel, Frances told us her story, the story of which we had guessed a good deal, but of which she had told so little—how, after her father's death, she had gone to live with the Crippses because, as she thought, they wished her to do so from motives of generosity and kindness.

"They are not really relatives of mine," she said. "I am glad of that. Mrs. Cripps married a cousin of my father's; he died and then she married Mr. Cripps. After Father's death they wrote me a very kind letter, or I thought it kind at the time. They said all sorts of kindly things, they offered me a home, they said I should be like their own daughter. So, having nowhere else to go, I went to them. I lived there nearly two years. Oh, what a life it was! They are very churchly people, they call themselves religious, but I don't. They pretend to be—perhaps they think they are—good, very good. But they aren't—they aren't. They are hard and cruel. Mr. Cripps owns several tenements where poor people live. I have heard things from those people that—Oh, I can't tell you! I ran away because I had learned what they really were."

Hephzy nodded. "What I can't understand," she said, "is why they offered you a home in the first place. It was because they thought you had money comin' to you, that's plain enough now; but how did they know?"

Frances colored. "I'm afraid—I'm afraid Father must have written them," she said. "He needed money very much in his later years and he may have written them asking—asking for loans and offering my 'inheritance' as security. I think now that that was it. But I did not think so then. And—and, Oh, Auntie, you mustn't think too harshly of Father. He was very good to me, he really was. And DON'T you think he believed—he had made himself believe—that there was money of his there in America? I can't believe he—he would lie to me."

"Of course he didn't lie," said Hephzy, promptly. I could have hugged her for saying it. "He was sick and—and sort of out of his head, poor man, and I don't doubt he made himself believe all sorts of things. Of course he didn't lie—to his own daughter. But why," she added, quickly, before Frances could ask another question, "did you go back to those precious Cripps critters after you left Paris?"

Frances looked at me. "I thought it would please you," she said, simply. "I knew you didn't want me to sing in public. Kent had said he would be happier if he knew I had given up that life and was among friends. And they—they had called themselves my friends. When I went back to them they welcomed me. Mr. Cripps called me his 'prodigal daughter,' and Mrs. Cripps prayed over me. It wasn't until I told them I had no 'inheritance,' except one of debt, that they began to show me what they really were. They wouldn't believe it. They said you were trying to defraud me. It was dreadful. I—I think I should have run away again if—if you had not come."

"Well, we did come," said Hephzy, cheerfully, "and I thank the good Lord for it. Now we won't talk any more about THAT."

She left us alone soon afterward, going to my room—we were in hers, hers and Frances'—to unpack my trunk once more. She wouldn't hear of my unpacking it. When she was gone Frances turned to me.

"You—you haven't told her," she faltered.

"No," said I, "not yet. I wanted to speak with you first. I can't believe it is true. Or, if it is, that it is right. Oh, my dear, do you realize what you are doing? I am—I am ever so much older than you. I am not worthy of you. You could have made a so much better marriage."

She looked at me. She was smiling, but there was a tiny wrinkle between her brows.

"Meaning," she said, "I suppose, that I might have married Doctor Bayliss. I might perhaps marry him even yet, if I wished. I—I think he would have me, if I threw myself at his head."

"Yes," I admitted, grudgingly. "Yes, he loves you, Frances."

"Kent, when we were there in Mayberry it seemed to me that my aunt and you were almost anxious that I should marry him. It seemed to me that you took every opportunity to throw me in his way; you refused my invitations for golf and tennis and suggested that I play with him instead. It used to annoy me. I resented it. I thought you were eager to get rid of me. I did not know then the truth about Father and—and the money. And I thought you hoped I might marry him and—and not trouble you any more. But I think I understand now. You—you did not care for me so much then. Was that it?"

I shook my head. "Care for you!" I repeated. "I cared for you so much that I did not dare trust myself with you. I did not dare to think of you, and yet I could think of no one else. I know now that I fell in love with you when I first met you at that horrible Briggs woman's lodging-house. Don't you see? That was the very reason why. Don't you see?"

"No, I'm afraid I don't quite see. If you cared for me like that how could you be willing for me to marry him? That is what puzzles me. I don't understand it."

"It was because I did care for you. It was because I cared so much, I wanted you to be happy. I never dreamed that you could care for an old, staid, broken-down bookworm like me. It wasn't thinkable. I can scarcely think it now. Oh, Frances, are you SURE you are not making a mistake? Are you sure it isn't gratitude which makes you—"

She rose from her chair and came to me. Her eyes were wet, but there was a light in them like the sunlight behind a summer shower.

"Don't, please don't!" she begged. "And caring for me like that you could still come to me as you did this morning and suggest my marrying him."

"Yes, yes, I came because—because I knew he loved you and I thought that you might not know it. And if you did know it I thought—perhaps— you might be happier and—"

I faltered and stopped. She was standing beside me, looking up into my face.

"I did know it," she said. "He told me, there in Paris. And I told him—"

"You told him—?"

"I told him that I liked him; I do, I do; he is a good man. But I told him—" she rose on tiptoe and kissed me—"I told him that I loved you, dear. See! here is the pin you gave me. It is the one thing I could not leave behind when I ran away from Mayberry. I meant to keep that always—and I always shall."

After a time we remembered Hephzy. It would be more truthful to say that Frances remembered her. I had forgotten Hephzy altogether, I am ashamed to say.

"Kent," she said; "don't you think we should tell Auntie now? She will be pleased, I hope."

"Pleased! She will be—I can't think of a word to describe it. She loves you, too, dear."

"I know. I hope she will love me more now. She worships you, Kent."

"I am afraid she does. She doesn't realize what a tinsel god I am. And I fear you don't either. I am not a great man. I am not even a famous author. I—Are you SURE, Frances?"

She laughed lightly. "Kent," she whispered, "what was it Doctor Bayliss called you when you offered to promise not to follow me to Leatherhead?"

I had told her the whole story of my last interview with Bayliss at the Continental.

"He called me a silly ass," I answered promptly. "I don't care."

"Neither do I; but don't you think you are one, just a little bit of one, in some things? You mustn't ask me if I am sure again. Come! we will go to Auntie."

Hephzy had finished unpacking my trunk and was standing by the closet door, shaking the wrinkles out of my dinner coat. She heard us enter and turned.

"I never saw clothes in such a mess in my life," she announced. "And I packed this trunk, too. I guess the trembles in my head must have got into my fingers when I did it. I—"

She stopped at the beginning of the sentence. I had taken Frances by the hand and led her up to where she was standing. Hephzy said nothing, she stood there and stared at us, but the coat fell to the floor.

"Hephzy," said I, "I've come to make an apology. I believe in dreams and presentiments and Spiritualism and all the rest of it now. You were right. Our pilgrimage has ended just as you declared it would. I know now that we were 'sent' upon it. Frances has said—"

Hephzy didn't wait to hear any more. She threw her arms about Frances' neck, then about mine, hugged us both, and then, to my utter astonishment, sat down upon the closed trunk and burst into tears. When we tried to comfort her she waved us away.

"Don't touch me," she commanded. "Don't say anything to me. Just let me be. I've done all kinds of loony things in my life and this attack is just natural, that's all. I—I'll get over it in a minute. There!" rising and dabbing at her eyes with her handkerchief, "I'm over it now. Hosy Knowles, I've cried about a million times since—since that awful mornin' in Mayberry. You didn't know it, but I have. I'm through now. I'm never goin' to cry any more. I'm goin' to laugh! I'm going to sing! I declare if you don't grab me and hold me down I shall dance! Oh, Oh, OH! I'm so glad! I'm so glad!"

We sat up until the early morning hours, talking and planning. We were to go back to America as soon as we could secure passage; upon that we all agreed in the end. I was the only one who hesitated. I had a vague feeling of uneasiness, a dread, that Frances might not wish it, that her saying she would love to go was merely to please me. I remembered how she had hated America and Americans, or professed to hate them, in the days of our first acquaintanceship. I thought of quiet, sleepy, humdrum old Bayport and the fear that she might be disappointed when she saw it, that she might be lonely and unhappy there, was strong. So when Hephzy talked of our going straight to the steamship offices next day I demurred. I suggested a Continental trip, to Switzerland, to the Mediterranean—anywhere. I forgot that my means were limited, that I had been idle for longer than I should have been, and that I absolutely must work soon. I forgot everything, and talked, as Hephzy said afterward, "regardless, like a whole kerosene oil company."

But, to my surprise, it was Frances herself who was most insistent upon our going to America. She wanted to go, she said. Of course she did not mean to be selfish, and if Auntie and I really wished to go to the Continent or remain in England she would be quite content.

"But, Oh Kent," she said, "if you are suggesting all this merely because you think I will like it, please don't. I have lived in France and I have been very unhappy there. I have been happier here in England, but I have been unhappy here, too. I have no friends here now. I have no friends anywhere except you. I know you both want to see your home again—you must. And—and your home will be mine now."

So we decided to sail for America, and that without delay. And the next morning, before breakfast, Hephzy came to my room with another suggestion.

"Hosy," she said, "I've been thinkin'. All our things, or most of 'em, are at Mayberry. Somebody's got to go there, of course, to pack up and make arrangements for our leavin'. She—Frances, I mean—would go, too, if we asked her, I suppose likely; she'd do anything you asked, now. But it would be awful hard for her. She'd meet all the people she used to know there and they wouldn't understand and 'twould be hard to explain. The Baylisses know the real truth, but the rest of 'em don't. You'd have all that niece and uncle mess again, and I don't suppose you want any more of THAT."

"I should say I didn't!" I exclaimed, fervently.

"Yes, that's the way it seemed to me. So she hadn't ought to go to Mayberry. And we can't leave her here alone in London. She'd be lonesome, for one thing, and those everlastin' Crippses might find out where she was, for another. It may be that that Solomon and his wife will let her go and say nothin', but I doubt it. So long as they think she's got a cent comin' to her they'll pester her in every way they can, I believe. That woman's nose can smell money as far as a cat can smell fish. No, we can't leave Little Frank here alone. Of course, I might stay with her and you might go by yourself, but—"

This way out of the difficulty had occurred to me; so when she seemed to hesitate, I asked: "But what?"

"But it won't be very pleasant for you in Mayberry. You'd have considerable explainin' to do. And, more'n that, Hosy, there's all that packin' up to do and I've seen you try to pack a trunk too often before. You're just as likely to pack a flat-iron on top of a lookin' glass as to do the other thing. No, I'm the one to go to Mayberry. I must go by myself and you must stay here in London with her."

"I can't do that, Hephzy," I said. "How could I?"

"You couldn't, as things are, of course. But if they were different. If she was your wife you could. And then if that Solomon thing came you could—"

I interrupted. "My wife!" I repeated. "Hephzy, what are you talking about? Do you mean—"

"I mean that you and she might be married right off, to-day perhaps. Then everything would be all right."

I stared at her.

"But—but she wouldn't consent," I stammered. "It is impossible. She wouldn't think of such a thing."

Hephzy nodded. "Oh, yes, she would," she said. "She is thinkin' of it now. She and I have just had a long talk. She's a sensible girl, Hosy, and she listened to reason. If she was sure that you wanted to marry her so soon she—"

"Wanted to!" I cried. "Hephzy!"

Hephzy nodded again. "Then that's settled," she said. "It's a big disappointment to me, I give in. I'd set my heart on your bein' married at our meetin'-house in Bayport, with Mr. Partridge to do the marryin', and a weddin' reception at our house and—and everything. But I guess this is the best, and I know it's the most sensible. But, Oh Hosy, there's one thing I can't give up. I want you to be married at the American Ambassador's or somewhere like it and by an American minister. I sha'n't feel safe if it's done anywhere else and by a foreigner, even if he's English, which don't seem foreign to me at all any more. No, he's got to be an American and—and, Oh, Hosy! DO try to get a Methodist."

I couldn't get a Methodist, but by consulting the hotel register I found an American clergyman, a Congregationalist, who was a fine fellow and consented to perform the ceremony. And, if we were not married at the American Embassy, we were at the rooms of the London consul, whom Matthews, at the Camford Street office, knew and who was another splendid chap and glad to oblige a fellow-countryman, particularly after seeing the lady he was to marry.

The consul and his wife and Hephzy were our only witnesses. Frances' wedding gown was not new, but it was very becoming—the consul's wife said so, and she should know. Also she said she had never seen a sweeter or more beautiful bride. No one said anything concerning the bridegroom's appearance, but he did not care. It was a drizzly, foggy day, but that made no difference. A Kansas cyclone and a Bayport no'theaster combined could not have cast a damper on that day.

When it was over, Hephzy, who had been heroically struggling to keep her vow not to shed another tear during our pilgrimage, hugged us both.

"I—I—" she faltered, "I—I can't say it, but you know how I feel. There's nothin' I sha'n't believe after this. I used to believe I'd never travel, but I have. And there in Mayberry I believed I'd never be happy again, but I am. HAPPY! hap—hap—Oh dear! WHAT a fool I am! I ca—I can't help it! I expect I look like the most miserable thing on earth, but that's because I AM so happy. God bless you both! Now—now don't so much as look at me for a few minutes."

That afternoon she left for Mayberry to do the "packing up" and my wife and I were alone—and together.

I saw London again during the next few days. We rode on the tops of busses, we visited Kew Gardens and Hampton Court and Windsor. We took long trips up and down the Thames on the little steamers. Frances called them our honeymoon trips. The time flew by. Then I received a note from Hephzy that the "packing up" was finished at last and that she was returning to London.

It was raining hard, the morning of her arrival, and I went alone to meet her at the railway station. I was early there and, as I was walking up, awaiting the train, I heard someone speak my name. I turned and there, immaculate, serene and debonair as ever, was A. Carleton Heathcroft.

"Ah, Knowles," he said, cheerfully. "Thought it was you. Haven't seen you of late. Missed you at Burgleston, on the course. How are you?"

I told him I was quite well, and inquired concerning his own health.

"Topping," he replied. "Rotten weather, eh—what? And how's Miss— Oh, dear me, always forget the name! The eccentric aunt who is so intensely patriotic and American—How is she?"

"She is well, too," I answered.

"Couldn't think of her being ill, somehow," he observed. "And where have you been, may I ask?"

I said I had been on the Continent for a short stay.

"Oh, yes! I remember now. Someone said you had gone. That reminds me: Did you go to Paris? Did you see the girl who sang at the Abbey—the one I told you of, who looked so like that pretty niece of yours? Hope you did. The resemblance was quite extraordinary. Did you see her?"

I dodged the question. I asked him what he had been doing since the day of the golf tournament.

"I—Oh, by Jove!" he exclaimed, "now I am going to surprise you. I have been getting ready to take the fatal step. I'm going to be married."

"Married!" I repeated. "Really? The—the Warwickshire young lady, I presume."

"Yes. How did you know of her?"

"Your aunt—Lady Carey—mentioned that your—your affections were somewhat engaged in that quarter."

"Did she? Really! Yes, she would mention it, I suppose. She mentions it to everybody; it's a sort of hobby of hers, like my humble self, and the roses. She has been more insistent of late and at last I consented to oblige her. Do you know, Knowles, I think she was rather fearful that I might be smitten by your Miss Morley. Shared your fears, eh?"

I smiled, but I said nothing. A train which I believed to be the one upon which Hephzy was expected, was drawing into the station.

"A remarkably attractive girl, your niece," he went on. "Have you heard from her?"

"Yes," I said, absently. "I must say good-by, Heathcroft. That is the train I have been waiting for."

"Oh, is it. Then, au revoir, Knowles. By the way, kindly remember me to your niece when you see her, will you."

"I will. But—" I could not resist the temptation; "but she isn't my niece," I said.

"Oh, I say! What? Not your niece? What is she then?"

"She is my wife—now," I said. "Good-by, Mr. Heathcroft."

I hurried away before he could do more than gasp. I think I shook even his serene composure at last.

I told Hephzy about it as we rode to the hotel in the cab.

"It was silly, I suppose," I said. "I told him on the spur of the moment. I imagine all Mayberry, not to mention Burgleston Bogs, will have something to talk about now. They expect almost anything of Americans, or some of them do, but the marriage of an uncle and niece ought to be a surprise, I should think."

Hephzy laughed. "The Baylisses will explain," she said. "I told the old doctor and his wife all about it. They were very much pleased, that was plain enough. They knew she wasn't your niece and they'll tell the other folks. That'll be all right, Hosy. Yes, Doctor and Mrs. Bayliss were tickled almost to death. It stops all their worry about their son and Frances, of course. He is in Switzerland now, poor chap. They'll write him and he'll come home again by and by where he ought to be. And he'll forget by and by, too. He's only a boy and he'll forget. So THAT'S all right.

"Everybody sent their love to you," she went on. "The curates and the Samsons and everybody. Mr. Cole and his wife are comin' back next week and the servants'll take care of the rectory till they come. Everybody was so glad to see me, and they're goin' to write and everything. I declare! I felt real bad to leave 'em. They're SUCH nice people, these English folks. Aren't they, Hosy."

They were and are. I hope that some day I may have, in my own country, the opportunity to repay a little of the hospitality and kindness that my Mayberry friends bestowed on me in theirs.

We sailed for home two days later. A pleasant voyage it was, on a good ship and with agreeable fellow-passengers. And, at last, one bright, cloudless morning, a stiff breeze blowing and the green and white waves leaping and tossing in the sunlight, we saw ahead of us a little speck—the South Shoal lightship. Everyone crowded to the rail, of course. Hephzy sighed, a sigh of pure happiness.

"Nantucket!" she said, reading the big letters on the side of the little vessel. "Nantucket! Don't that sound like home, Hosy! Nantucket and Cape Cod are next-door neighbors, as you might say! My! the air seems different already. I believe I can almost smell the Bayport flats. Do you know what I am goin' to do as soon as I get into my kitchen? After I've seen some of my neighbors and the cat and the hens, of course. I'm going to make a clam chowder. I've been just dyin' for a clam chowder ever since we left England."

And the next morning we landed at New York. Jim Campbell was at the wharf to meet us. His handshake was a welcome home which was good to feel. He welcomed Hephzy just as heartily. But I saw him looking at Frances with curiosity and I flattered myself, admiration, and I chuckled as I thought of the surprise which I was about to give him. It would be a surprise, sure enough. I had written him nothing of the recent wonderful happenings in Paris and in London, and I had sworn Matthews to secrecy likewise. No, he did not know, he did not suspect, and I gloried in the opportunity which was mine.

"Jim," I said, "there is one member of our party whom you have not met. Frances, you have heard me speak of Mr. Campbell very often. Here he is. Jim, I have the pleasure of presenting you to Mrs. Knowles, my wife."

Jim stood the shock remarkably well, considering. He gave me one glance, a glance which expressed a portion of his feelings, and then he and Frances shook hands.

"Mrs. Knowles," he said, "I—you'll excuse my apparent lack of intellect, but—but this husband of yours has—I've known him a good while and I thought I had lost all capacity for surprise at anything he might do, but—but I hadn't. I—I—Please don't mind me; I'm really quite sane at times. I am very, very glad. May we shake hands again?"

He insisted upon our breakfasting with him at a near-by hotel. When he and I were alone together he seized my arm.

"Confound you!" he exclaimed. "You old chump! What do you mean by springing this thing on me without a word of warning? I never was as nearly knocked out in my life. What do you mean by it?"

I laughed. "It is all part of your prescription," I said. "You told me I should marry, you know. Do you approve of my selection?"

"Approve of it! Why, man, she's—she's wonderful. Approve of YOUR selection! How about hers? You durned quahaug! How did you do it?"

I gave him a condensed and hurried resume of the whole story. He did not interrupt once—a perfectly amazing feat for him—and when I had finished he shook his head.

"It's no use," he said. "I'm too good for the business I am in. I am wasting my talents. *I* sent you over there. *I* told you to go. *I* prescribed travel and a wife and all the rest. *I* did it. I'm going to quit the publishing game. I'm going to set up as a specialist, a brain specialist, for clams. And I'll use your face as a testimonial: 'Kent Knowles, Quahaug. Before and After Taking.' Man, you look ten years younger than you did when you went away."

"You must not take all the credit," I told him. "You forget Hephzy and her dreams, the dream she told us about that day at Bayport. That dream has come true; do you realize it?"

He nodded. "I admit it," he said. "She is a better specialist than I. I shall have to take her into partnership. 'Campbell and Cahoon. Prescribers and Predictors. Authors Made Human.' I'll speak to her about it."

As he said good-by to us at the Grand Central Station he asked me another question.

"Kent," he whispered, "what are you going to do now? What are you going to do with her? Are you and she going back to Bayport to be Mr. and Mrs. Quahaug? Is that your idea?"

I shook my head. "We're going back to Bayport," I said, "but how long we shall stay there I don't know. One thing you may be sure of, Jim; I shall be a quahaug no more."

He nodded. "I think you're right," he declared. "She'll see to that, or I miss my guess. No, my boy, your quahaug days are over. There's nothing of the shellfish about her; she's a live woman, as well as a mighty pretty one, and she cares enough about you to keep you awake and in the game. I congratulate you, Kent, and I'm almost as happy as you are. Also I shall play the optimist at our next directors' meeting; I see signs of a boom in the literature factory. Go to it, my son. You have my blessing."

We took the one o'clock train for Boston, remained there over night, and left on the early morning "accommodation"—so called, I think, because it accommodates the train hands—for Cape Cod. As we neared Buzzard's Bay my spirits, which had been at topnotch, began to sink. When the sand dunes of Barnstable harbor hove in sight they sank lower and lower. It was

October, the summer people, most of them, had gone, the station platforms were almost deserted, the more pretentious cottages were closed. The Cape looked bare and brown and wind-swept. I thought of the English fields and hedges, of the verdant beauty of the Mayberry pastures. What SORT of a place would she think this, the home to which I was bringing her?

She had been very much excited and very much interested. New York, with its sky-scrapers and trolleys, its electric signs and clean white buildings, the latter so different from the grimy, gray dwellings and shops of London, had been a wonderland to her. She had liked the Pullman and the dining-car and the Boston hotel. But this, this was different. How would she like sleepy, old Bayport and the people of Bayport.

Well, I should soon know. Even the morning "accommodation" reaches Bayport some time or other. We were the only passengers to alight at the station, and Elmer Snow, the station agent, and Gabe Lumley, who drives the depot wagon, were the only ones to welcome us. Their welcome was hearty enough, I admit. Gabe would have asked a hundred questions if I had answered the first of the hundred, but he seemed strangely reluctant to answer those I asked him.

Bayport was gettin' along first-rate, he told me. Tad Simpson's youngest child had diphtheria, but was sittin' up now and the fish weirs had caught consider'ble mackerel that summer. So much he was willing to say, but he said little more. I asked how the house and garden were looking and he cal'lated they were all right. Pumping Gabe Lumley was a new experience for me. Ordinarily he doesn't need pumping. I could not understand it. I saw Hephzy and he in consultation on the station platform and I wondered if she had been able to get more news than I.

We rattled along the main road, up the hill by the Whittaker place—I looked eagerly for a glimpse of Captain Cy himself, but I didn't see him—and on until we reached our gate. Frances said very little during our progress through the village. I did not dare speak to her; I was afraid of asking her how she liked what she had seen of Bayport. And Hephzy, too, was silent, although she kept her head out of the window most of the time.

But when the depot wagon entered the big gate and stopped before the side door I felt that I must say something. I must not appear fearful or uneasy.

"Here we are!" I cried, springing out and helping her and Hephzy to alight. "Here we are at last. This is home, dear."

And then the door opened and I saw that the dining-room was filled with people, people whom I had known all my life. Mr. Partridge, the minister, was there, and his wife, and Captain Whittaker and his wife, and the Dimicks and the Salterses and more. Before I could recover from my surprise Mr. Partridge stepped forward.

"Mr. Knowles," he said, "on this happy occasion it is our privilege to—"

But Captain Cy interrupted him.

"Good Lord!" he exclaimed, "don't make a speech to him now, Mr. Partridge. Welcome home, Kent! We're all mighty glad to see you back again safe and sound. And Hephzy, too. By the big dipper, Hephzy, the sight of you is good for sore eyes! And I suppose this is your wife, Kent. Well, we—Hey! I might have known Phoebe would get ahead of me."

For Mrs. Whittaker and Frances were shaking hands. Others were crowding forward to do so. And the table was set and there were flowers everywhere and, in the background, was Susanna Wixon, grinning from ear to ear, with the cat—our cat—who seemed the least happy of the party, in her arms.

Hephzy had written Mrs. Whittaker from London, telling her of my marriage; she had telegraphed from New York the day before, announcing the hour of our return. And this was the result.

When it was all over and they had gone—they would not remain for dinner, although we begged them to do so—when they had gone and Hephzy had fled to the yard to inspect the hens, I turned to my wife.

"Frances," I said, "this is home. Here is where Hephzy and I have lived for so long. I—I hope you may be happy here. It is a rather crude place, but—"

She came to me and put her arms about my neck.

"Don't, my dear, don't!" she said. "It is beautiful. It is home. And—and you know I have never had a home, a real home before."

"Then you like it?" I cried. "You really like it? It is so different from England. The people—"

"They are dear, kind people. And they like you and respect you, Kent. How could you say they didn't! I know I shall love them all."

I made a dash for the kitchen. "Hephzy!" I shouted. "Hephzy! She does like it. She likes Bayport and the people and everything."

Hephzy was just entering at the back door. She did not seem in the least surprised.

"Of course she likes it," she said, with decision. "How could anybody help likin' Bayport?"

CHAPTER XIX
Which Treats of Quahaugs in General

Asaph Tiddett helped me to begin this long chronicle of a quahaug's pilgrimage. Perhaps it is fitting that Asaph should end it. He dropped in for a call the other afternoon and, as I had finished my day's "stunt" at the desk, I assisted in entertaining him. Frances was in the sitting-room also and Hephzy joined us soon afterward. Mr. Tiddett had stopped at the post-office on his way down and he had the Boston morning paper in his hand. Of course he was filled to the brim with war news. We discuss little else in Bayport now; even the new baby at the parsonage has to play second fiddle.

"My godfreys!" exclaimed Asaph, as soon as he sat down in the rocking chair and put his cap on the floor beneath it. "My godfreys, but they're havin' awful times over across, now ain't they. Killin' and fightin' and battlin' and slaughterin'! It don't seem human to me somehow."

"It is human, I'm afraid," I said, with a sigh. "Altogether too human. We're a poor lot, we, humans, after all. We pride ourselves on our civilization, but after all, it takes very little to send us back to savagery."

"That's so," said Asaph, with conviction. "That's true about everybody but us folks in the United States. We are awful fortunate, we are. We ain't savages. We was born in a free country, and we've been brought up right, I declare! I beg your pardon, Mrs. Knowles; I forgot you wasn't born in Bayport."

Frances smiled. "No apology is needed, Mr. Tiddett," she said. "I confess to having been born a—savage."

"But you're all right now," said Asaph, hastily, trying to cover his slip. "You're all right now. You're just as American as the rest of us. Kent, suppose this war in Europe is goin' to hurt your trade any? It's goin' to hurt a good many folks's. They tell me groceries and such like is goin' way up. Lucky we've got fish and clams to depend on. Clams and quahaugs'll keep us from starvin' for a spell. Oh," with a chuckle, "speakin' of quahaugs reminds me. Did you know they used to call your husband a quahaug, Mrs. Knowles? That's what they used to call him round here—'The Quahaug.' They called him that 'count of his keepin' inside his shell all the time and not mixin' with folks, not toadyin' up to the summer crowd and all. I always respected him for it. *I* don't toady to nobody neither."

Hephzy had come in by this time and now she took a part in the conversation.

"They don't call him 'The Quahaug' any more," she declared, indignantly. "He's been out of his shell more and seen more than most of the folks in this town."

"I know it; I know it. And he's kept goin' ever since. Runnin' to New York, he and you," with a nod toward Frances, "and travelin' to Washin'ton and Niagary Falls and all. Wonder to me how he does as much writin' as he does. That last book of yours is sellin' first-rate, they tell me, Kent."

He referred to the novel I began in Mayberry. I have rewritten and finished it since, and it has had a surprising sale. The critics seem to think I have achieved my first genuine success.

"What are you writin' now?" asked Asaph. "More of them yarns about pirates and such? Land sakes! when I go by this house nights and see a light in your library window there, Kent, and know you're pluggin' along amongst all them adventures, I wonder how you can stand it. 'Twould give me the shivers. Godfreys! the last time I read one of them yarns—that about the 'Black Brig' 'twas—I hardly dast to go to bed. And I DIDN'T dast to put out the light. I see a pirate in every corner, grittin' his teeth. Writin' another of that kind, are you?"

"No," I said; "this one is quite different. You will have no trouble in sleeping over this one, Ase."

"That's a comfort. Got a little Bayport in it? Seems to me you ought to put a little Bayport in, for a change."

I smiled. "There is a little in this," I answered. "A little at the beginning, and, perhaps, at the end."

"You don't say! You ain't got me in it, have you? I'd—I'd look kind of funny in a book, wouldn't I?"

I laughed, but I did not answer.

"Not that I ain't seen things in my life," went on Asaph, hopefully. "A man can't be town clerk in a live town like this and not see things. But I hope you won't put any more foreigners in. This we're readin' now," rapping the newspaper with his knuckles, "gives us all we want to know about foreigners. Just savages, they be, as you say, and nothin' more. I pity 'em."

I laughed again.

"Asaph," said I, "what would you say if I told you that the English and French—yes, and the Germans, too, though I haven't seen them at home as I have the others—were no more savages than we are?"

"I'd say you was crazy," was the prompt answer.

"Well, I'm not. And you're not very complimentary. You're forgetting again. You forget that I married one of those savages."

Asaph was taken aback, but he recovered promptly, as he had before.

"She ain't any savage," he announced. "Her mother was born right here in Bayport. And she knows, just as I do, that Bayport's the best place in the world; don't you, Mrs. Knowles?"

"Yes," said Frances, "I am sure of it, Mr. Tidditt."

So Asaph went away triumphantly happy. After he had gone I apologized for him.

"He's a fair sample," I said. "He is a quahaug, although he doesn't know it. He is a certain type, an exaggerated type, of American."

Frances smiled. "He's not much worse than I used to be," she said. "I used to call America an uncivilized country, you remember. I suppose I— and Mr. Heathcroft—were exaggerated types of a certain kind of English. We were English quahaugs, weren't we?"

Hephzy nodded. "We're all quahaugs," she declared. "Most of us, anyhow. That's the trouble with all the folks of all the nations; they stay in their shells and they don't try to know and understand their neighbors. Kent, you used to be a quahaug—a different kind of one—but that kind, too. I was a quahaug afore I lived in Mayberry. That's who makes wars like this dreadful one—quahaugs. We know better now—you and Frances and I. We've found out that, down underneath, there's precious little difference. Humans are humans."

She paused and then, as a final summing up, added:

"I guess that's it: American or German or French or anything—nice folks are nice folks anywhere."